The Shadow of Water

The Charismatics Series

Explore the dark, mystical streets of Edwardian London with The Charismatics, a supernatural historical fantasy series full of deadly mystery and arcane powers.

—

The Fire in the Glass
Book One of The Charismatics
Books2Read.com/FireInTheGlassDigital

Lily's visions could stop a killer if she'll trust a reclusive aristocrat with her darkest secret.

The Shadow of Water
Book Two of The Charismatics
Books2Read.com/TheShadowOfWater

A dangerous prophecy threatens London. To stop it, Lily must uncover the truth behind her mother's murder.

Bridge of Ash
Book Three of The Charismatics (Coming in 2021)

When a ruthless man discovers their secret, Lily and Strangford are faced with an impossible choice.

What the Ravens Sing
Book Four of The Charismatics (Coming in 2022)

In the maelstrom of the Great War, only Lily can stop an ancient and terrible charismatic ability from tearing the world apart.

The
Shadow of Water

THE CHARISMATICS

BOOK TWO

Jacquelyn Benson

VAUGHAN WOODS
PUBLISHING

Copyright © 2021 by Jacquelyn Benson
Cover design by Sara Argue of Sara Argue Design
Cover copyright © 2020 by Vaughan Woods Publishing
Typeset in Minion Pro and ALS Script by Cathie Plante

First edition: April 2021

Library of Congress Catalog Number: 2021901761
ISBN: 978-1-7345599-3-4

Published by Vaughan Woods Publishing
PO Box 882
Exeter, New Hampshire 03833 U.S.A.

Stay up-to-date on new book releases by subscribing to Jacquelyn's newsletter at JacquelynBenson.com.

Content warnings for *The Shadow of Water*:
Contains alcohol use, kidnapping, violent fights, brief incarceration, death of a loved one, bombing, hospitalization, vehicle accident. References to prostitution, human trafficking, sexual assault, terrorism, medical procedures, torture, war.

"No one could understand the secret of this weaver who,
coming into existence, spread the warp as the world;

He fixed the earth and the sky as the pillars,
and he used the sun and the moon as two shuttles;

He took thousands of stars and perfected the cloth;
but even today he weaves, and the end is difficult to fathom."

KABIR, THE BIJAK OF KABIR
(TRANSLATION BY LINDA HESS AND SHUKDEV SINGH)

~

"Wade in the water, children.
God's gonna trouble the water."

TRADITIONAL SPIRITUAL

ONE

CROUCHED BEHIND A HEDGE, Lily Albright tried to know when the most dangerous cargo in England would come rattling up the road.

The grass was long and dry, seed-heads tickling the back of her neck. Crickets buzzed, the only other sound besides the whisper of the field. The Kentish countryside sprawled around her, rolling pastures lined with hedgerows and dotted with gnarled oak trees. She could smell the sea, the briny scent of it carrying to her from the marshes a couple of miles away.

A gull wheeled lazily overhead.

Sweat beaded on her skin. She was dressed in twill trousers and a light wool jacket, the ensemble she wore when riding her Triumph motorbike. It was more practical for an ambush than a linen lawn dress but somewhat less comfortable in a summer heat wave.

The road was visible through a gap in the tangled hedge of wild plums and brambles. It was a country lane, barely wide enough for two vehicles to pass each other without pulling into the ditch. The dirt and gravel surface was dry and prone to dust. Clouds of it had drifted over her twice since she had hidden herself here earlier that morning.

Both times something had driven by, Lily had been twisted into knots of anxiety.

She knew she was only a failsafe. The more reliable source of warning that their target was approaching sat beside her in the form of a wooden box, a makeshift telephone wired to a watch post a half mile up the road.

In some ways, the box was a rebuke. It shouldn't have been necessary. Knowing the difference between the vehicle they waited for and some farmer on his tractor shouldn't have been a tall order for someone who could see the future.

Then again, Lily's powers had never been very reliable.

Her visions weren't obedient pets that came when she called them. They surfaced or not as they pleased. One might pop up during tea with the gory details of a shipwreck that would take place three weeks later. Another might wake her from sleep, drowning her in a sea of obscure symbols that only made sense months later when the disaster they represented came to pass.

Lily mostly foresaw disasters.

It was only over the last few months that she had started to seek her power out instead of desperately avoiding or ignoring it. Her mentor, Robert Ash, had warned her that her clairvoyance would never answer to her beck and call, but he believed she could learn to tune in to more information than the horrors that forced their way into her awareness. With training, practice and patience, she might routinely pick up on knowledge from a little further down the timeline—not just a parade of awfulness but information that could actually be helpful or useful.

Lily knew Ash wasn't promising the impossible. She had experienced that just-before awareness once. It had been exhilarating. Knowing the next move of an enemy—what step he would take, which way he would turn—had felt as natural in that moment as looking before crossing the street. Her body had sung with the awareness, resonating like it had been waiting for this all her life.

Then it was gone.

She hadn't come by it honestly. The moment was a stolen glimpse of what she might be able to do someday if she worked at it long and hard enough.

Since March, she had been practicing diligently, facing the early mornings, the tedious exercises, the piles of reading.

There had been glimpses of progress, little flashes of success, but they were rare enough to feel like chance.

Finally, even Ash had admitted that Lily was not progressing as well as he might have hoped.

"You have spent years building up your defenses," he said. "It should not surprise me that rote methods of study are incapable of breaking them down. I believe that for you to truly open to your own potential, we must raise the stakes."

After that, her regular exercises and practice were interspersed with wild challenges. Most of them ended in some combination of failure, physical discomfort and humiliation.

Lily rubbed at the flecks of paint stuck to her hand. Bruises dotted her back under her jacket. The marks were evidence of last evening's training session.

It had not gone particularly well.

The stakes today couldn't be higher. The cargo Lily was here to intercept had already caused untold suffering.

If it got past her, it might inflict a far more terrible damage.

The mission was too important to risk on the fickleness of her power.

A sheep pasture sprawled behind her, the summer grass chewed down to tufts. The flock was gathered in a woolly cluster by the gate that opened onto the lane. It was not an unusual sight in the late afternoon when a farmer might be arriving any minute to lead his livestock in for the night. At least, it seemed normal enough until one looked closer and noted that the gate was already swung wide open.

Not a single hoof crossed the line from the field to the road. The sheep waited on the verge with uncanny patience.

Knowing why the animals remained in place didn't stop the goose-bumps from racing over her arms. No matter how many times she witnessed it, Sam Wu's power still unsettled her.

Sam looked suspiciously like he was napping. The tall, dark-haired young man slouched against the tumbled remnants of a stone wall, his flat cap pulled down to shade his face. Lily was tempted to give his lanky form a prod with her walking stick. Doing so would unleash a stream of East End invective that reflected nothing of his Chinese heritage, but at least Lily would be far enough away to avoid Sam knocking her with a stray fist.

Sam's social status was almost as ambiguous as Lily's. Was he Robert Ash's chauffeur or another of his students? Servant or pupil? She had been around for months now and she still wasn't sure she knew how to answer that question.

Lily had made up her mind about Sam's role in her own life early on.

"I ain't sleeping," her friend muttered lowly, arms crossed comfortably over his chest.

"I didn't say you were," Lily countered in a low whisper.

"I could feel them daggers you were looking. Just making myself comfortable. You might try it yourself."

Lily didn't respond. She returned her attention to the road, forcefully ignoring the ache in her legs. She didn't want to make herself comfortable. She needed to be ready to leap into action. There was no telling how much warning they would have before they had to act.

Probably very little.

The hum of insects was joined by a low, distant rumble. Lily zeroed in on the sound. It drew closer and distinguished itself as the noise of an engine.

Her heart began to hammer. She looked to the makeshift telephone in the wooden box that sat between her and Sam.

A whiz with all things mechanical, Sam had rigged it up in the garage the day before, demonstrating how the bell inside could be rung by spinning a winder in its sister contraption up the road.

"The winder takes an extra few seconds to charge the magneto, but it'll be more reliable than a battery," Sam had said. "The last three I bought could barely hold a charge."

Even a battery was more reliable than Lily's knowledge of the future.

The rumble of the engine came closer. The wooden box remained silent.

However much Lily doubted her effectiveness, she would try to play her role in this. She took a deep breath and recalled her training.

Stop thinking. Ignore your mind's attempts to analyze. Focus inward. Listen to what lies inside the silence. Accept knowledge instead of grasping for facts.

The vehicle was getting closer.

She listened to the silence. It distinctly lacked any ringing telephone bells.

Her concentration shattered as a mud-splattered diesel tractor rumbled into view. It rolled slowly past her, towing a cart full of baled hay.

She sat back in the grass, ignoring the way it itched at her exposed skin.

"You can keep your block on," Sam said. "They ain't going to be here for at least another hour."

"You don't know that."

"Lambeth to Kent's a sixty mile run, and what proper courier ain't going to pop off for a bit of nosh along the way?"

"This is a military transport," Lily countered.

Still sprawled comfortably on the grass, Sam shrugged.

"Bloke still needs to eat."

Lily couldn't share Sam's complacency. She comforted herself with the thought of their friend Dr. Gardner crouched somewhere up the road, his hand on the crank of Sam's telephone. Gardner was big, solid, and steady. He would fulfill his part of their plan. Their success wouldn't depend on Lily.

She went back to her training, ignoring the pang of the bruises she'd earned with her failure the night before.

Feel, don't think.

She cycled it through her mind like a mantra until she became one with the whisper of the grass against her hands, the heat of the sun beating down on her through her coat.

Insects chirped. A blackbird fluttered onto the branch of the plum tree woven into the hedge in front of her.

Feel don't think.

Deep inside of her something started to resonate like the hollow tone after a bell had already rung.

"It's coming," she said evenly, feeling the truth of the words vibrate through to her fingertips.

She wanted to take it back as soon as the words had left her mouth. No sound broke the quiet of the pasture, not so much as the clod of a pair of hooves. The makeshift telephone beside her was silent. Sam was likely right about the drive taking longer. He was a chauffeur. He would know the timing better than anyone.

The outburst was the whim of a moment. It would ruin everything.

Sam peered at her from beneath the brim of his cap. Then he flipped to his feet with cat-like grace.

"The bell hasn't rung," Lily whispered urgently, doubt twisting her into knots.

Sam looked down, his lean frame silhouetted by the glare of the midday sun.

"Machines break. Wires can be cut. Is it coming or not?"

The knowing pulsed through her, bone-deep, urgent with need.

"Yes," she hissed, forcing out the word.

"Right, then."

Sam adjusted his cap. He strode over to where the flock of sheep lingered by the open pasture gate.

The animals circled around him, nudging soft pink noses into his hands, shaking their fleecy tails. Sam bent down, whispering into their ears, scratching and stroking their wool.

The flock trotted out into the lane. They turned there in eddies and little collisions, the smallest ones running in circles and letting out an occasional cry of excitement.

The chaos resolved itself into a barrier of sheep six rows deep, facing uniformly east, at which point the animals went still.

Their eyes were on the road. Waiting.

Sam plopped back down beside her.

"What if I'm wrong?" she asked quietly.

"Then we're about to bowl over some clodhopper," Sam replied.

An engine coughed in the distance.

Lily felt her muscles tense. Sam was coiled in readiness beside her. They waited in silence as the rattle of the engine drew closer.

A dark green military lorry ground to a stop in front of them.

Lily gripped her walking stick. She had trained for years in how to use the yew staff for self-defense and it had served her well in that capacity more than once.

6

The engine idled as the vehicle faced the wall of sheep. Lily jumped as the driver honked his horn. Sam's flock stirred, the odd sheep bleating, but held firm across the road.

The door slammed. The driver hopped down, dressed in a khaki service uniform. He strode over to the animal barrier.

"On with you, now! Move along!"

He waded in, waving his arms toward the pasture. The sheep closed around him, woolly bodies pressing against his legs. Lily saw his arms wheel as he fought to keep his balance.

"Now," Sam announced. He dove forward, slipping through the gap in the hedge and making a beeline for the lorry.

Lily ran behind him, her motoring jacket protecting her from the scrape of the brambles.

They had rehearsed this. Sam was going to hop into the driver's seat while Lily ran around to the passenger side of the vehicle. As soon as she had climbed in, he would reverse the lorry back up the road and take off for the rendezvous.

As she emerged from the hedge, instinct rang through her, stopping her short. Every fiber of her rattled with the knowledge that *something would be different.*

She didn't question it. There wasn't any time.

Instead of racing to the far side of the vehicle, she stayed on Sam's heels. When he yanked open the driver's door, Lily was right behind him, staring over his shoulder into the eyes of a clearly flabbergasted stranger.

He was perhaps forty with a thick, neatly-trimmed beard and mustache. He wore a summer suit with a carefully wrapped turban on his head.

A knife appeared in Sam's hand with a silver flash. He leapt into the car, forcing the passenger to slide up against the far door.

There was no time to think. Lily scrambled up behind him, dropping into the driver's seat and slamming shut the door.

The plan had changed. Lily would need to drive.

Her eyes flew over the unfamiliar pedals and levers. This was not her Triumph motorbike, the only motorized vehicle she had ever piloted.

On the road in front of her, the soldier pushed toward them, tripping over the thick white bodies of the flock, shouting loud enough to be heard over the noise of the engine.

"Clutch, brake, accelerator, gears," Sam shouted, pointing with his free hand. "Go!"

Lily stomped on the clutch and threw the vehicle into what she hoped was its reverse gear, then hit the accelerator.

The soldier shoved his way clear of the sheep. He hurtled toward them.

The road was straight as an arrow from their hiding place to the crossroads a quarter mile away. Lily gritted her teeth and pressed the pedal down to the floor.

The lorry flew backwards, dust pluming to either side of them. Their surprise passenger gripped the dashboard, his dark eyes moving from the screaming soldier through the windscreen to the knife in Sam's hand.

She blasted through the crossroads. Lily slammed the brake and shifted the lorry into forward gear. The clutch groaned and coughed. The soldier was still racing toward them, moving with fierce determination. She pressed the pedals again, felt the clutch catch, and the lorry lurched into motion. She yanked the wheel to the left and sent them hurtling around the bend.

She risked a glance out the window to the road behind them. The soldier jogged to a stop, pressing his hands to his knees and panting. He disappeared in a cloud of dust and Lily returned her attention to the road, easing up on the petrol.

"Is that really necessary?" she asked, glancing at Sam's knife.

Sam's hold on the weapon remained steady.

"We don't know who he is or why he's here," he returned.

"Singh," Sam's prisoner replied. His voice was steady, though he kept his back pressed to the passenger door as though he hoped it might swallow him. "Doctor Akal-Ustat Singh."

"Doctor of what?" Sam demanded.

"Hematology. University of Edinburgh," he added, as though the qualification should impress the young tough with the knife enough to get him to lower his weapon.

"So you're a toff," Sam said. "But you ain't military. What are you doing in an army lorry? You have any idea where you were going?"

"To a new War Office research center outside Graveney. I have been contracted to work on a very special project there. I'm afraid you'll find that the cargo you have stolen is both worthless to the black market and very important to the War Office. If you know what's best for you, you'll leave both me and the lorry and get very far away from here before the British Army realizes what's happened."

Lily adjusted her grip on the steering wheel.

"We know what your cargo is. Far better than you do," she said quietly.

The memories came whirling back.

The burnt-out shell of a clinic in Southwark, echoes of torture ingrained into what was left of its walls. The haunted voice of a woman in a hospital bed, feverish hands convulsively gripping the sheets.

A pile of forgotten suitcases, layered with dust and ash.

The body of a beautiful widow sprawled across blood-flecked sheets.

Yes. Lily knew better than anyone what sat inside the wooden crates filling the bed of this lorry.

"I'm surprised a bloke like you would take the job," Sam said. He looked deceptively lazy, relaxed in the center of the bench as the lorry rattled down the road, but the knife in his hand never wavered. "Given what the man who started your 'special project' thought of the likes of you and I. You make for an odd eugenicist."

"I am not a eugenicist," Singh retorted. "But your question is irrelevant. The personal beliefs of the scientist are of no matter to the value of the science."

"Women died for this science," Lily said.

"It is an unfortunate truth of medical progress that sometimes lives are lost along the way," Singh replied. "We work as we do in order to save more people in the future."

"That isn't what I meant."

She saw the flicker of surprise in his eyes. Apparently the dark history of torture and murder had been left out of whatever briefing he had received from the War Office. Not that he was about to admit his ignorance to a pair of thieves holding him at knife-point.

"How do you propose to manage this?" Singh demanded. "Are you going to kill me for what's back there?" He jerked his head toward the back of the lorry. "Would you take a man's life for a batch of papers?"

Lily shifted down a gear and pressed the brakes. The lorry lumbered to a stop on an isolated stretch of road. A stand of lime trees shaded the lane, an old farmhouse just visible in the distance. The fields sprawled out around them, thick with uncut hay.

"No. We'll just boot you out," she announced.

"What, so he can tell the toffs at the War Office all about the auburn-haired maid and the Chinese tommy what stole their goods?" Sam protested.

"By the time they find him, the papers will be beyond anyone's reach."

"I ain't worrying about the papers."

"What's the alternative?" she demanded. "Haven't enough people died for this already?"

Sam glowered. Then he reached across the doctor to twist the handle of the door. It swung open with a bounce.

"Go on, then," Sam ordered, waving his knife.

The hematologist scrambled down from the lorry, stepping awkwardly back onto the verge.

"You might destroy one man's work, but once knowledge is within the grasp of civilization it will come out," he called up at them, adjusting his jacket. "Progress is like water. It will always find a way. You can't stop it."

"Maybe so, Doc, but we can bloody well inconvenience it," Sam retorted before slamming shut the door.

Lily pushed the lorry back into gear, leaving the incongruous figure of Singh watching them through a cloud of dust.

~

She set a more moderate pace as they navigated the twisting country roads. The last turn was easy to miss. She well might have flown past it if she hadn't been made familiar with the spot the day before.

The narrow dirt track broke off from the road to plunge into a shadowy stand of oak trees. They bounced through the little wood, emerging on the far side at the edge of a shining silver creek.

10

A diesel fishing boat waited there. It wore weathered blue paint on its hull. Beyond it, the Graveney marshes stretched to the horizon, a flat landscape of waving grasses and pale water.

On the boat, James Cairncross put a mark in his book and rose to his feet.

Cairncross was a tall man, lean as a bone and unbent by his advanced years, his blue eyes keen over a white mustache trimmed with military precision. The Scotsman served as librarian to Lily's mentor, Robert Ash, though he was often called upon to fill other household duties. Lily had known these to include translator and chemist as well as personal assistant and occasional drill sergeant.

He was also responsible for the paint on her hands and the bruises under her jacket.

Don't reason. Don't guess. Know.

Those were Ash's words at the start of the practice session the night before. Lily had stood blindfolded and barefoot on the sand, the roar of the sea drowning out any more subtle sound. She tried to connect with her power while Cairncross moved around her with a slingshot in his hand.

The first rubber ball full of paint hit her in the thigh. A second struck her lower back, followed by a third. The fourth had nailed her on the wrist.

By the twelfth Lily had pulled off the blindfold and stalked off of the beach. The sun had just been peeking over the horizon. Ash had watched her go, arms behind his back, showing neither surprise nor disappointment.

Lily still harbored a healthy irritation at the librarian, who slipped the book into his carry-all as the lorry skidded to a stop.

The other person on board was not someone Lily recognized. He was short and sturdily built with the ruddy complexion of a man who made his living under the sun. This must be Mr. Adler, the old friend of Cairncross's who had provided them with the boat. He stood in the stern, reeling up a flashing silver fish. As Lily stepped down from the lorry, he neatly removed it from his hook.

"I don't care what your book says," Mr. Adler noted, tossing the fish back into the water. "Ain't no such thing as having half a soul."

"The phenomenon is extremely rare but I can assure you it has been documented, and not merely in faerie stories," Cairncross replied.

"Don't start with the faeries," Mr. Adler retorted, making an instinctive sign against evil influences.

Cairncross plucked a crowbar from the deck and hopped onto the banks with a nimbleness that belied his advanced years.

"Any hiccups?" he asked.

"Nothing we couldn't sort out," Sam replied.

Cairncross raised a silver eyebrow.

"Something went off with the telephone line," Sam said.

"And yet here you are," Cairncross noted. The librarian's cool blue gaze shifted to Lily.

"There was also another man in the lorry. A hematologist. We left him in a field about three miles back," she said. Somehow talking about the stranded Singh was easier than enduring Cairncross's knowing look.

"Would he be able to identify you?" he asked.

"He didn't hear any names," Lily replied.

Cairncross considered this.

"There are enough auburn-haired women in London to make you sufficiently difficult to locate," he concluded. The look he flashed to Sam was a bit more troubled.

Sam shrugged.

"If they're after a Chinese bloke what drops his 'haitches' they ain't going to go looking for him in Bloomsbury."

It was true. Sam's accent was clearly that of an East Ender. The tidy middle-class streets of Bloomsbury were likely the last place anyone would look for someone matching his description.

"And we shall be long gone from here by the time the doctor finds his way back to civilization," Cairncross concluded. "Now let us see what this little endeavor has netted us."

He lifted the metal latch and swung open the rear doors of the lorry. Seven wooden crates sat inside, still smelling of fresh sawdust.

He thrust the crowbar into the first of the crates and gave it a wrench. The lid popped loose.

Lily braced herself for what she would see as Cairncross lifted it away.

There they were, set into neat bundles—the notes and papers of Dr. Joseph Hartwell.

Seven crates of files, the life's work of one of Britain's most respected scientists. The legacy of an avowed eugenicist who had believed that his nation's future lay in creating a master race of supermen.

She thought of the crowds of people fawning up at him as he held court in a crowded gallery. The whispers of a Nobel Prize for his seminal work on distinguishing different types of blood.

The papers detailed all of it as well as his final, secret project—an effort that had nearly cost Lily her life.

If Hartwell had been allowed to continue, his discoveries might well have resulted in the deaths of millions.

But he hadn't.

In the end, the choice had been hers. Lily had stood poised between two possible futures—one uncertain, the other soaked in blood.

In that moment on a snow-covered rooftop in Hampstead Heath, Lily had known exactly where the difference lay between one possibility and the other. One nudge, one push, was all it would take to determine what path the future would take.

She remembered the cold bite of frosted metal under her fingers, the soft hiss of a body sliding across ice.

The crates stacked in the back of the lorry were the last loose end. They detailed everything Hartwell had learned through his crimes— the legacy of one of the leading minds of England.

The life's work of the man she had killed.

"Let's get this rotten stuff onto the boat," Cairncross said.

TWO

$\mathcal{M}$R. ADLER'S BLUE BOAT chugged through the narrow waters of Graveney, loaded with crates of stolen papers.

Lily had never been to the marshes. Graveney was neither sea nor land but an endless space of waving green grass and wheeling seabirds, of mud flats and canals that wove maze-like across its expanse. She had never known somewhere so liminal, so undefined and yet entirely sure of itself.

Something about it felt familiar, even though it was as different from her home in London as a place could be.

"You know the marshes?" Mr. Adler asked.

"No," Lily admitted.

"You ever find your way out here again, stick to the path," he said. "Can't trust the rest of it, however much it might look like solid land from a distance."

It was clear that Mr. Adler knew the waterways by instinct, navigating through narrow channels that Lily thought could not possibly accommodate their craft. She wondered if perhaps fishing were not the only source of income for Cairncross's friend. This isolated path to the sea would have been a handy route for smugglers.

It was more or less what they were doing now—smuggling official state property out of England, an act just as illegal as the crimes of the old brandy runners who had haunted these canals centuries ago.

The crime shouldn't have been necessary.

Hartwell's papers had been willed to his alma mater, King's College Hospital in London. Dr. Gardner had a colleague at King's, Dr. Saunders, a physician with a strong antipathy toward the eugenics movement. She quietly assured him that any notes relating to Hartwell's darker experiments would remain uncatalogued. They would sit in their boxes in the King's archives with no index and therefore no means of being accessed, left to the rats and the rot.

Lily and her friends were not the only ones who believed that research drenched in blood could not be the basis of good science.

It was Dr. Saunders who sent Dr. Gardner word that the War Office had declared Hartwell's records to be of vital state interest. The papers would be confiscated and transferred into Army custody. It was a stroke of luck that the King's College physician had managed to overhear that the papers were to be taken to Kent.

It made Lily's blood cold to think of why the War Office might have been interested in Hartwell's work.

Whatever their plan, her actions today had put a stop to it. The contents of these crates were the only record of Hartwell's illicit work, and they would not be returning from this voyage.

The boat glided into a wider creek. A heron watched their progress, elegant head turning on its elongated neck, as unperturbed by their presence as a god out of ancient myth.

The marsh stretched around them, its grass the most vivid green Lily had ever seen.

She looked down at the shining surface of the water. Light sparkled in the ripples that pulsed from the prow of the boat.

The rhythm of that movement was hypnotic. Lily let herself fall into it. It felt good to let her mind slip into silence. She was wrung-out by the pressures of the day, by the enormity of what had been at stake in this endeavor, by the memories it dragged back up.

The water danced. The light flickered. Lily felt the sinking pull of it. A shadow took shape beyond the surface—but not here. Not now.

Somewhere else.

Somewhere later.

A distant part of her brain warned that she was on the verge of a vision. The water could do that to her. She had learned the name for it six months before—*scrying*.

Six months before, she would have lurched away from the threat of another foresight. She would have fought against the inexorable gravity of the vision. The habit of that still lingered, quickening her pulse.

She refused to give in to it. Things had changed.

There was always a choice. She might not control what she saw, but she could control what she did about it.

Lily let her gaze stay anchored in that shining movement of the water.

. . . and she is beneath it. Light flickers on the surface over her head, a dance of green flame. Water presses down and around, playing with the strands of her hair. Her lungs are pain, her heart slow and urgent.

On the far side of the water, a shadow stands framed in a glowing door.

"Miss Albright?"

Mr. Adler's voice shattered the vision. Lily blinked down at the waves, feeling as though she had just washed up into the boat. She gripped the rail, her mind buzzing.

"You're looking a bit peaked. Need me to slow her down?" Mr. Adler asked.

Lily released her white-knuckled hold on the boat and sat back.

"That isn't necessary. I'm fine."

Cairncross glanced up from his book, his long mouth briefly creasing into a frown.

Lily looked away from him, directing her gaze firmly out over the marsh.

What had that been? Lily's visions were always strange, an amalgamation of symbols rather than the literal truth of what the future held. It was as though her mind had to translate a language she could not know into the memories and knowledge she already possessed. The result was always a mess of strange approximations that taxed her ability to interpret them.

This one was no different. The meaning of it skipped away from her like the ripples on the water. The old frustration roared back. Her power was never of any use.

"Not to be rude, mate, but why's your boat smell like rotten eggs?" Sam asked.

"That's not my boat, son. That's the marsh," Mr. Adler replied cheerily. "You get to like it after you've been out here long enough. I've made my living off this place for forty-six years, ever since I was in the Lancers. Ain't that right, Sergeant?"

It took Lily a moment to realize that Mr. Adler was addressing the wiry old librarian reading his book in the stern of the boat.

"Sergeant?" she echoed with a surprised look at Cairncross.

"What, don't you know?" Mr. Adler exclaimed. "Your Mr. Cairncross is a bloody berserker. There we were, just two hundred cavalrymen on the plains of Kabul, facing down ten thousand mad Afghans—"

"I think that's enough of that old story, Eddie," Cairncross said mildly without looking up. He thoughtfully turned another page.

Lily was used to thinking of Cairncross as a scholar. He was a polyglot with an encyclopedic knowledge of mythology, folklore and ancient history. She would never have imagined him in a battle unless he was standing at the outskirts of it calmly and accurately recording the details.

It didn't sound as though that was where Mr. Adler's story was going.

She thought of her training sessions and how quietly the old librarian could move when he wanted to, how sharp his aim was.

"There should've been a medal for him," Mr. Adler finished. "Pity he's such a geezer. We might've loaned him out to the Serbs to put the fear of God into those Austrians."

"The Serbs don't need him. They ain't stupid. They'll back down before it comes to a war," Sam offered. He was lying across a pair of Hartwell's crates, practicing tying knots with a bit of rope.

"Bit late for that," Mr. Adler retorted cheerfully.

"Austria-Hungary declared war today," Cairncross said. "There was a special late edition of the paper. It reached the inn after you left."

The pundits had been warning of a possible war in Europe ever since the assassination of the Austrian archduke, Franz Ferdinand, by

Serbian nationalists the month before. The slow-lit fuse was finally starting to burn.

"Let 'em fight it out, that's what I say," Mr. Adler cut in. "The Russians and the Germans too. France even. Let 'em knock each other about while we run the seas, and who do you think'll be at the top of the pile when it's all said and done? Old Britannia, that's who."

"The geopolitical ramifications are a bit more complicated than that," Cairncross noted.

"It's a bunch of noise about nothing," Sam said. "The whole of Europe ain't going to go to war over one dead archduke."

Lily stayed quiet. She knew more about the subject of the war than she cared to admit. It was too terrible and too unclear.

The water before them opened into the wide blue expanse of the Swale. They had emerged from an unmarked channel in the marshes. A glance back showed her that it looked just like a dozen other little spills of water merging the wetlands with the sea.

The boat picked up speed, the diesel engine rumbling loudly enough that between it and the flapping of the wind, conversation was pointless.

Sam held on to the brim of his hat. Cairncross stubbornly turned the pages of his book, even though they were flapping in the breeze.

Mr. Adler whistled a tune Lily remembered hearing in her mother's flat when she was a girl. As a former music hall star, Deirdre Albright had known an extensive repertoire of songs. Lily remembered some of the lyrics to this one and knew why Mr. Adler had opted not to sing it out loud.

A bawdy music hall jingle should not have been a melancholy sound, but memories of Lily's mother were always complicated. A shadow hung over all of them, even the songs or the ringing clarity of her laugh. It painted everything with an edge of guilt and grief.

Lily supposed it must be like that when remembering anyone who'd been murdered.

⁓

The coast of Kent was a long green line on the horizon when Mr. Adler dropped the engine into idle. The boat rocked noticeably here in the open water. Lily wasn't certain whether she found the swaying rhythm soothing or disorienting.

"We're far enough out that no one on shore can see what we're up to," Mr. Adler announced.

"Then we might as well get about our business," Cairncross said.

Sam plucked the crowbar from the deck and wrenched the top off of one of the crates, tossing it aside. He looked down at what lay inside.

"Odd that a bunch of papers could cause so much trouble," he noted.

Cairncross plucked up a handful of files.

"Nothing is more dangerous than knowledge," he replied.

"Are we sure this is all of it?" Sam asked.

"I have reviewed the entirety of Hartwell's published works and articles, everything I could find of his correspondence, and there is not a whisper of his experiments related to eugenics and charismatic ability," Cairncross said. "It's all philosophy or the legitimate blood science that made his reputation. He kept the stuff built on murder close to his chest."

"So this is it, then." Sam swept an arm over the crates.

"This is it," Cairncross confirmed.

The old archivist plucked a handful of papers from the crate Sam had opened. He leaned over the rail of the boat and plunged them down into the water. Then he let go.

Lily watched the pages drift apart, spreading into curls and fans suspended in the rocking movement of the waves. Slowly they scattered, sliding into the murk.

Cairncross went back for another bundle.

"Why are you handling them like a burial at sea? Can't we just toss them over?" Sam demanded.

"Not if you want to make sure they don't float back to shore," Mr. Adler replied.

"Still don't see why we couldn't have burned the lot of them," Sam grumbled.

"Every additional mile that lorry drove increased your chances of being caught," Cairncross retorted. "How long do you think it would've taken the army to start watching the roads after they discovered the shipment was missing? Nor would a plume of smoke from a burn close to the theft have been likely to go unnoticed."

"A great many things have met oblivion in the arms of the sea," Mr. Adler added.

"What—you turning poet now?" Sam snapped.

"Only when talking about my mistress," Mr. Adler replied. "Now mind your cheek, lad."

The other crates opened with the press of a crowbar and a squeal of nails.

Lily picked up a handful of files. She read the names on the tabs, written in the elegant hand she recognized as Joseph Hartwell's.

Amanda Robertson

Berta Schmidt

Edna O'Rourke

She did not know the names, but she suspected she knew their stories. She prayed they were some of the ones who made it out alive.

Lily climbed onto the bench at the stern. Holding the rail in one hand, she slipped the files into the bracing chill of the North Sea.

They fell from her fingers, shimmering their way down into the darkness.

~

By the time the crates were empty, Lily's knuckles were red from the salt and the cold, her shoulders tired.

"What about the crates?" Sam asked.

"Toss them," Mr. Adler said. "The tide is turning. Like as not they'll be in Belgium by tomorrow."

The silence of the sea was shattered by the rumble of Mr. Adler's diesel engine. The noise startled a few gulls who had gathered on the water by the stern, hoping the fishing boat was plying its usual trade. They flapped up into the sky on lazy wings, glaring down balefully.

Mr. Adler turned the craft toward shore and picked up speed. The boat loped over the waves, cutting through them at an angle as the sunlight shifted toward golden on the horizon.

Cairncross sat down beside her.

"I am not usually one to celebrate the destruction of records, but what Hartwell started . . . that was best consigned to oblivion," he said. "You should be proud of your part in that."

Lily gave him a nod, but her mind was elsewhere. It had gone back up the canals to the remote stretch of roadside where Doctor Singh stood in the dust, his last words echoing in her ears.

You can't stop progress.

THREE

Later that afternoon
Whitstable, Kent

$\mathcal{T}$HE TOWN WAS AN image off of a postcard, brightly painted fishing shacks and lovely summer houses lined up in a tidy row along a gentle green rise above a long, sandy beach. As they approached the harbor, Lily could see the ladies in their pastel gowns and parasols strolling along the promenade. The calls of the ice sellers sang through the late afternoon air, and along the strand a pair of boys in short pants were racing with a bright red kite.

A familiar figure stood at the pier.

Dr. Gardner was an enormous man with a soft presence. Though he might easily have broken up a fight in an alley if he chose, Lily had seen him talk a small child into swallowing a tablespoon of vile medicine with a smile. His rough Ulster accent betrayed his working-class roots, but he was more of a gentleman than most nobles Lily had been unlucky enough to encounter.

He easily caught the boat line as they approached, tying them off once Mr. Adler had expertly piloted them into place.

"Did it get past us?" Gardner demanded once they were near, his voice unusually urgent.

"Miss Albright managed it," Cairncross replied, hopping nimbly off onto the pier.

"Of course she did," Gardner noted. "Blasted tractor passed over the crossing and hooked the line. Snapped it right out of that contraption you'd rigged together," he said with a nod at Sam. "I would've legged it after the lorry to warn you if I hadn't been afraid that the sight of a bolting Irishman might've raised their alarm. So it's done, then?"

"It's done," Cairncross confirmed solemnly.

"And we'll all rest easier for it. I'm grateful to the lot of you," Gardner said.

"It's you slung us the tip," Sam noted as he swung himself over the rail.

Cairncross reached back into the boat to shake Mr. Adler's hand.

"Your assistance in this matter is appreciated, Eddie."

"Least I could do for my old sergeant," Adler replied. "Now stay out of trouble, would you?"

"I am long past trouble," Cairncross replied.

"I doubt that very much."

Mr. Adler's eyes twinkled. He reversed the boat back into the harbor, piloting it out into the sea.

"There's an hour or so till dinner," Gardner commented. "Shall I walk you up to the inn?"

"You lot go on," Lily replied. "I left the Triumph here, so I'll ride."

Sam lingered behind as the two older men headed up the rise. Lily caught a pair of girls eyeing him with interest as he leaned against the lamppost. She suspected it was less surprise at seeing an East Asian man in Whitstable and more due to his dashing looks and vaguely disreputable figure. That tended to be an irresistible combination for young women of quality.

"You alright, then?" he asked.

"Why wouldn't I be?"

"Maybe because we just sunk the work of the bloke who tried to kill you. Seems to me a thing like that might leave a body rattled. Ladies," he added, acknowledging the passing girls with a tip of his hat and a charming smile. They giggled, hurrying past him.

"I just need a bit of air," Lily replied. She unlocked the chain around her bright green Triumph. She paused to look back at him. "But thank you for asking."

"See you at dinner," he said, then loped up the road after Cairncross and the doctor.

Lily swung her leg over the side of the Triumph. She pedaled the engine into igniting and tore off down the harbor road, ignoring the surprised looks of the promenaders as she raced past.

It took only a few minutes to leave the village behind her. The road wound like a ribbon along the shore, the sea glittering to one side, the low hills and fields rambling along the other. The salt air filled her lungs and tugged at the pins in her hair. She relished in the feeling of it stinging against her cheeks, needing this space, this momentum.

She found a sandy rise that projected out over the water. She stopped there, looking across the sea.

There was a war in Serbia. Though the others on the boat had dismissed it as inconsequential, Lily was less certain.

Only one other person she knew seemed to share that doubt.

Edward Carne, the Earl of Torrington, was one of the most powerful men in England. Though he held no official position in government, he wielded a great deal of influence in the House of Lords. Torrington was known for effectively brokering deals and compromises behind the scenes. He was extraordinarily well-connected and extremely well-informed.

He was also Lily's father.

Her mother wasn't the countess but an Irish music hall star Lord Torrington had kept on the side.

The earl had not maintained a particularly fatherly role in Lily's life even when Deirdre Albright was still alive. Her death had not improved matters.

It was only a few months ago that Lily and her father breached over a decade of estrangement to begin, tentatively, to build a relationship with each other.

Torrington wasn't good at talking about his feelings. It was a trait Lily had inherited. That made their occasional meetings a case study in awkward conversation. Torrington asked Lily about how she had been spending her time, and since she couldn't exactly tell him about having paint bombs lobbed at her or spending hours staring into silver mirrors, she didn't have much to say.

Torrington wasn't about to share stories of the exploits of his sons, Lily's half-brothers, with the daughter who was excluded from that family. There were four Carne boys altogether, only one of whom Lily had met. That had not gone very well.

For all his personal failings, Lily could not fault her father's political acumen. Lily suspected not all of Torrington's information came through official channels. He could not wield such influence if he did not have access to knowledge the moment it became available, or perhaps even a little earlier.

Torrington saw far more danger in the European situation than the newspapers, who were generally the first to trumpet any threat as a major crisis for the sake of selling a few extra sheets.

"The whole of Europe is a powder keg waiting for a spark," he said at their last appointment earlier that month.

The previous few times they met, he had taken her to lunch. They would go to one of the fashionable and quiet restaurants he haunted. Lily could see how they were noticed. There were covert glances from gentlemen in bespoke suits at neighboring tables, their women exchanging whispers behind their menus. If they did not already know who Lily was—Torrington's bastard—what they guessed about their relationship was likely even worse.

When he apologized that he only had space in his schedule for a walk along the Thames this time, Lily had been relieved. They had stood by the great obelisk on the Embankment, looking out over the muddy water busy with ferries and freighters.

"It isn't just the alliances that entangle us. It's the arrogance—too many of the men holding the reins think they are invincible. The Germans have a plan, the Russians have a plan—because we have all seen it coming for so long, this possibility of war, everyone has a plan. Each plan guarantees its maker will decisively win. Every one of them was developed on pen and paper based on maps and timetables, and all of them would fall apart the minute actual humans became involved instead of just schedules and numbers. But if you are convinced of victory, what is to stop you from striding into conflict?"

He had looked tired. Lily noted the hollows under his gray eyes. That same steel hue stared back at Lily every time she looked in a mirror. The exhaustion showed in his choice of topic. Torrington usually refrained from talking to her about politics. She suspected it was his way of trying to be thoughtful, but since everything else they might discuss was a landscape fraught with emotional land mines, politics—even the politics of a possible war—felt something like a relief.

"But I cannot get anyone to look to the continent. The Irish question dominates all discussion these days. The Catholics want Home Rule, a government of their own in Dublin. The Protestants want to preserve the union of Great Britain and Ireland. It is a four-hundred-year-old argument that now we must somehow resolve in a fortnight."

Lily had heard of the conflict over Ireland, of course. It was all the papers talked about. Opinion pieces railed on either side of the debate, and hovering over all of it was the threat of civil war. That spring, thousands of Protestants in Ulster had taken up arms, threatening revolt if the British government gave in and allowed Ireland to form its own Parliament in Dublin. The coffee houses and taverns of London were ringing with gossip about the threat of an uprising. The king himself had taken the unusual step of personally weighing in, summoning representatives of both sides for a conference at Buckingham Palace to take place next week.

Lily understood that the threat of an Irish war was real. She should have felt it more acutely, being the daughter of an Irishwoman herself, though she had never stepped foot on Irish soil. Next to the racket ringing through London about Ireland, the threat of a European war was more or less a vague noise in the background.

Yet it was Europe that kept her up at night, buzzing with an anxiety she could not quite name.

Torrington sighed, rubbing his temples.

"Perhaps these Home Rule talks the king wishes to broker might illuminate the way to a compromise. But none of it will matter a whit if Britain is at war with the world."

"Do you really think it will come to that?" Lily asked.

"Austria, Russia, Germany, France . . . they are all entangled in alliances, as are we. The nations that lie between cannot possibly be left uncompromised. Could Britain really stand idle in the face of that?"

He had looked at her as he asked it, and Lily had been aware of what he was not asking—whether she had foreseen anything that would tell him whether a war was coming and who might be involved.

She wasn't sure how she would have answered.

"You are keeping well, I hope?" he said instead.

"I'm fine," she replied, both relieved and disappointed.

~

Twilight was spreading across the land as she rode back to Whitstable, the sky fading to purple in the east, lengthening the shadows over the hills as Lily pulled her motorbike up to the inn.

The lovely brick building was perched on a rise with wide views of the sea, window boxes spilling with summer blooms. It would have been an ideal spot for a romantic holiday, were it not currently serving as a convenient base of operations for hijacking the property of the British Army.

She killed the engine of the Triumph and walked the motorbike around to the carriage house. She stowed it there and headed for the garden rather than the front gate, thinking that her wind-blown, trouser-clad appearance might attract a little less attention if she used the back way in.

As the gate swung shut behind her she realized that she was not alone.

It should not have surprised her to find a trim older gentleman with a silver beard and a charcoal suit sitting on the flagstones of the garden, his legs crossed over each other in a tidy triangle.

Robert Ash, Lily's mentor, did not spend his days in the same routine as other men of his class. Instead of afternoons at the club sipping sherry and discussing the races, Ash might more readily be found studying some ancient manuscript or practicing the Chinese art of tàijíquán. That he was spending the hour before dinner meditating in the garden was more or less to be expected.

Lily rubbed at the paint stain on her hand.

"How did it go?" he asked without rising from the place where he sat.

"The papers are all destroyed."

"You were able to successfully identify the right vehicle."

The easy certainty in his words fanned her anger.

Ash's theory that Lily required "higher stakes" to overcome her defensive habits and activate her power occasionally proved itself true. Nor was Lily particularly fond of the alternative to it, a mind-numbing routine of practice and study.

She still wasn't ready to celebrate the successes. The whole thing left her with a feeling of simmering resentment she knew wasn't entirely fair.

Perhaps it was simply that she felt powerless to refuse the absurd challenges he set for her. Ash had a certain tone of voice, a kind of perfect and unquestioning certainty of his own authority, that compelled you to go along with whatever he was proposing. It wasn't until Lily had sand between her toes and the first paint ball stung her spine that she stopped to consider whether she might simply have said no.

Lily knew she was not the only one susceptible to it. She had seen Ash use it on Sam before as well, always eliciting the same snap-heel response.

Shì, Lâoshī.

Lâoshī. Teacher or master—Lily still wasn't sure exactly how to translate the title Sam used for Ash, perhaps because their relationship seemed to straddle so many lines.

"It might have been a lucky guess," she replied thinly.

"I don't believe it was."

He sounded completely sure of himself. Lily's patience, already frayed by the humiliation of the paint ball exercise and the demands of the day's undertaking, snapped.

"You know as well as I do that this khárisma I have can't be relied upon. If it weren't for that telephone line Sam built—"

"The telephone line failed. You did not."

"It shouldn't have come down to me," Lily ground out. "What if I'd flagged the postman to Sam or some poor unsuspecting farmer? Or worse, if I'd let the lorry drive right past us without raising any alarm at all? Hartwell's papers would be in that manor in Graveney tonight, locked up behind barbed wire and guards. The consequences of that are unthinkable. And you left that up to chance."

"No. I left it up to you," Ash replied.

"I'm not sure there's any difference."

"If you cannot have faith in yourself, Miss Albright, then I shall do it for you until you can."

His answer infuriated her. She had no answer to it.

Ash rose from the flagstones. He unfolded himself gracefully. There was no need for him to brush off his trousers. Somehow, he had chosen a spot on the patio without any dust. He looked once again like a proper English gentleman so long as one didn't glance down at his bare toes.

"You think today's exercise was extreme," he noted.

"It wasn't an exercise," Lily countered.

Ash was not a tall man, but he cast a long shadow across the stones.

"I would not demand anything of you I did not know you were capable of," he replied. "Even if you are not yet aware of it yourself."

"I should go dress for dinner," Lily retorted. She turned and stalked into the inn.

～

Lily descended the stairs a half hour later, her dusty trousers and motoring jacket exchanged for a skirt and lace blouse. The hair at the back of her neck was damp from the quick washing she had given herself to scrub off the dust of the pasture and the road.

She was still stewing over her conversation with Ash. Was she being unfair? She didn't know. In the end, she had pulled off the task he had set for her. Contrary to the retort she had thrown at Ash in the garden, Lily knew it had not been a lucky guess. The knowledge about the military lorry had come in a form she recognized. Perceiving the future was like knowing the tone of a particular musical note. Once you learned it, you could not mistake it for any other sound.

She was still fuming over it when she reached the bottom of the stairwell, so distracted that she nearly walked into the man standing there.

He reached out before she could collide with him, black-gloved hands catching her shoulders.

Lily knew those hands.

"Strangford," she breathed in surprise, a familiar warmth blooming through her.

"Hello, Lily," he replied, his mouth quirking into a smile.

With his sober black suit and his dark hair curling over-long around his collar, Lord Strangford looked less like an aristocrat and more like a Yorkshire poet fresh from walking the moors.

Lily's relationship with Strangford was unavoidably complicated and not just because he was a baron and she the bastard daughter of an Irish actress. Five months ago, they had decided to give things a try anyway. Where it would lead was a future Lily could not guess at, never mind foresee, but Strangford's presence still had the power to set her nerves tingling.

"You aren't supposed to be here," Lily noted.

"That is rarely a deterrent."

He steered her to the side, making room for a couple of elderly holiday-makers to move past. The front desk was just visible at the end of the hall. A clerk stood behind it, watching the guests make their way toward the dining room.

"But what about Ireland?" Lily demanded. "I thought you would be there for at least another week."

Strangford made most of his modest income from translation work, transcribing contracts, letters, books and sermons from French and German into English, with an occasional dab of Latin. The family's estate in Northumberland hadn't made a profit in decades, still reeling from a double blow of estate taxes when Strangford's father had died of a stroke just eight years after inheriting the title himself. His mother, Lady Strangford, had determined that their best hope of restoring the family fortunes lay in establishing Allerhope Hall as a prime horse stud.

It might have seemed a long-shot had Lily not heard so much about the lady's tenacity and hard-nosed practicality. That, and she had seen Strangford on a horse. Riding was clearly in the family's blood.

Though Lady Strangford managed the stud, she was pragmatic enough to know that a man sometimes stood a better chance of successfully negotiating at the auctions than a woman, even a titled one. Strangford was therefore occasionally tasked with setting aside his translations to try to acquire some promising piece of horseflesh.

"The mare my mother was after went up two days ago. I had just shipped her off to Allerhope when Cairncross's telegram found its way to me. I came as quickly as I could but by the time I reached London the next train to Kent didn't leave until half past four. I considered commandeering a bicycle but I'm not entirely sure I could have overcome the suffragette who was riding it. I hear they have been training."

"Have they?"

"Some form of ju jitsu," Strangford confirmed. "Which I believe is significantly more martial than my tàijí."

The tàijí in question had its roots in the art of self-defense, but Strangford had other reasons for practicing it. That meant the careful, controlled movements were usually more like a graceful dance than a weapon.

Usually being the key word.

"Perhaps you could have soothed her into submission."

"I am a man of diverse skills," Strangford agreed.

Lily knew it to be true, though she had so far only scratched the surface of what she suspected lay beneath those words.

The telephone rang. The clerk turned to answer it, his attention pulled from the hall to the row of letterboxes behind his desk.

It was an irresistible opportunity.

She turned the knob of the door behind her and pulled Strangford through it.

It was a breakfast room, shadowy with twilight and entirely deserted.

Strangford was close to her, his face half obscured by the shadows.

"I must caution that this situation begs a scandal." His voice was low, the murmur of it palpable across the brief distance that separated them.

"I know," Lily admitted. She ran a finger along the soft wool lapel of his suit. This one was in better shape than some of his others. Strangford always resisted replacing them until dragged to it. The suits were not something he could buy off the rack. The longer he wore them, the more comfortable they became in a way that had nothing to do with the fit.

"And?" he prompted.

"And I'm not sure I care right now."

It had never moderated—this crackling tension between them. They spent a fair amount of time together, but those meetings were bound by propriety when even a walk through the park could be cause for comment. As a bastard, Lily had little reputation to speak of, but she was painfully conscious of those scraps of it she retained. Knowing eyes, whispers when she passed by . . . these had always struck her with more force than they might someone assured of their worth in the eyes of the world.

They struck her, but they did not necessarily stop her. The motorbike was evidence of that. So, at the moment, was the dark-eyed baron in the breakfast room.

"Do you need me to care for you?" he asked.

"Why don't you tell me what I need right now," Lily replied.

It was both a challenge and an invitation, and Strangford knew it. He responded by carefully tugging the black gloves from his hands and setting them aside.

He touched her face.

The frisson of it electrified her, tiny fires of awareness burning across her skin. Her neck sang with contact as his fingers brushed across it, sliding into the thick auburn of her hair.

His gaze had gone distant, pupils unfocused like those of a blind man. It lasted for a moment before he returned to her, his eyes locking onto her own with a renewed intensity.

"Ah," he noted.

Then he leaned in to kiss her.

Lily drank him in, the taste of him washing away the pain and tension of the day—the bruises from her training, the dusty heat of the field, the shaking in her chest as the lorry rattled backwards.

The weight of Hartwell's papers in her hands before they slipped into the cold dark sea.

His hands ran along her spine, brushing all of it to the floor. That tightly coiled thing inside of her relaxed, allowed itself to unravel a little as her fingers became lost in the dark silk of his hair.

Behind them, something hit the floor with a small thud.

They broke from the kiss but not from each other. Lily glanced over for the source of the sound. A sugar bowl had fallen from one of the tables. It lay on the carpet, the tiny white grains glittering in the thin light through the windows.

"That was risky." Strangford's voice was rich and close in the darkness. "Not accounting for whether there might be someone else in the lorry."

It was the complicated thing about loving a man who could read the past with a touch, whose hands pulled thoughts and memories from anything and anyone they came into contact with. Lily could not choose what she revealed to him any more than he could choose what parts of her mind he might see.

There would never be any secrets. That was the price Lily paid for moments like this.

"Sam and I managed," she replied.

"I still wish I had been there."

"There was very little notice," she countered. "You could hardly have been expected to fly from Ireland, even if Cairncross's message had reached you in time."

"You don't know that. I might have commandeered a balloon. Befriended a flock of eagles."

"Sam says eagles are snobbish," Lily replied.

"I can be very charming when I want to be," he returned.

"I will not argue that. But at any rate, there wouldn't have been any room for you in the lorry."

She felt the smile tug at his mouth. She reached up and ran her fingers along it.

"I found a new painting," he said.

"Oh?"

Strangford was a passionate collector of art, as much as his limited finances allowed. His tastes were eclectic, questing after work that exposed to the eyes something of how he must perceive the world through the power in his hands.

"The artist is living in a garret on Achill Island. Chap by the name of Henry. The piece is called The Watcher. There's a woman in red by a storm-tossed sea . . . a poor fisherman's wife or a siren. All of those things at the same time." He sighed. "I'm sorry, you know how terrible I am at describing them. You'll have to see it."

"I'll look forward to that," Lily replied.

"You heard about Austria-Hungary?"

Lily let her hand drop.

"They've gone to war."

She didn't have to tell Strangford what that meant.

He knew about all her conversations with her father. He knew about the tense muddle of hope and fear and resentment those meetings inflicted upon her, and he knew about the politics they discussed to avoid speaking about things more difficult than civil war in Ireland or the potential disintegration of Europe.

Strangford also knew about the visions Lily had endured while under the influence of the contents of a strange blue bottle she had stolen from Ash's kitchen.

In between and through an overwhelming cascade of truths, she had foreseen Strangford in a muddy uniform, crouched in the shadows of a hole dug into the mud. Seen him fall back as the wall in front of him exploded, burying him in heap of dirt and splintered wood and barbed wire.

She could not know when it would be, or what it really meant. Her visions were rarely literal, made up of symbols her mind pasted together to fill in for truths she couldn't yet know. They were obscure and unreliable things, but the news of war in Serbia still sent a chill of fear through her.

He ran his fingers over her palm, his touch exquisitely delicate.

"It was good work you did today," he said. "I can still feel the echo of those files in your hands. There was that much pain in them."

"I should wash them."

"That sort of thing doesn't wash off." He lifted her hands to his lips, pressed a kiss to them. "But it will fade in a little time."

A jaunty knock sounded on the door behind them. The risk of what they were doing came back to her. Whispers could reach London even from distant Kent.

She could almost hear the voices.

No better than her mother.

She told herself it shouldn't matter, but it did. The quick panic came and then immediately subsided in the face of a warm flash of knowing, a sure and simple awareness of what they would find when they opened that door.

Her power was like that. It cropped up when she wasn't asking, when her guard was down, or perhaps—if she was lucky—when she desperately needed it to.

What it did not do was answer to her will.

"It's alright," Lily told Strangford and turned the knob.

Estelle stood on the threshold.

Lily's friend and downstairs neighbor had joined their expedition to Kent with a declaration that "one never knew when another pair of hands might be needed." A tall woman of an indeterminate age somewhere over forty, she was dressed for dinner in an elegant caftan patterned like a peacock's feathers. A neatly-wrapped turban sat on her head, secured with a glittering brooch.

"Hello, darlings," she said, her hazel eyes flashing with mischief. "This establishment serves dinner at six. You are on the verge of being late, and you are scandalizing Mrs. Forbes."

"Mrs. Forbes?" Strangford echoed, arching a dark eyebrow.

"Formerly the lady of the house and of rather conservative sensibilities that do not extend to unmarried couples canoodling in the breakfast room."

Lily knew that Estelle was not talking about some retired great aunt kept around the place out of sympathy. *Formerly the lady of the house* meant *until she choked on a fishbone and was buried in the churchyard down the road.* Estelle was a powerful medium. More often than not, her information came from deceased sources.

"She has been rattling my pipes for the last five minutes. I am surprised they did not spring a leak. However much privacy you think you have stolen, the dead are always around."

Lily glanced back at the toppled sugar bowl.

"It is enough trouble dodging the living," Strangford countered, tugging his gloves back on. "I think the dead may have to fend for themselves."

"Dinner," Estelle returned, then glided down the hall in full anticipation they would follow.

"May I escort you?" Strangford offered, extending his arm.

Lily hesitated. To wander in to dinner felt oddly casual after what she had done that day. Thoughts of the past crowded in—the cracked mirror, the call of a raven. The voice of a dead woman speaking from the lips of a friend. There had been so much horror. Drowning Hartwell's papers changed none of it.

She looked to Strangford. His dark eyes were steady.

"I know, Lily."

She slipped her hand through his arm.

"Let's go."

FOUR

SHE IS NOT DREAMING, and it is winter.

Lily stands on a cliff, a sandy rise that projects out over the water. From the top, she looks out over the sea to Germany, Belgium, France. They are lost in the haze that clouds the horizon, the gray line of it blurring the space where the sea meets the sky.

She is on a motorbike, but it is not the one she knows. It is a thicker machine, heavier and more powerful. Lily does not wear her usual canvas trousers and jacket but a uniform of thick wool. The wool cuts the cold but itches where it extends past her shirt to rub against her wrists.

There is something in her pocket that pulls on her like lead. She opens the flap to look down at the slender piece of yellow paper.

A low buzz sounds in her ears. She looks up to see the great, bloated shapes of the zeppelins flying in a neat line overhead. Cold flakes spin down from the sky, landing icily on her cheek.

Lily reaches up to wipe one them away. Her hand comes back streaked with gray.

It is not snowing. It is raining ash.

The wind picks up, whips the salt spray into her eyes. Lily raises her arm to shield herself.

When she lowers it again she is in Hell.

It is a blasted place. The flat landscape is punctuated by the burnt and twisted remains of trees. Bloated corpses float among waves of torn earth, humming with flies. Snakes of black wire slither across the ground.

In the distance, she can see the beasts. They are black and hulking monsters that move with a sound like shrieking metal.

A raven, fat and glossy, flaps noisily onto the blackened branch of what was once a sprawling oak.

Lily.

The word is a breath against her ear, close enough for her to feel the wind of it on her cheek. It is Strangford's voice, soft with urgency.

Something flies past her cheek, near enough that she can feel the wind of it. It is a small brown thrush. It races through the gloom ahead of her, then stops with an audible thud. The bird crumples to the ground as though it has just struck some invisible wall crossing the barren landscape.

Lily runs to it. The thrush lies twitching, its neck clearly broken.

She reaches out to touch a barrier she knows is there but cannot see. As her hand makes contact, she slips through it to the other side.

The room around her is warm. Ornamented pillars soar to an elegant ceiling, its rich colors cloaked in gloom. The floor is lit up like a stage. Beyond the pillars, cloaked in shadows, enormous gears turn. It is the interior of a vast clock, and also the palace from a fairy tale, the sort of place foolish children wander into and never leave again.

The air around her trembles, full of movement and something she feels sure would have been noise, had she been able to hear it.

Instead there is only silence and the thin line of a song. It echoes off the high walls, a woman's voice, the tune achingly familiar.

Lily follows the sound of it down a twisting stairwell into darkness. She can just make out the words.

And a thousand blades were flashing at the rising of the moon . . .

Lily knows this song. She knows the voice. The truth of it lies just around the corner, tied up with memories of a silver brush pulling through long auburn hair, the smell of lilacs and a laugh like tiny bells ringing.

Lily continues down the hall.

A vast black lake lays before her, capped by arches holding up a low ceiling. It is a cathedral flooded nearly to the brim and trapped in an eternal night. It stinks of rot.

A man sits in the center of the lake on a theater seat plumped with tattered and faded red velvet. He lounges on it like a throne, desperately pale but nattily dressed. A broad-brimmed and stylish hat blocks her view of his eyes.

His suit is white linen save for the twin rivers of blood running from the stab wounds in his chest.

"Come along now, a stóirín. We mustn't be late."

Lily knows those words. She knows the dancing accent, the Irish endearment. She heard them before on the most terrible night of her life, the night that everything she knew was safe was taken away from her. The night that shaped everything that would come after.

We mustn't be late.

She recalls the tune that led her here, but it cannot be right. Lily sees the future, not the past.

At the rising of the moon, at the rising of the moon.

The sense of urgency surrounds her, threatening to drown her with its desperate importance. She must not let this slip away. She needs to *know*.

Ash has been teaching her. There are lessons for this, a science she must not forget.

Time . . . she must find a time.

Lily wills a clock onto the wall. It takes the form of a full, fat white orb, cratered with pale shadows. The hands point to the hour: 11:17.

"Well, aren't you the clever one," the man in the chair smirks.

Black pipes open in the walls. A stinking flood pours in. The water rises up to consume her.

She sinks beneath the murk. Her lungs burn.

Green flames dance across the surface.

Somewhere above, a shadow steps before a doorway blazing with light . . .

. . . and Lily sat up in Kent gasping for air.

The room was dark. The sea hushed in the distance, the sound carrying through the open window along with the cool relief of a breeze. Moonlight poured across the floor, carving out the shape of Estelle

41

lying on the next bed. Lily's friend wore a sleep mask, the soft, short down of her pale brown hair exposed.

Lily struggled to calm her ragged breath, the pounding of her heart, willing herself to be quiet.

"Bad dream?" Estelle asked.

"You're awake," Lily acknowledged.

"When one reaches a certain age, darling, sleep is like an old friend who never writes anymore. Was it just a dream, or something else?"

"Something else," Lily admitted.

She always knew the difference. A nightmare was painted in another palette entirely from what she had just experienced. The vision could not be mistaken for anything other than what it was.

Estelle didn't press her for more. The medium knew that Lily's relationship with her visions was a tumultuous one.

Lily would have preferred not to talk about it. Her first instinct was always to bury her visions as deep and far as she could in what she knew was a fruitless attempt to forget they had ever happened.

She knew better now, but that didn't make it any easier.

"I think this one is a bit more in your court than my own," Lily admitted.

Estelle sat up, pushing her eye mask into her hair.

"Why is that?"

"I saw a dead man," Lily said.

"That isn't unusual for you," Estelle noted. She was well aware that Lily's visions usually foretold disasters. There had been plenty of bodies. Estelle had very nearly been one of them herself.

"I mean someone who is already dead," Lily corrected her.

Estelle raised an eloquent eyebrow.

"I gather that is more uncommon."

"It's never happened before," Lily admitted.

"This is someone you knew?" Estelle guessed.

"Yes."

The older woman considered this.

"It isn't unheard of. The recently deceased are prone to that sort of thing. One doesn't have to be a full-blown medium for it to happen, particularly in a dream."

"This wasn't a dream," Lily said. "And he wasn't recently deceased."

"Well," Estelle said. "That is rather curious."

Something banged against the window. It struck the upper part of the glass, a flashing black shadow.

Lily threw back the covers.

She put her head out through the open lower half of the window and looked down.

A bird lay on the ground two floors below, just within the pool of illumination cast by the lantern at the inn door. It was a small brown thrush, neck broken, wings twitching.

Robert Ash stepped out onto the pavement, Cairncross following behind him. The two older men looked down at the bird.

Ash's eyes rose to Lily.

"This was part of it," she said numbly, surprise and unease spilling the words from her mouth.

Estelle plucked her dressing gown from the hook on the wall.

"Perhaps you'd best share exactly what else you saw."

~

The group assembled in the empty hotel parlor in the small hours of the morning completed Robert Ash's circle, the men and women he referred to as *charismatics*.

Estelle Denueve was swathed in purple silk, lounging on the settee. The medium was not the least bit self-conscious to be here without the makeup and turban she usually wore. The fine bones of her face were adornment enough.

Sam Wu leaned against the fireplace. Both Ash's driver and his student, he had thrown a jacket on over his pajamas. His dark hair was mussed with sleep but his eyes were alert.

Strangford stood behind Lily. He had dressed before coming down—he was not a man to be caught without his armor. He rested a gloved hand on the back of her chair.

Ash and Cairncross still wore their clothes from the day before. Lily suspected they had never gone to bed. It was not unusual for the two men to keep odd hours, staying up till dawn discussing a single line in the Koran or urgently studying a map of the Tiān Shān.

Cairncross was not a charismatic, though his encyclopedic knowledge of the contents of Ash's enormous library bordered on the uncanny. Lily did not know how Cairncross, a rank-and-file war veteran from a family of Scottish tradesmen, had come to be the companion of an upper-class gentleman scholar, but suspected there was quite a story behind it. She did know that the pair had traveled together for decades, crisscrossing the world before Ash was finally ready to return to England.

The only one missing was Dr. Gardner, who had left after dinner to take the evening train back to London. The son of a Belfast tailor, Gardner had worked his way to a position at St. Bart's, one of London's most storied and respected hospitals. He would cheerfully do without sleep to keep a shift in his ward. The disparity in class between himself and his esteemed colleagues caused enough trouble for the doctor without adding into the mix his knack for diagnosing medical ailments with a touch.

Gardner's khárisma was an intuition of the body. By laying on his hands, he could feel out whatever was amiss inside of a person. It should have been a boon for a doctor, but Gardner knew better than to share the truth of what he could do with his patients or fellow physicians.

Nor did knowing what was wrong necessarily grant him the power to heal it. Gardner spent much of his day treating ailments he could diagnose but never cure.

Lily wasn't sure whether Ash had collected them all like some naturalist pinning butterflies to a board, or whether they had gravitated to him, each of them hungry for others that would understand what it was like to know things the rest of the world thought impossible.

Perhaps it was a little of both.

He had built a place where they could find knowledge and acceptance. They called it The Refuge. It was the closest thing to home Lily had known since she was a child. Like any home, it came with complications.

A telephone rang back at the check-in desk. Lily heard the night clerk answer. Overhead came the scrape of furniture against the floor, a low rumble of laughter.

The inn dozed around them, full of people with no notion of the impossibilities being discussed in the quiet of the parlor.

"You say the man in the chair is dead," Cairncross asked. He was taking notes in a slender book.

"Yes," Lily confirmed.

"And he was familiar to you?"

"I know who he was," she admitted. She could feel Ash's eyes on her as she spoke. "He died with my mother."

The memories were sharp. Just uttering the words pricked them to the surface—the wet pavement, the scattered gems glittering like stars around the warp of a broken thread.

Her mother's ivory gown turned to red.

Lily had seen all of it, every horrible detail . . . two weeks before the attack took place.

She had tried to stop it. She had failed.

"The Irish costumer," Strangford filled in, knowing the story more intimately than anyone else in the room, for obvious reasons. "The one who accompanied her to the theater that night."

"Patrick Dougherty," Lily confirmed.

She had not known him particularly well. Deirdre Albright maintained a wide and colorful social circle. On any given night the rooms on Oxford Street that Lord Torrington rented for her could be found packed with opera singers, playwrights, painters, stagehands and street performers. There were men who wore gowns in their off-hours, hopeful poets with sheafs of paper, gruff foreign light riggers and chorus girls who sat with arms draped over each other's shoulders.

Patrick Dougherty had blended comfortably into that eclectic crowd. Lily recalled him as tall, elegant and unruffled, a man in a gorgeously tailored suit he had likely sewn himself. Perhaps a decade older than Deirdre, he attracted longing gazes from young actresses who didn't know any better and the occasional disappointed sigh from those who did.

That it had been Dougherty and not one of the others who ended up lying in the alley with his throat cut had always seemed to Lily a matter of rotten chance. Deirdre was a creature of whims. She might just as easily have picked the hopeful poet to join her at that evening's performance, or one of the chorus girls.

It was Lily herself who had insisted Deirdre not go alone. The frame of her vision had been confined to her mother's prone corpse on the black ground. It had never occurred to her to wonder what that scene might have excluded, like the well-polished wingtip shoe of a handsome costumer.

Lily had also begged Deirdre to go without the jeweled necklace Lord Torrington had given her a few weeks before. It was Patrick Dougherty who insisted she don an excellent costume piece instead, paste gems cut so brilliantly they drew more eyes than the real thing.

Paste that must have drawn the wrong eyes.

"This gentleman passed fourteen years ago?" Cairncross asked.

"That is correct," Lily said.

"Rather late for a visitation but I suppose it is not impossible," the librarian mused thoughtfully. "As I recall, there is a 17th-century account of John of the Cross encountering the embodied spirit of St. Teresa of Avila while convalescing at the monastery at Ubeda. That would have been nearly a decade after her death."

"Miss Albright did not encounter a spirit. She saw the costumer because her mind connected him to the future—to some event which is yet to come," Ash quietly declared. "He is not a man. He is a symbol for something Lily doesn't yet know."

"Does that mean that whatever is going to happen is connected to her mother's death?" Strangford's voice was low behind her.

"It is a possibility," Ash replied.

Lily tried not to let the notion shake her. Her mother was the victim of a random crime, murdered for the fake jewels she wore around her neck. What more was there to know?

"What about the rest of it?" Estelle demanded. "Tell us again about the place."

"A black lake. Somewhere underground." Lily frowned, reconsidering. "No—not underground. Inside. There were arches, a ceiling . . . like some vast windowless room. It was large enough that I couldn't see the end of it."

"You said there was a smell. Sulfurous? Acrid?" Cairncross was looking at his notebook.

"It was just rotten. Like the marsh this afternoon."

"The Greek geographer Pausanias described encountering a series

46

of subterranean lakes in the caves outside Kastria in the second century A.D.," Cairncross mused.

"She said it had a ceiling. It couldn't be a cave," Strangford said.

"Perhaps the basilica reservoir in Istanbul? Though I believe that is mostly kept drained. There is also a section of the catacombs in Paris that flooded twenty or so years ago, if I am not mistaken."

"Mightn't we look a bit closer to home, James?" Estelle chided.

"I would have an easier time of it if we were back at Bìfēnggǎng," he retorted. "There are several excellent atlases in the library."

Zìzhīzhīmíng Bìfēnggǎng was the true name of The Refuge, a string of Mandarin Lily was still learning to properly pronounce. It most neatly translated to "the sanctuary of coming to know one's self." In either language, it was a mouthful, and therefore generally abbreviated.

Cairncross flipped back a page.

"You accessed this place by descending a twisting staircase from a room you describe as 'palatial'. Ornate columns and iron screens, painted in colors like a circus caravan."

"Yes," Lily confirmed.

"Hold on," Sam demanded, raising his head. He had been outside when Lily had described the first half of her vision, respectfully disposing of the remains of the swallow. "A black stinking lake under a room glazed up like Christmas candy? Sounds like Cistern Chapel."

"The what?" Cairncross frowned.

"The Cistern Chapel. The Cathedral of the Marshes. Y'know—the sewage-lifting station down at Crossness."

"Ah yes. Of course. The Southern Outfall Works," Cairncross mused.

"The place is tricked out like a whore's parlor—pardon, ladies— and there's a big pit just under the lawn where they pump the stuff up to sea level to wait for the outgoing tide."

"Sam, were you reading sewer plans for fun again?" Estelle's tone was teasing.

"It's right genius how Bazalgette worked it all up," Sam retorted.

"You know there are other ways a young man of your charms might spend his time," she said.

"I get to that too," he replied. "So is that it, then? We looking for a dead man in a lake of sewage?"

As soon as the words had left his mouth, his expression flashed to one of dismay. His attention snapped to Ash as though expecting some reaction.

Cairncross did it too. Lily caught how his gaze flickered over to the man who sat quietly beside him, lines of concern briefly furrowing his brow.

Lily wondered what it was about Sam's words that had sparked their reaction.

For her part, Estelle looked conspicuously oblivious, her usually dynamic expression carefully restrained.

If there was something in what Sam had said that should have unsettled Ash, he gave no sign of it.

"What does the vision tell you, Miss Albright? Should we pursue this?" he asked.

It was not an easy question to answer. This connection between the vision and her mother's death made the whole thing feel so desperately personal. Were she to answer yes, she would be dragging her friends into taking wild risks to settle a matter that must be intimate to her own history with no guarantee it mattered at all to anyone else.

But Ash was not asking for her judgment. He was asking for her sense of the truth—for what the vision had communicated to her of its own urgency and necessity.

She did not have to dig far to find it. That demand for her attention, that sense of importance had been vibrating through her skin since she woke up.

"I think we should," she admitted. "If anyone is willing to help."

"Silly girl," Estelle said, hitting her with a couch pillow. "As if you even need to ask."

FIVE

*C*OMMERCIAL STREET WAS FLOODED with demonstrators. They blocked the entirety of the road as it entered Whitechapel, a dignified procession carrying banners and signs emblazoned with *Ireland demands Home Rule* and *Rule from Dublin is Rule for Ireland*. The procession forced Ash's Rolls Royce Silver Ghost to a halt, blocked into a wall of lorries and horse-drawn carts. The motor car stood out, drawing a few admiring looks from the East Enders gathered on the pavement. One of the men decided Lily was worthy of a shout of admiration as well from what he could see of her through the window glass. She ignored him from where she sat beside Strangford in the rear seat. In front of them, Cairncross consulted a map and his watch while Sam leaned back with his arm draped casually across the wheel.

"There's still time," Sam commented.

"I'm simply exploring whether there might be a faster route," Cairncross returned.

"There's another route, but it ain't faster unless it turns out every Irishman in East London has come out for this soiree," Sam replied.

There was genuine reason for concern about the time. Lily's vision the night before had come down to the exact minute. Deciding when to leave The Refuge and start the journey to Crossness had involved a fair bit of wrangling between Sam and Cairncross. The goal had been to arrive after dark had fallen so that their presence near the sewage plant could go unnoticed, and yet early enough to grant them a comfortable buffer before the events in Lily's vision came to pass.

Traffic across the city had proved much heavier than anticipated. The sun was already dipping below the horizon as they reached the East End. This Home Rule demonstration had now cost them another twenty minutes.

The protesters had drawn a crowd of onlookers which included a few clusters of policemen at opposite sides of the crossroads. They appeared to be merely enjoying the show, but Lily noted the gleam of their helmets and the way their hands rested casually on their truncheons.

A window popped open in one of the buildings that lined the road. A buxom young woman emerged, unfurling an orange sash and pinning it defiantly to the frame. As a symbol of the Protestants of Ulster who opposed Irish Home Rule, it did what it had clearly been intended to do, inciting a few violent epithets from the demonstrators.

The woman answered them with the toss of a glass bottle. The projectile landed in the center of the crowd, smashing with a crystalline pop and a cluster of screams. The orderly march of the protest dissolved as a group of the younger men launched missiles of their own up at the Unionist window.

The police whipped out their batons, swinging in toward the young men as other protesters linked arms and began defiantly singing "The Wearing of the Green."

Sam perked up in his seat.

"Right—this'll be on for a while," he determined. He turned, glancing back over his shoulder through the rear glass of the canvas top at the long line of vehicles blocking the road behind them. "That'll do," he concluded.

"What will do?" Cairncross asked crossly.

"Don't tell Mr. Ash," Sam ordered, then threw the automobile into reverse. He wove it neatly backwards, threading the needle between a four-seater hackney and an omnibus, the gleaming finish of the Rolls mere inches from those vehicles on either side. He veered sharply to the right, bumping the motor car up onto the pavement, then switched to a forward gear. Narrowly avoiding an orange girl flirting with a dandy, he swerved around a lamppost and then turned hard into a narrow lane.

The Rolls zipped away into the bowels of Limehouse.

The roads were clear and quiet. Sam navigated the maze of streets by instinct, gliding them past the tidy laundries and boarding houses with Chinese characters painted over the English on their signs. Limehouse was his old borough, the place where he and his family had lived for years before Robert Ash entered their lives.

Ten minutes later, they were diving into the mouth of the Thames Tunnel, crossing beneath the river to reach Kent.

Beyond the suburbs, out in the countryside, the silver Rolls Royce flew along the twisting roads. The stars were paled by the glow of a full moon, casting ghostly shadows across the fields. Ash's automobile was a gleaming missile, sleek and quiet even as Sam pushed it to nerve-rattling speeds.

The lights of the city were a distant glow on the horizon, the darkness of the fields broken only by the occasional glowing shape of a lit window in some isolated farmhouse.

Lily rode beside Strangford in the darkness of the rear seat. Her awareness of him complemented the lump in her gut over what they would find when they reached their destination. In the front, Cairncross tried to study the map with only the light of the moon through the windshield for illumination.

"What time is it?" Strangford asked.

"Ten fifty-three," Cairncross replied after a close peek at his pocket watch.

The time Lily had conjured into her vision had been seventeen minutes after eleven. They were cutting things far closer than she would have liked.

Fields turned to marshes, pervaded by the scent of low tide.

Ahead of them, beyond a turn in the road, rose a palace out of the Arabian Nights.

It was isolated against the inky backdrop of the marsh, sparkling with gaslights. The great structure sat majestically on a hill, the rise suspiciously uniform and unique against the flat ground stretching for miles around. A thin tower rose over it like the minaret of a mosque.

"You'd never guess what it was full of," Sam quipped before pressing on.

They passed the well-lit sign that marked the tree-lined drive for the Crossness Southern Outfall Works. The Rolls glided along what Lily could now see was a man-made embankment. They passed a dark and shuttered school building and stopped a bit short of an abandoned farmhouse.

The dark shadow of the Thames was just visible in the distance, a lower and blacker line in the landscape.

They climbed out of the Rolls, carefully shutting the doors. Sam pulled a canvas bag from the boot and slung it over his shoulder.

The sound of a bell echoed softly across the open landscape, a clock at the industrial complex in front of them sounding out the hour.

"This way," Cairncross said, setting off toward the glow of the works.

Lily and Strangford followed him, Sam taking up the rear.

A set of concrete stairs led them to an evenly-paved footpath. It lay arrow-straight behind a row of terraced houses identical to those one might see in one of the new developments in Stepney where parts of the old slums had been leveled. The sight was a bit more unsettling here where the close, tidy buildings stood alone in the middle of acres of nothing.

An inexplicably large green lawn lay between the two terraces, broad as a football field and unbroken by so much as a shrub.

Conscious that families were sleeping behind the shining dark glass of the windows, Lily and the others moved quickly and silently along the path. She prayed that the works forbade its employees from keeping a dog.

Cairncross slipped into the shadow of a great open vat that stank of sewage. He raised his hand in a silent signal. Lily and Strangford tucked themselves in behind him, Sam melting into the darker wall of a nearby workshop.

Footsteps clapped the pavement. Someone strolled by, whistling a tune, a toolbox in his hand. He disappeared into one of the maze of buildings that surrounded them.

"He won't be the last," Sam warned in a whisper. "The works runs through the night."

Across the courtyard, an enormous building hulked.

"The boiler room?" Cairncross asked.

"Likely enough," Sam replied.

They raced across the brightly-lit, open expanse of ground, Lily painfully aware of how exposed they would be should another night worker happen by. The building itself provided more cover, casting a dark shadow over a square of well-trimmed lawn.

Cairncross put his hand on the knob of the door.

"Here we go," he warned and twisted it.

Heat blasted her. Rows of electric lights illuminated the great black mountains of the iron boilers. Their bulk turned what should have been a vast space into something close and tight. The night outside had been warm, made tolerable by the breeze blowing from the river across the marsh. The boiler room was sweltering.

Lily had only a moment to take it in before racing after Cairncross as he ducked around a corner.

They stopped behind a shelf of tools, Lily taking the opportunity to catch her breath.

The electric bulbs were not as bright as gas lamps would have been, but they were everywhere. While the ceiling of the enormous space was lost in shadows, every aisle and corner of the floor felt illuminated. Each move they made was a dash across what felt like acres of open space in the heat of those hulking industrial gods.

"There's someone at the door to the engine house," Cairncross warned. Lily risked a glance around the corner of the shelf and saw the man in question, a heavyset fellow in a chair at a small table, eating a sandwich and flipping through the pages of a magazine. An unassuming door was visible over his right shoulder.

"Do you think he's alone?" Lily asked.

"He's got the look of a supervisor about him," Sam said. "Which means there must be other blokes around doing the real work."

"We need to entice him to move without making a fuss," Cairncross said. "Any suggestions?"

Sam scratched his head under his hat. He looked up at the shadows cloaking the high, angled ceiling.

"Like as not, there's bats up there," he commented. "Let's see what we can stir up."

He stepped apart from them, eyes tracking the shadows of the rafters. He put his fingers to his lips and whistled—or at least, that's what it appeared he was doing. Lily couldn't hear a sound.

A few patches of darkness detached themselves from the shadows cloaking the rafters. They fluttered down to where Sam stood, circling him in uneven orbits. Sam extended an arm and one of the bats grasped it, climbing to his shoulder with tiny claws at the ends of its leathery wings.

The creature let out a stream of chirps and squeaks. Lily was conscious of the guard by the door and wondered if he would hear them over the ever-present roar of the boilers.

"It's alright, then. See?" Sam said to the animal. He scratched it gently behind its small pointed ears. The bat leaned into it. Had it been a cat instead of a rodent, Lily would have expected to hear it purr.

"A little more speed might be helpful," Cairncross noted.

Sam glared at him.

"I can't just order them about. I have to make friends first."

Another bat landed on his hat. Lily saw Sam consciously contain the urge to flinch. It started kneading the tweed.

The one on his shoulder had crawled up to his neck. It leaned in and started licking Sam's cheek.

"What are they doing?" Lily demanded, resisting the urge to back away.

"Grooming me," Sam replied tiredly. "Right then, I think that's enough."

He plucked the bat from his hat and brought it to his lips. Both it and the one at his cheek paused in their ministrations as he whispered to them, their delicate ears cocked with rapt attention.

A moment later they took off, black wings flapping toward where the supervisor sat with his lunch.

The bats swooped at the man's head. His hands flailed in response, the sandwich falling to the floor.

More dark shadows dropped from the ceiling, circling down to where the man sat.

"They're right neighborly with each other," Sam remarked beside Lily, watching the growing swarm.

"So it appears," Strangford noted as the supervisor lurched to his feet, knocking over his chair.

Lily heard a string of curses. The man ducked and waved his arms. He skidded to the left, the bats continuing to haunt him, until finally he sprinted down the long hall.

Sam ambled over, three more of the bats flapping curiously around his head. He shooed them away gently and adjusted his cap.

"Right, then. Shall we?" he said and opened the door.

The engine house was loud. Lily realized she had been hearing the rumble of it even from within the boiler house, but once they passed through the door in the wall the rumble became a roar. Enormous machines plunged and turned all around her, the clatter of their gears echoing off the brick walls.

There were electric lights here as well, but they were spottier in their coverage than they had been in the boiler house. Pools of light were interspersed with wells of gloom.

Lily's sense of urgency was growing. There must only be a few minutes before their deadline. They had to find their way underground.

As they moved toward the heart of the building, their surroundings became more absurdly ornate. From soot-stained bricks and machinery, it changed to wrought-iron pillars and elaborate metal screens. The paint that covered them must once have been circus-bright, but age and use had weathered it. It gave the place a feeling of corruption as though the wonder that had once stood here had been abandoned and turned to grubby use.

Before them, in the center of a pool of electric light, lay a circular opening in the floor surrounded by an elegant railing.

That must be their destination.

Cairncross was leading them toward it, moving silently along the shadow of the hall, when a warning instinct hummed through Lily. It was like a tuning fork being hit, a sudden leap from stillness to a vibrating awareness.

Lily's power to detect a close threat was unreliable and intermittent, as the lingering bruises from her paint ball session attested. Despite Ash's best efforts and Cairncross's careful aim, Lily could not command that particular variety of foresight at her own convenience. It came or it didn't as it pleased, marching to a tune that was something distinctly other than Lily's will.

When it did come, the feeling was unmistakable.

"Sam," she hissed in warning.

The younger man grabbed Cairncross by the arm, pulling him back behind a console.

Strangford did not miss the urgency of her tone. His arm slipped around her waist and he tugged her into the narrow space between the wall and an enormous pump, the lever of it rising and dipping, intermittently blocking her view of the aisle.

"I'm off for a smoke," a voice called from above.

Lily waited, holding herself still, her back pressed to Strangford's chest as they crowded into their hiding place.

Footsteps echoed quickly off the wrought-iron girding of the upper floor. Someone descended the stairs.

A moment later he strolled down the aisle, a slight man with a flat cap tossing a tin of cigarettes in his hand.

A door closed at the far end of the building.

"He wasn't talking to himself," Lily whispered.

"I know," Strangford breathed in reply.

He inched himself back out into the open. Lily could see now that a narrow maintenance track ran the full length of the wall, providing a slender access to other parts of the machinery the engine room housed.

Strangford followed it, moving carefully and silently, his dark jacket and trousers blending into the shadows that fell thickly on these outer reaches of the room. Lily knew he was capable of handling himself should it come to a fight but the notion still made her feel ill.

Her own chances were somewhat hampered at the moment. She had left her walking stick at home, knowing that it might be too ungainly to carry where they would be going.

Sam and Cairncross were lost to her, their hiding place invisible from where she stood.

Lily followed Strangford along the narrow walkway, barraged by the clanking noise of the engines.

The room converged around a central well, brightly illuminated by electric light. The absurdity of the ornate construction was more glaring here. The interior of the building looked more like an arcade at a seaside pavilion than a sewer works.

The space was empty, deserted save for the rush and noise of the surrounding machinery.

She could see now that the hole at the center of it was indeed a stairwell leading down into darkness.

The floor around it glowed in the glare of the bulbs, exposed and bare.

"Where are the others?" Strangford murmured.

Lily shook her head.

She tried to feel for some other threat, fishing inside herself for any sense of unease. It was a little too easy to find and distinctly colored by her own nerves.

She was painfully aware of the time slipping past them.

"I think we have to try for it," she said.

"Quick and quiet, or like we belong here?"

"There is no chance anyone will believe I belong here," Lily pointed out.

"Quick and quiet, then," Strangford agreed.

He darted toward the stairs, Lily following.

"Hold on, then! You shouldn't be here."

The voice called down from above. Lily turned to see a surprised stranger standing at the wrought-iron rail that ringed the upper portion of the well.

"You stay right there," he ordered, pointing at them. He took a step back, clearly planning to call for help, when Sam materialized behind him.

The younger man's foot flashed out, kicking the stranger's legs from underneath him. Sam knelt down on his back, twisting his arm up at an angle that made Lily wince.

"Keep shouting and I'll pop it out of your shoulder," Sam warned cheerfully.

Cairncross came out into the light. He held a length of wire in his hand.

"He'll need a gag. I am afraid someone will have to sacrifice a sock," he said tiredly.

"Why us? Use one of his," Sam countered.

"I suppose he might find that preferable," Cairncross admitted.

~

They left the engineer trussed on the upper landing and hurried down the curving iron stair into the darkness of the lower level.

There was nothing palatial about this part of the works. It had the feeling of a crypt, low brick tunnels dark with the damp. The electric bulbs were placed farther apart, the light of one nearly completely lost by the time another came into view.

The stench became more apparent, a rich and murky miasma.

Cairncross led the way, having committed the schematics to memory before they left. The twists and turns of their path left Lily disoriented, feeling like a rat in a maze.

The tunnel ended at a low iron door. Instead of a handle, it was closed with a great wheel. It seemed to Lily like something she would see in the bowels of a ship.

The smell was more intense here, making her light-headed. Lily pressed her sleeve to her nose, but it did little to help.

Sam dropped the canvas bag he had been carrying and pulled it open. He handed her a bizarre apparatus.

"Put this on."

It was a mask worked in leather. Lenses provided space for the eyes. The nose of it was like an elephant's trunk, a long tube that hung near to the floor.

Lily slipped it over her head. Sam turned her around, adjusting the straps until the contraption clung almost painfully to her head.

Now the stink smelled of rot covered over with lavender and

eucalyptus, but the stomach-spinning quality of the air seemed to have lessened.

"Any better?" Sam demanded.

"A bit, yes," Lily replied.

"These remind me of the old plague doctor masks. Fourteenth or fifteenth century," Cairncross noted as he examined the one Sam had provided him. He sounded happy.

"Dr. Gardner said the methane was the clincher, knocks you flat if you breathe too much of it," Sam said. "The stuff rises, so keep the tube down near your feet. That way you'll be breathing the cleaner air."

"Delightful contraption," Cairncross concluded.

Strangford pulled his own mask over his head, the familiar lines of his face disappearing into something from a child's nightmare.

Sam lifted a pair of tin safety lanterns from his bag. He knelt on the floor to light them, then tugged on his breathing apparatus.

"Ready, then?" he asked, his voice floating up to her from where his tube hung at the floor.

Lily nodded and he spun the great metal wheel. The door swung open.

They emerged onto a narrow metal landing looking out over a scene of Gothic proportions.

The space in front of Lily was enormous. Row upon row of blackened brick arches extended as far as the light would go, marching off into the darkness.

Beneath them stretched an endless expanse of black water. The lantern-light shimmering on its surface revealed just the slightest of currents—a constant, quiet eddying of a great dark sea.

This was the enormous cistern that lay under the grand open lawn between the terraces of workmen's housing. The sewage of the better part of south London lingered here, pumped up from lower levels to wait for the tide to turn to outgoing. Then it would be released into the Thames and carried out into the North Sea.

Even through Sam's contraption, the smell was a force.

Cairncross held his pocket watch up to the light.

"Twenty-four seconds to go," he announced.

They looked out over the cistern and waited.

Each second ticked by with painful regularity. Twenty-four passed and then some, the strange black water in front of them unchanged. Lily was painfully aware that they had left a man bound with wire and gagged with a sock in the room above. How long would it take his colleague to smoke a cigarette? When he returned, would he notice right away that someone was missing, or go back to his work oblivious?

"There's nothing here," she finally announced.

"Perhaps you misread the time by a minute or two," Strangford offered.

"I might have misread everything," Lily said.

"What exactly are we expecting?" Sam demanded. "It's not like we think a dead man in a chair is going to come floating by. So what is it?"

It was hard to think through her growing dismay. Lily was always afraid on some level that her visions would steer others into pointless disaster. Because they spoke in figures and symbols instead of simple truth, there was too much left to interpretation. Ash told her she needed to learn to trust her instincts about the meaning of what she saw, but Lily didn't have much faith in her instincts. Now they had led people who trusted her to the brim of a lake of London's foulest detritus—and for what?

"We should go. We'll run out of time," she said.

Strangford touched her arm.

"It's alright, Lily. Just try."

She took a deep, unsteady breath, ripe with lavender and filth. She closed her eyes, trying to reach inside of herself the way Ash had taught her—centering, he called it. She felt the gravity of it, drawing her down toward a deeper place at her core.

"It's a dead man. There should be a dead man here."

"You mean a literal corpse," Cairncross asked.

"Yes," Lily confirmed, ignoring the slight tremor in her voice.

"You wouldn't get a corpse up here in the reservoir," Sam said. "All this has been pumped up from forty feet down. Everything's filtered before it hits the pumps, otherwise it risks clogging and burning out the engines. If some geezer's got himself washed up into the sewers, we'd find him caught in the gates by the pumping well."

"How do we get to the pumping well?" Strangford asked.

"We go down," Sam answered, and led them back through the door.

They followed another twist of hallways until they dead-ended at a blank wall. Instead of a door, there was a hole in the floor surrounded by a metal safety rail.

A ladder inside of it descended into darkness.

"In for a penny," Sam announced and hopped inside.

Lily went in after Strangford. Sam's lantern was some distance below, granting just enough illumination for her to see that she was descending a dank, narrow tunnel of mildewed bricks. The air here was cool and close.

A closet-sized space at the bottom of the ladder housed another iron door, identical to the one that had opened into the reservoir.

Cairncross was the last to land, his head nearly grazing the low ceiling.

Lily felt the time crushing down on her, as heavy as the earth over her head. Their gagged and wired hostage must have been discovered by now. He had witnessed her and Strangford heading for the staircase. He must be capable of guessing which way they had gone. How long would it be before they heard boots echoing down the hallway or the shrill cry of a policeman's whistle?

Sam spun the wheel of the door.

It opened onto another metal platform. This one was bolted into the wall of a narrower pit, perhaps a tenth of the size of the great black lake above. It still looked enormous. The smell here was like a punch to the gut even through the herbs of the mask.

Sam held his lantern out over the water.

"That ain't right," he muttered.

The liquid that filled this well was obviously less clear than the stuff they had seen earlier. There were torn shreds of newspaper and orange peels floating about, along with other things Lily preferred not to identify. The bloated shape of a dead cat bobbed against the wall on the far side of the pit.

It was the only corpse she could see.

Sam peered forward into the gloom.

"The gate's up. That ought to be down unless they're directing the outflow straight into the Thames, like they would during a flood."

"What does that mean?" Strangford asked.

"None of the big stuff's getting filtered out like it ought to be," Sam replied.

An alarm shrilled.

It came from behind them. Lily made a rough judgment of the distance and guessed it was set in the hall at the top of the tunnel they had descended.

"What's that?" she demanded.

"Whatever it is, there'll be a twin to it wired somewhere into that console in the engine house," Sam said.

"Some kind of security alert?" Strangford suggested.

"It'll be trouble with the works," Sam countered. He leaned over the rail for a better look, nearly toppling himself over the side. He snapped back up. "It's got to be one of the pumps. Something's jammed in there and blocked the flow."

"What does that mean?" Cairncross asked.

"Someone upstairs'll have to shut down the engine and backwash the pipe. Otherwise it'll burst the pipe or blow out the engine."

"And we left the man upstairs tied up on the landing," Strangford pointed out.

The blare of the alarm silenced. Lily felt a rumble in the iron rail under her fingers. She gripped it a bit more tightly.

"Turn around!" Sam ordered.

She obeyed, putting her back to the pit as a concussive rush of air pressed at her. The sewage below stirred into a tumult, waves splashing against the stained bricks as a jet of water shot out from somewhere beneath them.

Then it was done, save for the ringing in Lily's ears.

"Guess that other bloke got back from his break," Sam said.

His tone was light, but Lily did not miss the implication. If the smoker had returned to his post, it would not be long before he found his gagged and bound colleague on the upper landing—if he hadn't already.

Their time had just become very limited.

The foul tumult in the pit settled. Something broke to the surface, dark and mangled.

They stared down at it.

"Well done, Miss Albright," Cairncross said.

The corpse was barely recognizable as a man. The remnants of his suit were torn and stained. Pale limbs hung limply at impossible angles. One arm appeared to be staying in place solely because it was caught in the sleeve of a jacket.

Lily knew that the body could not be that of the man who died with her mother, a man who had been consigned to the ground fourteen years earlier. Nothing about this place bore any connection to the alley in Covent Garden where they had been stabbed. Lily's power had knit together these disparate moments in time, and their opportunity to determine the rhyme or reason for that was rapidly disappearing.

"I'll go in," Strangford announced, removing his mask.

The horror of what he intended hit her like a wave.

He shrugged out of his coat, laying it on the rail, then pulled off his gloves and held them out to her.

"Hold on to these for me?"

"You can't," Lily stammered.

"We need to learn as much as possible about this and there isn't any time," he countered.

He was calm, his dark gaze steady, but Lily knew that could not be the whole of it. He would be afraid of what he was about to do, unimaginably repulsed.

She accepted his gloves, tucking them carefully into her pockets. He flashed her a smile that was meant to be reassuring. It was transparent, rapidly swallowed by something grim.

He dropped through the hole in the platform and descended the ladder.

The dead thing floated lazily in the lingering current of the cesspool, trailing flags of torn pinstripe.

Strangford reached the bottom. The sewage rose to his chest. He waded through it to where the body drifted face-down in the murk.

Voices echoed to her distantly from the outfall works tunnels above them.

In the pit, Strangford reached the corpse.

Lily could see the man's face in the thin light of the safety lanterns—what was left of it. Skin was torn, his nose flattened. It was impossible to tell how much of the damage had come from being stuck in the pipes and how much had already been there.

The dead man was a stranger, no one she had ever seen before.

Why were they here?

Strangford took an uneven breath and put his hands on the body.

Cairncross stepped into the landing, listening, but it wasn't necessary. Even inside the pit, Lily could hear the shouts. They were getting closer.

"We need to go," Sam warned.

"Strangford," Lily hissed, knowing that to cry out to him would only alert the searchers above to their location.

Strangford didn't move.

He was standing by the body, the pale skin of his hands glowing against the bloodstained fabric, the bloated chest. His eyes were closed, his face contorted as though in pain.

The fear that had been fluttering inside her since he descended clenched, turned solid. Her grip whitened on the rail.

He couldn't hear them.

"I'll get him," Sam said. He tore off his mask and jumped into the well.

He splashed forward and grabbed Strangford's shoulders, shoving the corpse away. It spun lazily, drifting across the black water.

"He was murdered," Strangford gasped. "I saw—"

"No time," Cairncross cut in. "They're coming."

"Shut the door," Sam ordered.

Cairncross pulled the heavy iron closed. Lily winced at the soft clang of it.

"It won't lock from in here," Cairncross said.

"There," Sam pointed to a large black hole set into the far wall. It was nearly level with Lily's eyes, cut just below the ceiling. "That'll be the overflow line."

Another set of metal rungs in the wall led to the tunnel. Sam pushed Strangford toward them, following close behind.

"How do we get there?" Lily whispered as she watched Strangford reach the top and haul himself inside.

Cairncross was eyeing the distance between the end of the platform on which they stood and the rungs of the ladder.

"I recommend a jump," he concluded.

Behind her, she heard boots clanging against metal.

"Toss the lantern," Sam hissed from inside the hole in the wall.

Cairncross swung one of the safety lanterns at the tunnel. Sam caught it, cursing at the heat as he shifted his grip to the handle.

Lily kicked the other light off the platform. It sunk into the murk of the pit.

She yanked off her mask, tossing it aside, then ran to the end of the metal walkway and swung her legs over the railing. That left her clinging to the precipice over the shimmering murk of the pumping well.

She reached out. The rungs hung a tantalizing few inches from her fingers.

A muffled shout sounded from the far side of the door behind her.

Lily jumped.

She grasped the rung with both hands, her body slamming into the wall hard enough to knock her teeth together. Her boots scrabbled against the bricks until they found the purchase of another rung. She scrambled up, Strangford and Sam gripping her arms as she reached the top. They pulled her up into the brick-lined pipe.

Strangford did not release his hold on her. His hands were conspicuous in their nakedness, even smeared with filth.

"There's something you should know," he said.

"Time for that later," Sam shot over in a hush. "Best keep quiet."

Cairncross arrived, levering himself up easily. He wiped his hands on a handkerchief from his pocket and then discarded it.

They plunged into the darkness of the tunnel.

The sounds of the chaos back at the works echoed softly around them as they made their way along that dark length. Lily thought she could distinguish the rise in alarm as the workmen entered the pumping well and discovered the battered corpse floating in the water. That would certainly distract them for a while. By the time they remembered to keep hunting for the intruders, she and the others would be gone.

The light of the safety lantern danced off the soil-stained bricks, then flashed on the black rivets of a set of enormous metal doors.

They blocked the entirety of the tunnel, solid and impenetrable.

"It's a one-way valve," Sam announced. "Give us a bit of weight."

The four of them pressed together, shoving at the rough iron. The wall of metal split down the middle and swung open on oiled hinges.

The change in the air was a benediction, the muddy scent of the Thames flooding in. Low tide had never smelled so fresh.

They emerged on the mud flats. Behind her, the outfall works was lit up like a holiday parade. Shouts drifted distantly to where they stood, the small shadows of running figures visible against the glowing array of buildings.

"This way, then," Cairncross announced and led them squelching toward the darkness of the marsh.

SIX

One hour later
The Refuge, Bedford Square

$\mathcal{L}$ILY SCRUBBED HER HANDS. The basin was made of tin covered in cracked ivory enamel. It was decorated with the painted image of a snake. The beast wore a crown and appeared to be thoughtfully devouring its own tail.

The room behind her was just as eccentric. The bed was Chinese, narrow and low to the ground with carved wooden screens on three sides. It was covered with a colorful Mexican blanket. On the wall hung a beautifully sculpted wooden mask of a Yoruba ancestor next to a framed illuminated page from a Persian manuscript where a group of white-bearded sages huddled over the form of a sleeping phoenix.

The wallpaper was a very English Morris print of twining green ivy.

Every room at The Refuge featured its own oddities and wonders, conforming only incidentally to British expectations for furnishing and decor. It was the outcome of Ash's three decades of travel to some of the most remote corners of the globe. The journey had been sparked by the untimely death of his wife, Evangeline. Lily had never learned the details of her end, and despite thirty years' distance from the loss, Ash's grief was still too real for it to be polite to ask.

Lily didn't know exactly what Ash had been searching for on that journey or whether he had found it, but he had returned with Cairncross, a pile of odd artifacts, and an extensive library of works relating to the history of extraordinary human ability.

Now all of it was housed here in a pair of fashionable row houses on Bloomsbury's Bedford Square. The walls between the two buildings had been broken through to turn them into one elaborate warren of training rooms, archives, sanctuaries and eclectic guest quarters like the one Lily stood in.

The place had seemed so strange to her when she first encountered it several months ago. Since then, it was The Refuge that had begun to feel ordinary while the rest of the world felt off-kilter.

Lily was barefoot, stripped to her knickers and a chemise, the only articles of clothing that had escaped their expedition to Crossness unscathed.

The water in the basin looked clear. Lily had gone through two changes of it already. She shook the last drops off of her fingers, then ran the damp flannel around her neck and ears. It felt deliciously cool. The air was thicker here in London than it had been on the marshes.

The door behind her opened and the small, sturdy figure of Mrs. Liu appeared in the mirror. Ash's housekeeper bent to collect the dirty clothes Lily had left in the basket by the bed.

"Thank you, Mrs. Liu. I apologize for the state of them."

Mrs. Liu muttered a line of Mandarin in response.

"She says at least you didn't go swimming in it," Sam's voice called cheerfully from out the hall.

Mrs. Liu whirled on her grandson with a more forceful stream of Mandarin, pulling the door sharply closed behind her.

"I wasn't looking, Năinai!" he protested.

Lily winced in sympathy.

—

Lily walked down the upstairs hall, now decently clad in a spare skirt and shirt. She passed the studio, a wood-floored room empty of all furnishings. An array of weapons, both ancient and modern, hung on its walls. They were not there for purely decorative purposes.

At the bottom of the grand central stair, she followed the bright chatter of voices into the library.

It was by far the largest room in The Refuge, extending from one end of the house to another and rising a full two floors. Ladders mounted on the walls provided access to volumes on the higher shelves. Reading tables and display cases held an assortment of curios, from an orrery gleaming with brass gears and knobs to a ten-armed statue of Kali carved in ebony.

Both sets of windows, upper and lower, flooded the space with light during the day. As it was just after two o'clock in the morning, the world outside those long panes of glass was cast in shadows. It made the glow of the library look that much warmer.

Cairncross hung from one of the ladders, scanning the shelves. His desk on the far end of the room was covered with newspaper upon which rested a bejeweled mummified hand, the skull of some animal that had sported a single curved horn, and an obsidian mirror. The last item made Lily feel distinctly cold when she looked at it.

"What are you after, James?" Estelle demanded. She was comfortably arrayed in one of the leather armchairs that surrounded the library's fireplace, a hearth Lily knew was there for strictly architectural purposes. Ash did not risk his collection to the vagaries of fire, relying on electric lights and radiators.

"A firsthand account of the 15th-century witch trials at Metz."

"Dare I ask why?"

"It was an unusually cold summer," Cairncross replied. "The town went into a witch panic and burned twenty-eight people at the stake. I believe several of them may have been charismatics. There was one gentleman who was said to have the power to find lost jewels. A rather rare form of khárisma. The only other case I have heard of was an unsubstantiated account involving a young lady of good breeding in Devon a century or so ago."

"I meant why are you looking for it now?" Estelle asked patiently.

"Oh," Cairncross said. "I am quite convinced I mis-shelved it. It's like having a thorn in one's shoe."

"Perhaps you might find something a bit more useful?" Estelle suggested.

Cairncross considered the matter.

"I do have a French translation of *The Washing Away of Wrongs* by Sòng Cí."

"Which is?"

"A 13th-century study of the forensic sciences."

"There's not much forensics you can do when you don't have the body," Dr. Gardner commented. He sat beside Estelle. Though the two worn armchairs were identical in size, his looked significantly smaller.

Lily smiled at him.

"Hello, Dr. Gardner," she said.

"Miss Albright," the doctor replied, rising from his chair. "I trust the evening's entertainments have left you undamaged?"

"I'm quite well, thank you," Lily assured him.

"You should tell me if you experience any dizziness or shortness of breath. We don't know much about the long-term effects of exposure to sewer gasses. I won't worry about digestive troubles with you. Cairncross tells me you were wise enough not to jump into the stuff. You fools are lucky there hasn't been any cholera outbreak this summer," he added, raising his voice and moving his gaze to Sam as he strolled into the room.

Sam's hair was still damp. He had required something more than a wash at a basin to rid himself of the evidence of the evening's adventure. He plopped down in one of the other chairs, dropping a lidded bucket onto the ground beside him.

"Is that a chamber pot?" Estelle asked suspiciously.

"Not at the moment," Sam retorted. "Ooh, brandy snaps."

He plucked five of them from the plate on the table and scarfed them down in a bite.

"That was shocking awful," he announced through the biscuits.

Cairncross set the mummified hand onto a nearby tea tray to make room for the book he'd retrieved. Gardner helped himself to a biscuit, then set his big feet up on the ottoman.

It felt right, every piece of it—like the place she had always been waiting to come home to. It had been that way ever since she accepted Ash's offer.

The door of The Refuge will be open. It will always be open to you.

When Ash first said those words, Lily's instinct was to run away.

The notion of sharing this secret and strange part of herself with anyone seemed impossible and frightening. It still was impossible and frightening, but she had chosen to do it anyway.

Strangford came in, toweling the water from his dark hair, his hands still bare.

Even such a mundane activity carried a certain grace when Strangford did it. Lily wondered if it had been ground into him by the need for constant physical caution because of his ability. At any point, a stumble or sharp movement could force him into contact with something or someone rife with history he would rather not experience. Or it might have been his training in tàijíquán. Ash used the Chinese art of movement and self-defense to try to help Strangford learn to better control his psychometry.

Ash had not introduced Lily to tàijíquán. Instead, he had set her to studying meditation and visualization, telling her she must learn to clear her thoughts of fear and logic, doubt and reason.

She was not very good at it. Tàijíquán would almost certainly have been more fun.

Strangford was dressed in another of his plain black suits. This one was getting a little frayed around the cuffs. Lily knew that his fashionable sister, Mrs. Eversleigh, would be after him soon to retire it. If left to his own devices, Strangford would happily have worn his clothes until they fell apart. They were hard to replace as every thread had to come from carefully selected sources to avoid triggering unpleasant revelations when they brushed against his skin.

Lily studied him for some indication that he was suffering any negative consequences from his reading of the corpse. The last time he had used his power to pull secrets from the dead, it hadn't gone well.

He had not seemed troubled as they fled the pumping station, but conversation had been next to impossible. Silence was a requirement on their return to the automobile with the sounds of the search for them at the works still echoing across the marshes. Then Sam had pushed the top down on the Rolls as a precaution against the stench he and Strangford carried with them. The tarpaulins covering the seats flapped noisily as they drove, coupling with the wind to more or less deafen them.

Strangford noted her attention. He came over to where she sat and slipped an ungloved hand over her shoulder. She felt the soft electric buzz of his touch.

"I'm fine," he assured her.

Lily settled back against him, letting her fear dissolve and knowing that he would feel that, too.

The murmur of mixed conversation died as Ash entered the room. He was dressed in a tángzhuāng long coat of a rich midnight blue with a high collar and frogged clasps down the front. Ash had acquired a preference for Chinese food and clothing during the years he spent studying in the Wǔdāng mountains.

Her mentor seemed entirely comfortable in the foreign attire, but it always struck Lily as a bit off to see him in Chinese silk next to Sam clad in trousers and a tweed waistcoat.

"Good evening, everyone. Miss Albright, Lord Strangford. Sam," Ash added, his tone just formal enough that Sam straightened up in his chair.

It was easy to forget sometimes that Sam was not a colleague but a servant, an impoverished immigrant who owed Ash his employment and, Lily suspected, that of the rest of his family. The lines between masters and those in service were usually thickly drawn, but Ash's tone with Sam often sounded to her more like that of a foster-father.

Often, but not always.

From across the room, she could see that Sam was trying very carefully to continue chewing.

"I am glad we all returned safely from this evening's expedition. Miss Albright, if I had not said so already, you did well to pinpoint the time. I am glad to see that some of our training is taking root."

It was a compliment, but at two in the morning after slogging through a sewer, it didn't feel much like one.

"Lord Strangford, you are not suffering from any ill-effects after your reading of the corpse?"

"No," Strangford confirmed. He stood close enough that Lily could feel the low vibration of his voice. A thought crossed her mind that was not at all in keeping with the mood and theme of the occasion.

Strangford's fingers tightened on her shoulder. He coughed, clearing his throat, and Lily had to fight the urge to smile.

No secrets.

"That was a significant risk," Ash cautioned.

"I know," Strangford said, recovering. "But we needed to learn as much as possible about the man in very little time. It seemed the only option."

"I doubt it was the only option, but your choice was not unjustified," Ash replied. "As for Sam, it would have been preferable to distract the man you found in the control area rather than attacking and restraining him."

"There weren't so much as a pigeon in that place," Sam protested.

"I did not mean that you should use your khárisma," Ash pushed back, using the ancient Greek term he believed best expressed what their various abilities were—gifts of grace, both a boon from the gods and a grave responsibility. "But a physical confrontation must always be the last resort. Do you understand?"

"Shì, Lâoshī," Sam replied. There was a reflexive deference in his tone.

"You cannot know what surprises your opponent might have up his sleeve, and when you enter close quarters you necessarily increase the chances you will be seen and then identified. Be cleverer than him, not quicker with a fist. You may be capable of both, Sam, but one carries far less risk than the other."

"Now that's settled, can we finally hear what you discovered?" Estelle cut in. "What did the dead man have to say for himself?"

"It wasn't a drowning or accidental death," Strangford said. "The man in the pit was murdered. He didn't see who did it. They ambushed him on his way home from work and threw a bag over his head. I heard three of them working together." Strangford frowned, digging into his memory for more details. "At least one was Irish. I feel the accent was a bit like yours, Dr. Gardner, but it's hard to say. I was experiencing them through his ears."

"So possibly an Ulsterman, then," the doctor commented.

"They dragged him down into the sewers, put his head under the water and held it there."

Strangford's voice was even as he told the story, but Lily knew it was not so simple for him. He would have learned all of this not as a distant observer but inside the skin and mind of the man whose body he held in his sensitive hands. Strangford's power wasn't to witness. It was to be immersed. He would have experienced the horrors he described, living through them in all their vivid atrocity.

She suspected that was why his hand was still on her shoulder. Their connection was one-way. That touch did not reveal his thoughts to her, but physical contact with her might offer him some protection against what would certainly be a vivid and terrible memory.

As Strangford related the story of the man's death, that odd tension returned to the room again, the same one Lily had noticed in the parlor of the Whitstable inn. It was more subtle this time, but she could still see it in the change in Cairncross's posture, the careful focus of Estelle's attention.

There was another story here, one that some of her friends knew but had reason not to share. Whatever it was, Lily could sense that now was not the time to ask about it.

"There is something else," Strangford added carefully. "The dead man recently met with Lord Torrington."

Lily stood, pulling herself from under Strangford's hand. It was an instinct, an urgent need to make certain he couldn't feel her reaction to this.

How long had he waited to share this? It had been over an hour since they left Crossness. He had carried that knowledge inside of him all this time and she'd had no clue, no sense of it. Granted, the circumstances hadn't been conducive to conversation, the engine of the Rolls roaring and the top locked down to keep them all from being choked by the smell.

None of that would've mattered if it had been Lily keeping the secret. Strangford could have learned it all from her with a brush of his hand across her cheek.

The truth of that burned, leaving a sick feeling in her stomach.

Yanking herself away from him would allow her reaction to this news to be private for now, but it was more or less a futile gesture. Strangford would learn everything she was feeling the next time she got close to him.

He had warned her long ago that a relationship between the two of them could never take place on a level playing field.

She could see from the uneasy look on Strangford's face that more must be coming.

"Was this incidental, or do you believe it was significant to the man's death?" Ash asked.

"I know that he was terrified. He wasn't sure he could trust Torrington but he needed someone who was powerful. He was taking a chance."

"A chance on what?" Lily demanded.

"I don't know," Strangford replied. His look was a quiet plea, a request for her to trust him, because in the end it had to come down to trust. If there was something in that dead man's mind he didn't want to share with Lily, he didn't have to.

"He was thinking about names, about protection," he went on. "He felt threatened. He was offering a deal but he didn't know whether he was offering it to someone who could help him or to his enemy. I'm sorry . . . I don't have many details. I might have found more if there had been more time."

His hands were clenched at his sides as though they remembered the awfulness of how he had come by the information he was sharing.

The dead man had come to Torrington with some sort of conspiracy. Then he had been murdered.

Had her father been involved?

She did not want to think it might be true, but for fourteen years—most of her adult life—Lily and her father had not spoken. However earnest he seemed in his desire to build a relationship with her now, he was by all rights a stranger.

A powerful, well-connected stranger.

"I don't suppose you caught the fellow's name?" Dr. Gardner asked.

"No," Strangford replied.

"Nothing else that would help us identify him? His home, his workplace . . ." Cairncross pressed.

"I saw his death and I saw the meeting."

"In the absence of any intention on your part, you would have seen the experiences most important to him at the moment of his death. Those with the most potent emotionality or significance," Ash said.

"Murder and a meeting with Lily's father," Estelle mused.

"Good thing I nabbed this, then," Sam offered.

He lifted the lid of the chamber pot at his feet and plucked out a thick leather wallet. It stank. He waved it casually.

"You picked the corpse's pocket?" Cairncross sounded both moderately horrified and approving.

"Weren't like it was going to do him any good," Sam retorted.

"It might have made it a bit easier for the police to report his death to his family," Gardner pointed out.

"So we send the Peelers an anonymous note from a concerned citizen. Not like they would've shared anything with our lot if they'd been the ones to find it," Sam said. "You're lucky I caught Năinai before she tossed my trousers into the wash."

"Cairncross?" Ash said.

The librarian plucked a pair of tongs from the biscuit tray and used them to lift the wallet from Sam's hand. He carried it over to his desk, setting it down on the newspaper he had spread out beneath the assorted artifacts.

He pulled a set of gloves out of one of the drawers and slipped them on. He opened the folded leather.

Lily moved closer. Sam was more shameless about it, perching himself on the windowsill and peering over Cairncross's rounded shoulder.

"Some of it's dissolved to pulp," he warned, carefully examining the contents. He slid a slender metal tool into one of the pockets, running it carefully along the leather. Holding that with one hand, he took a pair of tweezers in the other and slowly worked a stained bit of paper out of the wallet.

It was a photograph. The thicker, glossed paper had mostly withstood the rigors of the sewer, though its shape was somewhat deformed. The image was one of an elderly couple seated with two younger men standing behind them. They looked a touch overweight and dully respectable.

Cairncross flipped it over.

"Prinz family. Leonard, Charlie, mister and mistress," he read. "June 10, 1913. And the name of a photography studio in Islington."

"Is one of them our man?" Gardner asked.

"Hard to say." Sam frowned down at the picture. "He was well banged up."

Strangford came to the desk and extended his hand.

Cairncross raised an eyebrow, but placed the soggy photograph onto his palm.

"This was carried by someone who saw his own face in it. The fellow in the back on the right," Strangford said after a quiet moment.

Cairncross retrieved the image with his tweezers.

"Charlie Prinz, then," Cairncross announced.

"What's Prinz? Russian?" Sam asked.

"German," Strangford replied. "Prinz is 'prince' in German."

"Some end for a prince, turned bloater in a ponking cesspool," Sam said.

Cairncross went still. He stood abruptly, pulling off his soiled gloves and moving to one of the bookshelves that lined the room.

"What is it, James?" Estelle asked.

"Reminds me of something. Don't mind me. Have to check or it'll drive me mad," Cairncross said. He stared at the books for a moment, lost. "Ah yes," he said and strode to a glass display case next to one of the reading tables. He pulled a set of keys from his pocket and fit one of them to the brass lock in the lid.

Lifting the top, he removed an old manuscript, its leather cover black with age. He set it into the plush book rest on the table and carefully turned the pages.

"Perhaps we could go to the studio, see if the photographer there has an address for the family," Estelle said. "We might learn a bit more if we can speak to them."

"Kodakers don't take down an address unless you're having the images mailed on. Most people just call back to collect 'em," Sam said.

"It wouldn't hurt to check," Estelle returned.

"If the man had family, they might also have reported him missing to the police," Gardner offered.

"Ticcfad amrear no dúbach ro cumanzh, brónach, déanach . . . " Cairncross cut in.

"Not all of us are fluent, James," Estelle chided.

"Sorry. Middle Irish. 'There shall come a time of dark affliction, of scarcity, of sorrow and of wailing.'"

"This your idea of a bedtime story?" Sam said.

"It is the sixteenth stanza of the prophecies of St. Amalgaid of the

Skerries, addressed to St. Brendan. Irish, ninth century. This manuscript is a later transcription, of course. There are some who argue he successfully predicted the great comet of 1680 and the Battle of Clontarf, as well as a locally notorious cattle raid in Armagh in the mid-seventeenth century."

"You have gone six steps ahead of us again," Estelle said. "Retrace and tell us how you got here."

"Let me read the rest of it. 'And in the time where men sail the sky with iron wings, shooting bolts of fire, the prince will be found drowned in the cesspool of the slaves. Three days hence at sunrise will come the cataclysm that devours Lunnainn, the babes turned to ash in their mothers' arms, the streets run with blood and fire. For the wrath of the Almighty against the men of that unholy time shall come . . . leis an mbráith-theine.'"

"You lost me on that last bit," Sam said.

"It's a mite complex to literally translate, but the meaning is more or less 'with the endless fires of the apocalypse.'"

"Charming," Sam replied.

"And Lunnainn translates to?" Strangford's voice was quiet.

"London," Cairncross replied. "I knew I recalled a reference to a prince drowned in a sewer."

"You are ever so handy to have around," Estelle blithely noted. "Was this just a lark or are you suggesting this is a reference to our Mr. Prinz?"

"I don't know that I'm suggesting anything," Cairncross countered. "I just recalled the reference. It's most likely that name is merely a coincidence."

Gardner's voice rumbled in.

"Unless your St. Amalgaid wasn't just a zealous nut, but someone like—"

"Me," Lily finished for him.

Silence descended. Sam slumped in his chair. Estelle picked at a loose thread in her caftan.

"It would be hard to say," Cairncross replied at last. "Amalgaid's prophecies are written in verse. They are strong on symbols and short on specifics."

"That's how it always is," Lily noted.

"You are not the first." Ash's words cut through the room. He stood by the window, gazing out at the ink-dark garden. "What you do is not new. All of you follow in the footsteps of others who have come before."

Lily knew this. Ash had expounded on the theme before. He insisted that many of the saints, witches and heroes of old were in fact charismatics like her and the others gathered in this library. It was the subject that filled most of the volumes that crowded these shelves. There were hagiographies and broadside ballads full of miracles and impossible feats.

And, of course, there were prophecies.

She could not say how much of it was true. The lines between history and fantasy were often blurred. A bishop might have been attributed the power to heal with a touch decades after he died by an abbot hoping sainthood would make the relics under his altar more valuable. Widows of property were made witches by inquisitors hungry for their land.

Other stories might simply have been true.

The suggestion that this St. Amalgaid fell into that latter category unsettled her. Lily wasn't sure she liked the notion of sharing her khárisma with a fanatical ninth-century saint.

Never mind that his text declared that Doomsday would fall upon London in three days' time.

"I don't suppose there is any reference to a cataclysm in Mrs. Ash's mural upstairs," Gardner asked.

The mention of the mural chilled Lily more than the ravings of the saint. While St. Amalgaid's charismatic credentials were questionable, there was no doubt that Evangeline Ash had possessed a strange and terrible gift.

My wife had an ability to perceive the imperceptible . . . the ineffable order of all things.

Those were Ash's words months before when he first described Mrs. Ash's power to Lily. She had since heard Cairncross use another term—*fatumspex.* Fate seer.

As an artist, Evangeline Ash had not tried to communicate her impossible knowledge with words. She had woven it into her work.

The entire attic of both buildings that made up The Refuge had

79

been cleared to form a single massive room. Every inch of its walls and ceiling were covered in her paintings. It was the most uncanny place Lily had ever been, one she did not relish ever going back to. Simply being reminded of its existence made her feel its enormous presence overhead. Mrs. Ash had been dead for thirty years, but her creation still felt very much alive.

Had Lily ever wondered whether Evangeline Ash's gift mirrored her own ability to see the future, the mural would have set her straight. It spoke of much more than glimpses of what was to come. It rang with meaning, with significance—echoes of a conversation between Ash's wife and something else, something ancient and immense Lily was not entirely sure she wanted to understand.

"Lord Strangford," Ash said. "Were you able to grasp any sense of where the meeting between Prinz and Torrington took place?"

"Parliament," Strangford replied. "Somewhere inside Westminster Palace. I don't know the room, but it is on the main floor and overlooks Tower Gardens." He frowned thoughtfully, his gaze going distant as he probed his memory for more. "Small but well-furnished. Not just a random office. Books all up and down the walls. There's something set in a glass case in the corner. It caught his eye because it looked old and important. A tall silver staff topped with a crown . . ." Strangford cut himself off, eyes clearing. "The mace. He was looking at the Lords' mace."

"What, a mace? Like for clocking people on the bean with?" Sam demanded.

"I believe its use is largely ceremonial now," Gardner said mildly.

"So he was in the Black Rod's Library," Cairncross said, frowning.

"What's that, then?" Sam asked.

"Part of a suite of rooms belonging to the Black Rod, set on the main floor of the Lords' side of the Palace of Westminster," Cairncross replied. "The Black Rod being one of the chief ceremonial roles in Parliament, charged with a broad range of duties that include the security of the building and personally attending to the sovereign himself."

"I did hear a rumor that Lord Torrington made himself at home in one of the Black Rod's rooms," Estelle offered. "He hasn't one of his own since he holds no official position beyond 'lord', but of course he must have someplace near the House of Lords to do all his . . ." she waved her hand expressively, searching for the right word.

"Meddling?" Gardner offered.

"That will do," Estelle replied.

What sort of meddling had Lily's father been doing when he met with the dead Prinz? It was an uneasy question. Lily could not forget that her vision had connected Prinz to Patrick Dougherty, whose blood had mingled with her mother's in a Covent Garden alley. There must be a connection between the two men, and she could not dismiss the possibility that it was a line drawn straight through the heart of Lord Torrington.

Cairncross pulled a rolled paper from a cubbyhole on the far side of the room. He unfurled it on one of the reading tables. Ash joined him there, Sam peering over their shoulders.

From where she stood, Lily could make out the labels on some of the larger rooms—The Royal Court, Central Hall, Victoria Tower.

It was a map of the Palace of Westminster.

"This is the Black Rod's Library, here," the librarian said, pointing to a place on the page. "It can only be accessed by passing the peers' libraries and entering the private hallway to the Lord Chamberlain's rooms. There will almost certainly be a guard stationed here, just past the door to the Royal Court. There is also a stairwell just outside the room, but any public entrance to that will likely be monitored as well."

"So if you was inclined to view the place, you'd have to get a guard or two out of the way," Sam mused. "Could be I know a trick or two for that."

The implication of their conversation settled in. Lily felt a flush of alarm.

"You want Strangford to read the room," she blurted.

Ash looked at her evenly from across the table.

"It is a possible avenue for learning more about Prinz's connection with your father. Is that line of investigation worth pursuing?"

Ash was not asking what she thought or believed, but for the deeper and more certain knowledge that emanated from her power. Yet how could her own thoughts not enter into this? They were talking about her father, the man who once betrayed and abandoned her. A man who looked at her with shattering remorse. The only family she had left in the world.

This was necessarily personal, necessarily complicated. Could she see past that? Would anyone in the room believe it if she did?

Strangford waited patiently for her answer along with the others. There was nothing of judgment in his expression, but Lily was painfully aware that every reading he did potentially exposed him to all manner of uncomfortable or horrific revelations. Was it fair of her to ask him to take such a risk so Lily could learn whether the man who sired her was somehow complicit in a murder?

Ash's question was not about fairness. He was asking for a fact. An impossible fact.

"Yes," Lily blurted, knowing it was true. "We should go to Westminster."

SEVEN

Thursday, July 30
Early afternoon
Westminster, London

$\mathcal{T}$HE PALACE OF WESTMINSTER, home of the Parliament of the United Kingdom, rose like a confection from the banks of the Thames.

It was early afternoon when Lily approached it. She had slept till nearly noon after last night's strange and urgent meeting at The Refuge, exhausted by their ordeal at Crossness.

She stepped out of the omnibus at the edge of the Old Palace Yard. Men in important suits mingled on the broad pavement at the foot of Westminster's elaborate facade, gossiping about the fate of nations or what they'd be serving for supper at White's.

Sam stood out like a goose in a bevy of swans. He was clad in tweed and suspenders, a flat cap perched rakishly on his dark hair, and was conspicuously loitering by the enormous brass statue of Richard the Lionheart. The dead king held aloft a five-foot-long sword and was mounted on a ferocious warhorse.

A pair of constables were eyeing Sam suspiciously, clearly considering all manner of nefarious reasons for him to be leaning against the crusader.

Lily hurried over before one of the authorities riled himself up into demanding to know why Sam was there. Her friend wasn't one to hold back his tongue or his fists in a confrontation. Today's endeavor would be little served by the need to rummage up Sam's bail.

"Mr. Wu," Lily said, slipping her hand under Sam's arm.

The constables were not so easily dissuaded. The pair of them approached, blocking Lily's path.

"Morning, miss," one said with a brief tip of the hat before turning less polite attention to Sam. "You, there. You a British subject?"

"I'm Chinese, mate," Sam retorted. "What's it to you?"

"No foreigners permitted to loiter in the yard," the other policeman announced.

"Good thing I ain't loitering then," Sam replied.

Lily's heart pounded with both fear and fury. She contained them both. They could not afford an incident, not if they were to accomplish what they had come here to do.

"Mr. Wu is assisting me with important business at Parliament today," she said. She put all her authority into the tone, infusing it with every aristocratic cell of her half-blue blood. "Is there to be a problem?"

She could see the constable waver, torn between deference to a member of the upper classes and a native contempt for women and foreigners.

"Oy, Reggie," his companion cut in softly. He nodded across the road at a small cluster of demonstrators.

They were older men dressed in sober suits, a few of which were accented by a bright orange sash. That marked them as Unionists, Ulster Protestants determined to preserve the union of Great Britain and Ireland, just as clearly as the banners they held protesting Home Rule. A few placards carried a gruesome symbol Lily knew was associated their movement. It was the icon of an uplifted hand, cut off at the wrist and painted a blazing and vaguely gory red.

The gathering was silent but Lily could feel the weight of their judgment throw itself against the walls of the palace where Parliament had been debating allowing a vote on the question of Irish Home Rule.

The constables weren't staring at the protesters. Their eyes were on a handful of ragged boys lurking nearby.

As Lily turned to look, one of the lads plucked a worm-eaten apple from the grass under a tree and lobbed it at the demonstrators.

"Sinn féin, ya buggers!" the boy yelled.

"Come on, then," Reggie the constable determined, abandoning Lily and Sam to hustle across the busy street toward the more obvious troublemakers.

Sam made a distinctly Limehouse gesture at the backs of their heads.

"You didn't need to do that," he said, letting his hand drop. "I could've handled myself."

"That is exactly what I was afraid of," Lily replied. She kept her tone light, but it took effort. "We have important things to do today."

The pair of them looked up at the walls of the Houses of Parliament . . . and up. The building was enormous, an ornate and monstrous monument to importance.

Lily had been inside of it once before, seeking help from her father. It had not been a very comfortable experience.

"The whole bloody pile looks ready to tip into the river," Sam commented.

"Let's hope it doesn't do it in the next three hours," Lily replied.

A familiar figure rounded the corner from Great George Street. Though he bore a superficial resemblance to all the other black-suited men dropping from crested carriages into the yard, Lily knew immediately that it was Strangford. Even the unusual presence of a top hat respectably covering his dark hair didn't throw her.

"Good afternoon," he said as he stepped up to them.

"Your lordship," Sam replied cheekily. "I trust you're rested?"

"I believe I might have dozed off over the paper for a moment or two before Roderick came in with the parrot."

"You don't have a parrot," Lily noted.

"That is what made the situation rather alarming," Strangford replied.

"Well, then. Best get on with the invasion," Sam declared. "I believe I know my part in it? You'll just need to excuse me for a minute while I give the word to Sylvia."

Sylvia was a fat gray pigeon perched on Richard the Lionheart's shoulder. Sam sauntered to her side. He took a pinch of seeds from his pocket held up his hand.

The bird hopped onto his arm and quickly gobbled up the snack. Sam tucked her into his coat, managing to do so without capturing

85

any notice from the busy crowd moving through the yard. He peered down at her, presumably to ensure she was comfortable, then returned to where Lily and Strangford waited.

"Tally-ho and all that," he announced in his best posh accent.

The Peer's Entrance to the House of Lords was a small door set in an intimidating frame. Strangford led them to it, merging them into the trickle of other black-suited bodies making their way inside.

Lily felt the gaze of the stern-faced sentries at the door move to her and Sam as the flow of noblemen brought them closer to the entrance.

Sam's coat was moving though his hands remained in his pockets. Lily was conscious of the bird he concealed under his lapel.

"Miss Albright, Mr. Wu," Strangford said as they reached the door. "After you."

Strangford didn't have the instinctive air of privilege shared by most of his fellow peers. Even with the addition of a top hat, he still had the low-heeled look of a country preacher about him.

The doormen of Westminster Palace were well trained to defer to their betters, however bohemian those betters might happen to be.

"M'lord," the sentry at the gate said with a respectful nod at Strangford, and they passed inside.

The entry was a press of bodies. Top hats obscured Lily's view of the smoke-stained oil portraits that lined the walls. The carpet was worn, the conversation an incomprehensible roar.

She could feel Strangford tense beside her. He was never comfortable in a crowd, even when safely wrapped in a suit and gloves. Lily suspected that sensitivity went beyond the possibility of stumbling into someone and inadvertently capturing all their secrets. Strangford was so carefully attuned to everything that surrounded him—to the nuance of a voice, the beauty in the curve of a leaf. When too much hit him all at once, it inevitably rattled him.

He steeled himself against it and led their way through the throng, skipping the cluster of bodies by the cloak room for the relative safety of the hall.

It was high-ceilinged and silk-papered, still busy with aristo-crats but with enough room to spare that Strangford appeared to breathe again.

More dull portraits lined the walls, interspersed with the busts of similar-looking craggy old men. Lily could smell tobacco smoke and the mud of the Thames. The river lay on the far side of the building and the tide was down.

She was finely aware that her father could very well be inside. Lily just hoped he wasn't in his commandeered office.

The peers of the realm milled up and down the hall, mostly ignoring them. They had the glossy air of men confident of their value to the world, even the ones who were obviously a mite tipsy.

Lily's path was blocked by a pair of gentlemen who stopped in the center of the hall to chat, either oblivious to the way this interrupted the free movement of those around them or unconcerned by it.

"You say the plane took off successfully? With a mounted weapon?"

This was the slighter of the two, a trim fellow with a thick mustache, prominent ears and a Welsh accent.

"Yes, yes. A drum-fed Lewis gun mounted within reach of the pilot."

The larger man had a receding hairline and cherubic cheeks, with a voice of cannon-like proportions.

"Air cooled with a 97-round magazine. Enough firepower to bring an enemy plane to the ground. No waiting for the fools to buzz our fortifications," the larger fellow went on enthusiastically.

"If you don't mind blowing your own propeller off," Sam cheerfully cut in.

The two gentlemen turned in surprise.

"If you want to use the thing without blasting yourself out of the sky, you'd have to synchronize the firing mechanism with the propeller."

"There! You see? The lad has hit it on the nose," the Welshman said.

"We'll get round to that soon enough. British ingenuity omnia vincit," the bigger man declared.

"My apologizes, Chancellor Lloyd George. Admiral Churchill," Strangford said. "Mr. Wu and I were just moving on."

"Lord Strangford, isn't it?" Churchill asked.

"Yes, Admiral," Strangford confirmed.

"Have you a line besides landowning?" Lloyd George demanded.

"Translations," Strangford replied.

"Well, that's honest enough work," Lloyd George confirmed approvingly.

"What tongues?"

The question came from Churchill.

"French and German," Strangford replied.

"And a bit of Latin," Sam offered helpfully.

"Is that so?" There was an odd glint of interest in Churchill's eye, and a strange energy raised the hairs on Lily's arms. The walls around her shifted, bending into someplace she knew far better, while the same big man stood before her, an echo of his voice dancing through her mind.

. . . would prefer a whiskey and soda . . .

"We are about to be late," Lloyd George announced, frowning at his watch.

The words snapped Lily back to herself.

"Of course," Churchill agreed. "Please excuse us."

The pair strode down the hall together toward the Commons, parting waves of important men like a prophet dividing the sea.

Lily, Strangford and Sam squeezed past enormous, richly decorated rooms that looked as though they were rarely used, then turned into yet another hallway. This one had windows looking out onto a dull gray courtyard. They were opened as much as they could be, though it offered little relief to the stuffy interior of the building.

Strangford pointed to a similar row of windows on the far side of the gap.

"That's it," he announced. "The Peers' Tea Room. The door to it is just shy of where the guard to the chancellor's quarters will be standing."

Lily could make out the shadowy figures of noblemen mingling inside, the glow of white tablecloths and occasional flash of silver.

"That'll do," Sam said. He sounded pleased.

"How much time do you need to prepare?"

Sam poked his head out through the window. He looked down at the flat asphalt of the courtyard, then turned and craned his neck for a peek at the tall Gothic spires of the upper floors.

A lord of extremely advanced years stared at Sam with shock from the end of the hall.

Sam pulled himself back into the building and the lord toddled off hurriedly in the other direction.

"Shouldn't take Sylvia more than ten minutes to round up the necessary resources," he announced.

"Let's make it a full quarter hour to be safe," Strangford said.

Sam gently removed the pigeon from his coat pocket, scratching the feathers at the back of her neck. She cooed in his hands.

"There's a good girl, my lovely Sylvia," he said, offering the pigeon a few more scratches. "Aren't you just the prettiest little bird?"

His tone was uncharacteristically mushy. Lily raised an eyebrow.

"Go on with you, then. Knock it on the head, my fine clever Sylvia."

Sam released the pigeon out the window. When it had fluttered up out of view, he shot Lily a glare.

"So? The girls take a bit of flattery. Can't just boss 'em around for nothing."

"I didn't say a word," Lily returned blithely.

Lily wondered what the elderly lord would have done had he stuck around to see that bit.

"Might as well move ourselves into position," Strangford said.

They turned the corner to a hall lined with close-packed offices, small rooms almost certainly belonging to very important people. They had made it halfway along when Lily was abruptly aware that something dangerous was about to turn the corner.

Without questioning the instinct, she ran three doors back, grasped the knob and ducked inside.

The room was tall, narrow, and unoccupied. A desk took up most of the wall that faced the courtyard, the rest of the space lined with bookshelves. They were heavy with files and thick leather-bound tomes.

With the lights off, it was shadowy, even in the middle of the afternoon.

"My lord."

Lily could hear Strangford's voice clearly through the narrow crack in the door. She did not miss the subtle tension in it, something a bit more than his general discomfort at being jostled around a crowded building. A moment later she knew why.

"Lord Strangford," her father said in reply.

The sound of his voice triggered a tumult of emotion, as it always did. It dragged up memories of her mother's rooms at Oxford Street, of long fingers ruffling her hair as he passed by.

Of a promise he made on the day they buried Deirdre Albright. *All will be well.*

It had not been well, and yet there was still that longing—the dream of the father who was there instead of the one who disappeared, swallowed by his obligations.

"I trust you've been well?" Torrington asked.

"I have," Strangford replied.

"What brings you here today? You don't sit on any of the committees."

He was making small talk. It was odd to hear the great Earl of Torrington sound as though he weren't sure what to do with himself.

"Just giving a friend the tour," Strangford said.

"I played that role myself today. Would this be Mr. Wu?"

"The same, m'lord," Sam replied.

"I have heard a great deal about you. A pleasure to finally make your acquaintance."

Lily could hear the sincerity in her father's voice.

"Be sure to show him the secret tunnel to Downing Street," Torrington noted.

"I'm not sure I'm familiar with it," Strangford said.

"Oh. I see. I should be happy to direct you. It's just past the—"

"Torrington! A word?"

The voice of another party echoed along the hall.

"Another time, perhaps," Torrington apologized. There was a hitch of hesitation before his next words. "Will you be seeing Miss Albright?"

"Er, yes," Sam coughed.

"Please pass on my regards."

It was not a perfunctory courtesy, but something genuine. Lily felt the pang of that. It recalled the brush of those fingers in her hair.

Then he was gone.

Sam was the first to duck into her hiding place.

"Good find. This'll do nicely for monitoring our Sylvia's

performance," he announced, moving immediately to the narrow, dirty window and looking up at the sky over the courtyard.

Strangford came in behind them.

"Did he look well?" Lily asked.

"A little tired," Strangford replied.

"Well. That's to be expected with everything that's going on," Lily said, moving to the desk.

It was a way of busying herself and of putting distance between her and Strangford. She did not want him to touch her just then. She would rather he did not know what she was thinking.

The move wasn't lost on Strangford. On the other side of the room, he put his gloved hands deliberately into his pockets. He turned to study a painting that was not at all to his taste, a dull scene of unremarkable British countryside.

Lily leafed idly through the papers on the desk. Behind her, Sam perched himself on the windowsill. She wondered if someone would spot him there through one of the windows across the way and wonder what a working-class Chinese lad was doing lounging in some toff's office.

"What you reading?" he asked.

Lily hadn't been reading, but she gave the page she currently held in her hand a better look so she would have a way to answer him.

"Security briefing."

"Anything good?"

"Moderate threat of an armed uprising in Ulster?" she offered.

"Psst. Everyone knows that. What else would they do with all those guns they smuggled into the place last April?"

Lily recalled the story. It had been splashed across the papers that spring. An enormous shipment of rifles had been sailed into the port of Larne in Ireland's County Antrim and passed off to a citizen army that had raised itself up in Ulster. They called themselves the Ulster Volunteer Force, an organization of Unionists who were threatening armed revolt if Parliament voted in favor of Home Rule.

It struck Lily as absurd—threatening revolt against the government you were ready to fight to belong to.

"What else have you got?" Sam demanded.

She scanned the page.

"They're heightening security for the king's Buckingham Palace talks on Home Rule. Apparently there's been a substantiated report that the Irish Republican Brotherhood will try to disrupt the conference on Sunday morning, the day before the talks begin."

The IRB—or Fenians, as they were more colloquially known—were on the extreme end of Irish politics. While the Ulster Volunteers were arming themselves and threatening war if the United Kingdom allowed Ireland to form its own Parliament in Dublin, the IRB claimed a Home Rule government wasn't enough. Home Rule in Dublin would still be overseen by the United Kingdom. The IRB's stated purpose was to fight for Ireland to be a nation of its own, completely independent of Britain.

"Bunch of bosh," Sam declared. "I've had the odd run-in with the Fenians and that lot couldn't disrupt a county fair. They wouldn't stop arguing long enough to agree on how to go about it."

"How did you end up involved with Irish extremists?" Lily asked.

"Weren't like that," Sam replied. "Just . . . a mutual acquaintance. Of sorts."

The conversation clearly made him uncomfortable. Lily decided to let it drop. There was rather a lot about Sam's past that she didn't know. For someone who hadn't quite completed his second decade of life, he'd had a hard run of it. London was not kind to penniless foreigners.

Lily set the papers aside.

"Good girl, Sylvia. She's done the job to a treat," Sam announced.

Lily looked over his shoulder into the courtyard.

The flat gray rectangle of pavement was covered in pigeons.

It was an unsettling assortment of birds, thick enough that the ground was barely visible between their feathers. Across the way, Lily could see a few pale faces against the windows of the Peers' Tea Room staring down at the menagerie.

"You two ready?" Sam asked.

Strangford looked to Lily.

"Yes," she replied.

"Give us two minutes," Strangford said. "Once you've done your bit, make your way back out of the building."

"As calmly and respectably as possible," Lily added.

"Right, right." Sam cut her off. "Bob's your uncle. Go on, then!"

Strangford held the door for her.

As they rounded the corner, Lily saw a sign for the Peers' Tea Room. Beyond it, the corridor ended at an unassuming door, the entrance to the Lord Chamberlain's private hallway. As they had anticipated, it was guarded. Only a single man stood at the post, but that would be enough to raise an alarm if they tried to push past him.

Strangford stopped at a large painting mounted on the wall. It was a dreadful and gory depiction of some ancient British king holding his sword aloft over a battlefield. He rested his left foot on the bloated torso of a black knight.

The only virtue it could be said to have was its proximity to the door at the end of the hall.

"You have to say something," Lily whispered beside him as Strangford stared at the painting.

"Sorry?"

"Talk to me about the painting so it sounds like we have a reason to be here."

Strangford contemplated the artwork in question as one might a dirty sock.

"Can I say what I really think?"

"No," Lily admitted. "Just speak loudly and sound important."

Strangford was saved from that by a rumble from the tea room.

It came with a tinkling of broken glass, then a murmur of surprise. The murmur rose to a roar punctuated by heavy thumps and clattering dishes.

The heads of a few lords emerged from the libraries that lined the hall, looking back and forth to each other in confusion. Others lingering in the hall had stopped gossiping, glancing toward the tea room as though unable to process what was taking place inside.

Then a tall man in a dark suit stumbled out the door, slapping wildly at a pigeon flapping around his head.

Another crash resounded through the halls of Parliament.

Lily could picture what was happening on the other side of the wall where a hundred or so pigeons were undoubtedly streaming through the opened windows and whirling around the peers of the realm at their refreshment tables.

The security detail at their end of the hallway bolted. To his credit, he ran toward the tea room rather than away from it.

Lily wasted no time. She tugged Strangford the last few yards of the corridor and through the forbidden door, closing it quickly behind them.

It was quiet here.

The chaos of the tea room was dulled to a murmur by the ancient oak boards. The space around them was narrow but high, papered in dark green damask. Old wood molding gleamed with wax, the air scented with the lemon of furniture polish.

A few of the doors around her were opened, offering glimpses into far more luxurious precincts than the little cell where she'd sought refuge from her father. No one was here, so far as she could tell, but the place had the feeling of a room someone had only just stepped out of and would any minute be returning to.

She tried to picture the map Cairncross had shown her in her head. The Black Rod's Library would be the last room at the end of this hallway.

They stopped at the door. Lily knew that her father had gone the opposite way. He could not possibly be inside. She felt a nervous twitch regardless. Pushing past it, she opened the door.

The room was small but finely furnished with an ancient oak desk and two leather armchairs worn to the point of comfort. The walls were lined with books save for the window that looked out over the green expanse of Tower Gardens and the wide brown water of the Thames.

It was also occupied.

EIGHT

A YOUNG MAN STOOD IN the center of the Black Rod's Library. He was a stranger with the look of an Oxford crewman about him, upright and fit with a golden, blue-eyed glow—and yet there was something about him that seemed familiar, tugging at the back of Lily's brain.

He held a long silver staff in his hand topped with what looked like a crowned silver bucket. A tall glass case stood open in the corner of the room.

As Lily watched, the stranger swung the silver rod out in a mock battle maneuver, crushing an imaginary skull.

"Take that, villain!" he announced, then noticed he was no longer alone. "Oh! Sorry. I was just . . . er . . ."

"Playing knight with the ceremonial mace of the House of Lords?" Strangford offered.

"Is that what it is?"

Lily had not thought it possible for someone to look both pleased and horrified at the same time.

Her thoughts scrambled. Who was this? She cursed her power for failing to alert her to his presence.

"We'll just pop that back," the stranger said cheerfully, returning the mace back to the glass case. He turned to them and stuck out a hand. "Lord George Carne."

The pieces fell into place.

The angular cut of his jaw, the prominent nose. The color of his eyes was wrong but the shape of them was the same Lily saw whenever she looked into the mirror.

This wasn't a stranger. Carne was the Earl of Torrington's surname. Lily was looking at her half-brother.

Strangford took his hand.

"Lord Strangford," he said politely, though Lily knew he must be aware of the tumult she was feeling.

Her father had four sons with his wife, the countess. The oldest, Torrington's heir, was Viscount Deveral. Lily had run into him before under less-than-pleasant circumstances that Deveral had made intentionally worse.

She knew far less about the others. They were mysteries, distant apparitions in a photograph on her father's desk—apparitions that shared half of her blood.

They were the children left at home with their mother when Torrington made his frequent trips to the rooms he kept for his mistress. The children who had grown up with him after the distraction of Deirdre Albright was no more.

Had he attended their football games? Helped them with their Latin? There must have been dinners around some enormous heirloom table, mornings with tea and noise and newspapers.

Lily knew what a family was supposed to look like, even if she had never had one herself.

There were four sons—Viscount Deveral living disdainful and debauched in one of their father's townhouses in Bayswater, a pair of twins still in school, and finally the middle child. The last Lily knew of him, he had been shipped off to some far away locale with the diplomatic service.

Apparently he had returned.

"Pleasure to meet you," Lily's half-brother said, shaking Strangford's black-gloved hand.

He cast a glance at Lily. Curiosity was clear in it, as though something about her jogged at his attention in a way he couldn't quite explain.

She wasn't sure whether she hoped or feared that he would figure out the truth.

"Am I in the way of something?" he asked, flashing a bright and authentic smile. "I must admit I'm not entirely sure I'm supposed to be here. Father—Lord Torrington, that is—told me to pop over to the tea room, but a plate of old kippers sounded a bit less appealing than capitalizing on a chance to poke about one of Great Britain's holy inner sanctums."

Something about this hurt. He was so different from Deveral, open where his older brother was cold, and he lacked the secret weight their father always seemed to carry. Lily felt an unexpected yearning, one that could not possibly be indulged in this time and place.

She slipped her fingers under Strangford's cuff, letting them rest against the skin of his wrist.

We belong here.

She willed it at him, hoping he wasn't too distracted by this unexpected guest to pick up her signal.

"We do have some business to attend to here," Strangford admitted.

"Jolly good," George agreed. "I'll be on my way."

"If you're in the mind for something other than kippers, there's another dining room upstairs. They make a halfway decent curry," Strangford offered.

"That's a rum suggestion. Lovely chat," George said. He looked once more to Lily, as though on the verge of saying something more, but settled for plucking his hat from the chair and heading for the door.

It closed behind him with a crack. George treated doors with the same enthusiasm he treated people.

"You could have told him," Strangford said quietly.

Lily moved away.

"There wasn't any time and it would only have complicated things. We'd best get on with this. We don't know how long we'll have the room."

If Strangford had further thoughts on the matter, he kept them to himself.

"The chairs," he said, nodding toward the two worn leather pieces that faced each other at the front of the narrow room. "That's likely the best option."

"Which one did Prinz sit in?"

Strangford nodded toward the one on the left.

He took off his gloves and tucked them into his pockets. Sitting down, he let his bare hands fall against the worn arms of the chair.

A moment later, he pulled them away and tore himself upright. He stood still in the center of the room, clearly working to collect himself.

Lily felt that familiar lurch in her gut.

"Something unpleasant?" she asked.

"Yes." His voice had gone ragged.

"Prinz?"

"No," he replied. "Someone else. Years ago. Long dead now. This place is rotten with history."

The way he said it in his low, soft voice made it sound like a curse.

"I could try the other one," he offered, shaking off the lingering effects of whatever old horror he'd just witnessed.

Lily glanced to the other chair—her father's chair. She nodded.

Strangford sat down. His hands hovered over the leather.

"If he sits here often, it might take me a while to find the right moment," he warned.

"I'll . . . try to know if someone is coming," Lily offered.

She moved to the door as though proximity to it might better attune her gift.

Behind her, Strangford set his hands down on the chair.

Lily decided that perhaps cracking the door open would improve their chances.

The hallway was quiet, cool with shadows and smelling of age. After peering out and finding it empty, she pressed her back to the wall by the narrowly opened door and tried to sense whether anyone was coming.

Concentration was a challenge when Strangford was sitting there reading her father's secrets.

He looked calm, so at least there was no violence here. He was sunk into the reading, his eyes closed, body still. Bits of dust danced around him, illuminated by the afternoon light slipping through the window.

Voices sounded from the hall.

So much for her khárisma.

Lily darted to the chair and yanked Strangford to his feet. Wordlessly, she rushed him out into the hallway. They darted into an opening across the way, a dimly-lit stairwell.

Strangford took the lead, bringing them down as the voices drew closer.

The stair twisted to an end at a rusted metal door. Strangford drew back on his gloves as Lily tried the handle. It turned and the door swung open to reveal a dim hall lined with pipes.

"We must have more shells. When's the next shipment?"

The voice belonged to Churchill, the admiral that they had met below.

"Another trainload from the Midlands will arrive in Dover by Sunday afternoon."

Lily's father's voice floated down to them from the top of the stairwell.

She and Strangford shared a look, then darted into the basement and closed the door.

A rat promptly ran across her boot.

It was more startled than she was, but Lily had to bite her tongue to stop from screaming.

The path ahead was narrow. Lily couldn't actually make out the walls through the thick layers of conduits and wires. Electric bulbs provided lighting, but they were spread thin, leaving deep pools of shadow between them.

"Which way should we go?" she asked.

"I would suggest forward," Strangford replied. "Given that there isn't any other option."

They made their way along, stepping around still puddles sunk into the floor. The whole place smelled of damp. Lily spotted other rodents scurrying for the dark as they approached.

"It had to do with guns," Strangford said as they walked. "Prinz's meeting with your father."

Lily wasn't sure why that made her feel relieved. Perhaps it was because guns had nothing to do with Patrick Dougherty and the stabbing death of a music hall star in a blood-soaked alley fourteen years ago.

"Prinz worked for the War Office. I saw that much clearly. He was concerned about some oddity with a shipment of rifles from Canada. All of what was ordered arrived in England. Only half of it went on to its destination."

"What about the other half?"

"Prinz believed they went . . . somewhere else. Somewhere they weren't supposed to go."

"Have you any sense of how many rifles were involved?"

"I have the number," he replied evenly.

"How on earth did you manage that?" Lily exclaimed.

Strangford's power, like Lily's, was a matter of symbols and impressions, fading echoes of other people's memories. Emotions often came through powerfully. He would know whether a sword was raised in rage, or what someone was feeling the last time they wore a certain hat. Facts, figures—these were not what made the greatest impressions on the objects he touched, because they were not what made an impression on the men who used them.

"Your father's mind is . . . different," Strangford said. "Strangely organized. The number mattered to him."

"Why?"

"Because it was twenty thousand."

"That does seems like rather a lot to just go missing," Lily noted.

"It wasn't that. The number made him think of Ireland, very clearly and with quite a bit of concern. Also the month of April."

"How odd," Lily mused as she stepped over a cable that lay snaking across the ground.

Then she stopped.

Pieces began clicking into place.

"That smuggling incident was in April. A load of guns shipped to the Ulster Volunteer Force. How many rifles were involved in that?" she asked, but she already knew the answer. She could recall seeing it splashed across a news headline months before.

Twenty thousand.

"But how did they end up in Ulster?" she demanded. "Did Prinz think they were stolen by the Unionists?"

"He was very concerned about papers. Official sorts of papers, papers that should have been very dry. Receipts or manifests . . . something of that sort. Numbers weren't adding up the way they were supposed to. Documents had been signed. The whole thing felt terribly bureaucratic. That makes it hard to grasp any details but your father felt all of it was very significant."

"That doesn't sound like a simple theft."

"Some kind of accounting error, perhaps?" Strangford suggested.

"How does an accounting error end up smuggled to Ulster? Did it feel like an accounting error?"

"No," he admitted. "It felt dangerous."

Lily let that sink in. If Prinz could be believed, the British Army had allowed twenty-thousand rifles—valuable crown property—to somehow fall into the hands of an army of potential rebels.

She knew the Unionists had strong ties to the government. There was a great deal of public sympathy for their cause among members of the Conservative party, who believed that allowing Ireland to form its own Parliament was a step towards the dissolution of the empire.

She suspected there were quite a few others who were willing to help Ulster's cause more quietly.

Did that include officers of the British Army? Did it include her father?

And if it did . . . what lengths would he go to in order to conceal the truth?

"If he'd found the rifles were missing, why did Prinz come to my father? Why not go to the police?"

"He was afraid," Strangford replied.

"Afraid of what?" Lily demanded.

He shook his head. "I don't have the whole of it. Just a pair of words."

"What are they?"

"Red Branch," he replied.

She searched her mind for some sense of significance, some notion of why those words—*Red Branch*—would inspire such terror in Charlie Prinz. She could think of nothing.

"What did he want my father to do?"

"I don't know," Strangford replied.

The line of his mouth was grim. Lily could feel his frustration.

"If I had more time, I might be able to distinguish things more clearly," he said.

"We were already seen in there. If Lord George thinks to tell our father he met you, Torrington will be suspicious. You couldn't possibly have been looking to speak with him or you would have done it when you ran into him in the hall. The Black Rod's private suite isn't exactly on the tour list. He'll know we must have been there to spy on him."

"You could talk to him," Strangford suggested quietly.

"And he could lie to me," Lily replied. "If he has something to hide in all of this, I will have tipped him off that we suspect him."

"Do you think he could be a threat to you?" Strangford asked. There was a low tension in his voice Lily had not heard before.

"Not to me," Lily admitted, knowing it was true. "But perhaps to others. And it would give him a chance to cover things up."

"If he has something to hide in all this," Strangford countered.

"Does he?" Lily asked.

Strangford's face was long in the gloom.

"I don't know."

They had come to a crossroads. Their corridor ended in a junction. A tangle of wires and fuse boxes blocked the way ahead, two dim and pipe-lined hallways marching off in either direction.

Lily fought against a rising headache. It was too much of a coincidence to think the British Army would somehow misplace twenty-thousand guns, only to have the same number of firearms turn up off the coast of Ulster—firearms which ended up in the hands of a renegade army threatening armed revolt against the crown.

"What else can you tell me?" she asked. She tried not to make it sound too much like a plea.

"He was thinking of a woman."

"Who?"

"Someone he didn't entirely trust. She's tangled up with . . . information, secrets. What Prinz said made Torrington think that he would need something from her, and he was worried about her price for it."

"What else?"

"He was frightened, Lily." Strangford's voice was low. "A word kept running through his head."

"What was it?"

"Treason," Strangford replied.

Lily felt a chill that had nothing to do with the gloom of the basement.

The quiet rerouting of British Army rifles to a group of Ulster rebels. If it was true, it was absolutely treason. But why did the word strike her father full of fear? Did he fear what it could cost his nation? Or was he afraid of being caught?

Traitor or defender. Which role did her father play?

Lily knew he was devoted to his country. He was also a realist, clear-thinking and sharply pragmatic. It was possible that he might bend moral rules if he thought it necessary for the greater good. Which good did he serve here? How far would he go to protect it?

Lily didn't know the answer to that. She could not go off of any public stand he had made for or against Home Rule—and he had made none, so far as she knew. If he was a conspirator, he would be far too clever to broadcast his support for a cause he was willing to commit treason for. Or murder.

"Is that all of it?" she demanded.

"No," Strangford admitted. Something in his tone made her pulse skip. She was aware of the mice skittering through the shadows.

"He was thinking about your mother. And about Patrick Dougherty, sitting in the same chair as Prinz."

Patrick Dougherty had met with her father. But when? Why? What possible reason could an Irish costumer have had for meeting with the powerful Earl of Torrington—and in the Black Rod's Library?

And why did Prinz's tale of treason and conspiracy cause her father to recall his meeting with the man who had died with her mother?

She held her temples. The hall was too narrow, the ceiling too close.

"Lily . . ." Strangford began.

"I'm fine," she cut back. "I will be fine."

She took a deep breath, fighting to still her spinning thoughts, and voiced the question she had been avoiding.

"Was he involved in the murder?"

She could read the answer on Strangford's face.

"You don't know."

She rested a hand against one of the thick black pipes running through the corridor, arteries pumping the strange and dirty life of this enormous place.

"And when he thought of my mother, and of Dougherty . . . what was he feeling?"

"Guilty," Strangford quietly replied. "I'm sorry, Lily. I wish I could have done more. Or less. Something other than just enough to confuse things." He looked down at his hand, flexing his fingers inside the black gloves. "What I am . . . it's both too much and not enough."

She didn't need to be a psychometric to feel his frustration.

Lily took a deep breath.

"Which way should we go?" she asked.

"I don't know where we are," Strangford admitted.

"This way, then," Lily declared, and turned to the left.

NINE

$\mathcal{T}$HE SUNLIGHT WAS A benediction as they stepped into the Old Palace Yard, washing over Lily's skin. She had almost begun to doubt there really was another world outside the dim labyrinth of the maintenance corridors. They had finally escaped by following the clink of glassware and the rumble of self-important voices through a kitchen and into a long, low barroom. Though he had not been to it before, Strangford recalled it was located near the chapel, and was able to navigate the rest of the way to the exit.

They made their way through the summer crowds in the palace yard to the green oasis of Tower Gardens, set against the Thames just west of the Palace of Westminster.

The Buxton Fountain was near the center of the park. It looked a bit like the top had been lobbed off a cathedral spire and set in the middle of the wide lawn. Sam sat by it as planned, but he was not alone. A pretty woman stood beside him holding the leash of a small, fat dog.

It was not unusual to see pretty women stopping to chat with Sam, but this one was dressed far more finely than the type that usually showed interest in him.

The woman turned as they approached, her face lighting up into a brilliant smile as she waved them over. Lily realized her mistake. This wasn't a flirtation. It was an ambush.

The petite brunette in the elegant blue dress was Virginia Eversleigh, Strangford's sister.

Mrs. Eversleigh was a few years older than Strangford and far more fashionable. It helped that instead of inheriting the family estate and the inadequate income that came with it, she had married the handsome heir of a steel company.

Mrs. Eversleigh had decided to approve of Lily from the moment they first met on Strangford's front steps. Lily still found this somewhat surprising. After all, Lily was the unacknowledged bastard of an Irish music hall star, and had worked as a chorus girl herself during one of the more desperate periods of her past. Anyone else of Mrs. Eversleigh's class should have given Lily the cold shoulder. The ton—the cream of London society—viewed being disrespectable as something contagious. Lily had caught it from her mother and was capable of passing the infection to anyone who associated with her.

Mrs. Eversleigh was immune to it. Like Strangford, she refused to allow her life to be dictated by the beat of society's drum, but there was a key difference. Strangford was oblivious to most class pressures and stubbornly resistant to the rest. Mrs. Eversleigh navigated them like a salmon leaping over a waterfall.

The dog should have given her away the moment Lily saw her. Mrs. Eversleigh was perpetually accompanied by her aging pug, Horatio. The animal was sprawled over the grass at Mrs. Eversleigh's dainty feet. It let out a deep and meaningful sigh as they approached.

"Hello, Anthony," she said, rising gracefully from the bench with a shimmer of cobalt silk and hand-stitched lace.

"Virginia," Strangford said, kissing her offered cheek. "I didn't expect to find you here."

"Roderick said you'd gone to Westminster, so I knew you must be at the Lords. It's not as though you go anywhere else. I thought I'd catch you at the door and saw Sam coming out. I grabbed him instead. I knew he would make for excellent bait."

"Don't mind being on your hook, Mrs. Eversleigh," Sam commented, reclining on the bench and offering her a charming grin.

"Lily, darling, I am very pleased to have caught you as well." Mrs. Eversleigh took Lily's hands and pulled her in for a kiss. Lily was enveloped in a cloud of delicate and tasteful French perfume.

"It is always nice to see you as well, Mrs. Eversleigh."

"Virginia," the smaller woman corrected her. "I have asked you to use my name before and now I must insist on it."

"Of course," Lily said, feeling both charmed and uncomfortable. It was an experience she thought many must share when speaking to Strangford's sister.

"How is Mr. Eversleigh?" Strangford asked.

"Walford? Useless. He secured some enormous government contract two months ago and has been flat out ever since."

"What's he building?"

"I haven't the foggiest idea. They have apparently sworn him to secrecy. I would love to think it's something dramatic like submarine periscopes or airplane wings but it's most likely much duller than that. Whatever it is, it has completely tied up the Hugglescote factory, so on top of it all Walford must to negotiate over delays for his usual clients."

Eversleigh had several steelworks in the Midlands, but his factory outside the quaintly-named town of Hugglescote in Leicestershire was by far the largest.

"I'm just looking forward to Sunday afternoon," Virginia said with a sigh.

"What's on Sunday afternoon?" Strangford asked.

"It's when I'll get my husband back. He's shipping all of this whatever-it-is on a special train through Blackfriar's at quarter past six on Sunday morning, and it should be at its destination by mid-day."

"Have you anything planned?" Lily politely asked.

"Oh, yes," Virginia replied with a devilish glint in her eye. "But enough about my troubles." She turned to Sam, handing him a large coin from her purse. "Sam, would you be a dear and buy me a posey from that flower girl over there?"

She nodded toward a pretty young thing at the far end of the park.

"But of course, madam," Sam replied, plucking the silver from her fingers.

"No need to rush about it," Virginia called after him. "We have a little family matter to discuss. You can entertain yourself for a few minutes?"

"I know a thing or two might keep me occupied," Sam replied with a cat-like look at the flower girl.

"Good lad."

Virginia winked, Sam tipped his hat, and Lily was left alone with the two siblings. The smaller woman wasted no time getting down to business.

"You have a visitor," she announced.

"I do?" Strangford said. Visitors were not a common occurrence in Strangford's townhouse in Bayswater's Lancaster Gate. Despite the fashionable address, the house survived on a skeleton crew that consisted of a hapless footman, a competent but somewhat overbearing housekeeper, and her niece, who acted as either maid or extra furnishing depending on her mood and the day.

"It's Mother," Virginia said.

Strangford looked concerned.

"Is something wrong?"

"That is a matter of personal opinion," she replied. "But she's perfectly healthy and there is nothing amiss back home, if that is what you're asking."

Home was Allerhope, the family ancestral seat in Northumberland, where Lady Strangford lived her preferred life of hard work and glorious solitude. Lily had never met Strangford's mother, but based on what she had heard of the woman, she pictured her in Wellington boots and tweed, galloping across the moors on some exquisite piece of horseflesh with a herd of sheep trailing obediently behind her.

"Then why is she here?" Strangford asked. He sounded genuinely bewildered.

Virginia did not offer an immediate answer. Instead, her thoughtful eyes flashed to Lily.

"Lily, would you take a turn with me on the river walk?" she asked.

"If you like," Lily blurted, surprised by the twist in the conversation.

"I take it I am not invited to join this promenade?" Strangford's tone was dry.

"You are not," Virginia retorted. "Stay here and contemplate the beauty of the grass or whatever else it is you do to entertain yourself."

"Right now, I am contemplating tossing you into the river," Strangford replied.

"It would hardly be the first time. Come along, Lily," Virginia ordered. She slipped a dainty hand under Lily's arm and marched her toward the Thames with a strength that defied her size, the fat pug dragging along wearily in her wake.

"I admit that I am very glad you happened to be here as well," Virginia said as they strode across the green. "I much prefer to discuss this with you rather than my brother. In my experience men can be ridiculously obtuse about these matters, Strangford more than most."

She stopped short at the railing that overlooked the water. Horatio collapsed gratefully onto the pavement. She turned to Lily, her gaze direct.

"May I have your permission to speak frankly?"

"Of course," Lily said.

"You know that I hold you in very high regard, so please don't take what I'm about to ask you the wrong way."

"Go on," Lily said.

"What are your intentions regarding my brother?"

Lily's discomfort rose.

"I am . . . not entirely sure how to answer that question."

"Anthony is intelligent, reasonably attractive, and extremely kind-hearted. Add to that a title and there are any number of women who would be pleased to have set a hook in him. Many have tried. He would rather gaze at a painting of some Frenchman's deconstructed mistress or sit alone in that drafty house reading incomprehensible poetry than entertain any of them. I had rather despaired of him until you came along. I might have been happy to see him get that gleam in his eye for any female but you are something more than that. You are not some heiress grasping for a title or a starry-eyed debutante dreaming Strangford into something he patently is not. You would take him for exactly what he is."

The last words hung in the air with a heavy meaning.

Strangford had once told Lily that no one in his family was aware of his unique abilities. It was a secret he had kept entirely to himself until he met Robert Ash—and then Lily.

It struck her then that it was hard to believe that anything so significant as the power to read the past with a touch could have slipped past someone with a mind like Virginia Eversleigh's.

Not that Lily would ask. She knew nothing for certain, and that secret was not hers to reveal.

"For any normal man this sort of thing would've been settled in half the time," Virginia went on, her tone light and quick once more. "But I am well aware that my brother is anything but normal. You are very fond of him?"

Lily's guard was up, but she resisted it, holding her defenses under careful control. She did not believe that Virginia was her enemy, no matter how closely this chat kept dancing toward dangerous ground.

"Yes," Lily admitted frankly.

"You hope to continue to spend time with him? Perhaps even to allow him all of the inordinate duration he requires to make up his mind about something that should be entirely obvious by now? Never mind that last part. I am overstepping, however accurately. You want to keep seeing him?"

"Of course I do," Lily snapped.

Virginia seemed pleased with her answer, however curtly delivered.

"Good. Then we shall make certain that you may do so."

Virginia took her arm again, propelling her along the river.

"My mother has come to London because he intends to talk Strangford out of your relationship," she announced. "Some nosy gossip—Lady Carollton, if I had to guess—has written to tell her that he is courting the illegitimate daughter of an Irish actress and she is convinced it means disaster for the family." Virginia stopped short, giving Lily a frank look. "My mother is not inherently prejudiced. She would not judge a person's character solely by their birth, but she is eminently practical. She does not comprehend whimsy, dreams, or passion. Her concern is that by marrying you, Strangford will put himself beyond the pale of polite society."

The rage was as quick as it was unexpected. None of this should have been any surprise to Lily. She had initially objected to entering into a relationship with Strangford for exactly the same reasons. Why should it surprise her that his mother was concerned?

It was entirely predictable and yet there the anger was, refusing to bow to Lily's rational knowledge that this was all more or less as she had thought it would be.

"Strangford doesn't care about polite society," she replied, making an effort to keep the sharpness from her words.

"I know that. So does she. But she believes that will change, particularly were he to become a father."

Her tone softened as Lily felt the quick blow of what those words implied.

"It is one thing to care little about your own standing with the haute ton," Virginia went on, more gently. "It might be another matter to see your children looked down upon or excluded. There is real power in belonging to the higher circles of the world, opportunities my mother does not want to see her grandchildren excluded from."

The words burned, all of them true. Lily knew that better than most. She had felt the sting of inherited shame. It was a lonely burden.

She also knew that however much Strangford was indifferent to high society, he cared very deeply for his family. Open opposition by his mother to their relationship was bound to put him in a painful position, however long it took him to recognize that.

"Thankfully there is a simple solution," Virginia chirped. She paused, her eye caught by a flat stone that some child had left elegantly balanced on the round iron rail of the river walk. She plucked it up and flicked it out over the water with a strong and elegant turn of the wrist.

The stone skipped across the high waters of the Thames ten times before Lily finally lost sight of it.

"We must simply show my mother that you can be accepted by the ton."

Virginia's easy declaration sparked another flame of anger.

On the far side of the summer-bright park, Sam chatted up the blushing flower girl. Strangford stood by the fountain, frowning down at the surface of the water as a pair of children raced around him in noisy circles.

Families picnicked on the green lawn. Members of Parliament strolled the embankment. Lily felt dangerously close to causing a scene, a notion which horrified her.

"I don't see how that's possible," she replied carefully.

"It is not unprecedented," Virginia went on. "There is the example of Lady Sackville to consider. Her mother was a dancer and Spanish to boot, and she rose to become mistress of an ancient house, her company sought after by princes and kings. The world will be that much more ready to accept you if you follow a trail that has already been blazed. The first step is both the most important and the simplest to arrange."

"And what is that?"

"Your father must publicly acknowledge you as his daughter," Virginia replied.

There was nothing simple about what Virginia was asking. Lily's tentative relationship with her father was complicated by a history of guilt and betrayal. His son and heir, Lord Deveral, despised her. How would he react were Torrington to claim her in the eyes of his peers? What would Torrington's wife, the countess, say?

Lily and Torrington stood in the center of a web of complex and delicate relationships, any thread of which might break and send the whole thing tumbling to the ground.

Behind it all loomed the threat of treason and the ghost of a dead Irishman promising some hidden truth about the death of Lily's mother.

"Two nights from now, Lord Bexley is throwing a ball at his house in St. John's Wood. It is to be the event of the season, attended by anyone who matters. You will come and your father will introduce you. Bexley is a lord-in-waiting to the king and there are rumors Asquith will name him to be Secretary of State for War. His wife is a notorious snob. If they accept you, others cannot possibly help but do the same. And they cannot do other than accept you with Lord Torrington standing at your side."

The scenario that Virginia painted filled Lily with dread. There were a thousand reasons it would not work.

"I shall arrange the invitation. Lady Bexley's secretary owes me a little favor. You find a time between now and Saturday to speak with your father. You will need a gown, of course. You are always well turned-out but this demands something extraordinary. I have already spoken to my dressmaker. She is quite the miracle-worker and I have an uncanny eye for measurements."

"I don't think this is a good idea," Lily said.

Virginia took her arms, meeting her gaze fearlessly.

"You must trust me. It will work, and my mother cannot possibly

THE SHADOW OF WATER

object to you once you have waltzed in Lord Bexley's ballroom. Leave the details to me."

She glanced quickly to the little gold watch on her wrist.

"I must dash. I am late for tea—one must start laying the groundwork for a battle of this nature early. Tell Strangford I love him and that he should cut his hair. Good day, dearest Lily—you will find me a formidable ally."

She gave Lily another quick kiss and sped off in a flash of blue silk.

TEN

*T*HERE WAS NO OPPORTUNITY to discuss Virginia's revelations on the ride back to The Refuge.

Lily and Strangford shared a cab with Sam. He was riding high thanks to the twin victories of successfully invading the inner sanctum of the British Empire and convincing the flower girl to go out for a walk with him. He peppered Strangford with questions about what he'd learned from Torrington's chair, sang the praises of Sylvia the pigeon and questioned whether they were going to stop on the way back for chips.

The carriage disgorged them in front of the gleaming white facade of The Refuge. Sam spilled out first and detoured to the carriage house. That left Lily and Strangford standing by the steps.

He moved closer to her, making way for a woman pushing a pram.

"I should go to Bayswater and check on my mother," he said.

"You haven't asked me what your sister and I talked about. Do you want to know?" she asked.

"I'm not entirely sure," he admitted.

A pair of well-dressed men were strolling through the private green at the center of the square. Two houses down, a group of students lounged on the steps, their voices echoing across the street. It was not the place for a private conversation, and yet Strangford needed to know what he was walking into.

Lily held out her hand.

Strangford let out a low breath, then tugged off his glove and slipped his fingers against her palm.

She felt the dancing energy of his touch and tried to focus on Virginia by the riverside.

Strangford cursed softly. His eyes regained their focus. He released her hand. The air felt cool where he had been touching her skin.

"That doesn't matter to me," he said.

"I know," Lily replied.

"But you're afraid that will change."

It was not a question. He knew it was true. He would have pulled that from her skin along with everything else.

"What do you want me to say?" she asked.

"What I want is for you to trust me."

She could hear the anger in him. Her own temper flickered to life in response, a threatening spark.

"I do," she replied.

"How can you say that and think someday I might turn around and resent you for what I've known all along that you are?"

"You don't know what might change in the future."

"Do you?" he retorted.

The anger was burning now. It was a foreign thing invading her careful self-control. Lily was conscious of the men in the park, the boys on the steps. For the moment, none of them were paying her and Strangford any mind, but that would change quickly enough if she started shouting at him.

And yet she knew it was not Strangford she was angry at. It was not his practical mother, either. She could not name the target of this steady, intense fury, the thing it yearned to lash out at.

She pulled herself together. It took an effort.

"Not like that," she replied, carefully controlling her response. "That isn't how it works. As you know."

He ran his hand through his hair roughly. She could feel the frustration seething off of him.

He looked away.

"I need to go. Forget all that madness Virginia has dreamed up. I'll settle matters with my mother."

"You will not let this drive a wedge between you and your family," Lily snapped, the words coming out before she could think better of them.

He raised a dark eyebrow, his own anger close under the surface.

"They aren't that fragile," he replied.

He could have said more—that Lily didn't understand how family worked because she had never had one. He didn't. She felt it there between them anyway, and the size of it blocked any retort she might have made.

"I'll send word once I've settled things at home," he said. "Then we can talk about what to do next. About the murder."

And your father, he might have added.

Lily felt holes all over this conversation, deep pits they were barely navigating around.

He wanted to say something more. She could see it in the way he hesitated. She could not guess what it was—there were too many possibilities, all of which felt dangerous.

"Good afternoon," he finished tautly, then turned and walked away.

Lily mounted the steps of The Refuge.

She paused at the familiar bright blue door, needing a moment to gather herself.

Strangford could read her feelings like a book. He kept his own locked safely away. *It wasn't fair.* Couldn't he see how vulnerable this relationship was? How easily it could crack?

But she knew he did. It was why that exchange had so quickly sparked him to anger. It cut too close to what he'd feared about their entanglement from the start.

This is not a level playing field.

She leaned forward, reaching out to rest her weight against the door. She felt too heavy all of a sudden, weighed down by terrible uncertainty.

The surface beneath her hands shifted.

The air is cold, the square empty.

Blue paint flakes away under her fingertips, drifting down to the dry leaves that cover the front steps.

Lily blinked.

The door was smooth, the steps swept clean.

A chill ran down her spine. She had seen something else, something not-yet-there. Something that would be.

She closed her eyes, forcing herself to face it.

The weathered surface of the door, wood showing through the neglected paint. Rust edging the brass plaque mounted on the wall, the one engraved in Chinese characters that spelled out the true name of this place. Debris covering the ground, making it clear that no one had passed this way in a very long time.

The Refuge empty. Abandoned.

But when? What did it mean? The vision had come over her too quickly, without any warning. There'd been no time to conjure up a clock, a newspaper with a date conveniently stamped into the corner. All she had was a glimpse of this place left hollow as a shell— this place that was more home to her than the one where she slept at night.

It was like seeing the ghost of someone who had not yet died.

She opened the door and stepped tentatively inside.

Part of her expected the paper to be peeling from the walls, cobwebs draping the grand stair, but the hall was as clean as it ever was. Ash's artifacts still hung on the walls, the bust of Isaac Newton glowering sagely from his pedestal.

Mrs. Liu was at the end of the hall, dusting the corner of a picture frame.

"Hello, Mrs. Liu," Lily called.

The older woman turned.

"Need anything, Miss Albright?"

"No," Lily replied, shaking off the chill. "I'm sorry. I'm fine."

"You look pale. I'll bring you tea," Mrs. Liu announced.

"Really, that isn't necessary," Lily countered quickly.

"Very well," Mrs. Liu said, clearly skeptical. She returned to her work.

The sound of familiar voices drew Lily into the library.

"'And in the time where men sail the sky with iron wings, shooting bolts of fire.' That's what it says. Even you must admit that sounds suspiciously like a description of this war plane flight," Cairncross said as she came in. He was holding up a newspaper.

"I admit nothing of the sort."

The argument came from the softly plump and pretty woman hanging off of Cairncross's ladder. Miss Gwendolyn Bard was Lily's other downstairs neighbor, Estelle's flatmate and companion. The two women were quietly devoted to each other.

Miss Bard's round face was smooth and unlined, but the threads of gray in her rich dark hair betrayed that her age could not be very different from Estelle's.

She was a staunch suffragette and a renowned folklorist, publishing under an androgynous pseudonym to avoid having her papers summarily rejected.

"There are myths of flying men in half a dozen cultures I can think of off the top of my head, Icarus being the most common example," Miss Bard went on. "Or the ba bird of ancient Egypt. I personally think it's a reference to Bladud."

"No one else here knows what that is," Estelle sang from one of the chairs.

"The legendary English king whom Geoffrey of Monmouth claimed built himself a pair of artificial wings," Cairncross retorted. "Some of us are also aware that Monmouth claimed Bladud promptly fell out of the damned sky. And anyway Amalgaid was Irish."

"An Irish monk with a scriptorium at his disposal. You don't think they had a copy of Monmouth chained up in there somewhere?" Miss Bard neatly replied.

Cairncross was clearly working to keep his temper.

"The point is," he went on, tapping the newspaper to punctuate his words. "If Amalgaid's words are a reference to this war plane flight, then we have corroboration of two of his prophetic cues in as many days. War plane, and drowned prince. If Amalgaid got that much right, don't we have to address the possibility that he was a genuine clairvoyant and was also right about the bit where a cataclysm drowns London in blood and fire in three days' time?"

"Or he might have been a half-mad religious fanatic during a time when Christianity was gobbling up and assimilating pagan traditions left and right," Miss Bard retorted. "With a volume of Monmouth in his library. I know which theory I find more plausible."

"Miss Albright, would you pass me the manuscript?"

Ash's voice startled Lily. She had not realized that he was in the room, standing quietly by the fireplace, looking down at the empty hearth.

The others quieted. Cairncross handed Lily the book, which was surprisingly heavy. She carried it to Ash.

"How did things go at Westminster?" he asked as she came over.

"Not as well as they might have," she replied.

"These are shadowy waters. Navigating them will not be straightforward, but you are capable of finding the way through. Even if it is hard to see that at times. Thank you," he added, taking the weight of the ancient book from her.

"Thank goodness," Estelle said, pushing herself up from the chair. She hooked her hand through Lily's arm. "These two are driving me batty with their monks and kings. Let's take a turn about the grounds."

Lily glanced back at Ash, but his thoughtful eyes were on the book in his hands. He opened it and moved to the door, studying the pages as he slipped out into the hall.

Behind them, Cairncross tossed an accusation at Miss Bard.

"It seems to me you have a weakness for Geoffrey of Monmouth."

Miss Bard tossed a book at him. Cairncross neatly caught it.

"That is a first edition!" he snapped.

"Escape. Now," Estelle ordered, propelling Lily out of the library.

They sought the quiet of the garden.

When Lily had first seen the open space behind The Refuge, it had been sleeping with the brown and gray of winter. It was different now, an oasis framed by high brick walls stretching the length of both of the buildings that made up Ash's home.

Fruit trees were heavy with pears and quinces, and other fruits Lily did not know. Ivy draped the walls, setting off the bright hues of flowers.

The garden was not planted with the usual assortment of roses and hydrangea. Sam's father, Mr. Wu, had charge of the place, and had filled it with seeds and roots and cuttings he had brought with him from their home in the Hubei province of China. Lily knew that protecting those plants on the long journey from the east must have cost no small effort. It spoke to the sort of man she suspected Mr. Wu was—someone who took a long view of things and had the patience to wait for the rewards of his work.

Even the ever-present sound of London's traffic was fainter here, lost in the twitter of birdsong and the splash of the fountain. The sky overhead was a hazy pink, the late afternoon light casting a golden sheen over everything.

They were not alone. Mr. Wu squatted by one of the beds, a pail beside him and a gardening fork in his hand. He was digging out the root of a tall plant topped with stems of bright purple bell-like blooms.

"Good afternoon, Mr. Wu," Estelle said.

The gardener stood.

"Miss Deneuve," he said with a nod to Estelle. "Miss Albright."

Sam's father was tall, like his son, but where Sam exuded charm, something about Mr. Wu felt heavy, as though the slender man carried a weight that was palpable in his presence.

"What is that you're working on?" Lily asked politely.

"Harvesting wūtóu. Monkshood," he replied.

"Harvesting a flower?" Lily was surprised by the idea, as the blooms in front of her looked like the sort planted purely for ornamental purposes.

"For Mr. Ash's hands. The pain in his bones."

"Arthritis," Estelle clarified. "Not that he'll admit it."

Lily reached out toward the plant, thinking to run a finger over the soft foliage of its leaves.

"Don't," Mr. Wu said, laying a firm hand on her arm. "It is poisonous to the touch."

"Oh," Lily replied, taken aback. "What about this one?" she asked, pointing to another bloom beside it. This one was complex, the petals arranged in folds and layers of snow white and red. The flower rose from sleek green leaves.

"That is not poison. It is gāo liáng jiāng," he replied.

"It has a lovely bloom," Lily commented.

"It is not grown for the bloom. It is grown for the roots," he replied. "They dispel the cold."

Despite the warmth of the late summer afternoon, Lily felt it as he spoke—the thick chill of English winter, the weight of the gray skies and the sting of drizzle on her skin.

She did not know very much about China, but it occurred to her then that a land that produced flowers like the one in front of her must be one of abundance.

London did not likely show well by comparison.

The roots of that beautiful plant were not for Ash. Lily suspected they were grown for Mr. Wu and his family, to warm them against the pervasive and unrelenting chill of the place they now called home.

"If you will excuse me," Mr. Wu said.

There was an awkward pause as Lily realized that he was waiting for an answer.

"Of course," she said quickly.

He gave her a bow, then picked up his basket of roots and the fallen stems of the beautiful, dangerous monkshood.

He left for the kitchen.

"I will never understand how Sam came from someone so serious," Estelle noted once he had gone.

She took Lily's arm and steered her to a bench by the fountain, plopping down beside her. Dragonflies buzzed around them, stopping for water before zipping off in search of prey.

"What a day!" Estelle exhaled, reclining. "First was the trouble with Desdemona."

"What was the matter with Desdemona?" Lily asked.

Desdemona was a magic lantern slide of a pale odalisque Estelle used to project a ghostly image onto the curtains of her seance room. Though Estelle's abilities were genuine, the clients at her open seances were accustomed to a show. Estelle obliged them, since that was what it took to acquire the private consultations where she could pass on more meaningful messages from the dead.

"It's these newfangled batteries. They're dreadfully unreliable. The last one I had worked fine until I spilled tea all over it. This one charges well enough, according to that little gadget Sam gave me."

"What gadget?"

"An ammeter. Clever thing. It very accurately tells me exactly when my useless battery is about to spontaneously drop all of its charge. I think it's the brand. Don't buy anything with *Zing!* on the label. Really, I ought to have known better," Estelle noted dryly. "And all of that was before I spent three hours with the solicitor. It is enough to drive one to one's vermouth."

"A solicitor? What for?" Lily asked.

"A former client of mine is threatening to file a complaint about me with the magistrate. His departed mother had strong words for him about some rather poor life decisions he has made of late and I was foolish enough to pass them along. The rotter means to see me jailed for fortune telling."

Lily was aware that what Estelle did for a living was technically a crime. The Vagrancy Act, which prohibited fortune telling and claiming to commune with spirits, wasn't routinely enforced, but could easily enough be brought to bear by someone who wished to cause trouble for a medium.

It had occurred to Lily before that technically her own khárisma was also a violation of English law. As she kept its existence strictly to herself and those between the walls of The Refuge, she had not felt the threat all that keenly.

It was different for Estelle, who paid her rent on her gifts. Though her advertisements were discreet, she couldn't survive without being public about what she did.

"What will you do?" Lily demanded.

"Pay him off," Estelle replied. "It leaves a bitter taste but Mr. Budge assures me that the expense will be far less than the cost of enduring a trial . . . never minding that he gave me perhaps a fifty percent chance of avoiding imprisonment."

The injustice of it infuriated her.

"It's a pity there's no khárisma for curses," Lily ground out.

"One never knows. Half of Europe certainly believed it was possible a few centuries ago, though of course the end results of that were some highly unpleasant bonfires."

Lily let that reminder roll over her. She had heard Cairncross and Ash discussing the witch hunts of the 15th and 16th centuries, and their theory that many of those caught up in the panic had been charismatics.

"But enough of all that nonsense. Now that I finally have you to myself, you must tell me everything about Lady Torrington," Estelle ordered. "What's she doing in London?"

"How did you know she was in London?" Lily blurted.

"Darling, really." Estelle waved dismissively.

It was admittedly a foolish question. Estelle was a master at knowing what everyone in a ten mile vicinity of the Thames got up to. It was her primary hobby, one that might have raised suspicions from those already skeptical of how Estelle made her living.

"It's because of you, isn't it?" Estelle prompted.

"Yes," Lily admitted, because it would have been pointless not to.

"Concern about the offended mores of a bunch of dowagers is not going to sway Strangford's opinion."

"No. Of course not."

Estelle leaned back, her hazel eyes thoughtful.

"But it complicates things," she suggested. "And things were already complicated."

Lily watched the water tumble from the fountain. The drops were both regular and unpredictable, random patterns lacing across the shimmering surface.

The swallows had come out overhead, dark winged shadows chasing after the dragonflies.

"I love Gwen," Estelle mused, leaning back against the weathered boards. "Very much. She knows me better than anyone, and yet there are still places in my soul I would rather keep entirely to myself. Choosing what to share is the greater part of what makes any relationship work over the long term. That isn't an option for you. You don't need any more troubles to wrangle and yet here they are. The question is, what are you going to do about it?"

"Mrs. Eversleigh believes I should ask my father to introduce me at Lord Bexley's ball."

"Hmph," Estelle commented. "Mrs. Eversleigh is clever but fatally optimistic."

That was the truth of it. Virginia's plan had the sound of a well-constructed plot, but any number of things might knock out the pillars on which it rested. Not the least of which was the drowned Prinz and a possible connection between his murder and Deirdre Albright's death.

Estelle's mind was clearly running down the same track.

"I don't suppose your little excursion today revealed whether Torrington was involved in Mr. Prinz's death?" she asked.

"No. It fell something short of that . . . but perhaps there might be another way we could find out," Lily said, the idea coming to her as the words left her mouth.

There was, after all, more than one way to see into the mind of the dead. If you couldn't read their secrets in their skin or the things they had touched . . . why not simply ask?

ELEVEN

$\mathcal{T}$HE POISONOUS BLOOMS OF Ash's remaining monkshood danced in the evening breeze.

"I see," Estelle said thoughtfully, quick enough to know where Lily was going. "Communicating with Mr. Prinz on the far side of the veil is certainly a possibility, though it is always a bit more challenging to reach someone with whom you have no personal connection."

Lily considered this. Of course, there was another option—someone else who might be able to offer insight, though the idea of trying to contact him filled her with an uncomfortable dread.

"What about Patrick Dougherty?" she asked.

Estelle looked thoughtful.

"Yes. That could do. Though I must caution you that once you throw open a door to the other side, there is no telling precisely who will walk through it."

Lily felt a chill.

"You mean something dangerous?"

"Tosh," Estelle replied. "Nothing of the sort. I mean that the living can ask to speak to the dead, but it's the dead who do the talking. They have more say than we do as to who gets to take the spotlight. We may ask for Dougherty, but someone else might have more to say to you. Are you sure you want to hear it?"

Lily thought of the men she had killed.

Lieutenant Waddington. Mr. Northcote. Joseph Hartwell. As she always did when she thought of them, she saw their faces in the moment before their deaths. One was rage, the other terror. The last wore a look of surprised indignation as though offended by the notion that a mere woman could get the better of him.

She thought of the many others she had failed to save. They haunted the greater part of her past, the people whose deaths she had foreseen. That was a burden she had only recently begun to move beyond. It was a journey that was far from complete, and their faces were still burned into her memory.

One more so than the others.

She recalled the echo of an old song, a thin thread of remembered tune.

By the rising of the moon, by the rising of the moon . . .

"We need to exhaust every possible source of information," Lily said.

"Fair enough. Would you rather the others weren't aware of what we're doing? It would be fine if you were. Most people prefer their readings to be private, once they've accepted that conversing with the spirits is even possible. The dead know all sorts of inconvenient secrets."

Lily nodded.

"Mr. Wu should be done for the day. We can make use of the potting shed," Estelle announced.

The shed stood in the back corner of the garden, adjoining the carriage house. It felt airy despite its diminutive size. The space was meticulously organized. A few bundles of herbs hung from the ceiling to dry. Clay pots were neatly stacked on the shelves. Tools hung from a pegboard at the back. Unlike any other potting shed Lily had seen, there was not a speck of dust to be found, and she could not spot a single cobweb.

The potting bench itself also served as a desk. A tin box held neat rows of seed packets. A paraffin boiler and a cheap but pristine tin teapot sat to one side next to a pretty china cup. On the other was a folded newspaper printed in Chinese characters.

The single chair in the room was pulled up to the bench, and

Lily found she could easily picture Mr. Wu here, sipping his tea and reading the paper when he claimed a bit of time for himself.

There was also a photograph. Lily examined it in the fading light. A family stood in front of a prosperous-looking house nestled on a hillside among ancient trees and thick palms.

She could clearly make out the faces of a younger Mr. Wu, with Mrs. Liu—Sam's grandmother—standing to his left. A young boy stood on the other side, his dark hair oiled into submission, hands tucked behind his back as though it were taking an immense effort for him to hold still for the long seconds required for the exposure.

It was not hard to recognize Sam in that boy.

The last figure in the portrait was someone Lily had never seen. She was a girl of perhaps fifteen, clearly beautiful. There was something fierce about her gaze as though she were daring the image to try to subdue her.

Was she Sam's sister? The physical resemblance between them was undeniable. Why had Lily never heard of her before? She wondered if perhaps the girl had died. It seemed the most likely explanation, though Lily found it strange that a dead sister wouldn't have merited so much as a mention through the months she had known Sam.

Looking at those blazing eyes it was hard to imagine anything being capable of snuffing such a determined creature out of existence.

"I'm afraid I will have to claim the chair," Estelle apologized as she lit the lamp hanging from the rafters. "I can't really do this unless I settle myself down, and it's hard to manage that while standing or leaning on a table."

"Of course," Lily said, making way for the older woman to sit.

She had lived upstairs from Estelle for years now and had heard countless seances through the thin floorboards of her flat. She knew that much of that sound was a response not to the presence of the dead but to the tricks and flash that Estelle used to impress her newer clients. There had also been moments in her conversations with the medium where Estelle casually mentioned some bit of information she had gathered from somebody deceased. Lily recalled the offended Mrs. Forbes in Whitstable, the former landlady who disapproved of her brief tête-à-tête with Strangford.

She knew that the dead were a regular presence for Estelle, something she might note in a room the way others would pick up on a fine wallpaper print or the smell of cinnamon.

For all that—for all the years she had now known Estelle—she still did not have the foggiest idea how this would work.

"What do I need to do?" she asked.

"If you don't mind it terribly, you could hold my hand. It isn't strictly necessary but I do find it sometimes helps to focus if I'm in physical contact with the person I'm reading for. Otherwise there is a particularly tenacious great aunt of mine who has a tendency to try to bully through."

Lily knelt down by Estelle's chair. The concrete floor was swept clean, so she had no fear for her skirts. She set her hands into Estelle's.

She remained quiet as Estelle closed her eyes. The medium breathed deeply and slowly, her usually animated body uncharacteristically still. This was not the performance that elicited screams from an eager audience. It felt like something more akin to what Robert Ash was doing in the sanctuary of The Refuge, that empty room in which he would sit for hours with no company but the low rush of water and the light moving slowly past the windows.

The potting shed was quiet save for Estelle's even breath. The shadows lengthened outside and the little tin lamp burned brightly overhead.

"A white dress. A warm room. Something to do with Strangford . . . she is pushing his image at me very strongly. There's a pretty little knife, the sort of thing a gentleman opens letters with. Jewels," Estelle added thoughtfully. "Initials on the hilt. I cannot get the letters but I believe they would be significant to you if I could."

Lily felt cold. She knew that knife. Knew the white dress. She remembered a bell-bright laugh, a woman with black hair who drew every eye in a crowded room.

They belonged to Annalise Boyden, the woman Strangford had once loved. The woman he and Lily had found sprawled in her bed with her throat cut.

Yes, she would know the letters on the hilt of the blade.

"This isn't who we've come for, is it?" Estelle asked, her tone quintessentially wry. It comforted Lily to hear that tone, because things had suddenly gone very strange in a way she was not entirely ready for.

"No," Lily confirmed.

"Would you like to know what she wants to say, or shall I move her along?"

Lily had not liked Annalise Boyden when she was alive. She would not have trusted her. She had failed utterly to save the woman's life.

"You can say it," she replied. "Whatever it is."

Lily knew that the unheard conversation happening in front of her did not take place in words. It would be an exchange of feelings and symbols, signs pulled by the dead woman from the library of Estelle's mind.

"The gas lamp man," Estelle went on. "She knows you killed him. There is a ferocious sort of joy in her over that. She doesn't exactly mince away from vengeance, this one—that much is quite clear—and she feels you were the hand of it. I gather it has raised her opinion of you somewhat."

"I see," Lily said carefully.

"And that is what she wanted you to know," Estelle concluded. "Well. It is rare to see a spirit maintain such utter self-interest even after passing into the next realm, but the world endlessly surprises."

She looked down at Lily, her blue caftan falling regally around the plain wooden legs of the chair.

"We really ought to have done this sooner," Estelle chided. "There is quite a muddle of presences trying to get through to you. I gather the one we are trying to reach was not particularly close to you?"

"No," Lily admitted.

"And he passed some time ago. I have his name, of course, but might help if you were to think of him as best you can remember. It will give us a bit more to go on in order to cut through the chatter."

"I'll try," Lily said.

She took a deep breath, nerves fluttering in her chest, and tried to focus on what she could recall of Patrick Dougherty.

The memories were slender things, light little pieces that slipped away from her as she tried to grasp them. There was the figure of a man, tall as her father but slender and more elegant. The flat brim of an unusual and fashionable hat. Something about his laugh—it had been very distinctive, a quick bark that was inherently laced with sarcasm.

The fragments kept slipping. The laugh flipped into a woman's throaty humor, the scent of lilac perfume. Auburn hair pulling through the bristles of a silver brush, kohl-lined eyes smiling at Lily through a mirror.

Lily forced those images aside. She grasped at something more recent, at the vision of Patrick Dougherty holding court above a pool of filth, bloodstains darkening the pallor of his suit.

Come along now, a stóirín.

"How anyone could wear tweed in July," Estelle muttered. "Here, lad, for a kiss. *The boy I love is up in the gallery . . . merry as a robin that sings on a tree.*"

It was a fragment of a song, one Lily distantly recalled. Estelle sang it with a rich baritone, ringed with the hint of an accent that was not her own.

The chill settled deeper into Lily's bones. She knew what this was. She had seen it before in a warehouse with fire licking up the walls—Estelle speaking someone else's words in someone else's voice, the language of a dead woman who looked through Estelle's eyes at the face of the man who had killed her.

Thief. Murderer. Alukah.

What was happening now was not a mere reading. This was the medium as conduit, a road laid down between Lily and a man who had been murdered fourteen years before.

"Patrick Dougherty," Lily said.

Estelle went quiet, her head tilted at an angle, listening.

Lily was consumed by the uncanny awareness that she was sitting in a potting shed with a dead man.

"What do you have to do with Charlie Prinz?"

"Red Branch," the dead man said with Estelle's voice.

Ice shot through Lily's bones. She thought of Strangford in the labyrinthine basement of Westminster Palace.

He was afraid of something . . . Red Branch.

"What does that mean?" Lily demanded.

"Ask the Brothers. *At the rising of the moon, at the rising of the moon . . .*"

"Don't sing that," she snapped, the rebuke spilling out of her.

"Look to your father," the dead man replied.

"Why? What has my father got to do with it?"

"Treason. Sorry, little bean. All my fault, poor songbird . . . *At the rising of the moon . . .*"

"What about my father?"

Estelle didn't answer. Something in her was shifting. Her posture changed, softened, her voice lightening.

" . . . *at the rising of the moon. And a thousand blades were flashing . . .*"

This was not the Irish costumer. Brashness was replaced with grace, the wry edge melted into a dreamy distance.

Gooseflesh raced up Lily's arms, crawled across her neck. She knew it—that grace, that dreamy distance. Knew the voice singing that strange old tune.

Estelle looked down.

"Lily," someone said through her lips.

Sam burst into the potting shed.

"Hey Bà!" he called before he realized it was not his father sitting in the chair. "Oh. What are you two doing in here?"

Estelle was rubbing her hand over her eyes.

"Goodness, that hasn't happened in a while," she said, the words entirely her own.

"Are you alright?" Lily asked, both concerned and wary.

"Fine," she replied. "Just wrung out like an old flannel. Channeling is extremely draining."

"What's that, then? You're channeling in the potting shed?" Sam asked.

"It's a perfectly good place for it," Estelle returned as she stood up. "If one wants a bit of privacy."

"Privacy? What'd you want that for?" Sam demanded.

"My point exactly," Estelle returned evenly.

Lily was glad to see that she seemed entirely herself, though she was clearly a bit worn by the experience. It was hard to reconcile the eeriness of what had taken place inside the shed a few minutes before with the ordinariness of it now. Lily was conscious of the planting pots and trowels, the rake leaning against the corner. Sam stood in the doorway in one of his flasher waistcoats, frowning at them in the light of the lantern.

"I think your father went to the kitchen," Lily offered.

"Fine," he replied, throwing up his hands. "Turn me out. Not like old Sam's got anything useful to offer. Dinner's on back at the house, if you're interested. Mr. Ash is taking it up in his room but Năinai made enough for the lot of you."

"What is it?" Estelle asked.

"Egg soup, bao and steamed greens."

"I'll be right in," the older woman announced with a determination that surprised Lily. Estelle was usually indifferent to food at best.

"You're staying for supper?" Lily asked.

"Serving as a vessel for the dead always leaves me famished," Estelle admitted.

Sam had left the door open behind him, the light of the shed spilling out into the long shadows of the garden. A few early moths fluttered in, dancing around the lantern.

"And what about you?" Estelle asked. "Are you any worse for our little chat with the departed?"

"I'm not sure I found what I was hoping for," Lily admitted.

"Their priorities are different than ours," Estelle said. "It can make any sort of direct inquiry rather complicated."

"What does it mean? Red Branch." Lily asked.

"I can't say," Estelle admitted. "That's the trouble with channeling. I'm less the intermediary and more just along for the ride. But I do sense that it wasn't a literal branch he was referring to."

"It's a symbol," Lily finished, knowing something of symbols herself.

"Yes," Estelle confirmed.

"He said to ask the brothers. Have you any notion which brothers he meant?" Lily asked.

"I can only tell you that he had rather mixed feelings about them, whomever they were. An odd and uncomfortable loyalty mixed with a healthy dose of contempt."

"That doesn't exactly narrow it down."

"No," Estelle agreed. She touched Lily's arm. "Mostly, he wanted you to know that he felt terribly sorry. About what happened to your mother."

"My fault," Lily echoed, repeating the dead man's words. They tasted bitter in her mouth. She had felt it herself for years after her mother's death—*my fault*. Because she had known it was coming and failed to prevent it. Because Lily's efforts to thwart fate had brought about the very circumstances that led to Deirdre Albright's death.

Outside the shed, crickets were singing, the sky over Bloomsbury shifting toward purple.

"It was the necklace," she told Estelle quietly. "Dougherty had a set of very fine paste jewels. He loaned it to her for the evening. The thieves mistook them for something real."

"No," Estelle countered gently. "That is not why he was sorry."

The words shook her, rippling some part of the foundation upon which she had constructed her life.

"What do you mean?"

"It wasn't the necklace. I'm afraid I can't say any more than that. Red Branch. That's why he was sorry. It was all tied up with the Red Branch."

"I see," Lily said numbly, though she did not. The shed had grown smaller and the night pressed in around them.

She needed to get home. She needed to be alone.

"You should eat," she said, pressing Estelle's hand.

"You aren't coming?"

"I just . . . there's something I need to see to."

"Ah," Estelle noted. "Then I will leave you to it."

She patted Lily on the cheek then sailed out of the shed, the rich colors of her caftan billowing around her as she moved through the twilit garden.

Lily sat back down in the lone chair. Her gaze moved to the photograph on the table, to the girl who stood beside Sam, a fierce-eyed secret.

Then she took a moment to cry.

TWELVE

Friday, July 31
Morning
March Place, Bloomsbury

 $\mathcal{L}$ ILY WOKE TO A pounding on the door.

It was later than it should have been. The slant of the light on the floor of her attic flat was wrong. The air was already hot, promising that London faced one of those rare sweltering English summer days.

She sat up in her bed, knocking over the warm sleeping bulk of Cat as she did so.

Cat was an enormous orange beast that belonged to no one in the house yet was impossible to eradicate. It was impervious to doors, turning up in places no reasonable animal should have been able to get into, like Lily's locked bedroom in the middle of the night.

She brushed the layer of orange fur from her nightgown. The pounding outside continued.

"Miss Albright! I said your ride has arrived."

Lily shrugged on a dressing gown and staggered into her little parlor, opening the door to reveal the bullish face of her landlady.

"What is it, Mrs. Bramble?"

"I said, your ride is here. He's waiting on the steps."

"Who is?" Lily asked, still rubbing sleep from her eyes.

"That Chinese boy," Mrs. Bramble retorted. "And what are you locking the door for? Afraid the ladies downstairs are going to sneak up in the night and assault your virtue?"

Lily was fairly certain the ladies downstairs—Estelle and Miss Bard—had done away with each other's moral standing some years ago and never looked back.

The truth was that the experience with Estelle in the potting shed had left her rattled. That was why she had locked the door to her flat. Glancing back into her bedroom, she could see the lamp still lit on her nightstand as Cat walked proprietary circles around her mattress.

"Tell Mr. Wu I will be right down," Lily said and closed the door.

—

She was feeling slightly more alert as she left the house, clad in a blouse and a linen skirt that were among the lightest in her wardrobe. They still felt too warm for the weather. She rather badly wanted a cup of tea, but whatever had brought Sam to her doorstep unexpectedly must be urgent.

She found him at the curb. He had brought Ash's carriage and appeared to be having a comfortable conversation with the horses. Ash had granted Sam the privilege of naming the beasts which is how the chestnut had come to be called Mary while the bay was given the slightly more eccentric name of Pickford.

The names were Sam's tribute to a doe-eyed brunette motion picture actress.

"I'm sorry that took so long," she said as she came out. "I overslept this morning. What's wrong?"

Sam frowned. "What do you mean?"

"You're here," Lily said dumbly. "So I thought something must have happened."

"I was told to collect you for training," Sam replied, stroking Pickford's neck contentedly.

"Training?" Lily echoed. "But I'm not training today. And I don't usually require a lift if I am. It's only five minutes' walk."

Sam considered this. Pickford gave a snort, irritated that Sam's hand had momentarily stopped its ministrations.

"Sounds like you've been summoned," he concluded. "That's the master of the house for you."

Lily could hear the edge to his tone. She thought longingly of that missed cup of tea.

As much as Lily respected her mentor, it sometimes felt as though Ash moved them all like pieces on an invisible chessboard where only he knew the rules of the game.

That was frustrating enough for Lily. She imagined it must be something more complicated for Sam, who was both nineteen—an age not known for emotional restraint—and someone who was obligated to Ash in a way that went beyond a bit of occult training.

Sam scratched the ear of the chestnut mare who stood patiently beside Pickford in the harness of the carriage. She whickered happily and pushed her nose against his hand.

"Go on with you," he chided, pushing back. "Well, you coming, then?"

Was this just a whim of Ash's? The notion made her want to crawl back into her room for another hour of sleep. Her night had been restless, her dreams ragged and unsettling.

"I'm coming," she said.

~

Ash was waiting for her on the steps of The Refuge.

"Miss Albright," he said as she stepped out of the carriage.

"Good morning, Mr. Ash," she replied.

"Sam, you recall the rest of my instructions?"

"Take care of the horses and then find someplace other than Bedford Square to occupy myself," Sam replied flatly.

He did not sound as though he particularly appreciated the order.

"At least one hour. Not more than two," Ash clarified. "I believe your father has gone to the mahjong house if you wished to join him."

"Shì, Lâoshī," Sam said and snapped the reins.

"You have given everyone the morning off?" Lily asked as Ash led her inside.

"We require the house to ourselves for this exercise," Ash replied. "This way."

He started up the stairs. Lily followed, though she was beginning to feel uneasy. What sort of exercise required everyone to be evicted from The Refuge?

"I appreciate your coming on such short notice. I am sorry for the abrupt summons," Ash said as they climbed. "A critical matter has arisen that requires prompt attention."

"Of course," Lily agreed. She noticed, absently, that he was actually wearing shoes. That was a rarity for him when at home. They were polished black oxfords, a bit worn in the soles.

They passed the studio, where she had expected they would go. The wood-floored room, bare of furniture but supplied with mats and other equipment, was where Lily usually did her training.

Instead, Ash stopped at the foot of the attic stairs.

The attic was an immense space, entirely open for the length of both of the buildings that made up The Refuge. It was empty save for one thing—a mural that covered every inch of the walls and ceiling, the final opus of Ash's dead wife.

Evangeline Ash's final work was . . . unsettling. It might be mistaken for the eloquent visual ravings of a madwoman or a gruesome experiment in the avant-garde if it hadn't felt so uncomfortably true.

It was also personal. Lily was one of the many figures Mrs. Ash had depicted. The portrait was stylized, its connection to Lily not one of face and feature but of symbol and significance. That ought to leave more room for skepticism, but having seen it for herself, Lily knew better.

Evangeline Ash, who perceived fate rather than the future, had somehow painted Lily years before she was born. She had woven the image out of the secrets that shaped Lily's life, then threaded it through with uncomfortable promises of what her destiny held in store.

Ash started up the narrow stair. He did not wait to see if she would follow.

The heat rose to meet her as she reached the top, a palpable force, thick enough that moving through it felt like pushing a knife through cold butter. It wrapped around her as she reached the top with oppressive intensity.

The attic smelled like the church Lily had attended with her mother when she was a girl, all dust and the strange incense of old paint. Where St. Patrick's in Soho had been comfortable as an old shoe, Evangeline Ash's attic felt more like a sacred relic, a temple to some long forgotten deity. Instead of a vague flicker of guilt for not coming around more often, the space filled Lily with a quiet dread.

The walls of the attic were covered by thick black curtains, open only around the narrow gabled windows that spilled pale light into the room. The yards of dark cloth whispered of the strangeness they concealed. Lily had glimpsed some of it in the flesh, other fragments in the throes of a vision. She wasn't sure she wanted to see any more of it and was glad that Ash had kept it covered up.

The room was normally empty, so Lily was surprised to find anything in it besides the heavy expanse of black fabric. A small table stood in the center of the floor. A very old book lay in the center of it beside a box of matches. A tin watering can sat on the ground. A sledgehammer leaned incongruously against the wall.

The floor itself was made of unfinished but smooth-worn planks. Lily could only see the outer edges of it. The rest was covered by a gray rubber tarpaulin.

Whatever training Ash intended for her today, it had clearly taken some preparation.

All she could see of the mural was the ceiling. It was familiar to her. This part of Mrs. Ash's work was always left exposed. The style was distinctly Egyptian, gold and silver stars on a rich blue background mingling with the figures of various gods, both small and immense. Ash had told her before that his wife had based it on the ceiling of the Temple of Hathor at Dendera in Egypt.

Lily looked up at it as she entered the attic. It was impossible not to. Evangeline Ash's work commanded the eye.

"The ceiling was the last thing she painted," Ash said, noting the direction of Lily's gaze. "She died the day after it was completed."

"I'm very sorry," Lily said.

"We honeymooned in Egypt," he went on. "She was different then. Her khárisma was less . . . pronounced. Looking back on it now I can see, of course, how completely it shaped her from the beginning, but at the time one might almost have mistaken her for . . ."

"Someone like everyone else," Lily offered quietly.

"She changed at Dendera."

Ash looked up, his eyes traveling over the rich cacophony of divinities dancing across the ceiling, the sunlight through the narrow windows picking out the cobalt blue and sparks of gold.

"Charismatics are not necessarily born complete," he said. "New charismatic ability can emerge at any point in life. It can manifest at any age in someone who has never before displayed any indication of supernatural power. And in someone who has, new powers may make themselves known. These may be deeper and more intense versions of previously identified inclinations, or they may be something entirely novel."

His gaze stopped on the figure of an immense goddess striding across the northern end of Evangeline's sky. She was a regal figure, her profile commanding and terrible. She carried a snake in her hand like a scepter, an asp that she pointed at the corner of the room where the painted rays of the western sun could just be seen spilling out from behind the thick black curtain covering the wall.

"My wife was always intuitive, with an uncanny instinct for the significant. After Dendera she was something else. It was as though that ancient pattern on the ceiling of the temple was the missing element that completed a circuit."

Lily's heart pounded. She thought of everything she knew about Evangeline Ash. There were the stories of the young debutante sought after by a range of powerful men despite her mixed racial heritage—a stain in the eyes of many in society—and modest fortune. To have called forth that level of admiration, Evangeline must have been something more than simply beautiful. She must have possessed the sort of charm that had seen Lily's mother rise from a dirt-floored cottage in Ireland to the center of the London stages.

That image did not reconcile with the woman's art. Evangeline Ash's paintings were not charming. They struck a blow. They were arrangements of symbol, both the shocking and the mundane, gathered in a way that paid absolutely no regard to propriety. These arrangements were not wild or random. They were rigorously organized in accordance with some system Lily could not perceive and was not sure she wanted to understand.

The image of a charming young girl was also contradicted by the tone people used when speaking of the late Mrs. Ash. It was not an air of nostalgia or admiration. It was uncomfortable, a mixture of awe and fear and perhaps just a little revulsion.

She changed at Dendera.

Lily looked up. The gods marched in untidy rows, figures all out of proportion, celestial lights spinning through and between them.

The Parliament of Stars. That was the odd name Ash had given fate when they talked on Tottenham Court Road months before. The phrase had stuck with her. The ceiling of the attic of The Refuge seemed to depict it perfectly.

"Why do you think this was so important to her?" she asked.

Ash closed his eyes. He looked tired.

"The ceiling of the Temple of Hathor at Dendera is a zodiac. Look at it closely and you will see three forces interacting with each other to shape the lives of men. There is the regular movement of the forces of nature, represented by the astronomical bodies. The enigmatic whims of the gods. And finally the free will of ordinary mortals."

The stars twinkled overhead, glittering against the darkness that lay between the strange and distant figures marching across the ceiling.

"Which ones are the mortals?" Lily asked, looking from a hawk-headed figure to the baboon with a quill in his hand.

"They're down here," Ash replied, waving a hand at the black-curtained walls of the room.

The walls, where the meat of Evangeline Ash's mural lived, where Lily's own portrait could be found. She knew there were others hiding beneath those curtains. She had glimpsed some of them before—a peacock-robed woman dancing in the arms of the dead, a halo-crowned warrior with black gauntlets over his hands.

Portraits of mortals who were something quite other than ordinary.

"I believe that when Evangeline saw that ancient artist's work, something which had always been there inside of her recognized it as true. It woke up, and she began to see that truth everywhere else she looked."

Ash's eyes met Lily's across the room, the table and the book standing between them.

"It is something that might happen to any of us. We may all be capable of more than we realize, waiting for the right stimulus to quicken us to strange new life," he said.

"Why are you telling me this?" Lily quietly demanded.

"Six months ago, you stole a South American shamanic potion from Cairncross's apothecary cabinet. The Wine of Jurema."

"Yes," Lily confirmed. It was not the first time they had discussed this. Ash had asked Lily to describe her experiences while under the influence of the Wine of Jurema early on in her training.

"I know that consuming it triggered a particularly intense and powerful series of visions. You have told me some of what you saw. It included an experience in a place you described as a hall of doors."

The memory of it flooded in. It was still fresh, burned into her brain—the feeling of that white, endless space, the countless doors marching into obscurity. The key she held in her hand, the brass weight of it shifting into a thousand different shapes. The wild, trembling sense of some limitless potential.

"What about it?"

"I believe in that moment you may have been glimpsing the potential emergence in yourself of a new form of khárisma."

"I'm sorry. I don't understand," Lily said, her heart pounding.

"What do you know about the future?" Ash asked.

"Right now?"

"No. I do not mean the specifics. What do you know about how it works? What *is* the future, Miss Albright?"

"I . . . don't know that I can answer that."

"You perceive it. You have lived with it all your life. Surely you must have some notion. Do you believe that it is preordained? That the course of our lives is set down before we take our first breaths?"

"No," Lily protested.

"Then why can't you change it?"

Ash asked the question in a matter-of-fact tone, but it cut at Lily all the same. It was too close to a point of vulnerability, evoking memory after memory of her failure to save people from the terrible things she had known were coming to them.

Ash knew that. She had trusted him with that history of guilt, of pain. His blunt question had a prick of betrayal however much she knew it was true.

"I don't know," she snapped.

"I have told you that my wife could perceive fate. Do you believe me?"

"Yes."

"So you must believe in fate, then."

"Is that where this is going?" Lily demanded. "Are you telling me that all of this is fated?"

"No," Ash replied. "And yes."

Her skin was slick with sweat. The heat of the attic pushed at her brain, eating away her patience. Lily headed for the stairs.

"I don't have time for this."

"That is correct."

Ash's voice cut across the attic, clear as a thunderbolt. He put his hand on the ancient book on the table.

"We have no time, which is why my methods must be something less gentle than I might have preferred. I have been reading Cairncross's translation of the prophecies of St. Amalgaid of the Skerries. It is my conclusion that Amalgaid was in fact a charismatic. A clairvoyant like yourself, Miss Albright. He predicted the destruction of London in a cataclysm of blood and fire and he has told us when this cataclysm will take place."

Evangeline Ash's ceiling pressed down overhead. The heat of the room suffocated her thoughts, rendered her numb.

"We have two days," Ash announced.

THIRTEEN

⸻

*T*HE SHOCK OF IT was like a bucket of water in her face.

"You can't possibly be serious."

"Would that I were not," Ash replied. "But the death of Charles Prinz and his discovery at Crossness, the recent armed Vickers aircraft flight—these and other signs surpass mere coincidence. Cairncross and I have identified a further six events between now and the early fourteenth century that St. Amalgaid predicted with uncanny accuracy. His precognitive power was as genuine as your own, Miss Albright, and there is no ambiguity in what he foresees for this city."

It was the gravity of his tone that convinced her. Even for Ash, who seemed oblivious to humor, it was unusually weighted. Lily could not doubt his seriousness.

Her brain struggled to accept it. The idea that London could be so suddenly and irrevocably changed seemed impossible. It was her home, its streets and alleys more constant than any other force in her life had ever been. It was the Russian baker on the corner of Tottenham Court Road who made the most divine pastries. The newsboy who called from the end of March Place at seven o'clock every morning. The pigeons that crowded the embankment and the dandies one could always find lounging on Oxford Street.

The faded playbills on the walls of Covent Garden. The way the breeze smelled of mud even as far inland as Clerkenwell. The calls of the bargemen as the sun rose over the river and the bells that rang out in sequence from the church towers as though each of them were deliberately just a few seconds off from the other.

London could not be destroyed, and yet Ash's words had come with that quiet authority Lily could never deny.

"We have to do something," Lily protested.

"Indeed," Ash agreed. "If we believe the future is unchangeable—that fate is carved into stone—then we should go very far away, bringing as many of those we love with us as we can. Would you agree, Miss Albright?"

"No," she blurted. "You can't just leave thousands of people to die."

"So you believe the future can be changed."

"Yes," Lily asserted, making her voice far more firm than she really felt.

"Then why have you failed at it so miserably?"

She had no answer. The blow of it left her speechless.

The failures paraded before her, flickering past her vision like scenes from a magic lantern show. All the lives she had failed to save. The pain she had failed to prevent. All the times she had tried and fought and struggled only to stand over the same pointless horrors she had foreseen weeks before, knowing that the effort had been for nothing. Worse—that it had left her feeling pointlessly responsible, burdened with the guilt that she had known exactly what was coming and had been incapable of using that knowledge to do any sort of good.

For Ash to wield it against her was a violation.

The rage rose up in her, quick and hot.

"How dare you," she said.

Ash picked up the tin watering can. He began to circle the table, pouring the liquid inside of it out onto the tarpaulin-covered floor. It was not water but something that looked darker and more viscous. The smell burned her nose.

"I loved a woman who knew fate," Ash said as he let the contents of the watering can stream down onto the ground. "And if I learned anything from her about it, it is that fate is not a book someone has already written. It is a complex and wildly nuanced interaction between immense forces, not the least of which is you, Lilith Albright. Fate does not rule the future. You did not fail to change what you foresaw all those many times because fate refused you. You failed because you were going about it the wrong way."

It was another strike, another hit. She felt every atom of it tearing loose old scars, resurrecting the still-fresh morass of guilt and grief.

"I tried everything," Lily protested, voice raw with the truth of it.

"No," Ash countered. "Clairvoyance is a spectrum. On one end, we have the Amalgaids, the Cassandras who warn us of the horrors to come as though they were unavoidable, as though the future were a single road laid out across the landscape of time."

The watering can was empty, its strange contents now spread about the floor.

"Then there is the other end of the spectrum," he went on, setting the vessel down. "A clairvoyance that sees not just one future, but all of them—all the many probable and improbable outcomes that stretch out from any given moment in time. The smallest acts in the present have consequences that ripple far into the future. One touch, one push can be the catalyst for tremendous change. I believe there have been—and are—those gifted with the power to identify those catalysts, to sense the points upon which one future or another pivots. Clairvoyants like Amalgaid merely see. These others are gifted with the power to reshape the direction of things to come."

She thought of the image hidden behind the dark curtains to her left. She could pinpoint the exact location on the wall where Evangeline Ash had painted it—the figure she had labeled *The Prophetess*, a flame-haired goddess with a yew staff in her hand, luminescent with power.

Except that Lily had never felt anywhere near that powerful.

"I don't see multiple futures," she retorted. "If what you say is true I think we both know what end of the spectrum I fall on."

"We know nothing of the sort," Ash returned. "I suspect there is more to you. I think you have hidden it from yourself because you are afraid of what it might mean. You fear the responsibility it entails."

Lily's anger flickered higher.

"I spent years being responsible. I fought for more lives than I can count. I lost all of them. You know nothing about what I am afraid of."

"You lost because you were fighting with your head," he said. "You are always clinging stubbornly to logic and rationality. It is precisely what we have struggled against since you began your training. Knowing the future requires a different sensibility. So does changing it."

"If that's true, it is clearly a sensibility I do not possess."

"I think you do possess it. I believe it has been hiding inside of you, waiting for the right stimulus to emerge."

"Surely I would have some inkling of it," she countered.

"My wife had no notion of her true power until Dendera."

"So what, then? You would have me go to Egypt?" Lily's tone was sharp with sarcasm.

If it struck a blow, Ash did not allow any sign of it. His expression was as serious as she had ever seen. If anything, it was apologetic.

"This is not how I would have chosen to approach the matter. Unfortunately the circumstances require haste. Amalgaid could not have foreseen an event so distant in the future if it did not have the weight of fate behind it. If we are to change the outcome—"

"How can we change an outcome if it's fated?" Lily cut in. "Doesn't that contradict the entire concept of fate?"

"Destiny cannot be a monolith," he said. "It must be a dance. We are partners in it and at any moment one or the other of us might lead. That is what I learned from Evangeline, who knew it better than anyone."

"Then how did she die?" Lily demanded. "If she could see fate and she knew it could be changed, wouldn't she have avoided her own death? Unless her power wasn't as great as you say it was. Unless she didn't know."

"She knew," Ash replied. "She painted it. It is behind that curtain."

He pointed to the wall at Lily's back.

She did not ask to see it. She did not doubt him. She could feel that it was true, an awareness that crawled up her spine.

"If she knew, why did she let it happen?"

"I do not know," he said.

Suddenly Lily understood. She knew the reason for the grief Ash still carried, the grief that could be heard every time he spoke of his dead wife. Lily knew why he had left England after she had died and spent decades wandering through the wilds of the world. He had been searching for an answer to the question she had just asked him.

And he had never found it.

"We are not going to Egypt, Miss Albright," he said. "St. Amalgaid saw a probable future in which London burns and thousands die. That disaster will take place in two days' time if we cannot find a way to change it. We must activate what I believe is inside of you, and your charisma has only ever answered to one thing."

"High stakes," Lily said, her sense of alarm deepening.

Ash took the box of matches from the table.

"Yes," he confirmed. "So that is what we must utilize."

He lit a match.

"Find a way to change this," he ordered and dropped it.

He stepped back as the floor exploded into a wall of fire.

Shock rooted her. The flames raced across the oily substance Ash had poured across the ground. They licked at the black curtains and flickered against the painted ceiling, the gods and stars beginning to blister.

He was burning down The Refuge.

The heat of the blaze pressed against her. Memory swelled up, and for a moment Lily was somewhere else.

Flames licked at shelves packed with shimmering glass.

Estelle sat on a table with her hand at her throat, blood running between her fingers.

A board was wrenched from Lily's arms, the nail at the end of it jammed into the skull of the man she had just killed.

The heat of an explosion threw her against the wall, ringing her ears.

They were more than memories, sucking her completely into that other place, that other time—the burning warehouse on St. Savior's Dock six months before. Her lungs screamed for air, panic firing her heart into a frantic gallop.

Lily struggled back to the present but the fear came with her, threatening to swallow her in a wave of blind terror.

This was not February. She was in The Refuge, not Joseph Hartwell's warehouse. A door lay behind her, one she could bolt through until she reached the safety of the pavement. She could stand there in the square and watch this place that had become home to her turn into ashes.

Ash stood on the far side of the flames, his path to the door blocked by the blaze.

"You're a madman," Lily shouted across the flames. "You're going to burn yourself alive."

"That seems the likely outcome," Ash calmly agreed. "Unless you find the pivot."

"I'm going for help," she declared.

"The Refuge is empty," Ash called as she turned for the door. "You will not find anyone in time."

Fury rose in her, mingling with the fear in a heat that rivaled the fire at her feet.

"You have no right to do this," she shouted.

"It is my house," Ash replied.

"That is not what I meant!"

The air had grown thick, choked with some chemical stink. The flames were spread the length of the room, long fingers grasping at the walls.

Lily grabbed the black curtain that hung nearest to her. As she took hold of it, she realized the fabric was wet with some thick, slimy substance.

She wrapped her hands in the folds and yanked, thinking to pull it from the wall and use it to smother the flames. The curtain did not budge. Metal grommets at the top were looped around an iron rod bolted into the wall.

"You are using your head again, not your power," Ash chided her from the far side of the fire.

"Shut up," Lily shot back.

Wood cracked behind her, black stains spreading across Evangeline's ceiling.

"Logic cannot stop this. Remember your training and reach for something else," he said.

It was getting hard to breathe. The smoke had grown thick,

dizzying her with its stench. She could feel the closeness of the flames and thought of how much this place meant not just to her but to those she loved. It was where Strangford felt safe enough to let down his ever-present guard. It housed Cairncross's library, the books and manuscripts he used to feed his voracious mind. It was Sam's home, however complicated his feelings about it were.

She could not let it fall.

The curtain still tangled around her hands, Lily leaned her head against the wall and tried to push herself into that other place, the one where she knew things without learning them. She tried to silence the panicked racing of her mind and listen instead to something else, something deeper.

She thought of the rooftop on Hampstead Heath, of Joseph Hartwell. Of the moment when it had seemed that a thousand different outcomes opened up in front of her. The paths to different futures were illuminated, all of them hopeless except for one—one that demanded she pay an unspeakable toll.

The hall of doors came back to her. She remembered the walls falling away, the possibilities marching off in every direction. The cold weight of the key in her hand.

For a moment it was more than a memory, the walls of this room tumbling back, the flames becoming irrelevant in the midst of so much space, so much time . . . and then it splintered, the connection broken, swallowed by something else.

London is hollow.

Lily gazes at it from the flat surface of a barge floating on the Thames.

Where the city should be, there is only a crater. It cuts deep into the earth, the edges of it jagged with the remains of brick-lined sewer tunnels, pipes spewing water or burning gas.

The sky overhead is a forced twilight, the sun dimmed by a thick veil of black smoke.

The hole in the ground has devoured everything from the Tower to the courts. Fleet Street, Chancery Lane, Holborn—these are vanished, replaced with a well of rubble simmering with the oily waters of the river.

The Old Bailey. The Embankment. The dome of St. Paul's.

All gone.

The destruction is not limited to the City of London. Lily glances behind her to see a gap carved out of Southwark. Beyond that, flames redden the smoke-filled sky, dancing from the blown-out windows of office buildings and blocks of row houses.

On all of the remaining structures—the empty walls of dead buildings, the shards of overpasses—Lily can see the same sign, repeated over and over again, the bloody mark of an upraised hand.

Overhead, smoke streams into the orange sky. The lines of it merge, divide, sprawl out to form an elegant network. As the sun sinks behind her, the smoke flashes to crimson, capturing the fading light of the day. It leafs out, birthing strange blooms.

Red Branch, she thinks in the voice of a dead man. *Red Branch.*

Terrible things float past her down the river, the bloated shapes of men and dogs. Somewhere up the wind, she can hear a woman crying, the long sobs of hopeless despair.

My fault. My fault.

It cannot be. It must not be. This is not some moderate disaster like the ones Lily has struggled with in the past, the devastation of a family deprived of a father or a child crippled for life. This is horror on a scale she could never have dreamed.

Her mind moves through murk, shock threatening to paralyze her. Lily refuses it, grasping for a way out. There is one, she recalls, clinging to the thought even as it threatens to slip into vagueness.

An artist in her attic, shaping a mural terrible in its truth. Paint on fingers that had long since rotted in the ground.

Lily recalls the voice of Evangeline Ash in a vision provoked by desperately swallowing an entire bottle of The Wine of Jurema six months before.

Stop fighting. Ask for what you want.

She remembers that lesson. She knows how to do this.

The black air burns in her lungs. The river is livid with the reflected flames of St. Amalgaid's cataclysm. Lily forces the words out past the pain.

"Show me how to stop this," she begs.

A hot wind slams into her, pushing her back. She tips over the side of the barge and falls, swallowed by the dark water of the river.

The walls are painted with flames.

Shadowy green fire dances over shelves of carefully organized glass, beakers and vials and sample jars Lily knows were destroyed in a blaze that ended six months before.

This is the warehouse—Hartwell's warehouse. It should be a ruin on St. Savior's Dock and instead it is packed with bodies, men and women in costumes of fantastic excess.

The room echoes with the wail of a horn. Glass breaks like the ringing of tiny bells. Screams rise up with the music, another element in a hellish orchestra.

Behind her in this place that should not exist anymore lies a hole, a square cut into the floor that opens to a dark pool of water three floors below. It is the water that Strangford fell into, the water that was buried under the collapsing roof of the building.

That warehouse is gone. This cannot be the same place. She knows it, and yet it blazes before her, singing of death.

A shadow swings across her line of vision, moving like the pendulum of an enormous clock.

A woman stands in front of her. Her hair is black, her pale skin shimmering, covered with iridescent scales. She is beautiful and terrible.

"Thank you," she says. "But I will not give you what you have come here for."

A shadow falls across her, cutting her in half.

No, Lily thinks distantly. *That must not be.*

She steps into the woman's arms and is enveloped by the scent of her, of rain-soaked leaves and black pepper, the musk of a predator and the salt of tears. Lily takes the lead in their dance and spins her around, out of the line of shadow.

The great pendulum completes its arc, striking Lily in the chest. She falls.

Three stories of air rush past her, the dancing green flames on the painted walls receding overhead.

She strikes water, the sting of it needling her back.

The water swallows her.

Her arms and legs are dead weights. Her brain refuses to pass them a command to move, to swim her back to the surface.

She sinks gracefully deeper.

The light grows brighter, flickering across the surface. At the far side of it stands a shadow framed in a blazing door, and Lily knows she is about to say goodbye.

The water burns into her nose, her throat. Her lungs explode with pain. Fireworks burst across her eyes, leaving patches of darkness behind until everything has gone to black.

Lily gasped into the smoke of the attic.

Her eyes were burning, her throat scorched. She had fallen to her knees, her palms scraping against the rough surface of the floor.

Behind her, the fire burned.

Death. She saw death. For the sake of some beautiful serpent Lily would fall into the water and drown.

There were no alternative futures. She had not gone to some mystical place where the secret to saving The Refuge unfolded before her.

The paint on the Dendera ceiling turned from stars into charred black bubbles.

Ash waited with infuriating patience on the far side of the fire. He was an arrogant lunatic. Lily had no secret power. The Refuge was going to burn into a pile of rubble.

She could not let that happen.

She grasped the black curtains once more, twisting them firmly and deliberately around her arms. Her fingers clawed into the soaked fabric until it was as much a part of her as her own skin.

She planted one foot up against the wall, then the other, putting the whole of her weight against the curtain. She pushed out through her thighs, her calves, her back, pulling against the fabric with every ounce of her strength.

"Miss Albright," Ash shouted from across the room.

Lily's teeth ground together, her body soaked with sweat. She wrenched against the curtain and felt it tear. The rip flew across the material, dropping Lily to the floor like a stone under a mound of black fabric.

Her head bounced against the tarpaulin. Flames danced at the corners of her vision. She could smell the reek of burning hair.

She rolled away, conscious of Ash moving somewhere behind

her. She flicked her hands through her hair, smothering the burning ends of it.

She grasped the drenched weight of the black curtain and threw it over the floor.

It knocked over the table, throwing Amalgaid's ancient prophecies to the ground. A portion of the fire smothered out with a hiss, while the rest of it around her curtain continued to burn.

A great knock resounded through the attic.

Lily turned to see Ash standing at the corner of the room with the sledgehammer in his hands. He had pushed aside one of the curtains, revealing the sunset Lily had glimpsed earlier, the one pointed out by the regal goddess on the roof.

Ash swung the hammer again and the plaster broke apart, revealing a slab of rusted metal.

He struck a third blow and the metal exploded.

Water blasted into the room.

It knocked Lily off her feet. She felt a sharp pain in her temple as she went down.

The vision swallowed her once more.

She floats under the surface of the black water, urgency gone. Silent fireworks flash at the corners of her vision, liquid burning warmly inside her chest.

Lily rose up sputtering, soaked through.

The fire was gone. The room dripped, stinking of smoke.

Ash stood by a ragged wound in his wife's last work, a black hole in the center of the setting sun. Lily could see that it opened into the rusted hulk of the water gravity tank.

He set the sledgehammer down carefully, leaning it against the wall where it had been before.

"It appears I was mistaken," he said.

Charred at the edges and bleeding from the head, Lily made him a far less polite reply.

FOURTEEN

$\mathcal{M}$RS. LIU MADE A snip with her scissors and another twist of auburn hair fell to the floor.

Lily was sitting in the kitchen of The Refuge. The room was at the back of the house on the ground floor. It was cooler here where the windows were shaded by the boxwood hedges that framed the garden, but Lily could still feel the heat of the day.

It had all the accoutrements of a typical English kitchen but was also clearly Mrs. Liu's domain. A bamboo steamer sat on a shelf over the cooker beside a tin can full of chopsticks. A long waxed paper scroll hung from the wall, decorated with a watercolor painting of a crane and rows of Chinese characters. An altar was set up on a little table in the corner. A few sticks of burnt incense rose from a jar of sand before a ceramic figurine of a plump man with a long black beard.

The cooker was cold, and Lily found herself grateful that Ash's housekeeper had little interest in using an oven.

An empty bowl of rice sat on the table. Lily had forced it down at Mrs. Liu's insistence, though her stomach recoiled from the thought of food.

She had seen the world end.

A pile of hair was heaped around her chair. It was not the same texture Lily knew from running her brush through it each morning. The strands were frizzled into tight twists, crisp and brittle.

Mrs. Liu cut again, her softly wrinkled hands moving with careful precision.

The city she called home would be blasted into a pit of mud and blood and fire.

Cairncross came in with a basket full of laundry. He set it by the door to the garden.

"It has officially stopped raining on the second floor," he announced. "And this is the last of the washing. Only the two western bedrooms were impacted."

Mrs. Liu made a curt reply in Mandarin.

"I am aware you cannot do the washing without running water, Mrs. Liu. Sam is ordering the parts for a new system. I am under the impression it will be an improvement over the old gravity tank on the roof. That was in dire need of replacement anyway."

"Very convenient," Mrs. Liu replied, her tone dripping with disdain. She neatly trimmed off another lock of Lily's hair.

Guilt flashed across Cairncross's long features, but he quickly schooled them.

"I am told that short hair is becoming quite fashionable," he said. "I believe the young women call it a 'bob.'"

Lily could not see Mrs. Liu's face but the look she gave Cairncross must have spoken volumes.

He cleared his throat.

"Yes. Well."

Lily had asked for a way to stop it. Her power had shown her a vision of her own death, dark water filling her lungs for the sake of a stranger, a woman with the skin of a snake.

Did the salvation of London lie on the other side of that choice? She could not know.

All of them were in danger, everyone she loved. Cairncross and Mrs. Liu, sparring across her cropped head. Sam. Estelle and Miss Bard. Her father and all the brothers she would never really know.

Ash. Strangford.

Would dying save them?

Dr. Gardner came in, carrying his black bag. His shoulders filled the narrow doorway to the kitchen.

"It seems I cannot complete a shift at the hospital without you lot concocting some disaster," he noted. His gruff voice was a comfort, but Lily was incapable of feeling it.

He set his bag on the kitchen table, plucked up a chair and swung it around to face Lily. He sat opposite her and leaned down to her eye level.

"Well, aren't you a sight?" he said kindly. His brown eyes traveled carefully over the skin of her face and neck, then down to her hands. "How's your breathing?"

"It's fine," Lily replied.

"No chest pain? Shortness of breath? Dizziness?"

"Not anymore."

"No burns, at least," he concluded.

"The fuel Mr. Ash used combusts at an exceptionally low temperature," Cairncross offered from across the room. "It is an old Islamic formula attributed to the alchemist al-Jabir."

"Fire is still fire," Gardner replied. "What the devil was he about, anyway?"

"It was an unconventional training exercise for Miss Albright," Cairncross replied.

"A training exercise?" Gardner's tone was clearly skeptical.

Training exercise. The words cut through the fog that muffled her feelings. A few sharp pricks of rage spiked through, mingled with fear and horror.

If she closed her eyes, she could see Ash's face in the gloom of the attic.

Then why have you failed at it so miserably?

Mrs. Liu offered Cairncross a response in Mandarin. It dripped with disapproval.

"That is not an entirely fair characterization, Mrs. Liu," Cairncross replied. "Mr. Ash has called for a meeting this evening. He will explain the matter then."

Ah, Lily thought. So that was how it was going to be. Ash would summon them all together in his elegant library and explain that the end of the world was nigh because Lily lacked the capacity to save it.

Gardner's attention was on Lily. "You appear to be undamaged, but I would feel better if I took a closer look. May I?"

Lily knew he was not talking about bringing out a magnifying glass.

She nodded.

Mrs. Liu held her scissors, prepared to wait.

Gardner put his hand to the base of her throat. He closed his eyes, his breath deepening. Lily had the familiar but still uncanny sensation of something happening at a level she could not feel or see.

At least this touch would not violate the secrets of her mind.

Sam barreled into the room. He slammed the garden door shut behind him hard enough to rattle the panes of glass in the nearby window. The sound made Lily wince.

"The constant pressure tank will be here tomorrow," he announced. "Which will be useful, as it turns out we still have a house to install it in."

"Careful, Mr. Wu," Cairncross said.

"I'm not the one who needs to be careful. It wasn't me nearly burned the place to the ground," Sam retorted. He looked to Dr. Gardner and Lily. "She alright?"

"I might be able to tell you if you cut that bloody racket," Gardner replied evenly, his eyes still closed.

"Sorry," Sam said, reining himself in. It was a precarious patience, more volatile than Cairncross's medieval Islamic fuel.

"Right, then," Gardner said, his eyes clearing. "You've come out of it relatively unscathed."

"She's covered in blood," Sam pointed out.

If his tone irked Gardner, the doctor didn't show it.

"Head wounds bleed like the devil," Gardner said. He turned his attention to Lily. "You've a bit of irritation in your lungs, but that ought to clear up on its own. Your wrist might be a mite tender for a day or two. The hair will grow back. That just leaves this." He put a finger gently to the bandage on Lily's forehead. "May I?"

"Go on," Lily said flatly.

The doctor carefully pulled the blood-soaked gauze away.

"Someone already painted you with iodine, I see," he said.

"We are not entirely ignorant of the basics of medical science," Cairncross retorted in response to Gardner's look.

The doctor prodded the wound gently. Lily could see Sam over his shoulder. He looked furious.

The sight of his obvious anger lent energy to her own. It stirred restlessly beneath the numbness that still overwhelmed her.

"It doesn't need stitches," Gardner concluded, taking a fresh piece of gauze from his bag. "Just keep it clean and dry. A bandage would be good for a day or two. Change it twice a day. You're a healthy young woman. You'll do the rest quite well on your own."

He taped the bandage carefully into place.

"No thanks to the master of the house," Sam concluded.

He slammed a paper bag onto the counter. It was full of small pieces of metal, parts for the repairs to the plumbing.

"Mr. Ash has his reasons," Cairncross said.

"He always has his reasons, don't he?" Sam replied. "He nearly burned Lily alive this morning."

"Nobody was going to be burned alive," Cairncross said. "The fuel combusts at a very low—"

"He lit the house on fire! He knocked a hole in the water tank! Do you think he asked her first whether she wanted any of that?" Sam demanded. "No. He just keeps pushing, trying to bully all of us into becoming whatever it is he thinks we should be. He never stops to ask whether it's what we want."

"That's not entirely fair," Cairncross warned.

Sam didn't hear it. The anger was loose in him now, and Lily suspected its roots went far deeper than this morning's fire in the attic.

"It's not enough for us to live a normal life. We have to be something great. After all, we're why he built this place. We're all his tribute to her. His wife walks into her own death and that's got to have a reason, so why not make it us?"

Cairncross stood.

"You go too far," he said.

For a moment, Lily wondered if it would come to blows. Something long simmering in Sam had boiled up to the surface. He seemed ready to break.

She did not miss the significance of what he had said.

His wife walks into her own death . . .

Why would no one speak of how Evangeline Ash had died?

The old soldier and the East End tough faced each other across the kitchen. Lily didn't doubt Cairncross's restraint. She was less confident of Sam. She was conscious of Gardner behind her, quietly ready to intervene.

"That is enough," she announced.

Her words cut across the kitchen, snipping the tension between the two men.

The house was fraught with a tangled and wild energy. She could feel it in the walls. It was no wonder Cairncross and Sam were edgy. What Ash had done . . .

Mr. Ash has his reasons.

Lily knew it must be true but at the moment it was hard to understand what they might have been.

"Lǚxíng zhízé," Mrs. Liu said calmly from behind Lily's chair, her eyes on her grandson. "The horses are hungry."

"Shì, Nǎinai," Sam replied. He cast a dagger-sharp glare at Cairncross, then exited to the garden.

Cairncross rubbed his eyes, dropping back into his chair.

"That boy is growing up fast," Gardner noted.

"It's hard to believe seven years ago he was just a wee sprout picking Ash's pocket," Cairncross distractedly agreed.

Gardner raised an eyebrow.

"Didn't realize the lad had actually robbed him," he said.

"It wasn't as though he succeeded at it," Cairncross replied, looking a touch uncomfortable.

Lily could tell he had not intended to bring up the story, but she had always known there was more to Sam and Ash's history. At the moment, she found she had little tolerance for secrets.

"What happened?" she demanded.

Cairncross glanced at Gardner as though looking for help.

"You're the one who brought it up," Gardner noted.

Cairncross leaned back. He looked tired.

"Sam set a couple of cats to fighting in the street. That was how he distracted his marks. He has told me one cannot ask a cat to do anything, but it is simple enough to get them irritated with each other. He would likely have gotten away with it if Mr. Ash had been alone, but I was walking behind him and caught him at it."

"How old was he?" Lily asked.

"Not more than twelve. Mr. Ash refused to turn him over to the constable. He was suspicious about the cats, you see. He asked Sam about it and of course the boy denied everything. Mr. Ash let him go but asked me to track him. I followed him to his home—if you could call it that. Pitiful little hole in a Limehouse tenement. Mr. Ash introduced himself to Mr. Wu. When he learned the family were from Hubei he offered him a position here at The Refuge. The Wu farm was perhaps two days' journey from the monastery where Mr. Ash spent several years studying the way of the Tao. He retains a fondness for the food and finds some of the Chinese herbs very useful."

Cairncross cast a glance at Mrs. Liu, who was standing behind Lily, making occasional delicate cuts to her hair. She remained quiet though Lily was sure she understood every word. She could feel the careful focus of her attention.

"Mr. Wu accepted Ash's offer of employment and the family came to live here at The Refuge," Cairncross concluded. "It isn't what they had before Sam fell in with the Brothers, but it is a sight better than what they were reduced to in Limehouse."

"Brothers?" Lily asked, the word catching at her mind, pulling her out of Sam's story. "Sam has brothers?"

"No," Cairncross replied carefully. "More a . . . fraternal organization, back in China. A story for another time, perhaps."

Mrs. Liu's scissors paused ever so briefly before they continued their regular, careful cuts at the back of Lily's hair.

Sam had told Lily once before that it was his fault his family had left China, something about falling in with a bad crowd. Lily had been left with the distinct impression that this "bad crowd" were somehow even worse than the Limehouse thug who had put him to work as a housebreaker and pickpocket when he was barely more than a child.

An organization that called itself a brotherhood.

Pieces clicked neatly into place, shaping a new truth inside her mind.

Ask the Brothers.

Patrick Dougherty's words when Estelle had channeled him in the potting shed. She and Estelle had been thinking of literal brothers, blood relations. What if Dougherty had been trying to tell them something else?

Lily recalled the old tune he had sung. The words to it were there inside her mind, an old memory waiting for the right trigger to recall it.

At the rising of the moon.

It was part of an old Irish ballad, a romantic tale of an uprising in Ireland against the English overlords. Dougherty had been Irish, like her mother, his voice still rich with the musical cadence of his homeland.

Lily had not known him well. He had been one of many colorful figures who passed through her mother's life, their stories brightening the salons she held in her Oxford Street flat.

She recalled the photograph on the shelf in the potting shed where Sam's father had made his office. That was the image of a prosperous family. They had left all of it behind for a Limehouse tenement because of Sam and his Brothers.

When Ash made his offer to employ the family, Sam couldn't possibly have opposed it—not if he was responsible for such a fall in their fortunes.

Not even if he suspected that Ash's interest wasn't primarily in Chinese cuisine and medicinal herbs but in a boy who could manipulate animals.

Lily had made a choice to walk through the doors of The Refuge, to accept Ash as her mentor. That had been challenging enough.

Sam never had any choice. It lent another layer of complication to his relationship with his mentor.

Patrick Dougherty spoke of Brothers. He could not have meant Sam's old accomplices in Hubei but rather something closer to home.

The Fenians called themselves a brotherhood. A more formal name had been listed on the memorandum she saw in Westminster— the Irish Republican Brotherhood.

Brothers who weren't brothers. Brothers for whom an old Irish song might be an anthem.

Brothers whom the memo claimed were planning a "disruption" the morning before the king's peace talks over the Home Rule crisis were to begin.

This Sunday morning. The morning Ash believed St. Amalgaid's cataclysm would take place.

Lily flinched as Gardner closed his bag with a snap.

"I'm afraid I have to return to the hospital. What time has Mr. Ash called this meeting?"

"Six o'clock," Cairncross replied. "Mrs. Liu will be providing supper."

"Mr. Liu's cooking is always much appreciated," Gardner replied. "I will be interested to hear what this is all about."

Cairncross didn't comment. He cast a glance at Lily, then looked away again.

He knew.

She remembered the thick, slimy fireproofing that had been applied to the curtains that covered Evangeline Ash's mural in the attic. It was hard to imagine Ash patiently painting that stuff on himself. Then there was Cairncross's intimate knowledge of the fuel Ash had used to start his fire.

An old Islamic formula . . .

Cairncross had helped him. She should have guessed as much from the beginning. His loyalty to Ash was unimpeachable, rooted in a long history neither man had ever shared with her.

He would also know about the rest of it—about St. Amalgaid and the cataclysm. About Ash's belief that London would die in two days' time.

That was the purpose of the meeting that evening. Ash was summoning the charismatics to The Refuge to tell them that the city they called home was about to be destroyed.

And that Lily would not be able to save them.

A spike of pain twisted inside of her. There would be more where that came from once this veil of shock burned away.

Mrs. Liu made a final snip, then set down her shears.

"Done," she announced. "Up with you."

Lily rose. Mrs. Liu moved the chair out of the way and began to sweep up the remnants of her hair. Lily watched the destroyed tangles of it pile into the dustbin.

Strangford stepped into the doorway.

His dark locks were more disheveled than usual, his boots scuffed. His gaze snapped straight to the bloodstains on her shirt. He took a step toward her then caught himself, holding back. Lily could see that it cost him to do so when his instinct must be to take hold of her and rip out the knowledge of what had just happened.

"Are you hurt?" he demanded.

"Not particularly," she replied.

"Head wounds bleed like the devil," Cairncross offered from his chair.

Mrs. Liu scoffed from the opposite side of the room.

Strangford's hands were clenched at his sides.

"I heard there was a fire."

"In the attic but the damage was minimal," Cairncross said. "It was set deliberately as part of a training exercise."

"Low temperature combustion," Mrs. Liu noted acerbically as she tipped her dustbin into the waste basket.

"I still don't understand." Strangford's words were thin.

"I am sure Miss Albright can enlighten you," Cairncross finished as he stood.

The words stung, though Lily knew Cairncross's callousness was born of his own conflict. He had to find a way to believe that what Ash had done that morning was right. It was clearly something that took more than the usual effort.

"I need to complete my assessment of the damage to the mural," Cairncross said. "As the curtains were all soaked in fire retardant, it appears to be confined to the Dendera ceiling and the northwestern panel, but I had best be certain no other intervention is needed to stabilize it. Unless there is anything else you require, Miss Albright?"

It was a formal expression, but Lily could read more in his tired blue eyes. There was concern there and perhaps a little shame.

"No. Thank you," she replied.

"M'lord," Cairncross said to Strangford as he left.

Mrs. Liu set the chair back at the table, the floor beneath it clear of any sign of Lily's mutilated hair. She came to where Lily stood, taking hold of her chin with her soft, wrinkled hands. She gently turned Lily's face to and fro.

"Still beautiful," she concluded, patting her on the cheek.

The older woman gathered up a stack of towels and climbed the stairs, leaving Lily and Strangford alone.

He stood at the window, his arms crossed over his chest, looking out at a wall of green boxwood.

"Where is Ash?" he asked.

"He went out after the fire," Lily replied.

She watched him for a long moment. The tension coming off of him was palpable.

"There must not have been any other way," he concluded out loud, and Lily understood.

It wasn't just fear for her safety that was tying him into knots. Ash was Strangford's mentor, too, someone he trusted and respected. His concern about Lily was running straight up against his feelings about a man who was both his teacher and his friend.

This was how he had decided to reconcile it—by believing that Ash knew what he was doing in the attic that morning.

Lily had trusted and respected Ash too, however much they had butted heads over the last few months of her training. She well understood that conflict.

His words still filled her with an uncomfortable fury.

"I need some air," she announced and stepped out into the garden.

The heat hit her like a fist. The sky was gray with haze, the sun a distant blur. Even the fountain splashing amid the hydrangeas looked limp. Lily felt the sweat break back out on her skin.

Strangford followed her outside.

"Lily . . ." he began.

She turned to face him and held out her hand.

"Read it," she ordered.

"Are you sure that's what you want?" he asked without coming closer.

Lily didn't answer. Her hand remained extended.

He came to her. Stopping just short of where she stood, he pulled off his gloves and tucked them into his pocket.

She felt it again, that intense response to his nearness. It had only grown stronger over the months since she had met him. Even now, when everything threatened to fall apart, it was there, burning through her as she faced him in the thick quiet of the garden.

He took her hand.

She closed her eyes, letting him move through her. That electric contact tingled from her hand up into her back, her neck. Every nerve fired with awareness, the inimitable sensation that told her he was inside of her mind.

She could see the impact of each revelation. They were written across his moving features—the pain and the horror of witnessing Amalgaid's apocalypse winding him like a blow. The way the impossible warehouse paled him, fear tensing his jaw.

Then the unavoidable truth of what came next.

The snake woman in a room of green fire. The black water drawing her down, swallowing her in darkness.

The electric connection spiked, then broke. His eyes cleared as he looked at her, widening with anger and desperation.

"No," he declared.

She took her hand back.

"To which part of it?" she demanded.

"All of it. Any of it."

"I asked for a way to stop the cataclysm," Lily quietly reminded him.

"You don't know that what you saw was an answer," he snapped.

"I don't know that it wasn't."

He held his head, struggling to contain everything he had just absorbed.

"We have to warn them," he blurted. "We have to get everyone away from here."

Lily didn't have to be a psychometric to know what he was thinking. She had gone through the same process of horror and denial and reason an hour before when she had first been dragged into the kitchen. If he had maintained his connection with her a little longer, it might have rendered this conversation unnecessary.

"We can't," she replied.

His eyes widened.

"Why not?"

"What would we tell them? That we found a prediction in an

ancient manuscript? That I had a vision of the future? They wouldn't believe us. Not enough of them. And the ones that did . . . Remember Joseph Hartwell." Even the sound of the name on her own tongue set her pulse racing, raising the bitter specter of an old fear. "You know what he did to people like us. *You saw.*"

The image of Annalise Boyden splashed across Lily's memory, her pale arms sprawled across blood-flecked sheets, her throat an angry red slash.

Strangford had born witness to it too, the horrific destruction of a woman he had once loved.

"Hartwell believed, and he wanted it for himself," she continued. "He didn't care whose lives he destroyed in the process. Half of them think we're the work of the devil and the rest are all certain we're liars or criminals. Estelle is being threatened with imprisonment for it *right now*. You haven't even told your own family what you can do."

The last was a blow. He flinched under the impact of it.

"I have twisted my mind around it a dozen different ways since the fire, trying to find a path that doesn't end in disaster. I can't see one," she snapped. "All I have is that vision. It's the only thing that feels somehow like hope."

"How can it be hope if it kills you?" he retorted.

"I don't know," she replied, letting her eyes close.

It was all too much, too overwhelming. She wasn't ready for any of it, but she didn't have any choice.

"You could go to Northumberland," he announced.

"Northumberland?" she echoed, disbelieving.

"What you saw in that warehouse. Whatever it was can't come to pass if you're not even in the same city."

"You don't know where it will happen. The warehouse doesn't exist anymore. It's a bunch of empty pilings at St. Savior's Dock. My mind must have substituted it for something I don't know yet, a place I couldn't yet imagine."

"It wasn't Allerhope," he returned stubbornly.

"I can't go to Allerhope," she protested.

"Why not?" he demanded. His dark eyes flashed.

"I'd be walking away from it. I'd be letting all those people die."

"It isn't your responsibility." His voice was rising.

"Because I couldn't do what Ash wanted me to do?" Lily shot back.

Strangford closed his eyes.

"He thought he was helping you."

"It didn't feel like help."

"You don't know what was in his head," he said.

"Neither do you."

"He wouldn't do something like that without a reason."

Strangford's words sounded like a plea. Lily wasn't sure she disagreed with him. She had always trusted that Ash knew what he was doing.

The image of him standing next to the jagged hole in the attic wall flashed back to her.

It appears I was mistaken.

She was angry. The anger had started under Evangeline Ash's Dendera ceiling and it had not yet dissipated. It felt as though it was growing solid, becoming a physical thing inside of her, another organ crowding her liver, her heart. The oppressive heat of the day fueled it, whipping the flames higher.

"Maybe I'm just not what he hoped I was," she said.

"We have to tell the others," he concluded.

"Cairncross already knows. Ash has called a meeting tonight to inform the rest of them."

"I'm not talking about the cataclysm. I'm talking about your dying," he said.

"No," Lily replied.

He stepped away. Tension rippled off of him. He stared down at a fig tree in a terracotta pot.

"I can't let their fear of something happening to me compromise their actions," she went on. "We'll need everyone if we're going to find a way to stop this."

"You told me."

"You would have found out anyway," she said.

It was the truth but it struck a blow, as she knew it would. She could see the impact of it between his shoulder blades.

"So that's it, then. You're going to walk into your own death out of some misplaced sense of sacrifice."

"I'm not walking into anything. I'm not looking to martyr myself."

"Then leave," he growled.

Running had never worked before. Dodging and manipulating, issuing dire warnings—none of it had ever saved any lives in the past. Why should it be any different this time when she herself was the victim of what the future held in store?

Though she said she had no interest in martyrdom, Lily knew the vision of her death had come as an answer to her question.

How did she stop the cataclysm? By saving the life of a stranger and losing her own in the process.

It made no rational sense, but the knowledge didn't care about being rational. It was there nonetheless.

She could picture it so clearly—climbing onto a train with Strangford, running away with him to the wide green moors of his home. They would be far from warehouses that shouldn't exist anymore, from the woman who was also a snake and the horrific devastation of London. It could all happen in the distance while she walked with Strangford in peace.

"No," she replied.

His boot shot out. It was a brutal gesture with nothing of the grace of his tàijí. The polished leather struck the fig tree. The pot shattered, roots and soil spilling into a heap.

It shocked her, that burst of physical rage. Strangford held everything tightly coiled, wrenched into restraint, yet Lily had always known things ran deep under that quiet surface.

"You wouldn't have told me, would you?" he said. "If you weren't afraid I'd find out anyway, you would have kept all this to yourself."

His words cut. Lily knew there was truth in them.

"There isn't much point in playing games of might-have-been," she returned.

She caught herself before she voiced the rest.

Because it is impossible for me to keep anything to myself.

Could she live like this? She wasn't sure she could answer that.

In the light of what she had learned in the attic, the question might be irrelevant.

She forced herself to focus on what mattered.

"St. Amalgaid's vision. You saw what I saw."

"Yes," he admitted.

"Then you know I have to do whatever I can to prevent it."

He stared down at the broken pieces of the fig tree.

"That can't be the only way." He ground out the words.

Lily closed her eyes.

"I changed the future once before. I saved Estelle. I did it with what I have, not whatever Ash thought I might . . ." Her voice trailed off, the words for that disappointment failing her. Could this have been different if she had been what Ash hoped she might be? There was no way to know. The power he described terrified her. It was hard enough being what she was.

"It isn't impossible," she concluded.

"But if you're wrong, Lily . . ."

"I can't run away from this," she insisted.

She knew what came next would not be well received, but she had to say it anyway.

"You could go," she offered. "You could take Virginia and her family and your mother and go someplace safe. Someplace away from here."

The anger flared back up in him again, firing sparks behind his dark eyes.

"Do you honestly think I would do that?"

"No," she admitted. "But I had to say it."

The rage crumbled back. His shoulders slumped under the black wool of his suit.

She took a deep breath. There was no time to dwell on it anymore, the fear that thrummed under the surface—fear of Amalgaid's prophecy, fear of what she had foreseen in the attic.

Fear that she wouldn't have what was needed to stop any of it.

In the face of such an overwhelming burden, she could only find a foothold and start dragging herself up, one step at a time.

"I think there's a connection. Between Patrick Dougherty and the dead man in the sewers and St. Amalgaid's prophecy."

"That pattern you saw in the smoke in your vision," Strangford filled in. "I felt its significance."

"Dougherty called it the Red Branch," Lily said.

"But what is it?"

"I don't know," she returned. "Dougherty said to 'ask the Brothers.'

In Westminster I saw a briefing that said the Irish Republican Brotherhood were planning some sort of disruption, something to pressure the government against making concessions to the Unionists in Ulster. It's meant to take place the morning before the Buckingham Palace talks—Sunday morning. If they are the Brothers Dougherty was referring to . . ."

"Then perhaps this disruption is the cause of the disaster," Strangford concluded.

"It's all just . . . guesses. Coincidence."

"You know what Ash would tell you," he said.

She did. She could hear the words in her head, the same thing he had said to her dozens of times, most recently that morning as the attic burned around them.

Logic cannot stop this. Remember your training and reach for something else.

She was still angry at Ash for what he had put her through. That didn't make him wrong.

"We need to talk to the Brotherhood. We need to know what the Red Branch is and what their connection was with Patrick Dougherty. We need to know what they're planning for Sunday morning. Sam mentioned that he had a connection to the Fenians—to the Brothers. I know it isn't much but it's the best I've got at the moment."

"Then we should pursue it," he said.

In a way, it was a relief to be believed, to take such a leap of intuition and have it accepted as a matter of faith. It was also frightening. However sure Strangford was of her power, Lily herself was still wracked with doubt.

"I can't accept it, Lily," he said from his place by the broken pot. She knew he was not talking about Irish rebels and the song of a dead man.

"I know," she replied.

FIFTEEN

Six o'clock that evening
The Refuge, Bedford Square

*T*HE CONSERVATORY WAS A glass-framed room at the rear of the second of The Refuge's two buildings. It jutted out into the quiet of the garden, a box of windows webbed with iron, and could be reached through the dim and quiet of the sanctuary where Robert Ash retired to meditate.

In winter, the space was an oasis of potted palms, orchids, and spills of flowering vines. Many of those plants were moved out into the garden for the summer, like the fig tree Strangford had assaulted earlier that afternoon. The room was more open as a result, with space for a pair of small white wrought-iron tables and an assortment of chairs.

It could become stifling during the heat of the day, with the sun glaring down through the glass panes of the ceiling, the air thick with humidity. With the panes all swung open, the cooler air of evening spilled easily inside, a soft breeze stirring the verdant fronds of the plants that filled the shelves or hung from the rafters.

It was cooler here than the rest of the house, and the scent of smoke was less prominent. Lily could still smell it, even here, that distant whiff of burnt chemicals and wet wood. It was stronger back in the library and unavoidable on the upper floors.

She wondered how long it would take to fade.

Sunlight, golden with the slant of the hour, filtered in through the glass panes. It fell across the faces of the members of Ash's circle, charismatic and otherwise, who were all gathered here.

Bowls of rice and dumplings were crowded onto the tables, a simple supper that Mrs. Liu had prepared and which Ash had insisted they partake of before beginning the meeting. Lily had forced some of the food down, unable to taste it but knowing she needed fuel for whatever was to come.

Mrs. Liu's efforts were forgotten now, ignored as the assembled group absorbed the enormity of what Ash had just told them.

Estelle reached across the small gap that separated her chair from that of Miss Bard. She took hold of her companion's hand, the two women linked together, sharing their strength in the face of the horror of the future Ash had just revealed.

Dr. Gardner sat beside them, his elbows on his knees, face resting in his hands. The weight of Ash's news bowed his big shoulders.

Sam had not taken a chair. He leaned against the frame of one of the windows, looking fiercely away from the rest of them. His posture was one of coiled hostility. Lily felt that the slightest pressure would crack him open, unleashing a storm.

Behind Ash, Cairncross paced restlessly. The conservatory was not his domain. He was far more at ease when they gathered in the library, where the old Scottish soldier could pick through his books, searching for esoterica related to their discussion. His restlessness was more apparent here where there was no ready place to direct it.

Strangford stood by a potted fig. It was the same tree he had attacked earlier when they fought in the garden. Mr. Wu had transplanted it into a new vessel, a pot much simpler and less decorative than the one Strangford had destroyed.

As she watched, Strangford reached out to run his fingers across the leaves of the plant. Lily wondered whether he was fighting the urge to take off his glove and try to feel whether the plant was very deeply offended by the ordeal he had put it through.

It was Estelle who broke the silence.

"I suppose this was the reason for the incident in the attic this morning," she said. Her voice was firm and strong, unshaken, but she kept her hold on Miss Bard's hand.

"I had hoped that given proper stimulation Miss Albright's power might illuminate a solution," Ash replied.

Lily recalled the heat of the fire, the acrid stench of the burning paint. She was conscious of the strange weightlessness of her shorn hair.

"And you were unsuccessful." Sam's voice was sharp, edged with disapproval.

"That is correct," Ash replied.

He made it sound as though the failure were his own. That was not how it felt to Lily.

"I made enquiries this afternoon with an old acquaintance in the upper echelons of *The Times* and a relation of mine at the Home Office," Ash went on.

"What sort of enquiries?" Lily asked.

"I informed them that there must be an evacuation of London," Ash replied.

"And they very nicely put you out the door," Gardner filled in.

"I was aware that it must be improbable they would agree to alert the public when I could not tell them the exact nature of the threat nor how I had come to know about it," Ash admitted. "But the attempt had to be made."

"So what else is there to be done?" Gardner demanded. He sounded tired.

"Miss Albright and I spent the afternoon going over the symbols from her vision," Cairncross offered.

It had been a long afternoon.

As they worked, Lily had been conscious of Cairncross's role in the burning of the attic. His conviction that Ash's judgment was sound kept working its way into the conversation as though he sensed that Lily herself was less certain. It felt like evangelizing and by the third hour of it, Lily had to consciously restrain herself from throwing a Song dynasty Chinese puzzle ball at his head.

Instead, she had patiently answered his myriad and detailed questions about everything she had seen, over and over again as Cairncross poured through his books.

When Estelle joined them later in the afternoon, Cairncross's search had expanded to cover everything Patrick Dougherty had communicated to her and Lily in the potting shed.

Lily endured it though she was wrung-through with exhaustion and the work was mind-numbing. Uncovering the significance of those obscure signs and references could mean the difference between life and death for thousands of people . . . and maybe even herself.

"The most prominent symbol is clearly that of the Red Branch. In addition to appearing in Lily's vision, it was also referenced in both Lord Strangford's reading of Lord Torrington's chair and Miss Denueve's . . . interlocution with Patrick Dougherty." Cairncross slipped comfortably into his lecturing mode. "There are a number of possible references, but I am afraid few of them seem immediately relevant. Certain types of dogwood have crimson bark, or there is a variety of coral known as Red Branch. The dracaena cinnabari or dragon blood tree of the Arabian peninsula is known for its vividly red sap. Somewhat closer to home, there is the alder tree, worshiped by the Celts because its cut wood changes color from white to red."

"What about the Knights?" Miss Bard interrupted.

The folklorist had not been part of the research party in the library that afternoon. Miss Bard had spent the day at a women's suffrage meeting and received the summons to The Refuge late.

"Knights? What knights?" Cairncross retorted.

"The Knights of the Red Branch," Miss Bard offered. "A mythical band of elite warriors sworn to protect the ancient kings of Ulster in Ireland. The Red Branch was the name of the king's royal fortress."

"Well, yes, of course," Cairncross stuffily cut in. "I am more familiar with it in the original old Irish, Cróeb Derg. I have found 'Cróeb' more routinely transcribed as 'tree.'"

"That is not how Lady Gregory puts it," Miss Bard calmly returned. "And I do believe her knowledge of Irish may exceed your own, seeing as she was raised speaking the language."

"Do you know anything about the origins of the name?" Ash asked.

"I do," Miss Bard replied. "The Red Branch is a reference to the ancient Celtic practice of hanging the severed heads of one's enemies from a tree outside the king's fortress."

"Charming," Estelle commented.

Miss Bard ignored her and continued, clearly in her element.

"The practice served a dual purpose, warning off other potential troublemakers while also magically providing the king with some of the power of those he'd successfully overcome," she explained.

Gardner lifted his head.

"You said Dougherty might have had a connection to the Irish Republican Brotherhood," he noted, his voice low. "And Charlie Prinz was concerned about the Larne gun smuggling in April. The Ulster connection could be significant."

The conflict over Home Rule was directly centered on the Irish province of Ulster in the northern part of the country. While the rest of Ireland broadly supported the idea of an Irish Parliament in Dublin, Ulster was different. The majority of its population were Protestants, not Catholics, the descendants of Scottish families who had been deliberately settled there starting in the reign of Queen Elizabeth I. The settlers had been given homes and estates on lands confiscated from rebellious Catholic chieftains, sparking a history of resentment that would spill forward across the next three centuries.

"Are you familiar with any contemporary use of the term in Ulster, Doctor?" Ash asked.

The question reminded Lily that the doctor was a native of this province in Ireland that lay at the heart of the current political trouble.

"I suppose it must be in schoolbooks and history plays. Perhaps a sign on a pub somewhere. But no—I know of nothing that would be relevant to a threat to London," Gardner replied.

"You understand the conflict more intimately than the rest of us," Ash gently pressed. "Do you believe that the Irish Republican Brotherhood would resort to such a level of violence to further their cause?"

Gardner weighed the question. It was clear this was no light topic for him.

"It's an old fight," he replied at last. "Men have died for it before, and they have killed for it. I remember the riots in Belfast when I was a boy. A firebomb was lobbed through the window of my school. One of the girls burned her hands getting away from it. She'd still have the scars. My family are Unionists—I have an uncle in the Ulster Volunteers. For them, it's a matter of life or death."

"The Protestants of Ulster have always had close ties to those with power in the United Kingdom," Cairncross noted. "Their interests are heard. They must have little confidence of their prospects in an Ireland ruled from Dublin, a government that must be predominantly Catholic."

"And many of them are bigots," Gardner returned bluntly.

"They don't trust the Catholic Church," Estelle offered.

"They think all Catholics are rabid slaves to the pope," Gardner cut back. "And that under Home Rule the Protestants of the north will be forced to convert or be expelled."

"That's quite ridiculous," Miss Bard protested.

"You know that. And I know that. But when you've grown up with factions throwing bottles or stabbing each other in the street, with houses and shops blazing, you grow up afraid. And fear always wants a target." Gardner sighed. "Catholics are poorly treated in the north. They're left out when it comes to jobs and housing, and the nation as a whole has suffered under British rule. The memory of the great famine is still fresh, for all that it was nearly seventy years ago."

The list of grievances was familiar to Lily. She could recall hearing the stories in her mother's drawing room when she was a girl. Deirdre Albright had not been at all political, but many of the artists she surrounded herself with fancied themselves revolutionaries. Their conversation would sometimes fall into the crimes of history or the ills of colonialism instead of poetry, stagecraft, or gossip about who was sleeping with whom.

Lily remembered passionate rants about the famine, which some of her mother's friends had called an extermination where entire villages were starved to death or emptied through emigration. She had heard stories about the transportation of minor criminals to a harsh life in Australia, the repressive policies of Protestant landlords or the complicity of the police.

Would those men with their songs and stories have been capable of perpetrating the kind of apocalyptic destruction she had foreseen? The idea seemed ludicrous. They had been storytellers and showmen, not soldiers. If anything, they would have been more inclined to romantic self-sacrifice than wholesale slaughter.

"It's all moot, anyway," Sam cut in.

A little brown swallow fluttered in through the open window, perching on the iron frame beside him and regarding him curiously.

"Off with you," he ordered impatiently, waving his hand. The bird fluttered back a step and Sam continued.

"Even if the Fenians wanted to pull off something as big as what Lily saw, they couldn't do it. They don't have the men and they ain't that organized. What she saw weren't just some paint-pot nail bomb."

"Sam has a point," Cairncross said, looking to Ash. "I don't believe the Irish Republican Brotherhood has the capacity to create destruction on the magnitude of what Lily has described."

"It is still the best lead we have," Lily cut in.

Her words sliced through the room, ending the debate.

She looked to Sam.

"You said you had a connection to the Brothers. Could you contact them, arrange a meeting?"

"It ain't like that," Sam replied. There was a mulish set to his jaw. "I don't know any of them directly."

"But you know someone who does," Estelle suggested.

Sam didn't reply. His look had grown even more stubborn as though every atom of him resisted this turn of the conversation.

The sparrow inched closer to him, clearly hoping he would forget that he had told it to go away.

"Sam," Ash said. His tone was even, but still Lily heard the word for what it was—an order.

So did Sam.

"It's Cannon," he admitted at last. He threw a glare to both Ash and Cairncross. "Cannon's the one who could arrange it."

The two older men exchanged a significant look, and Lily's memory clicked into place.

Crawling through the wreckage of Hartwell's burned clinic in Southwark five months before—asking Sam about how he had come by his skills as a thief.

So who taught you how to pick locks?

Bloke named Cannon.

Cannon—a man who had plucked a desperate boy from the street and set him to picking pockets and shimmying through windows, risking imprisonment and who-knew-what other violence.

For as long as Lily had known him, there had been an edge to Sam, a brittle hardness. She suspected she knew who was responsible for that—for the hard and angry glint in his eye.

Cannon.

The notion of demanding Sam ask a favor of a man who had exploited and abused him as a child of ten made her sick, but the image of a gutted and smoldering London was still burned into her mind.

The horror of that was too vast, too terrible. They could not afford to be squeamish about whatever might be necessary to stop it.

"This Cannon. Could you reach him if you wanted to?" Lily asked.

Sam's glare shifted to her. She felt the urge in him to curse at her, or perhaps something worse, but he bit it back. His eyes flickered to her cropped hair, to the bandage on her forehead.

"I can," he replied flatly.

"Then arrange a meeting," Ash ordered quietly.

"He'll want us to go alone," Sam shot back.

"Out of the question," Strangford cut in. There was nothing tentative in the declaration, however quiet he had been for the rest of their meeting.

Sam blazed back at him.

"It ain't a matter for debate. You want your meeting, you'll play by Cannon's rules."

"Perhaps Lord Strangford and Mr. Cairncross could shadow you. Stay out of sight," Miss Bard suggested.

"He'll know," Sam stubbornly replied. "It's his borough. Nothing happens in Limehouse that Cannon don't know about."

"Sam knows the man better than we do," Ash said. "He and Lily will go alone if that is what Mr. Cannon demands."

Ash's words left no room for argument. Strangford did not reply, but his disapproval was a palpable thing, thickening the air of the conservatory.

A light breeze stirred the blooms on the hibiscus and the glossy leaves of the lemon trees as dusk began to spread across the sky beyond the glass.

"There is one other avenue we might pursue," Lily admitted. "I could speak to my father."

All the eyes in the room had shifted to her. Strangford clearly had an opinion on the matter, one he was forcefully keeping to himself. Estelle's gaze was tinged with a sympathy she was wise enough not to express.

It was not unjustified. Though Lily had offered the suggestion, it left her feeling just as wrenched and tangled as the talk of Cannon clearly did for Sam.

"We know that he is involved with this," she noted, forcing out the words.

"Right," Sam replied. "And the man could be all tied up in the Ulster gun-running or offing that bloke we found in Crossness. You sit down for a little chat with him and he'll know we're onto him. He might not hand it out to his own daughter but I doubt he'd have a touch of the seconds about the rest of us."

"Sam is correct," Ash said. "We cannot risk alerting Lord Torrington of our interest if there is a chance he's involved."

Lily did not feel particularly relieved. The tension remained coiled up inside of her as the distant sound of a train whistle floated through the open glass.

"There is another option," Strangford offered. His voice was cold. "I could read him directly."

"That would be far too dangerous," Estelle quickly protested. "Lord Torrington is not the sort of man who would fail to notice the change in your demeanor, however subtle. He has built his authority on such hints and tells."

"But could he possibly suspect what Strangford is doing?" Miss Bard countered. "It is something most men would not even consider possible."

"He knows such things are possible," Lily quietly replied.

She was conscious of Estelle's quick and careful look. Torrington was not the only one who could read the significance of subtle signs in a conversation. She was sure her friend's careful, clever mind was putting it all together.

Torrington knew charismatics were possible because he was aware of what Lily herself could do.

"That makes the risk exponentially more great," Ash determined.

"And what about the Fenians?" Sam cut back. "Ain't tipping them off that we're on to them just as much of a risk?"

"Patrick Dougherty said to ask them about the Red Branch," Estelle replied.

"And we're supposed to take his word on it?" Sam retorted.

Estelle was not offended by the sharpness in his tone.

"In my experience the dead generally have a more thorough sense of such matters than the living," she said.

Sam scoffed.

"We aren't going to ask them anything," Lily cut in. "We're going to offer them a deal."

"What do we have that the Fenians would want?" Sam demanded.

"We will tell them that if they call off their plans for Sunday morning, Lord Torrington will throw his support behind Home Rule for Ireland," Lily replied.

"The Irish Republican Brotherhood are nationalists, not Home Rulers. A Dublin Parliament that's subservient to one in London isn't enough for them. They don't want Home Rule. They want full independence for Ireland," Gardner pointed out.

"And you don't know that your father would do it," Strangford added bluntly. Lily knew the sharpness in his tone was driven by his disapproval of sending Lily and Sam into a meeting with a batch of Irish revolutionaries alone.

"I don't expect them to accept the deal," Lily returned. She was focused on Ash and Sam, knowing they were the ones she needed to convince.

Cairncross looked thoughtful, then quietly impressed.

"You're hoping to bluff them into revealing what they have planned for Sunday morning," he announced.

"By pretending that you already know," Miss Bard added, eyes bright. "Very clever."

Around them in the conservatory, the night-blooming flowers of jasmine and datura were slowly unfurling, adding an intoxicating sweetness to the air.

Lily waited for a verdict.

"Sam?" Ash asked.

He was letting the young chauffeur make the call. Lily did not miss the significance of that. Of course, it was Sam who had the most direct experience of both Cannon and the Brotherhood, but granting him the final word on whether or not Lily's plan would go forward still struck her as a mark of respect.

Sam held out his hand. The sparrow fluttered down from the rail, landing in his palm. He set it on his shoulder and the bird fluffed its feathers happily.

"It could do," Sam admitted carefully. "But there's an awful lot could go sideways."

"I believe it is worth the risk," Lily replied.

Sam raised his head, meeting Ash's gaze.

"That raw mess in the attic this morning. You were looking for Lily to find us another way around this," he said.

"I was," Ash admitted evenly.

The moment rushed back to her—the heat of the flames, the crisp scent of her burned hair and the acrid stench of blistering paint. The pain in her hands, in her head, and the black nightmare of her visions.

Amalgaid's apocalypse and what had followed it—the moment where she would lose her life in dark water painted with flame.

The lingering scent of the smoke mingled with the perfume of the datura, unmoved by the soft breeze stirring through the conservatory.

She could read so much in that silence—Miss Bard's frowning disapproval, Gardner's weary concern. Cairncross's stubborn loyalty and Estelle's careful thoughtfulness.

Strangford's face was the only puzzle she could not solve. Whatever he was feeling was still too complicated to settle into something she might recognize.

"What you were after up there. Is there any other chance in it?" Sam demanded.

Lily waited for Ash's answer, her heart pounding heavily in her chest.

"I do not believe so," Ash finally replied.

It was not a surprise. Lily had no reason to be disappointed. She ought to be relieved that it was over, that there would be no further ordeal aimed at dragging out of her a power she did not understand and certainly did not desire.

Yet there was still what waited for them on Sunday morning and a guilty tangle inside of her at the knowledge that she was not capable of offering them a ready way out of it.

She did not have some grand gift that could save them from St. Amalgaid's prophecy. She had only these smaller tools—her wits and her determination and this occasional power to peer an inch farther down the timeline.

It did not matter. She would use them to fight this. She must—no matter what it ended up costing her.

"We can't mug off Jack Cannon," Sam concluded. "He's dangerous. We do this, it's my rules. No questions."

"I understand," Lily agreed, and she could see that it was done.

Ash rose.

"The rest of us will remain in contact until Lily and Sam have concluded their meeting and can report the results," he declared. "I want all of you to understand that if they are unsuccessful, we must be prepared to exit London until the events of Amalgaid's prophecy have come to pass."

Gardner came to his feet.

"You can't be serious," the doctor said.

"You'll not be able to heal anyone if you're dead," Cairncross cut back.

"There is an inn on the road to Highgate," Ash continued as though no objection had been raised. "The Spaniards. It is sufficiently outside the city to offer protection but near enough that we may return to offer assistance."

Sam muttered a curse under his breath, and for once it did not elicit the requisite glare from Cairncross. The sparrow hopped from his shoulder back to the safety of the rail.

Gardner's expression was stormy. Lily found she had little hope that the doctor would wait out the coming storm from the safety of a suburban inn.

"Lily, is there anything else you can tell us? Anything else in your visions that might give us a clue as to how to stop this?" Miss Bard asked earnestly.

Lily knew that there was. She had kept one vital revelation to herself, a terrible secret about where all this might lead that only Strangford knew . . . and that not by her choice.

She could feel the dark energy radiating off of him as Miss Bard asked her question and the rest of the room waited for Lily to respond. Strangford's anger was a force so strong she was surprised no one else in the conservatory could feel it, but she knew he would not speak.

The true answer to Miss Bard's question was not his knowledge to share.

The guilt twisted through her. The men and women gathered in this room of glass were the nearest thing Lily had to a family. She did not want to lie to them but to tell the truth would be to put them under an impossible strain. In the battle to come, she could not allow them to be distracted by concern for her own welfare.

"No," Lily carefully lied. "I am afraid not."

SIXTEEN

Saturday, August 1st
Midday
Limehouse, East London

IT WAS THE HOTTEST day of the year. Brickfield Gardens sweltered in it, the noon sun blazing down as Lily and Sam entered the small green refuge in the heart of the East End.

The park sat in the center of a block of drab flats. On an ordinary Saturday, Lily suspected it would be busy with families picnicking and children racing about. The day was too hot for a picnic, so their only company were a pair of boys lounging in the shade of a tree and a man on a bench reading a book while eating a sandwich. A woman dressed too warmly for the weather was letting her dog drink from the fountain.

They had stopped on their way there. Sam ordered their hackney to the mouth of an alley just outside the limits of Limehouse. He had disappeared into the gloom of that narrow space between the tenements, reappearing ten minutes later claiming to have "made arrangements" for some backup.

Lily had some inkling of what those arrangements might have been. Even now, she could see the sleek brown bodies of the rats darting under the bushes of the park.

Lily had witnessed Sam claiming dominance over a mischief of rats once before. She found she did not terribly mind that he had excluded her from the process this time.

The mid-afternoon sun burned down from a hazy sky. Not a leaf stirred on the trees that surrounded them. Everything was covered in dust. Lily felt a bead of sweat drip down her back.

Six men entered the park.

They came from different angles—two from the north, another from Clemence Street.

The boys under the tree and the man with his sandwich looked up as the men came in. They just as quickly looked away again.

That, more than anything, told Lily just how thorough Cannon's control of his borough was—and how little hope they would have of assistance.

She had opted for respectable dress for this meeting instead of the trousers and boots of her motoring attire, which she generally preferred when faced with the possibility of a fight. She had not neglected to bring her walking stick along. As the six men approached the place where she and Sam were standing, she shifted her grip on the polished yew.

Sam did not miss the gesture.

"Leave it," he ordered. "If you fight them, you'll only make it worse."

"You can't possibly be serious," Lily said.

"You don't know these blokes like I do."

Her pulse pounding, she forced herself to stillness as their attackers loped in.

In the brief space before they arrived, Sam whistled softly. Lily caught a flicker of movement under a nearby rhododendron, the scurry of brown feet.

The first of the men to reach them greeted Sam with a punch to the gut. Lily heard the air rush out of him.

"Leave him alone!" she shouted, the protest an instinct. Watching Sam hurt felt like being hurt herself.

"Steady, Lily," he gasped out quietly, doubled over with the impact of the blow.

It was Sam's old borough and Sam's old boss. She knew she had no choice but to follow the strategy he had set for them, however much her hands itched against the familiar contours of her walking stick. She could almost feel how the kali would flow from it, how the moves she had practiced for years would crack the knee of the thug to her left, break the jaw of the man who had struck Sam in the gut.

The urge to defend both Sam and herself was overwhelming, but if Sam refused to fight taking on six men would sorely tax her capabilities.

You'll only make it worse.

Lily dropped the stick on the ground and raised her hands.

They took her arms and yanked them behind her back. A blindfold was tied around her eyes while her hands were bound.

She heard a diesel lorry rattle up beside them.

"Toss them in the back," one of the men ordered.

She was picked up and pushed roughly into the bed of the lorry. She could see just enough through the cloth over her eyes to know that it was enclosed. Slivers of light streamed in through cracks in the wooden slats.

The doors slammed shut, the engine coughing as it accelerated. Lily was thrown against Sam as the lorry looped around to reverse course.

"Can you see where they're taking us?" she asked quietly.

"Naw, they've blindfolded me as well," he replied. She could feel the vibration of his voice from where she had landed against his chest. "But I can hear it well enough. Catch the sound of those nippers playing?"

Lily could hear it, the echo of happy children's screams echoing off the close buildings nearby.

"Yes."

"That'll be St. Paul's School," he said. "And that smell is the Limehouse Cut. They must be taking us over the Burdett Road bridge."

Sam's deep knowledge of the territory they were being carried over was comforting.

"Should I be afraid?" she asked.

"It's generally best practice when Cannon is involved," Sam replied.

The lorry jerked to a stop. The doors were thrown open a moment later, sunlight streaming in through her blindfold. Lily was plucked off of Sam and hauled outside, stumbling to keep her feet.

"Oy, watch where you're putting those jelly snatchers," Sam barked from behind her. She felt him reach her side a moment later.

"A pleasure to see you again, Mr. Wu."

The voice was that of a stranger. Lily could just make out the silhouette of him in front of them, a figure no taller than herself but significantly more solid. He had a bold voice, the sound of someone clearly comfortable with his command of the situation.

"You'd see me better without this bloody sash about my head, Cannon," Sam replied.

"Still the young wit," Cannon noted. "I was pleased you reached out to me. Always happy to do a favor for an old friend."

Cannon sounded jovial, but Lily felt distinctly uncomfortable with the notion that she or Sam now owed this man a favor.

She only hoped it was worth it.

"Bring them inside," Cannon ordered.

Lily and Sam were marched forward. A door was opened and they passed from the relative brightness of the alley into darkness. The air that flowed over her was significantly cooler than the heat of the open afternoon.

It was a loud darkness. Machinery clattered around them, the air smelling of crushed grain and oil.

The smell of the grain tugged at some deep place in her mind, and abruptly she was somewhere else.

She feels it washing across her legs, the sea of dry golden seeds. She fights through waves of it as she struggles to move forward. The sky is painted with smoke, her ears ringing, the stench of something burning in her nose as worry twists inside of her. She must reach the far side of that rustling sea. Faster, she must go faster—

"Move along," one of her captors drawled, prodding her in the back. Lily tripped forward, hoping blindly that they weren't marching her into a wall or off a precipice.

There was no time to contemplate what that flash of foresight might mean.

From beside her, Sam shouted up the line, cockily defiant.

"Sounds like your crusher shaft is out of alignment."

"Shut up, ye wee prat," another of the men replied, cuffing Sam on the side of the head.

Lily heard the clang of another door and they were led out of the machine room to someplace where the air felt less close. It was still dark, but the roar of the engine was duller here. It smelled of yeast and Lily could make out enormous shapes looming around her through the gloom of the blindfold. A brewery, she surmised. They must be in the fermentation room.

She was pushed into a chair and heard Sam bite out a protest beside her. Sitting was awkward with her hands still bound behind her back. Lily knew better than to voice her discomfort.

"Greetings, Captain," Cannon bellowed from somewhere just in front of them.

"Mr. Cannon," came the reply. The voice was that of an older man, clearly Irish, who spoke with a careful authority.

It seemed for all the unnecessary roughness of their delivery, Cannon had made good on his promise to connect them with the Irish Republican Brotherhood.

"Thank you for agreeing to come blindfolded," the captain went on, this time addressing Lily and Sam directly.

"Weren't so much of an agreement," Sam commented from beside her.

"I thought I said to ask them," the captain said. Lily could hear his frown.

"We streamlined your process," Cannon replied comfortably.

"Then I must apologize for that." The captain directed his words to Lily and Sam again. "But we thought the blindfolds prudent given your affiliations."

"I think he means your old man," Sam noted to Lily. His voice was easily loud enough for everyone in the room to hear.

"We're wasting time. Ask 'em what they knows," a new speaker snapped. This one sounded younger. His working class accent matched Sam's, but where Sam was all lazy insolence this one was taut as a drum. A firebrand, Lily thought, one not afraid to speak up to his boss. Perhaps there was some dissent in the ranks. She made note of it. It might come in useful, depending on how the rest of this meeting went.

"I don't know nothing," Sam replied cheerfully. "I'm just her chaperone."

"Very bloody proper," a third voice offered. This was another young man, also Irish, and from his tone Lily could tell he fancied himself a wit.

"Pipe down, lads," the captain said. "You asked for this meeting, girl. Why?"

Lily straightened in her chair. It was hard to take on a posture of confidence and authority when blindfolded and bound, but she was determined to try.

"I am here to make you an offer," she announced.

"What sort of offer?" the captain returned.

"One regarding the future of your nation," she replied.

"And what might a wee English lass have to offer for the future of Ireland?" the captain said.

"The wee lass can offer her father's support for Home Rule," Lily replied evenly.

There was a quick mutter of conversation.

"She serious?" the wit demanded.

"We ain't interested in any Home Rule," the firebrand retorted. "Home Rule's a buzzard's game."

She could almost hear the captain silencing them with a movement of his hand.

"I assume you are aware of who my father is," Lily pressed.

"Aye, we know," the captain confirmed.

"Then you know that the votes he would bring with him would be enough to shift the balance in Parliament."

The machinery of the brewery continued to rumble in the background. Lily could smell hops drying somewhere nearby.

She wished she could see. Playing this game of words without her eyes was like fighting one-handed.

"If his lordship wishes to make a deal with us, why does he not come himself?" the captain asked. "Why send you?"

"I am sure you must realize how inappropriate that would be," Lily returned.

"So he sends his whore's-get instead?" the wit remarked. "Very noble of him indeed."

She did not let the slur impact her. She might be blind to their reactions, but they would be watching her own.

"And how do we know that he has authorized your visit here today?" the captain asked.

"If you agree to his terms, I will return here with proof," she replied. "You could hardly expect me to have brought that along before we have an agreement, given the nature of our intermediary."

Cannon's voice cut cheerily across the room.

"I never claimed to be a gentleman, Miss Lilith Albright."

The sound of her proper name in his mouth sent a bolt of discomfort through her.

"You said terms," the captain went on. "What does his lordship want?"

This was the moment. Lily was conscious of the thick beat of her heart, her blindness intensifying her sensitivity to that nervous pulse. She could feel the men in the room around her, sense them in the soft brush of cloth, the scuff of a shoe on concrete. She wished again, painfully, for her sight—to be able to read the subtle changes in expression on the faces of the men she spoke to.

There was no use agonizing over it. She would make do with what she had.

She let her voice ring out clearly through the room.

"It relates to your plans for Sunday morning."

There was an uncomfortable shuffling, a rush of whispers.

"What's she mean—the ten o'clock mass?" the wit burst out.

"Shut it," the firebrand snapped.

"What plans exactly would you be referring to?" the captain calmly asked.

Lily lifted her chin.

"We can stop playing. My father is quite aware of what you intend. His sources are very thorough," she said.

This next step was critical, the moment in which she would make her play. She prayed that she had read them right—that they would jump on the bait she was proffering.

"Even the Westminster security briefing this week contains an alert about it," she added casually. "Though of course they are less firm on the details."

They must rise to that. How could they not? They would want to know what the British authorities already understood of their plan. How could they possibly move forward with any confidence otherwise?

"What's she on about?" the firebrand demanded.

The confusion in his tone was genuine. Lily decided to use it.

"Seems you've been kept out of it," she called cheerily.

"You watch your gob," the firebrand snapped in return. "I ain't kept out of nothing."

"But what does it mean?" the wit pressed. "Are they going to come after us?"

"Whisht, both of you," the captain barked.

"Whatever you've planned, surely we need to call it off," the younger man rattled on. "Else they'll be waiting for us."

Lily could hear the fear in his voice.

"We ain't going to back down for a fear of a batch of peelers," the firebrand retorted. "Ain't that right, captain?"

"But that'd be cracked," the wit protested. "Captain—"

"Enough!" the captain shouted.

The word echoed off the great steel fermentation tanks, rattling through the rafters. The two younger men bit back whatever further words they had on the matter.

Lily heard steps approaching, quick and deliberate. A hand grabbed her chin, lifted up her face as though he meant to force her to meet his eyes.

It was a futile move given that she still wore a blindfold.

"Who told his lordship there was a plan for Sunday morning?" the captain demanded, his voice now coming from just above her.

Lily's pulse quickened. She was conscious that the trap she had set here could easily rebound on her.

"I am not privy to my father's sources," she replied.

"Bloody hell she ain't," the firebrand called.

The captain's grip tightened. It was not a controlled pressure, not the move of a man accustomed to such physical manipulations. Lily could feel the tremor in his fingers, a tension that wired up into his core.

He was afraid. But why? Was it the possibility that his plan had been exposed?

"Rough her up and you'll have her old man to answer to," Sam burst out from beside her.

"Shut your can," the firebrand cut in.

"The boy's right."

The words came from a new voice, one that had not yet made itself known in the room—a fourth member of the Brothers. Lily could hear that he was older. His silence this far into the meeting also spoke of a greater maturity than the two mouthier underlings.

The captain released his grip on her, turning to shout at this quieter colleague.

"I need to know what she knows!"

"Go about it that way and it'll cost you. It'll cost all of us," the quiet man returned.

Her mind raced as she listened to the pair of revolutionaries debate the wisdom of beating her.

What did this mean? Was the captain that desperate to know who had leaked their plan for Sunday morning—a plan so secret even his own lieutenants were ignorant of it?

Another possibility itched at the back of her mind, but she was not given time to consider it.

"Gentlemen," Cannon cut in smoothly. "You are going about this the wrong way."

"How's that, old timer?" the firebrand retorted.

"You don't need to hurt the woman to get her to talk. Just use the boy," Cannon explained.

"Who cares about some scaly pickpocket?" the firebrand shot back.

"She does," Cannon replied.

Lily felt her stomach drop.

"Put a little pain on him and she'll give you whatever you're looking for," Cannon easily suggested.

Sam called Cannon something colorful.

"Nothing personal, lad," Cannon replied.

"That isn't our way," the quiet man objected.

"It isn't?" the wit asked.

Lily would not be capable of giving the Brothers what they wanted of her, not without admitting the whole thing had been a ruse.

She doubted they would be inclined to laugh that off.

She was blindfolded and bound to a chair—and she needed to take control of the situation before it had gone past the point of no return.

Lily did not understand exactly how Sam's power worked, but she had her suspicions. Though Sam sometimes chatted aloud with the animals he interacted with, as often as not their exchanges seemed to happen on a level that flowed somewhere beneath words and sound—as though Sam talked to the pigeons and cats and swallows of London mind to mind.

She hoped she was right. Their lives might just depend upon it.

The captain and the firebrand had moved away, distracted by the debate over whether or not to torture Sam.

"Did any of your friends manage to follow us here?" Lily whispered, her voice low under her breath.

"Only a few," Sam breathed in reply.

Sam's tone made it clear that there weren't enough of his rats here to take on Cannon and the members of the Brotherhood directly.

Which left them with . . . what?

"Someone's setting us up," the firebrand snapped. "We need to know what she knows."

Setting us up.

Lily's mind spun. Of course it was possible. She had assumed that the young men's ignorance of the plans for Sunday meant that the secret was being kept to the topmost levels of the organization . . . but there was another plausible explanation.

That there was no plan for Sunday at all. That the report in the Westminster memo was merely a rumor . . . or a perhaps a deliberate attempt to discredit the Irish Republican Brotherhood.

She waited, her breath caught. The captain's answer would reveal it.

No, son. What we're after is a leak. Or perhaps it would be *leave this to your elders, boy.*

"The lad is right," the captain said.

The world shook. Lily's careful plan shattered around her, leaving a void behind.

The Irish Republican Brotherhood would not be responsible for the disaster on Sunday morning . . . because they had not planned any disruption.

The security briefing in Westminster was wrong, an error.

A substantiated error.

But how could that be?

She had come here to ask the wrong question. The voice of a dead man echoed through her mind, words shaped by Estelle's lips.

Red Branch.

Ask the Brothers.

She had run out of time for that. Now what she needed was to find a way out of here while blindfolded, bound, and short on rats . . . or she could watch while Sam was tortured to get her to reveal a secret that didn't exist.

An idea occurred to her.

It was mad. It couldn't possibly work. It would mean exposing her most dangerous secret to a band of thieves and rebels.

There was no time to think of anything better.

"Whichever of your friends are here," she breathed to Sam. "Tell them to get close to me."

"Sure you're up for that?" he asked.

"Just do it," she hissed.

Footsteps echoed through the room, coming near. There was the sound of a scuffle. Lily heard Sam shout in protest, chair legs scraping against the floor.

"It don't work if she can't see you!" Cannon called.

Someone grabbed the side of the cloth that covered her eyes, yanking it off roughly. Lily found herself looking up at a tall, lean man roughly the same age as Sam. His hair was dark, his brown eyes angry.

She quickly took in the rest of her surroundings. Yes, it was a brewery, the great steel vats rising like giants around the floor where she sat. Cannon stood to the side. He looked rather more respectable than Lily had imagined, with thick sandy hair and a well-cut suit.

The other Fenians were at the front of the room. She picked out the captain by his frown of disapproval. He had the air of a printer or a scholar about him rather than a soldier. His hair was mostly gray, his build slight. Round glasses perched on his prominent ears, a thick mustache covering his upper lip.

The wit was beside him. He was more or less Lily's age, with pomaded hair and sloped shoulders.

The fourth man, the quiet one, was also older, perhaps fifty, with the rough, hard-working air of a tradesman. He gazed at her with a look that struck her as deliberately impassive.

She was conscious of movement at the corners of her vision—small bodies scurrying silently in the gloom.

The firebrand whipped a knife from his pocket and pressed it to Sam's throat.

"Easy there, son," Cannon laughed. "It don't work if you kill him straight off."

"Tell me where Torrington heard it," the firebrand demanded. "Do it now or I'll cut him."

Lily felt the first of the rats reach her leg.

It tugged at her skirt, digging small claws into the fabric. The creature scrabbled up. It took an effort not to flinch, to rein in her instinctive repulsion.

She could feel the warm weight of the animal in her lap.

The firebrand looked down at the rat, his eyes wide.

They grew wider as the creature climbed to her shoulder, perching itself next to her shorn hair.

More came. Furry bodies wormed around her ankles, wriggled through her clothes.

"Sweet Mary!" the wit shouted. The captain was staring with obvious shock. The quiet man behind him took a careful step back.

She had their attention, could see the fear creeping at the edge of it. That fear was her lever, but she would need to press it harder to get her and Sam out of this.

Good thing she had a plan for that . . . if she could manage her part in it.

High stakes, she reminded herself as her heart pounded in her chest.

"They're just rodents," Cannon called. "What're you mincing back for?"

"I ain't afraid of them," the firebrand retorted, dread giving his anger a rougher edge.

Lily closed her eyes, reaching deeper. She sought the place inside of her where her power lived, pulling on every scrap of her training with Ash and a healthy dose of desperation.

Connection flared, and she knew.

The knowledge was terrible. She would use it anyway.

She opened her eyes, fixing the firebrand with her gaze.

"You'll be drunk," she said. "You pick a fight with another man. He takes you in the throat with a broken bottle."

Her voice rang through the room with the clarity of truth.

The firebrand stared at her, surprised to stillness with his knife still poised at Sam's throat.

"You bleed out in the street," she continued. "A dog watches from the alley waiting for you to die. Autumn," she added thoughtfully, pulling more detail from the scene playing out behind her mind. "Dry leaves on the ground. It comes soon for you, before the gray touches your hair."

She blinked, clearing her vision. She looked calmly around the room.

"Who would like to be next?" she asked.

Sam laughed. It was a dark sound.

The captain stared at her, his lips pressed into a grim line. The quiet stranger at the back crossed himself instinctively. The wit had his fist to his mouth as though to block the emergence of a scream.

Cannon looked quietly impressed.

The firebrand pulled the knife from Sam's neck to point it at Lily. The blade trembled.

"What the bloody hell was that?" he demanded.

"Just what you think it was, mate," Sam replied.

The ropes fell away from her hands, chewed through by the rats that still clung to her body.

Lily stood.

She could see it in each of them, the rot waiting for emergence.

The wit rasping in a cot, drowning in the fluid filling his lungs.

The captain in a green uniform before a blazing building like a Grecian temple, his body torn apart by machine gun fire.

The fourth man falling to his knees in a quiet country road, his right hand grasping his heart as though he could will it back into beating.

And then there was Cannon, his throat opened, the red mouth of it spilling blood. The quiet surprise in his eyes as he collapsed by a pair of familiar brown motoring boots.

Those look like my motoring boots, Lily thought distantly.

The vision itched at her, threatening more. She deliberately broke it, forcing herself back into the gloom of the brewery.

"Who would like to be next?" she repeated softly.

It was the captain who finally spoke.

"Go," he said with a jerk of his head. "Get on with you."

The rats had freed Sam as well. He wasted no time getting to his feet and yanking off his blindfold. He grabbed Lily by the wrist, dragging her toward the door.

"Come on, before they change their minds," he urged.

"I'll say hello to your sister for you," Cannon shouted after them.

Sam stopped as though struck. He whirled back, and now it was Lily who kept hold of his hand.

"Oh yes," Cannon went on, noting Sam's attention. "She's alive. Though perhaps you'd wish she weren't."

He flashed them a white-toothed grin.

Lily tugged on Sam's arm.

"We're leaving. Now."

She pulled him into motion, and at last his feet agreed to follow. They pushed through the doors into the machine room, the rats scurrying at their heels.

"Not this way," Sam said, yanking her to a stop. "Cannon's blokes will be watching." He whispered to the rat on his shoulder and it dropped amid the others of its kind that still clustered around Lily's ankles.

The animals pivoted. Lily and Sam followed, dodging through the clattering engines to a door she had not known was there.

SEVENTEEN

*T*HEY BURST OUT INTO the street, the heat hitting her like a wall. Lily could swear the air had become even thicker during the hour or so they were inside. Haze continued to obscure the sky.

Sam quickly assessed their surroundings.

"This way. Hurry."

She pulled back.

A dead man's words were still singing through her memory.

Red Branch.

Ask the Brothers.

"We need to follow one of those men."

"We barely got out of there with our skins!" he protested.

"The quiet one at the back. Use your friends."

Sam cursed under his breath, giving Lily an evil look. He yanked her into an alley then knelt down for a quick conference with the rats, who continued to tumble around his ankles.

The animals split, making twin paths around the looming brick facade of the brewery.

"They'll find us when they have him," he said. "Come on."

He grabbed Lily's arm and pulled her into a run.

She hurried to keep pace as he ducked them around tight corners strung with drying laundry, past piles of refuse where dogs nosed for treasures.

They reached a narrow building pressed into a close, grimy block. Newspaper covered the insides of jaggedly broken windows, soot staining the bricks black.

Sam grabbed the door and pushed it open. It gave without resistance. He propelled Lily up the narrow stairs.

She ran ahead of him past doorways hung with ragged curtains and the sound of crying children, jumping over the prone form of a man who reeked of sour gin. They burst out onto the roof, the typical reek of London a relief after the stench of the tenement.

"Just a little jump, now," Sam ordered.

He ran at the low wall bordering the edge of the building, stepping up onto it and leaping across the narrow space that separated the flats from the structure next door.

He landed easily on his feet.

"Quick!" he urged, waving her on.

Lily took a breath and followed.

Her boot struck the top of the low wall. She pressed through it, launching herself forward. She was conscious of a sheer drop five stories to the street beneath her.

Then she was on the other side, Sam catching her with firm hands.

"Back here," he ordered, leading her on.

They twisted around the bulk of a water tower, stopping at the far edge of the roof.

Sam crouched, peering over the edge to the street below.

"Sam," she said, catching her breath. "What Cannon said back there about your sister . . ."

"It's clear," Sam cut in.

He lowered himself onto the metal grill of a fire escape.

They climbed down, Sam kicking the last ladder to send it rattling the ten feet to the ground. He landed his boots solidly on the pavement, reaching back to give Lily a hand down.

They strolled onto a market street busy with carriages. Women lounged under the awnings of the storefronts, fanning themselves with newspapers. A few boys raced by, stripped to their trousers and barefoot. They were all soaking wet.

As they waited at the crossing for an omnibus to disgorge its passengers, something tugged at Lily's skirt. She looked down to see a rat gazing up at her unblinkingly.

"Sam?" she asked.

"It ain't a signal. She just wants you to hold her."

"Hold her?" Lily echoed, disbelieving.

"It's how they are once you make yourself part of the family," Sam explained. "Always wanting to cozy up."

Another rat chattered at them from the top of a rubbish bin. A passing newspaper boy's attention was drawn by the sound. He gave them an odd look.

Sam muttered a brief curse under his breath. With a quick glance to make sure no one was watching, he plucked the rat from the bin and slipped it into his coat.

Lily felt the tug at her skirt again.

"Must I?"

Sam shrugged.

"Up to you, but she'll likely not let up till you do."

Lily was conscious that the creature at her ankle might just have saved both of their lives.

Quickly, she bent down and plucked the animal from the ground. She held it to the pocket of her skirt. It crawled happily inside.

None of the people passing by on the street had stopped to stare at her. Lily could feel the weight of the rat in her pocket, warm and soft.

The omnibus pulled away and Sam set off, his hands in his pockets.

They wove through the afternoon shoppers. A man passed with a basket of fresh-baked bread. A tinker's cart rattled with a load of dented pots. A cluster of women outside of a printer's house roared with laughter, chattering in Russian.

"Her name was Zhao Min," Sam said at last.

Lily did not have to ask whom he meant. She could hear the weight of it in his voice.

"Your sister."

He nodded.

"Two more years and she'd have been safely married off," he said. His voice was tight. He stepped back to let a woman with a pram and a pair of toddlers pass. Lily saw how his eyes carefully scanned the street, looking for threats.

"Back in China, you mean," she filled in.

"I was more careless about it then—what I could do. Didn't know any better. Bragged to an older cousin about how I could get the monkeys to pick míhóutáo for me. A fruit," he explained, knowing she wouldn't know the word. "Fuzzy on the outside, sweet and green on the inside. It took some work. The monkeys don't like to share."

He led her across the road and around a corner, clearly familiar with where they were.

"My cousin was one of the Gēlǎohuì. The Elder Brothers—that was what they called themselves. Others knew them as . . . the Hatchet Gang."

Lily could hear that he was translating some of the words as he spoke. Since Sam was as fluent in English as she was, it could only mean that this wasn't a story he had told before.

She had wondered what brought Sam's family from China to London—what terrible thing had forced them to leave a life of prosperity for one of exclusion and poverty. She had never asked. It was not her place to probe at Sam's secrets.

He had chosen to share it with her now. Lily was conscious of the privilege of that and kept quiet, listening as they made their way through the close streets.

"The Gēlǎohuì thought the emperor was giving China over to foreigners. Granting them access to our ports, inviting them to set up homes in our cities knowing full well their goal was to carve China up like a melon into colonies they could pillage dry. They were drugging our people with opium, making themselves rich on the wealth of our land . . ."

He shook his head as though shaking off an ancient way of thinking that clung to him like a tentacle.

"The only foreigners in Hubei, outside of the city, were Christian missionaries, but the Brothers hated them too. Thought they were part of the whole foreign plan. I was so chuffed over how the accepted me . . . like they ever would've welcomed a ten year-old into their ranks if they hadn't a fine use for me."

"What was it?" Lily asked.

"Theft at first. Nicking grain from a Christian village nearby. Scaring people out of a church." He smirked. "I set a load of chuānshānjiǎ loose on them. They're funny little monsters with scales like a pine cone."

"And after that?"

He kicked an empty tin out of the way.

"Murder," he replied.

"Do you want to talk about it?" Lily asked gently.

"No," he replied. They waited for a tram car to huff past. The younger men were hanging from the sides of it by the doors to escape the heat of the interior. One of them carried a small dog under his arm.

"My bà knew I was running with the Brothers. Forbade me to do it. I ignored him. He tried everything to keep me home but short of locking me in a cage, but he couldn't stop a ten-year-old boy set on causing trouble. I'd snuck out to the village with my cousin again when this abbot—big Belgian fellow—got into a bit of a palaver with one of the local elders. The Brothers asked me to create a distraction, rile up the pigs at a neighboring farm. The rest of the monks scarpered. The Brothers cut the abbot into pieces."

Sam's tone was casual. His pace didn't falter, but Lily could hear something raw under the surface of it.

She pictured it—a child crouched at the edge of a village square, watching the men he trusted slaughtering a helpless stranger. The blood spilling into the dust.

It might have been a game to him until then. Being treated as one of a fraternity of important adults would be a dream come true to any young boy, and the crimes he described at first might have played like harmless pranks to someone not yet capable of understanding what fear and deprivation felt like.

But no child was immune to the horror of a killing.

"There was a local official hiding in one of the shops on the square when it happened," Sam went on. "He told my father. When I came back home that night, four of our neighbors wrestled me to the ground. Tied me up and threw me on a fishing boat. My father was there—my grandmother, my sister."

A newspaper lorry rattled by. It was nearly supper. The sausage cart on the far side of the lane was doing a lively trade.

"I fought them," he admitted. "Even though what I'd seen made me sick. The notion I was being taken away from the Brothers turned me wild. My bà must've known that would be the way of it after everything else he'd tried to do had failed. That's why he didn't just take us to my great uncle's farm near Xianning or even Beijing. The Brothers were everywhere in China. He knew they would find me again or that I would find them."

Sam stopped, looking down at his boots. He usually kept them polished to a dapper shine. They had picked up some scuffs since they had been plucked from the park earlier that afternoon.

"We followed the river all the way to Shanghai and my father put us on the first boat he found that would take us out of China. Happened to be a British merchant ship bound for London. He said he would rather I be an exile than a murderer."

"You were only a child," she said. "You couldn't understand how the Brothers were using you."

Sam didn't acknowledge her words.

"We had a fair bit of dosh from the sale of the farm, even after Bà paid for our passage. He was clever enough to have it in gold. We had to show it to the customs man when we arrived. A crewman— one of our own people—translated for us. He talked the geezer into stamping our papers, brought us to a lodging house. The landlady was White. That should've clued Bà in—there are Chinese places in Limehouse that take in new arrivals, help them get settled, but of course we knew nothing of that then."

A pair of well-dressed men moved past, chattering in Cantonese. They nodded to Sam and he tipped his hat at them automatically.

"Later that night we were robbed. I think it was the sailor tipped them off. Probably got a nice cut for it. Things got rough after that."

"And your sister?" Lily asked.

"She disappeared about a year after we landed. Bà was struggling with odd jobs here or there and I'd taken up with Cannon. Nǎinai was working at the laundry. Jiějie—my sister—she helped deliver the stuff. Went out on a run one morning and didn't come back."

Lily's heart was pounding. Sam didn't meet her eyes. He was squinting against the hazy glare of the sun, looking to the west.

"It was something you heard about—girls taken off the street and forced into the nastier sort of cat houses. Năinai was frantic. Bà talked some of the other men in the neighborhood into looking for her but nobody had seen a thing, or if they had they weren't talking. Course I could've found her easily enough if I'd wanted to."

"What do you mean?" Lily blurted, shocked.

He looked at her.

"You know."

And she did. Sam had told her once before about the cleverest of the animals he could communicate with. It was not a creature that served out of loyalty, like the rat still curled warmly in her pocket, or friendship, like the swallows he used to check on where Ash or his father were before he went off to do something he knew they'd likely disapprove of.

The ravens demanded payment for their work.

Lily had made use of them once before. When she had left two men dead in the snow of Hampstead Heath, the ravens had apparently considered it a proper bargain.

"They can find anything," Sam said.

"But you would have had to kill for it." Lily's voice was thin.

"It ain't like that," he countered. "They say the price is an eye. You can give 'em one from someone else. Or you can offer up your own. What matters is the sacrifice."

The chill ran light fingers over her skin despite the heat of the day.

"What sort of animal cares about sacrifice?" she asked quietly.

Sam's eyes were dark.

"Ravens ain't like other animals," he replied.

Lily could hear there was more to it but Sam did not elaborate. She was not sure she wanted him to.

"I went as far as hailing the black blighters down," he went on. "But when it came to it, I turned coward and called off. I begged Cannon to help me instead. There were a price to be paid for that as well," he noted, and something in his tone made her ill. "He came back two days later with one of her slippers. He told me one of the brokers got hold of her, used her in a line-up."

A line-up. Lily was familiar with the term. It was a horrific fate.

Sam's sister had been plucked from the street by the traffickers who hunted the East End, used against her will in one of the roughest forms of the sex trade.

"He said it was too much for her," Sam went on, the tension in his voice thick enough to cut. "Could've been different if I'd had the stomach to pay the ravens their price."

A woman was singing out the window of one of the flats nearby as she pulled in her washing. A girl across the street leaned against her beau, laughing at some piece of wit he'd uttered.

The horror of it twisted inside of her.

"You were a child."

"You keep saying that like it means something," Sam replied.

Lily had no answer to that.

"In the brewery, Cannon spoke as if your sister was still alive."

"So either he's lying now, or he was lying then." Sam's tone was dismissive, but Lily knew better. She could feel the pain writhing under his placid surface.

If Cannon had been lying all those years ago—if Zhao Min had survived—then there had been years where Sam could've done what was necessary to find and save her.

If there had been anything left worth saving.

Lily knew the horror stories of the brokers. When she had worked the theaters of Drury Lane, the seamstresses and chorus girls had spoken of them the way nannies told their charges nightmares of the bogeyman. If that part of Cannon's story was true, Zhao Min would have been subjected to unimaginable suffering and then discarded when there was nothing left of her to use up.

It might have been better had she died when Cannon originally claimed.

"What will you do?" Lily asked.

"Suppose I could ask the ravens now, if I thought Cannon might be telling the truth." His voice was hard.

"That's a heavy price to pay against the chance of a lie."

"Who says I'd pay it myself?" Sam countered. "Maybe I'll offer them Cannon instead."

There was an edge to his tone Lily had never heard before. It frightened her.

"It doesn't have to be like that," she said softly.

"No? And why not?" he shot back.

She reached out to touch his arm.

"Because you aren't alone."

He stopped. A pair of elderly ladies swerved to avoid bumping into him.

They stood in front of the gates of an elegant little church, its white bell tower rising over the low brick row houses that lined either side of the narrow street. The sun blazed down, its heat untempered even as the afternoon shifted toward evening.

Rats scurried at the edge of her vision, quick movements in the shadow.

"Yeah, well," he said at last, his tone just a touch uneven. "Enough about that old trouble."

Sam turned into the churchyard, a little oasis of green trees and soft grass. He sat down on a bench facing the scattered tombs and gravestones. It was shaded by the overhanging branches of a linden, which provided a bit of respite from the heat.

Lily joined him, conscious of the rat still slumbering contentedly in her pocket.

The field of the dead before her appeared similarly restful, all weathered stone and the chirping of small birds. The peace of the place belied the impact those who were gone continued to have on the living.

Sam's sister was not the only ghost haunting them that day. Another tugged at Lily's mind, as it had ever since Sam had blurted out his shocking words in the kitchen earlier that morning.

His wife walks into her own death and that's got to have a reason . . .

A lorry rumbled by somewhere beyond the churchyard walls. It sounded distant, an echo from a different world.

"Sam?"

"Yeah?"

"What happened to Mrs. Ash?"

"She was on the *Princess Alice*," he replied, dropping the name as though Lily ought to know what that meant.

On some level, she did. It had a familiar ring, one that was woven through with dread.

"Passenger steamer," Sam went on when she did not respond. "She was hit by a collier down Gallion's Reach . . . just after the Barking Works dumped millions of gallons of sewage into the outgoing tide. Ash's wife drowned in it," he finished, his voice sharp enough to cut.

Lily remembered. She had heard stories of the shipwreck on the eastern Thames when she was a child. Her mother's theater friends had spoken of it like a tale from a penny dreadful, a horror too terrible to be anything but fiction.

Hundreds of people had died in that wreck. Those uninjured enough to swim would have been poisoned by the toxic filth they were plunged into. Some had survived for days or even weeks only to succumb to chemical burns or an infection.

The strange looks she had seen Sam, Cairncross and Estelle give when she had shared her vision of Charlie Prinz's corpse now made sense to her. They had been conscious of how nearly the circumstances resembled the death of Ash's wife. They had been waiting for him to show the pain that reminder must have caused him.

"You said that she walked into it," Lily said. "What did you mean by that?"

"Well, she could see fate, couldn't she?" he retorted.

"But not the future," Lily countered.

"The *Princess Alice* was returning from Kent. Mrs. Ash had no call to be in Kent that day."

"You think she knew," Lily surmised with horror. "You think she understood on some level what would happen to that boat and chose to be on it anyway."

"Seeing fate," Sam replied, letting some of his defenses drop. "I don't know what that means. How's what I do compare to that? A bit of chatter with the birds, and there are still times I wished like anything it'd go away. Maybe she was just tired of it."

"If that were all it was, there would have been other ways to manage it," Lily replied quietly.

"And there lies the crux of our mystery," Sam returned. His tone was forcefully unfeeling, but Lily knew better.

This was the question Ash had sought to answer, the one that had sent him tumbling across the globe for the better part of three decades.

Had he ever found what he was looking for?

Sam clearly had a theory. He had revealed it in the words he threw at Cairncross across the length of the kitchen.

That's got to have a reason . . . why not make it us?

Lily had never known Evangeline Ash, and yet she understood that the woman had been extraordinary. The truth of that was carved into the canvases and walls she had painted, into the grief that her husband still carried.

How could a woman who perceived fate do anything without a reason? And if a person was that reason—the purpose for why such an extraordinary being stepped willingly into a premature and horrific end—it was an unspeakable burden to carry.

It was no wonder it had twisted Sam up into knots.

Lily was trying to think of a way to respond to that when something slid past her ankles.

She forced herself not to yelp and looked down to see a rat gliding past her to climb onto Sam's boot.

Sam hissed a reproof and the animal crawled back onto the pavement. Three more of them had climbed onto a nearby tomb, their pebble eyes reflecting the gold of the afternoon.

"They've got your man," Sam informed her. "Best follow before he moves on."

—

The rats led them to the mouth of the Limehouse Cut, where the canal met the waters of the Thames. Crowded wharves lay to either side, skiffs and fishing boats beached on the mud of low tide, ropes tying them to the row of buildings that rose above the banks.

Normally standing by the river brought the relief of a breeze, but the air here continued to hang thick and still, the heat unmoved even as the sun began its slow decline.

A warren of narrow stairs and ladders led from the walkway Lily stood on to the mud flats. It was normally a busy place, but the heat seemed to have lulled even the ever-present traffic of the river. Barges sat at the wharves still loaded with cargo, the watermen waiting in the shade for the cool of evening to do their work. A cluster of sailors outside a pub laughed over a joke in Hokkien. One of them, short and visibly strong, reminded Lily of Bay, the East Indian light rigger who had taught her how to fight.

The thought of him made her miss her walking stick, abandoned back at the park when they were accosted by Cannon's thugs.

The Thames was not a river for swimming, at least not this far to the east. Still, the ribbon of shimmering water visible between the rising masts of sailing boats and the smokestacks of the diesel steamers looked unusually appealing.

The rats darted past the shoes of a man who stood at the mouth of the Cut. He kicked at one of them with a curse before leaning back against the rail of the river walk.

The stranger turned to face them and Lily recognized him as the quiet man from the brewery.

"About time you turned up," he said as they approached. He looked narrow-eyed at Lily. "Your monsters have been trailing me for an hour. I suppose it shouldn't surprise me that you've the blood of the Sidhe in you, being the daughter of Deirdre MacBride."

"My mother's name was Albright," Lily replied, confused.

"Albright was the bloke she ran off with at sixteen. The one who took her to London. I doubt there was ever any Christian blessing of that union. She was a MacBride." He squinted at her. "Not sure what you are."

"You knew her," Lily said. The realization set her pulse leaping. She felt the rat stir in her pocket.

"I grew up in Dunfanaghy," he said.

"Dunfanaghy?" Lily echoed. The word felt strange in her mouth.

"It's your mother's home, girl."

"She never mentioned it," Lily admitted carefully.

"She couldn't get out of the place fast enough. Touched by the fae—that's what my aunt always said about her. They'll grant you beauty and charm but curse you to restlessness."

The stranger studied her frankly, his gaze stopping at the rats that lurked around her feet. She wondered what he would think if he knew of the one she could feel twitching in her pocket.

"You've a darker sort of boon, it seems," he said.

Her mind was spinning. Of course her mother must have had a history, but Deirdre had always seemed a creature of the present, sweeping from moment to moment without a backward glance. She rarely spoke of Ireland and if pressed to it, dismissed it as a someplace left behind and best forgotten.

But there would have been a village. There would have been family and schoolmates, rivals and young loves—grass to trample and rocks to climb. Her mother had been a person before she exploded onto London's music hall scene. Encountering a relic of that past existence shouldn't have felt so shocking.

"You set your creatures to following me. What do you want?" he demanded. "If you've come to play the banshee, I'll beg off. If the Brothers had listened to me they'd have ignored your invitation altogether. I knew nothing but trouble would come of it."

"The Red Branch," Lily said, dropping the words like a stone into still water. "I need to know what it is."

The question was clearly not what he expected. His gaze turned careful, and it was a moment before he answered.

"Best go forth in happy ignorance," he finally replied.

"That isn't an option," she returned.

"And if I refuse to tell you, what then? You reveal to me how I'll stumble off a cliff drunk in the dark? I already know what my end will be. You hold no threat over me."

His words were bold, but Lily had seen the fear in him back in the brewery. Still, the thought of threatening him with the future made her queasy.

"There is a very great deal at stake in this," she urged.

"You want to know about the Red Branch? Ask your father. He'll be right cozy with them if he isn't one of them himself."

She would not let him see how that revelation shook her. She focused her attention on the word that gave more of the truth away—*them.*

The Red Branch was not a myth. It was not an object. It was a body of men.

She needed more.

"I'm not asking my father. I'm asking you," she retorted.

"I owe you nothing, girl," he snarled. "Your mother couldn't wait to show the rest of us the dust of her heels, and your father's a grand lord who gets rich off the blood and sweat of my countrymen

working in his fields and his factories. You say so much is at stake . . .
what do you know of the plight of Ireland? You couldn't even name
the village where your mother was born."

His verbal blows hit home. Lily had to school herself not to flinch.

It was true. Ireland claimed half of her blood but it was as foreign
to her as Argentina. What she knew of its struggles came from newspapers, not experience.

And yet she doubted the man at the rail had the whole picture of it.
In her experience, the more bluster someone made about a cause, the
less nuance they admitted into their understanding. The truth didn't
come in neat bands of black and white. It was far messier than that.

"Is there a plan for Sunday morning?" she demanded.

"I don't know anything about that," he returned.

"You sure about that? They can sniff out a lie, you know," Sam said
casually, nodding at the rats that still lurked about his boots.

Lily was fairly certain the rats could do nothing of the sort, but she
kept that thought to herself. Sam's bluff had set a flash of fear in the
stranger's eyes, and they needed to make what use of that they could.

"There's nothing planned," the quiet man cut back. "Why would
we interfere? Home Rule might be short of full independence, but
it's a sight better than living under laws set by a batch of English rot-
ters in Westminster. My grandfather lost three sisters in the famine.
That's what English rule brought us—mass starvation and exile.
Those boys back there wouldn't admit it, but we'll take Home Rule if
we can get it, then keep pressing for what Ireland truly needs. This
is the nearest chance we've had in four hundred years. The young
bucks might mouth off about it but they're not such fools they'd give
England cause to side with the Unionists."

"What about the Unionists, then?" Sam demanded.

"Well, that's another story, isn't it?" the man retorted. "Home Rule
wouldn't do them any favors."

He was right. England had long shown support for the Unionist
cause. Only a few months ago, the possibility that the British Army
might be ordered to stand against Unionist guerrillas had nearly
led to a mutiny, with a bevy of officers saying they would resign
their commissions before they took up arms against the Ulster
Volunteer Force.

The ties between Ulster and Britain were too thick, too deep. Many high-ranking officers of the army were Ulstermen themselves. Others had brothers or cousins or in-laws among those threatening to take up arms for the Unionist cause. Then there were the men who supported the Unionists out of imperial ambitions. They thought the world was best served with England ruling most of it, spreading peace and prosperity under the shadow of the Union Jack.

If anyone had a reason to disrupt the Home Rule talks, it wasn't the IRB.

The tide was rising. Water lapped softly at the piers, melding with the distant sound of carriages and the echo of laughter from across the canal.

Lily took a breath. There was one other question she had for this man—this bitter revolutionary who had known her mother when she was still a laughing girl.

"Tell me about Patrick Dougherty," she demanded.

"He was a molly," the stranger retorted. "What else do you want to know?"

"What did he have to do with the Red Branch?"

"What—besides being done in by them?" he replied.

The seance in the potting shed echoed through her mind.

What do you have to do with Charles Prinz?

Red Branch.

That was the connection between Dougherty and the corpse Lily had found in the pit at Crossness—a group of men who were responsible for both of their murders.

No . . . more than that. There had been three.

Patrick Dougherty had not died alone. He had bled out in an alley beside an auburn-haired actress.

Lily's mother had fallen too . . . and now she knew who had held the knife.

She felt Sam's hand come up onto her shoulder, the warmth of it like an anchor that kept her from spinning out to sea.

Lily took a breath, forcing back the tumult. There was more here she needed to know.

Something in the stranger's gaze shifted, falling toward a flash of sympathy.

"You didn't know that," he stated.

Lily didn't answer him.

"Why?" she demanded.

He looked away, directing his gaze up the river through the tangled masts of ships to where the sun dropped low and orange in the west.

"I once thought she fancied me," he said. "Deirdre had a way of making a man feel like that. I don't know that she meant to do it. It was just what she was."

"Yes," Lily agreed as memories rolled over her of a rich laugh, snatches of song. The smell of lilacs and a smile that lit up the world, with you right at the center of it.

Looking at the man by the railing, she could almost see the boy he had once been. Dark hair, square jaw, that fiery determination in his eyes—it would have been undimmed by disillusionment back then.

"Dougherty wasn't one of us," he said. "But there was a connection through a cousin. He asked for a meeting, said he had information."

"About the Red Branch," Lily guessed.

"He wanted protection. He was Irish enough to want us to be able to use what he'd learned, but he was afraid. What could we offer him? We're a bunch of rats hiding in cellars." He glanced back at Sam, but his long-tailed followers had slipped into the shadows. "So he looked for it somewhere else."

Lily's pulse quickened.

"You mean my father."

He pushed back from the rail, standing.

"Three days later he was dead. And that's all I can tell you."

He stared at them defiantly. Lily doubted the threat of Sam's rats or her foresight were what compelled him to share as much as he had. He'd done it for an auburn-haired girl who had been dead to him long before she was stabbed in a Covent Garden alley.

"Dunfanaghy," Lily said, pushing the word past the lump in her throat. "Is there anyone still there?"

"The elder MacBrides passed years ago. There was a brother transported to Australia. Last I knew, you'd a great aunt still breathing, a handful of distant cousins. But none of them had anything to do with Deirdre after she went the Magdalene way."

"Thank you," she replied.

The stranger stalked off. He paused, glancing back.

"You've her voice," he finished.

Then he was gone.

"You alright?" Sam asked.

His hand was still on her shoulder. Lily leaned into it for a moment, letting herself fall against him as a shiver of grief passed through her.

Sam's arm slipped the rest of the way around her shoulders. He gave her a squeeze.

"Thought it might be like that," he said quietly.

"Thank you," she said. She pulled herself together, straightening.

"What now?" Sam asked.

The rat looked out from her pocket. Lily gently pulled it out and set it down on the ground.

"I think it's time I spoke with my father," she replied.

EIGHTEEN

Seven o'clock that evening
March Place, Bloomsbury

$\mathcal{T}$HE SUN HAD SUNK low in the sky when Lily made it back to Bloomsbury. The heat hung over the city like a blanket, thick and still. A bank clerk arriving home late for supper paused to remove his bowler hat and swipe a handkerchief across his forehead, stifling in his three-piece suit.

The members of a more bohemian household at the end of the road had given up any attempt at propriety and lounged on the front steps with shirtsleeves rolled up to their elbows, a dog panting beside them on the stoop.

Lily missed her walking stick. Her hands felt empty without it, but it seemed it had been well and truly lost in the encounter with Cannon's men. She and Sam had chanced a swing past Brickfield Gardens in their hackney on the way home, but the yew staff had been long gone.

She reminded herself that it was just a piece of wood she had plucked more or less at random from a playhouse attic. There was nothing special about it. It could easily be replaced.

It wasn't much of a comfort.

As Lily rounded the corner, she could glimpse a line of dark clouds hanging thickly over the western horizon. She wondered if they promised rain. The air ached for the relief of a storm.

It was too late to catch her father at home or in the halls of Parliament. Lily knew where she would find him. To get inside, she would require weapons for a different sort of war.

And once she reached him? There was one way she now knew she could gauge whether or not Lord Torrington was telling the truth. The thought of using it made her feel ill.

She climbed the stairs and pushed inside.

The post had arrived. It sat where it always did on the side table by the stairs.

The envelope she needed was there, marked in the sort of elegant hand one had to hire out for. Lily popped it open.

Your presence is cordially requested at The Night Sky—an evening's entertainment. Dance and dinner. Dress to theme. Lord and Lady Bexley, St. John's Wood

It was addressed to *Miss Albright, guest of Mrs. Walford Eversleigh.*

Virginia had succeeded in getting Lily an invitation to Lord Bexley's soiree and would apparently herself be serving as Lily's chaperone, at least so far as the guest list was concerned. Lily had not considered that she would require one. At twenty-four, she was not some fresh young debutante, and anyway the rules of the society marriage-mart had never been meant for the likes of her.

Whatever was required to get her in the door, she concluded grimly. Lily did not plan on looking for Strangford's sister once she arrived. There would be other pressing matters to attend to.

Beneath the note sat a white cardboard box. Lily knew what must be inside. She had nearly forgotten about the rest of Virginia's offer. Accepting that gift felt like an uncomfortable extravagance, but she admitted it would likely be as necessary as the invitation for getting her in the door.

She picked up both box and envelope and hurried up the stairs.

Once inside her flat, she pulled off her skirt and blouse, both stained from her ordeal in Limehouse.

She was at the basin in her chemise and drawers, scrubbing her face and hands, when the knock came at the door in her parlor.

"Lily?" Estelle called.

"Come in!"

Estelle slipped inside. She paused in the door to Lily's bedroom, quickly assessing the scene.

"I take it our Irish friends weren't able to tell you everything you needed to know," she concluded.

"I need to talk to my father," Lily returned.

Estelle noted the presence of the bruises on Lily's arms where Cannon's men had hauled her into the lorry. Something about that made Lily burn with embarrassment, but she refused to give way to it.

She set down her towel and met Estelle's eyes through the glass of the mirror.

"How much longer will you . . ." Lily's words drifted off.

It didn't matter. Estelle knew what she was asking.

"We are already packing," she replied.

The feeling of helplessness washed over her. Her friends were calmly preparing for a disaster and Lily, who was the one among them capable of seeing the future, could tell them nothing of what they faced or how to stop it.

"Dr. Gardner? Cairncross?"

"The doctor is at St. Bart's. You know he will stay there until the last possible moment. Cairncross is making preparations at The Refuge. And Ash is with him," she went on, anticipating Lily's next question.

"What about Strangford?" Lily asked. She kept her voice carefully neutral, though saying his name brought a lump to her throat. She could still see the look in his eyes when she told him she would not flee London for the safety of Northumberland. The memory of the conflict was as fresh as it was unresolvable.

"He is going to Lord Bexley's," Estelle replied.

"To a party?" Lily could not keep the surprise from her tone.

"It's not for dancing. I heard him mention your father's name."

It was a grim revelation. If Strangford was looking for Lord Torrington, it had to be for the same reasons Lily herself was tracking him down.

There was only one way that Strangford could pull information from her father that Torrington didn't want to reveal, and he could accomplish it with a shake of the hand.

When Strangford was a child, he had made a game of stealing secrets from the aristocrats who visited Allerhope, but that was ages ago. For the last twelve years, he had gone to great lengths to avoid physical contact with other human beings. Because Strangford's power wasn't a distant witnessing but an immersive experience, stumbling across the wrong memory could provoke a very clear and obvious reaction on his part. Lily had seen him sob, or laugh, or hover on the verge of a scream.

What would happen if he were to do that in the midst of a party crowded with the most powerful men and women in England? In front of her father, who might very well stand at the heart of the conspiracy they needed to thwart?

It was as rash as it was unnecessary. Thanks to the quiet man at the Limehouse Cut, Lily now knew how to get the truth from her father without Strangford's hands.

She had to stop him.

"It is hard to imagine that something so terrible could actually happen," Estelle said. "I keep asking myself whether it could possibly be that bad."

Lily closed her eyes.

"It is," she replied.

Estelle absorbed that with quiet dignity.

"Well," she said softly.

Lily turned to face her.

"I have to stop it," she said. "This matter with Patrick Dougherty feels like a trail of breadcrumbs but it's all I have to go on."

"Then we had best get you ready for the ball," Estelle replied, unbowed. "You won't get past Bexley's butler in your chemise. What have you got to wear?"

"Mrs. Eversleigh sent something." Lily indicated the white box, which she had set on the bed.

"That's very generous," Estelle remarked.

"She didn't give me the option to refuse—and it isn't as though I have something else in my wardrobe. I'm not the sort of person who receives invitations to balls."

"It's good I came upstairs, then," Estelle concluded. "These gowns are usually designed for a woman with a lady's maid on hand to lace, button, hook or stitch them into it. Let's see what we're up against."

Lily lifted the lid of the box, Estelle leaning over her shoulder, and unfolded the white tissue paper that concealed what lay within.

The fabric nestled carefully inside was a satin of the deepest midnight blue, like the space between the stars of Evangeline Ash's Dendera ceiling. It was run through with brilliant golden embroidery, the thread shimmering against the dark silk.

The pattern glittered up at her, tumbling swirls of hundreds of tiny golden keys.

Lily blinked and the keys were gone. The gold resolved itself into abstract whirls and ornaments.

She had simply imagined that the dress had the same pattern as the gown Evangeline Ash had painted onto her portrait of The Prophetess, the flame-haired woman on the attic wall with a staff of yew in her hand.

The woman Ash had thought held the keys to changing the future.

Lily was not what Ash had hoped. There was no new and strange khárisma hidden inside of her, waiting to emerge.

Perhaps there was still another way for her to swing the pendulum of fate and rewrite what that dead saint had foreseen.

"Chop chop, darling. We mustn't stand here gaping at it," Estelle ordered.

Lily lifted the gown from the box. As it unfurled, it changed from a compelling bundle of strangely lovely fabric to something entirely more.

"Bravo, Mrs. Eversleigh," Estelle said from behind her.

Virginia had not played it safe with her choice. The gown eschewed all of the adornments which had been so fashionable for the last five years—the chiffon sleeves, the waspish waistlines and layers of contrasting lace and bundled fabric.

The dress lacked any sleeves at all. It was cut flat across the bosom and held up over the shoulders by a layer of the sheerest gauze run through with streams of golden beads. The midnight silk fell in simple folds to someplace just shy of Lily's ankles in the front, with a longer spill of shimmering fabric in the back.

It was far more daringly modern than anything Lily would have chosen for herself, yet somehow timeless, like something out of one of the paintings in Strangford's gallery.

This was not a gown that would allow Lily to slip into Bexley's ball more or less unnoticed. It was a piece of clothing designed to command attention and admiration. Virginia clearly did not intend for Lily to make her debut into high society with subtlety.

It would not do at all for what she needed to accomplish that evening—a quick plunge into Bexley's ballroom to corner her father and determine what he truly knew about the deaths of Patrick Dougherty and Charlie Prinz.

And yet it seemed she had no choice.

"You won't need a bodice with this," Estelle noted. "There's just a row of hooks up the back. But you will have to lose your chemise." She glanced at the lower folds of the skirt. "And I hope you have some decent stockings."

Stockings were found and Lily shrugged into the dress.

"What about . . ." Lily's voice trailed off as she looked down at the purple marks on her arms from where Cannon's men had grabbed her. Virginia's elegant, modern gown did nothing to conceal them.

Estelle turned to the vanity. She quickly rifled the drawers and pulled out an old cake of foundation, a relic from Lily's theater days.

She rubbed the powder onto the discolored spots on Lily's arms.

"I can't imagine you'll be doing any dancing, so just be careful what you lean on. Now for this." Estelle laid a gentle finger on the cut on Lily's temple. "Perhaps we can cover it with your hair."

"There isn't much of it left," Lily noted.

"My skills are up to the challenge," Estelle replied.

She sat Lily in the chair and began to work. Lily could just glimpse her through the mirror out the corner of her eye.

It gave her an unexpected comfort to feel Estelle's fingers in her hair, to see her friend thoughtfully plucking a pin from the dressing table and setting a lock into place.

From the day Lily had seen her mother put into the ground, she had been alone, isolated within a whirlwind of schoolgirls who despised what she was, or surrounded by actors and scene-dressers who considered her something apart, knowing the importance and power of the man who had fathered her. It was not until she arrived here at March Place that Lily had known what it was like to be simply and unquestioningly welcomed—not until Estelle.

Lily was glad that she and Miss Bard were going to Highgate. Nothing about what lay before her that night would be easy, but some part of her was comforted knowing that at least the pair of them would be safe.

It was more than she could say for herself.

The memory of the vision flashed across the back of her eyes—the snake-skinned woman with the enigmatic smile, the swing of the pendulum, the shadow falling across the water as Lily sank down, down, down.

"Estelle?"

"Mmm?" Estelle replied through the pin in her mouth.

"Do you know what happens? You know . . . after."

Estelle paused, her fingers going still in Lily's hair.

"Only the dead know for certain," she replied. "But after communicating with them for over forty years I have a fair notion."

Lily pushed out the question that had been haunting her.

"Should I be afraid?" she asked.

"No," Estelle replied.

It was a plain statement, mere fact. She set a final pin in Lily's hair and came around to face her, crouching down to look her in the eye.

"I know it by feeling more than anything else. It feels like ring of the doorbell and on the threshold is the most wonderful friend you had forgotten you ever had. Or the first time you ride down a slide in the park when you are a child, only it goes on and on until you wonder why you ever wanted to do anything else. Or you are walking into a new house and realize that actually you have lived here all along, and nowhere else could ever feel so much like home. There are some who are confused by it for a little while. There are some who resist because they resist anything they do not themselves control. But they are never afraid. Fear is for those of us who are living."

Estelle stood. There was something grand about her even in the cramped space of Lily's attic bedroom. She was tall and resplendent in her rich blue caftan, in the ageless lines of her face and the clarity of her gaze.

"Fear the pain of grief. Fear neglecting to embrace life with both your arms and draw all the joy out of it that you can. Fear being stingy with your love or your compassion. But do not fear Death."

"Thank you," Lily replied.

Estelle smiled.

"Now. Let's get you off to the party."

Lily could hardly step off an omnibus at Bexley's doorstep. A hackney appeared to be the best available alternative, though Lily did not need Estelle to tell her that it was not exactly "done" to arrive at one of the most fashionable addresses in London in a hired cab.

She hoped that Virginia's undeniably expensive gown would go some way toward making up for it.

The dress felt strangely airy as Lily waited in the hall for Estelle to fetch her a ride. The fabric was strong enough to hold its elegant folds but breathed more easily than anything else in Lily's wardrobe. Even inside the close confines of the house on March Place, Lily could feel the air move over her bare arms and shoulders. It was an admitted relief when set against the lingering heat of the evening.

Miss Bard stepped out onto the landing at the top of the stairs. Her soft brown eyes widened as she looked down to where Lily stood.

"Oh!" she exclaimed, her round face warming with delight. "Aren't you a vision?"

Miss Bard was not a woman prone to flattery. Lily could see that her reaction was genuine. It offered another sort of comfort. If she had to plunge into the foreign territory of London's highest society, perhaps looking like a goddess off of Evangeline Ash's ceiling might have its benefits.

Estelle poked her head inside.

"Your transport awaits," she announced.

Miss Bard hurried downstairs. Lily clasped the smaller woman's hands as she reached the hall.

"Please be safe," she urged.

"I might say the same to you, but you look ready to take danger by the throat," Miss Bard returned.

Estelle threw wide the door and Lily stepped out, blinking at the glare of the dying sunlight.

There was no hackney. Instead, what waited on the curb was a gleaming silver Rolls Royce.

A familiar figure leaned against the hood, neatly dressed in chauffeur's livery.

"You scrub up well," Sam announced.

"What are you doing here?" Lily demanded.

"Well, he wanted a report once I was back, didn't he?" Sam returned. Lily didn't have to ask which "he" was meant. She could picture Ash waiting for Sam in the garden of The Refuge. "When I told him where you was off to, he told me to bring you the car."

Lily was grateful for Ash's gesture. The Silver Ghost was impressive enough to ease her entry into Bexley's inner sanctum.

She was also glad for the company. Knowing Sam would be nearby as she attempted this was a comfort.

Estelle touched her arm.

"It'll be too hot for the windows. You'll need something to block the wind," she said. She reached inside and plucked a scarf and a wrap from the coat rack. She handed them to Lily.

Lily tossed the scarf over her hair, knotting it around her throat.

"The wrap will keep the dust off," Estelle added. She leaned down to plant a firm kiss on Lily's cheek, squeezing her hand. "Now go!"

"And God speed you," Miss Bard called from behind her.

Sam held the door for her as she climbed into the car.

She looked up at the steps of the house as he hopped into the driver's seat, drinking in the sight of the two women standing there watching her, Estelle's arm slipped around Miss Bard's shoulders.

"Best hang on to something," Sam announced.

The engine roared to life. The squeal of the tires echoed off the high buildings as the Rolls peeled out of March Place, ripping around the turn toward St. John's Wood.

NINETEEN

Saturday evening
Eight-thirty
St. John's Wood, London

THE SKY WAS PAINTED blood red as they pulled into the lush confines of St. John's Wood.

Sam let up his breakneck pace, achieving something approaching respectability as they drove through the broad, quiet streets. This was the sort of place where a constable would not hesitate to wave down a vehicle being blatantly reckless.

The houses were enormous, set back from the road in nests of ancient trees, modestly concealed by ivy-covered walls or tall hedges. It was the sort of place that should be immune to the summer heat, but the potted ferns still drooped on front steps and the small white dogs panted on the ends of their leashes as chambermaids took them out for their evening walks.

They passed the Lords' Cricket Ground, empty of its cheering crowds, and turned onto a street lined with high elms. Lily could glimpse glittering windows and soft-burning electric lights through the gaps in the greenery—a finely arched gable, a spotless dining room glowing with the warmth of crystal and gilded trim.

The dark line of clouds had risen in the west, concealing the last fragments of the sunset. The heat ignored the onrush of evening, continuing to oppress.

Sam slowed the Rolls and Lily set Estelle's wrap aside, untying the scarf from her hair.

A footman waited at the curb at Bexley's address, dressed in full livery in defiance of the weather. He was clearly not permitted to sweat. He opened the door as Sam stopped the automobile and offered Lily a hand.

A carpet had been laid out from the pavement to the front gate, through which Lily could glimpse the secret bulk of the house, its true dimensions concealed by the brick privacy fencing and the overhanging trees.

She stepped down. She felt the magnificent gold and cobalt dress unfurl around her as she emerged.

The footman gestured toward the gate.

Lily risked a glance back at Sam. He offered her a deliberate tip of the hat, and she reminded herself that he would not be far—just around the bend where Bexley had arranged for the automobiles and carriages of his guests to wait.

Lily faced the gate.

She had trained for this for years at the finishing school she had been banished to after her mother's death. There was an earldom in her blood.

She held her spine straight, her head high, and walked through.

Beyond the privacy wall, the house revealed itself. A narrow entrance gave way to an enormous sprawl of stone, ivy, and glittering windows that would have impressed in the distant country, never mind the rigid confines of London.

The butler, an elegant man of African descent, waited at the door.

"Good evening, madame," he said.

He spoke with flawless courtesy, but Lily did not miss the quick assessing look he gave her as she came in through the gate. He had taken in the details of her dress, the presence of the Rolls Royce, silently measuring the likelihood that she belonged here.

"I have not yet had the pleasure of your acquaintance. May I see your invitation?"

Lily handed him the envelope.

234

He opened it and glanced at the thick, embossed card inside. He handed the letter to another footman who waited beside him.

"My apologies, Miss Albright. Lord and Lady Bexley will be delighted you have joined us. If you please."

He motioned her inside.

The footman called out as she stepped from the entry to the reception hall.

"Miss Albright, guest of Mrs. Walford Eversleigh."

The ceilings were at least twenty feet high. An enormous electric chandelier hung overhead, glittering crystal and gleaming brass. Richly dressed bodies crowded the floor, the chime of laugher mingling with the clink of glass and the roar of polite conversation.

It smelled of perfume and spilled champagne. Somewhere nearby, a violin was playing Vivaldi.

The space had been decked to support the theme Lily had seen on the invitation, "The Night Sky." Gold foil stars were suspended from a ceiling draped in black tulle. Hired servers carrying trays of drinks and canapes were draped in flowing costumes meant to represent the Greek constellations.

The guests appeared in varying states of fancy dress. There was a great deal of gold and silver. One woman had fashioned a headpiece in the shape of a crescent moon.

Everywhere she looked, she saw extravagance. Wealth oozed from the very pores of the room. Lily could not help but be aware that tomorrow, the tulle and the stars would likely be consigned to the dustbin, the rented palms shipped back to whatever greenhouse had birthed them.

She pressed forward.

A few heads turned as she entered the room, glancing her way with relative disinterest.

The interest sharpened once she had been seen. A few more heads turned.

Lily was aware of a low murmur of attention as she made her way across the hall.

It was the dress. It was sparking exactly the reaction Virginia had hoped it would—admiring looks or a hint of jealousy, the same question echoing through the little coteries of conversation.

Who is Miss Albright?

Before long, that question would find its way to someone who knew the answer. There would be people in this house who recalled the old gossip about Lord Torrington and "that Irish actress."

If she had been here to execute Virginia's plan, Lord Torrington would appear at her arm to escort her through the gauntlet before the rumor made its way across the party and the tenor of those curious glances changed.

That would not be the way of things tonight.

She didn't intend to be here long enough to see how the scandal of her presence at Bexley's party would play out. She wove through the crowd, scanning the room for a sign of the tall figure of her father.

"Not him. Gambling problem," an older woman said as she passed.

"What about Lord Cobham?"

"He comes with a mountain of debt. Mr. Arlington, on the other hand . . ."

The woman spoke across the head of a bored debutante in a silver-spangled gown.

"I believe Arlington keeps a set of rooms in Convent Garden," another replied carefully.

Lily knew well enough the significance of that delicately worded phrase.

"All the better. It will keep him occupied," her companion replied.

The debutante caught the gaze of another young woman tied to a dour chaperone. She flashed her a flirtatious smile.

The young woman blushed.

Her father was not here.

A large drawing room beckoned on the far side of a tight cluster of men in black evening dress.

"But of course who can speak better to the matter than our new Secretary of State for War," a shorter one boasted, his chest puffed out.

"The appointment has not been made yet." The sardonic reply came from a tall, aristocratic man with round gold spectacles. He wore a black waistcoat under his evening jacket richly and delicately embroidered with golden thread. The pattern was one of glittering stars and crowns.

"It will be public knowledge by tomorrow evening that Asquith intends to name you to the position, Bexley," the puffed chest replied.

Lord Bexley was her host for the evening, the owner of all the splendor that surrounded her. He looked utterly ordinary to her aside from the lavishness of his waistcoat.

A glint of light caught her eye. One of the men Lord Bexley conversed with wore a pin on his lapel in the shape of a pair of interlocked carats.

Lily knew that symbol. It was worn by members of the Society for the Betterment of the British Race, the eugenics club founded by Dr. Joseph Hartwell. Though Hartwell's life had ended on a rooftop in Hampstead Heath, his ideas continued to live on, finding plenty of favor even in the highest circles of society and government.

It made Lily feel ill.

The knot of men blocked her way forward.

"Excuse me," Lily said to the nearest of them.

Bexley turned to look down at her through his spectacles.

"I don't think I know you," he commented.

"I'm Miss Albright. I'm a friend of Mrs. Eversleigh's. I don't mean to interrupt, I just need to—"

"A fine woman, Mrs. Eversleigh," the puffed chest noted.

"We are blocking her way, gentlemen," said an elderly man in full military dress uniform. He shared Dr. Gardner's Ulster brogue.

"Astute as to the lay of things as always, General Taggart," Bexley replied.

Taggart—Lily recognized the name. She had heard her father speak of the man, the Quartermaster General of the British Army.

They stood before her in their perfectly tailored suits, the brokers of power in the realm, holding crystal glasses and regarding her with indifference.

A few miles away, a disaster loomed that would devour the heart out of their precious empire.

"Do go on, my dear," the puffed chest said with a polite bow, stepping aside.

He gave her an admiring look, the same sort of gaze he might bestow on a finely built racehorse.

She took the opening to move past them, slipping into the drawing room.

Brocade sofas were pressed against the walls, draped with elegant bodies. Tiffany lamps shone from walnut tables, the smell of cigars and French brandy thick in the air.

The younger set had collected here. Lily found herself trapped by another circle of privileged male flesh.

"Enjoy that while it lasts—it may be hard to come by for a while."

The speaker was handsome and athletic, nodding at the brandy in the hand of another icon of British manhood.

"I think we ought to get into it. Remind them all who's the real power in Europe."

"It is hardly worth the effort," came a laconic reply. "The whole business will be over by Christmas."

"There will be a small fortune to be made in the meantime in armaments," a third noted cannily.

They spoke of war. They made it sound like a sideshow or an opportunity. Memories of things which had not happened yet forced themselves into her awareness—the devastated earth, the fly-buzzed corpses. Overturned machines and knots of razor wire.

Strangford falling away from her in a blast of mud and splintered wood.

A spiral of ravens whirling up into the sky.

The light shifted, a veil falling from the room, revealing what lay beneath its surface. The vision washed over her where she stood in the center of all that elegance.

The handsome young men change. The ruddy tan of hours spent rowing the Thames or swinging a cricket bat drops from their faces. Lily sees hollow cheeks, bone showing where the ravens have ripped the flesh away. One of them is burned to a crisp, his black skin flaking to the gleaming marble floor as he raises his drink to his lips.

The entire room is infected with it. Every fifth one of the close-pressed bodies around her reveals itself as a walking corpse. They laugh with arms blown away, heads half-crushed and oozing.

Fewer of those with gray in their beards are impacted. It is the younger men who are changed. They are corpses plucking canapes from silver trays and eyeing a passing woman with a wasp-thin waist.

"Pass me a bit more of that brandy," says a man with a bullet hole in his forehead.

Lily's stomach lurched. A wave of dizziness swept over her, and she was struck by the horrible fear that she was about to either vomit or faint.

A firm hand slipped under her arm.

"Hello, there! You're looking a bit peaked."

Lily recognized that cheerful voice. She had heard it before in the Black Rod's Library, that narrow sanctum in the hallowed halls of Westminster Palace.

It belonged to her hale, healthy half-brother, Lord George Carne.

She closed her eyes, terrified that when she turned to look at him she would see his face half blown away, the maggots crawling through the place where his eyes once were.

It could not be avoided. She forced herself to look.

Her half-brother peered down at her, the tanned skin around his eyes creasing with concern.

The dead men were gone—or rather they still stood all around her, laughing and chattering without any notion of the rot that lurked inside of them, waiting for its inevitable moment to emerge.

"I'm fine, thank you," she said, glad her voice came out steadier than it deserved to be.

"Jolly good. You had me worried for a moment there."

Lord George took his hand from her arm now that he was assured she was not about to fall over. He looked almost bashful. Lily was quite certain this was not a common state for him.

"I'm rather glad I've run into you again. This may sound terribly out of place. If I'm mistaken, I hope you'll forgive me for it, but aren't you—"

"George?"

The voice came from the door to a long and elegant hallway on the far side of the drawing room. Lily followed George's gaze to see that the speaker was an elegantly turned-out woman of perhaps fifty. Her blond hair was piled elaborately on her head in a manner only a lady's maid could accomplish. She still carried the echoes of the prettiness she must once have possessed in youth. It should have been a package that sparkled even in this glittering company, but there was something timid in her despite her clear air of wealth and influence.

She was looking across the crowd at Lily's blond, blue-eyed half-brother—a brother with a dimple on his left cheek that echoed the one Lily could see on the woman's powdered face.

Lily realized whom she was looking at just as the woman's eyes shifted to the right.

The Countess of Torrington stared at her.

She was Lord George's mother, Lily's father's wife—the woman he had left in lonely splendor when he went off to make love to an actress in the suite of rooms he rented for her use.

The countess's expression as she saw who her son was speaking to made it clear that she knew very well who Lily was. Her reaction was not the visceral hate Lily had seen in the eyes of her eldest half-brother, Lord Deveral, the first time she had been properly introduced to him. It was something almost worse.

Fear.

"I'm very sorry. I have to go," Lily blurted. She turned from the surprise on her half-brother's face and dove into the crowd.

"Wait!"

She heard him call after her but ignored it, plunging through the French doors that opened onto the clear air of the garden.

She stepped into another world.

The garden was an unheard-of size for a home in London. Rich foliage framed it, mature trees arching overhead. The air smelled of roses, and Lily could see that blooms of a rich dark purple were set in pots around the grounds. She was certain they had been purchased specifically for the evening.

That was not the only adornment. The trees were hung with what seemed like a thousand lanterns. It was as though the stars had descended from the sky to hover around the guests who mingled in the soft glow of the lush green lawn.

The crowd was thinner outside, gathered in tight little circles of laughter and clinking glassware. It did not surprise her to discover that Strangford had found his way here. Weaving through the close-packed bodies inside the house must have been a certain kind of hell for him.

He stood alone by the fountain, his eyes on the regular fall of the water. She could see his lingering discomfort in the tight set of his shoulders.

As though sensing she was there, he turned.

For a moment, a shadow clung to his left eye, obscuring it in an unnatural darkness. Lily blinked and it shifted away.

She saw him take in the effect of her gifted evening gown. Something fierce in the look it provoked made her blood warm, but his gaze was also conflicted. Lily was conscious that their fight that afternoon had never been finished. The fate she had foreseen for herself, her refusal of his demand that she flee to Northumberland, the fact of his mother's purpose for coming to London all still lay between them.

She crossed the grass to where he stood.

"Have you seen my father?" she asked.

"Not yet," he replied.

His gaze dropped to her arms. He had an instinct for sensing where she had been injured. Lily was conscious that the makeup Estelle had applied would conceal the marks only from a casual look.

There was nothing casual in how Strangford looked at her. That he had seen through the powder was clear in the iron set of his jaw.

"Sam's old boss put on a show of roughness when we went to the rendezvous this afternoon," she told him. "I'm fine. So is Sam."

"Did you learn anything?" he asked.

"Not enough," she replied quietly.

A woman by one of the rose bushes threw back her head, releasing a throaty laugh. A plump gentleman stumbled into a bird bath, just managing to prevent it toppling over with the help of a quick-moving servant. A pair of young women tittered with delight over their glasses of champagne at something an elegantly turned-out naval officer had said to them.

A cluster of guests spilled out of the house behind them, two of the women shrieking as the heels of their shoes sunk into the soft ground.

Strangford flinched at the sound of it.

"Over here," Lily said, leading him deeper into the garden. The move took them into one of the little pockets of shadow she suspected had been deliberately left among the laurels and fruit trees.

It was a place designed for a romantic interlude. Lily was sharply reminded of how unsettled things between her and Strangford remained. His anger was still there, burning behind the careful facade of his expression.

"You shouldn't be here," he said.

Lily knew he wasn't just talking about Bexley's party. He was talking about London, about the disasters that loomed over them—over her.

"This isn't the time to discuss that," Lily returned.

"Then when? Tomorrow morning, when the world has fallen apart? When you've already drowned?"

"You don't know that what I foresaw will happen tonight," she countered.

"You said it was related to the destruction of London. That means tonight. You know there's a danger here and you keep racing toward it like you're fine with losing your life."

"You don't get a say in this," Lily retorted in a harsh whisper. "It's not your fate."

"You don't know anything about what's fated. That isn't what you do," Strangford snapped.

"I need to find my father," Lily said, ignoring the blow of that.

"I'll take care of your father," he said.

"You can't," Lily hissed. "He'll know what you're doing. You know what he's like. It isn't safe."

His eyes were dark fire, a barely contained fury.

"Don't talk to me about what's safe."

"There you are!"

Virginia Eversleigh's voice rang out across the garden.

Strangford schooled his expression with some effort as she approached. Lily tried to do the same.

Strangford's sister wore a gown of black silk sewn with thousands of tiny silver-beaded stars. It was less decisively modern than the one she had selected for Lily, but still extremely stylish and flattering.

"I wondered where you had gone, brother. I am glad to see you have collected Miss Albright." She smiled at Lily. "I must apologize for my husband. He would very much have liked to be here to support the cause, but this mysterious shipment is leaving the factory in Hugglescote tonight. Apparently there are matters that must be personally seen to by him in order to ensure that it is able to pass through London on schedule tomorrow morning. I swear I am considering traveling to Blackfriars rail bridge at quarter past six just to wave the thing on. I will be that glad to see the far side of it. How is our plan proceeding? Have you arranged matters with your father?"

"We don't have time for this right now, Virginia," Strangford cut in.

"You never have time for this sort of thing, and that is why I am forced to swoop in and help you," she replied breezily.

Of course Virginia would still be focused on the plan she had made to debut Lily to high London society. Lily felt the weight of that obligation. It was Virginia, after all, who had garnered her the invitation to tonight's party and sent the dress she now wore, all the in the name of the noble cause of making Lily a more suitable partner for the brother she loved.

Lily would have to disappoint her. There were bigger things at stake.

"I'm sorry, Virginia," she began, but stopped short as someone new joined their small circle.

The woman who stopped at Virginia's side was unmistakably Strangford's mother.

Lady Strangford was taller than her children but shared the same dark hair and black eyes. The lines of her face were stronger with a firm set that more resembled her son than her dynamic daughter. She had the air about her of someone who spent a great deal of time in the outdoors.

"Mother," Virginia said, putting on a brilliant smile. "Allow me to introduce Miss Albright."

Virginia's smile was a formidable weapon, but Lady Strangford was immune to its effects.

"Miss Albright," she said, her voice flat. "I am sure you are a very charming young woman but I cannot condone your relationship with my son."

Lily had not expected Strangford's mother to receive her with warmth, not after what Virginia had shared about her disapproval of their relationship. She still found herself shocked by what the woman had just said.

Lady Strangford had not spoken in rancor. There was no personal animosity behind it. It was simply a statement of fact by someone who clearly preferred not to mince words.

It felt as though the woman had stepped up to her in the middle of the party and calmly slapped her across the face.

"Dear Lord, Mother—must you be so blunt?" Virginia said.

Beside her, Strangford was dangerously quiet in a way Lily knew did not bode well for whatever was coming next.

"There is no point dancing around the matter," Lady Strangford replied. She returned her attention to Lily. "I believe my daughter when she tells me that you are not a social climber and that your feelings for my son are genuine. I am not unsympathetic to that but there is no way that this ends well." Her dark, steady gaze shifted to her son. "You will break it off, Strangford, or I will be forced to distance myself from you. I will not stand by while you destroy your standing in society and curse my grandchildren to a life of whispers and ignominy."

Had it been any other night, Strangford might have found a way to weather it—to redirect his mother's attention or quietly demand that the conversation be taken up at a more appropriate time.

But it was this night, a night where he was already worn thin by their fight in the garden that afternoon, by the threat of Lily's impending death and the cataclysm looming over London.

Lily didn't need to be a clairvoyant to know what was about to happen.

There was only one way she knew to stop it.

She took a breath, forcibly mastering her own roiling emotions, then reached out and grasped Strangford by the wrist, slipping her hand between the black leather of his glove and the cuff of his suit.

Her fingers wrapped around bare skin and she set all her focus into a single fierce thought—*not now. We can't do this now.*

She dropped it, not wanting to distract him further.

Virginia was looking at her.

Strangford had never told his family about what he could do. Lily knew he believed both his sister and his mother to be in complete ignorance of his power.

Something in Virginia's careful, intelligent gaze made her wonder if that were entirely true.

A flash of movement on the far side of the garden caught her eye. She glimpsed a familiar leonine profile illuminated by the light of one of the myriad hanging lanterns.

Torrington.

Lily faced Lady Strangford.

"You have no idea who I am," she said, her carefully banked anger giving the words strength. "Now if you'll excuse me, there is someone I need to see."

She brushed past Virginia and Lady Strangford, striding across the garden.

"We are not finished yet," she heard Lady Strangford say to her son.

Lily did not wait. Torrington was moving and she could not afford to lose sight of him again.

She wove through the women in their beaded gowns and the men with their top hats and ebony walking sticks, finally reaching the place where she had seen her father.

He was gone.

Lily looked around but there was no sign of him. Taking a chance, she pressed on in the direction she had seen him going.

It led her to a narrow gap between two holly bushes. Following that slender path to a darker, less public corner of the garden, she found herself looking at a little wooden gate set into the tall brick privacy walls that separated the estate from the teaming life of the city.

There was no sign of her father. Unless her instincts had led her awry, there was only one place he could have gone.

Lily took the chance and lifted the latch, slipping through the gate out into the night.

TWENTY

$\mathcal{S}$HE STEPPED INTO THE narrow, clean-swept mews that ran behind the grand houses. Ancient trees loomed over the high walls that bounded it, casting all in deep shadow.

Lily was forced to pause to allow her eyes to adjust to this deeper darkness. The air around her began to lift with the promise of the storm she could now see flickering on the horizon.

One of those fluorescent flashes revealed a tall, lean figure turning the corner at the end of the mews.

Lily moved to follow him, but her polished heels clicked against the cobblestones.

She cursed, pressing herself back into the deeper shadows that disguised the gate. The man at the end of the lane turned, glancing back.

Lily waited, willing herself to invisibility.

He moved on, disappearing around the bend.

She ripped away her shoes, pausing to unhook and tug off her stockings. She tucked the silk into one of the heels and deserted them by the garden gate, hurrying barefoot down the mews.

She emerged by the brick wall that bordered the silent cricket ground.

Her father was a block ahead of her, crossing Wellington Road. Lily followed. The big detached houses on their bright green lawns were dark at this time of night. The street was deserted.

Lily waited in the shadows as a single tram car rattled past. Once it had gone, she could no longer see her father.

The street was broad and empty in either direction. That left only one way he might have gone—into St. John's Wood Church Gardens.

The park lay directly before her across Wellington Road. It presented itself as an elegant row of thick trees, woven through with tidy pathways.

Lily dashed across the open expanse of the road and plunged into the depths of the park.

The trees here were old and thick. During the day, it would be popular with nannies pushing prams or young couples looking for a place to meet that their wealthy parents wouldn't find overly scandalous.

It felt different at night. The dark was thicker here. The air was still, the heat of the day lingering oppressively. The only sound interrupting the silence was the chirp of the crickets.

It was admittedly not the sort of park where shady characters would be prone to gather. The constables of D Division were particularly vigilant to that sort of thing in the posh districts they patrolled. Lily still cursed inwardly that her walking stick had fallen victim to Cannon's ambush. She would have felt significantly more confident pressing on into the park if she had known she could knock down anyone who caused her any trouble.

What was Lord Torrington doing here?

Her feet moved silently along the path, quickly reaching a fork in the way.

There was no sign of her father. She could only guess which direction he had gone.

To the north, slivers of light were visible through the trees. The park this way opened onto another fine street of respectable houses.

The other way led to a deeper darkness, the path twisting into the farther reaches of the park, toward the old church and unused cemetery from which this stretch of wilderness took its name.

Lily took the darker path, her feet soundless on the packed earth.

Low voices carried through the thick air.

She slowed down, approaching carefully.

Her father stood on the path that ran through the old cemetery. The stones leaned at odd angles, picturesquely overgrown with ivy and ferns. Lily could smell the wildflowers that bloomed here during the day.

Lord Torrington looked smart in his evening dress, his black coat contrasting with his white collar and tie. His shoes were polished well enough that they reflected a glimmer of light even here, with the clouds gathered thickly across the night sky beyond the overhanging branches of the old lime trees.

A woman stood beside him.

She was a little taller than Lily, elegantly dressed in a gown of dark purple, her face shaded by a dark veil that fell fashionably from the brim of her hat.

Lily faced the embarrassing possibility that she had stumbled into some sort of illicit rendezvous, but quickly dismissed it. The pair of them weren't standing close enough to be lovers. This was something else.

"As a show of good faith, I'll offer something to you gratis," the woman said. She had a rich, low voice. Her elocution was decidedly upper-class, but there was something just a little bit strange about it. Lily couldn't quite place what it was.

"It will be a bomb," the woman went on, and Lily stopped thinking about accents. "Tomorrow morning. Precisely at six-fifteen."

"Where?" her father demanded.

"I can tell you that it is an economic target. A disaster of the pocketbook. The impact is intended to be costly and disruptive but with minimal loss of human life."

Disruptive. The word sparked a connection to the memo Lily had read in that office in Parliament, the rumor of a disruption the day before the Buckingham Palace talks on Home Rule were to begin. So it was true—the IRB were to be framed for an attack staged by some other organization.

The Red Branch.

A bomb at sunrise tomorrow morning . . . it could not be a mere coincidence. It had to be related to St. Amalgaid's prophecy, but what Lily had glimpsed of that cataclysm did not sound like the economic disruption the woman was describing.

"For anything more than that, you will have to question the gentlemen involved," the woman went on.

"I presume you have identified them?" her father asked.

"I have a name," she replied. "You know my price for it."

Strangford had told her that her father was worrying about a woman, some sort of spy or informant. It was among the scraps of information he had gleaned from sitting in Torrington's chair in The Black Rod's Library.

This must be her. But who was she? Certainly not anyone who worked in an official capacity. She would not be asking for payment if that were the case.

"I can't give you what you're asking for," Torrington said.

"Then this meeting is a waste of my time."

"I had hoped you would consider financial compensation as an alternative," he offered. His tone was businesslike as though they were discussing a trade in stocks.

"I am trading in information today. Not currency," the woman replied.

An auto drove slowly past on the road outside the park. Fragments of light from the headlamps made their way through the trees and shrubs to where her father and the woman stood, briefly illuminating them.

Torrington looked tired. Lily could see the weight of it in the deeper lines of his face.

The veil concealed the features of the woman, all save the neat cut of her chin and the elegant slash of a mouth. It was barely a glimpse, and yet something about the stranger's features tugged at the back of her brain.

"If I were to give you what you are asking for, how could I be assured you wouldn't sell it to the Germans?" Torrington demanded.

"You can't," the stranger said.

A gust of wind rustled the leaves overhead. Lily heard a distant rumble of thunder.

Torrington didn't answer right away. Lily could read the reason in the set of his shoulders, the way his hands clenched at his sides. He was deeply upset.

The revelation shocked her. Her father was a consummate player of games like these. It was his stock-in-trade, collecting information, applying careful pressure, negotiating deals.

The only time Lily had ever seen him truly shaken was when their conversation slipped onto the dangerous ground of the past. The death of her mother. How he had abandoned Lily for the sake of the family he had already betrayed.

That the woman standing at the edge of the cemetery had rattled him that deeply spoke of desperately high stakes.

"You are asking me to risk our defeat in a war. I can't do that," her father finally said.

"What war?" the woman countered breezily.

"You know as well as I do what's been happening in Berlin, St. Petersburg and Paris today."

"And the rest of London will know within the hour," she replied. Lily could see a flash of white teeth as she smiled. "*The Evening Standard* has it. 'Germany declares war on Russia.' They are rushing out a special edition for it."

Lily could see that this struck a blow against her father. She felt it herself.

Germany declares war.

It was happening.

She had known it would come. Her father had warned her of it back in March, in the rich quiet of his study at his country estate in the Sussex Weald. She had been seeing the shadow of it falling across the world for months now—the visions of blasted landscapes, the dead men in Lord Bexley's drawing room.

It would be a disaster even worse than the one St. Amalgaid had raved about, but dispersed across a far greater time, infinitely more complex.

"Of course, if your fat MPs are to be believed, it's nothing for Britain to be concerned about. We shan't be involved in some European scuffle."

Lily could hear the sarcasm in her tone. Torrington did not even bother to refute it. It was clear both he and the stranger in the clearing knew the real implications of the headline about to scream its way across England.

"I wish I could impose upon your patriotism," he said. "Your general humanity."

"I am not English. And my humanity was taken away from

me a very long time ago. You may thank some of your fellow countrymen for that. I take it we do not have a deal?"

"No," Torrington agreed. Lily could see that it cost him to do so.
"Not until you change your terms for payment."

"Well, well. A man with honor. That is a novelty, if not a particularly useful one. You know where to find me if you are the one who
changes his mind."

She called back over her shoulder as she moved away.

"Best ask your shadow to come out now."

Beneath the veil, her gaze slipped to where Lily stood in the gloom.
She flashed a smile like a knife blade and then was gone.

"Lily," Torrington said, seeing her. His expression was one of tired
surprise.

Another hot gust of wind tugged at her hair, the folds of her gown.
She was conscious of her bare feet on the grass at the edge of the path.

"You shouldn't be here," he concluded.

A quick battle raged inside of her. She could feel his exhaustion
and dismay. He knew as well as she did what the news from the continent portended. The disaster he had been fighting desperately to
prevent was upon him, and Lily was about to throw another weapon
at him—now, when he was already worn thin by the weight of the
fate of the world.

She had no choice. Her own disaster loomed closer than his, and
the knowing thing inside of her told her there was still a chance that
future could be changed.

She had to get the truth out of him, and there was only one way
she could see to do that. She launched it at him without warning,
deliberately, knowing that catching him off-guard was the only way
to do this.

"What do you know about the Red Branch?"

The words were a test. Lily knew that two men had come to her
father with information about the organization before they died.

Charlie Prinz . . . and Patrick Dougherty.

If Torrington was complicit with the Red Branch, he would pretend not to know what she was talking about.

A denial would be as good as an admission of his own guilt.

He lowered himself to the bench at the edge of the path. He looked older.

"I swear to you I still do not know the truth," he said. "Was it just a random robbery or did your mother get caught in the crossfire of Dougherty's assassination?"

Lily recognized the weight she heard behind those words. It was one she knew too well herself, the burden of guilt and grief. The feeling that there had been something more to be done, some way to stop it from happening, and that failing to accomplish it left you as responsible as the man who held the knife.

"No one ever claimed responsibility, but then that isn't the way the Red Branch works. They don't trumpet their crimes as accomplishments the way others do," he said.

"Who are they?" Lily demanded, looking down at him.

"An oath-bound society sworn to protect the union between the United Kingdom and Ireland at whatever cost. The members are largely men of Ulster but not exclusively. I believe they were responsible for an attempted bombing in 1893 the last time Home Rule was raised in Parliament. Thankfully the device was discovered and diffused in time."

"Are you part of it?" Lily asked the question plainly. Her heart pounded as she waited for his response.

He looked up to meet her eyes.

"No," he replied. "I am not. But others in positions of high authority are."

He rubbed his eyes, his exhaustion apparent.

"Patrick Dougherty tried to tell me fourteen years ago, but he was hardly the most reliable source. I couldn't be certain whether he spoke from a dramatic turn of mind. He might even have been a Fenian plant, meant to send me spinning down the wrong path. I could not be certain whether his death—your mother's death—was just a terrible coincidence or something more organized."

"Until Charles Prinz showed up with the same story," Lily finished for him.

He stood.

"How do you know about that?"

She swallowed thickly. They were skirting close to a place Lily still wasn't comfortable dwelling.

"No one told me, if that is what you're asking," she replied.

"Then I suppose I know the answer," he said evenly.

He might have pressed for more. She knew part of him must want to. Her father understood something of what Lily was. She had exposed it to him with the carelessness of childhood when keeping her power a secret had been a game she wasn't entirely sure she wanted to win.

Did he suspect some of her friends at The Refuge shared her uncanny knack for knowing things that should have been impossible? If he did, he had never asked—and Lily was hardly going to offer the information.

"These men in positions of authority. Who are they?" she demanded.

"Neither Dougherty nor Prinz would give me the names without a guarantee of protection, and that is no mean thing to muster when any government office might harbor one of the conspirators. I cannot authorize or organize it myself. I hold no position beyond my title. I have influence, and what good is that when you cannot know who your enemies are?"

His pain was closer to the surface now. Lily could sense it in him, even from where she stood on the far side of the path.

The thunder rumbled again, becoming more insistent. The storm would come. It was only a matter of time before it broke.

"I made inquiries, quietly, after Dougherty came to me. And I have never been able to dismiss the possibility that one of those messages reached the wrong people and resulted in his death. In your mother's death. I may have wronged you even more deeply than you have ever suspected, Lily. I am so terribly sorry."

Regret roughened his words, rasped them like sandpaper.

"You couldn't know what would happen," she said softly.

She had known. She had still failed to stop it.

Waking in the night with the image of it blazed across her brain—her mother lying in the alley, crumpled like a paper doll. Dead eyes staring into an empty sky, her crimson gown scattered with jewels.

Now, Lily knew all too well what those symbols had meant. Crimson had stood for the blood staining her mother's ivory dress. The jewels were paste, a clever imitation loaned to her by the dead Irishman who lay just outside the frame.

"Tell me about the woman," she said.

"She calls herself Madame White. I know nothing else of her origins. I only know that she is able to acquire information no one else can find and that it is always accurate."

"You believe she truly has the names of the conspirators," Lily said.

"Yes," he confirmed. "She has them, but that woman owes loyalty to no one but herself. If there is an altruism in her to be appealed to, it is not for the likes of me. I think there is a hatred in her of my kind and I suspect it was likely well earned."

"Isn't there any way you can give her what she is asking for?"

"I can't." The desperation was clear in him, his face long in the dim light of the garden. "I am standing between two disasters. If a bomb goes off tomorrow morning and sabotages the Home Rule conference, we will very likely be dragged into the middle of a vicious civil war in Ireland at the same time that we are forced to intervene in an unimaginable conflict in Europe. We will be torn between two fronts, a situation we cannot possibly emerge from victorious. And yet if I pay her price, it could tell the Germans exactly how to defeat us. Either way we are going to lose. I have been trying to find these men since the moment Prinz stepped into the room and this is as far as I have managed to go."

"How did Prinz come by what he knew?" Lily demanded.

"He worked as an accountant in the War Office. He identified a discrepancy in the paperwork around a shipment of firearms."

"Twenty-thousand rifles," she offered quietly.

He absorbed the impossibility of her knowledge of that.

"Yes. Prinz had evidence that the guns were deliberately misdirected, not stolen or overlooked. Signatures on shipping receipts, the sort of thing only an accountant would notice. There are hundreds of men in power who sympathize with the Unionist cause. They make no secret about it, but this was something else."

"Treason," Lily filled in.

"Treason," her father confirmed. "The deliberate theft of government resources to arm an enemy threatening violent revolt against the will of the king."

"What about Dougherty?"

"He had a . . . relationship. With a Special Branch officer. Someone who revealed names in relation to the attempted bombing in 1893. Dougherty wasn't a rebel but his sympathies lay with the Irish nationalist movement. I believe he could not stomach knowing what he did without trying to do something about it. I know he went to the Fenians, but he must have doubted their ability to bring these men to justice."

"So he came to you," Lily said.

"I did not know him well," Torrington admitted. "I had only seen him a few times in the flat at Oxford Street, but I suppose because he trusted Deirdre he decided he could trust me as well."

He did not say the rest. He didn't have to. Lily could read it in the lines of his face.

Dougherty had trusted Torrington, and he may have died for it.

It felt as though the threads that held the world together were dissolving, exposing fault lines at every angle.

The Red Branch were setting off a bomb at a quarter past six tomorrow morning with the intent that the Irish Republican Brotherhood would take the blame for it, destroying hopes of Home Rule.

Madame White had said the blast would be aimed at an economic target, but either she was wrong or something was going to go horribly awry.

Lily had to find out where that bomb was being set, and she was running out of time.

She needed the names of the conspirators. There was only one living soul she knew had that information.

"Where can I find Madame White?" she said.

He didn't try to tell her it wasn't her fight or that she ought to stay safe. She was grateful for that.

"To arrange a meeting I send a runner to a chip shop in Soho with a note. I don't know how the messages get to her from there, but she always responds."

"You don't know where she lives?" Lily asked.

"She keeps that well concealed," he replied. "But she will answer your message quickly if she is inclined to answer it at all."

"How much hope have I of that?" she demanded.

"Some," he replied truthfully.

"Send your runner," she ordered. "Tell her I want a meeting. She can reply to Robert Ash's house on Bedford Square."

Her father looked down at her, the breeze ruffling his silver hair.

"There is something you are not telling me," he said.

Of course he would sense that. Her father was not one to miss the undertone of a conversation, especially one with the weight of the secrets Lily was carrying.

Might things have been different if she had trusted him? If she had believed from the start that her father could not possibly be involved in murder and conspiracy?

But Lily suspected her father was capable of a great many things. There was honor in him, but he was also deeply pragmatic. He lived his life in a gray space outside the clear lines of right and wrong. Who was to say what compromises he would make in the name of some greater need?

It was possible his influence would have been strong enough to convince the authorities to evacuate millions of people on nothing more than his word. Lily could not have given him anything else. All she had was a tangle of circumstantial evidence and instinct.

No—not instinct. Her knowledge of the connection between Patrick Dougherty's death and St. Amalgaid's disaster was more than instinct. It was a truth gained by way of a power the world could not understand and would not accept.

There was no time for playing might-have-been. The night was slipping away from her.

"If I told you that you had to leave London right now, this hour. Would you go?" she demanded.

The question shocked him. That in itself spoke words. Her father was not a man easily surprised.

"Why?"

"Would you go?" she repeated. Urgency leaked into the question. She was exquisitely aware of everything tomorrow morning might cost her.

"I presume the consequences if I did not are suitably dire?"

"Yes," Lily admitted.

She could see him processing it, his mind working through possibilities, weighing consequences.

"No," he said at last. "I cannot, Lily. Telegrams will fly back and forth from Westminster tonight that might prevent the deaths of millions. I must be there. Whatever that costs me."

She absorbed the blow of that. She had expected it. It meant something that he believed her. She could hear that in his words.

"I understand."

"Is there anything to be done about it?" he asked.

"I am doing it," she replied, meeting his eyes. "Find me Madame White. Send your note."

"I will," he vowed.

There was no more time. Lily knew she had to go. Whatever else there was must be left unsaid.

"If I should need . . ." she began.

"Send to Westminster," he replied. "I must go to the Prime Minister. Mark the message urgent with your name. I will tell the staff to be alert for it. Ask for whatever is required. My resources are not insignificant and they are at your disposal."

"Thank you," she said.

"Lily . . ."

His voice stopped her as she turned to go. She looked back.

"Can you tell me anything that might stop this war?" he asked.

She did not have an answer. She could see that her father understood what that meant.

He turned his head to the south as though he could see across Mayfair and Southwark to the far shores of Belgium and France.

"There is a darkness coming to the world, and I fear I will not live to see the light win through again."

His words danced a chill across her skin though the wind that gusted through the trees, spinning leaves across the path, was still thick with summer heat.

"Send the runner," she finished.

TWENTY-ONE

$\mathcal{L}$ILY HURRIED BACK TO Bexley's house, flying past the shadows of the park and the deserted cricket ground. She was driven by a sense of urgency. She had to find Sam and return to The Refuge as quickly as possible.

Sam was not the only one she would need.

The wind had risen. From eerie gusts it had gone to a steady tumult, tossing the branches of the trees that lined the mews behind Bexley's home.

Black clouds roiled overhead. She felt the first few pings of water against the bare skin of her arms as she reached the hidden gate in Bexley's privacy fence.

She picked up her shoes and pulled the gate open as the sky split, purple lightning sparking across the night. Thunder cracked a moment later.

A rush of delighted screams rose from the few guests still braving the garden. They ran from the imminent downpour. A man held his evening coat over the feather headdress of his companion as they dashed for the open doors of the drawing and dining rooms, which were still crowded with glittering bodies.

She spotted Strangford immediately. He stood at the back of those fleeing the outdoors, his gloved hand on the elbow of an clearly tipsy woman who had lost the heel of her shoe.

He looked back as though sensing Lily's presence by the holly. His dark gaze locked onto her across the length of the garden.

He turned away for just a moment to help the stranger across the threshold. Then he was crossing the manicured lawn to where Lily waited. The wind whipped at his dark hair and the black fabric of his evening coat.

"Where have you been?" he demanded.

"I found my father," she said.

"What did he know?"

"Not enough," she replied.

He was wound like a spring, the tension coiling off of him.

"You should have brought me with you," he said. "I could have learned more from him."

"I believe him, Strangford," Lily said.

"Then what happens now?" he demanded, his anger heating his words.

The sky cracked overhead, the wind pulling at her gown. It mirrored the tumult raging inside of her, a different sort of storm that felt near to a breaking point. In the throes of it, control deserted her, the truth spilling out as though it knew she stood before the one person she had never been able to hide anything from.

"I don't want to die."

"I know," Strangford replied, his voice raw with the feeling of it.

"But I can't run away from this," she admitted.

"*I know.*" The phrase came with more force this time. His eyes were fierce. "Even if I have no right to. Even if I took it from you when you would have kept it for yourself. I can't pretend that I don't. I can't pretend it isn't tearing me apart."

"I know," Lily echoed softly.

"Where does that leave us?" he demanded.

Lily didn't have an answer.

The storm broke over them. Rain pounded down onto the grass, drenching her in an instant. The thunder ripped across the sky, shaking them with its intensity.

She tossed her shoes aside and ran to him.

He caught her. She pulled his mouth to hers and the relief of contact burst over her. She tasted him through the freshness of the rain, shivering at the roughness of his jaw, the way he held her like a life-line, black leather gripping her bare skin.

She needed more than that. She needed to be known.

She took his arm and tore the glove from his hand, throwing it aside, then did the same again and drew his hands to her skin as she kissed him once more. His touch ran over her, electric, singeing at every point of contact.

The rain poured down, running over them like a waterfall. Lightning purpled the sky, thunder rumbling through the ground on which they stood. Lily let herself fall completely into all of it—the storm and the heat and him, always him.

He paused for breath, letting his forehead fall against her own. She could feel the warmth of his exhalation mingling with the torrent.

"I don't know how to do this," he said, the words tangled with pain and need.

"Neither do I," she whispered.

They could not crumble into this gulf, this fracture—not now. The world could not afford it. There was another battle to fight before the sun appeared once more on the horizon.

She pulled back to look at him. He was beautiful in the rain, his dark hair drenched, the water streaming down the planes and angles of his face. She let her fingers glide over him, fearless for the moment of what he might learn from that touch. Her other hand rested where she could feel the powerful rhythm of his heart.

She loved him. She felt that in her bones.

She did not know how anyone could survive without secrets.

She could not possibly let him go.

The threat of a decision hung suspended inside of her, enormous in its significance. She would not make it tonight. For tonight, they would stumble on as they were because a greater purpose demanded it.

"I need you for what comes next," she said. "Will you help?"

"You know better than to ask me that," he replied. "Where do we go?"

~

The silver Rolls Royce swept into the mews behind Bedford Square.

The rain had washed past, leaving behind damp streets and clear air. Sam stopped the motor car at the carriage house behind The Refuge, hopping out to roll open the bay doors.

Strangford had taken a different route, whisking his mother and sister back to Bayswater for a hurried and likely uncomfortable conversation about why they would need to change and hop on a late train to Richmond. Virginia's children were already there, sent to spend the night with Mr. Eversleigh's sister.

Lily did not envy him the task. She suspected that Lady Torrington would not submit to this seemingly mad request without a fight.

He had promised to return to The Refuge within the hour. Lily understood that it must take at least that long for her father's note to find its way to the enigmatic Madame White and for her reply to reach Bloomsbury. Strangford's absence still itched at her.

She climbed out as soon as they were inside the carriage house and handed Sam his damp coat. He had sacrificed it back in St. John's Wood to give Lily something to sit on when she arrived at the automobile soaked to the bone.

"You ought to hang on to that," Sam replied with a nod toward her still sodden gown.

Now that the storm had broken, the air had cooled considerably. Lily was admittedly chilled standing around in her wet clothes.

"Thank you," she said, shrugging the damp coat around her shoulders. It was an improvement, if a marginal one.

A racket sounded from the garden, the regular crack of a hammer.

Lily and Sam pushed out of the carriage house and into the garden, following the sound.

In the dim light, Cairncross was just visible perched atop a ladder leaning against the bricks of The Refuge. He was nailing a board over one of the tall windows to the library.

"Good," he called down, pausing to wipe his brow with a handkerchief. "This will be a damned sight easier with another set of hands."

Sam looked to Lily.

"Go on," she said. "You'll know when there's more to be done."

"Where's Bà?" Sam asked, setting a second ladder against the wall.

"Ash sent him and your grandmother on to the inn at Highgate. They left with Miss Denueve and Miss Bard. Dr. Gardner should be joining them there shortly once he's done preparing things at the hospital."

Lily was relieved to hear that Sam's family had escaped the city.

The sight of Cairncross boarding up the windows made the threat of tomorrow morning feel that much more real. Would his efforts make any difference? Lily recalled the monstrous destruction she had seen in her vision. She could not begin to guess whether Bloomsbury would still been standing.

"Where is Mr. Ash?" she called up.

"Still inside," Cairncross replied. "I know he wishes to speak to you. I believe you can find him in the attic."

She went in through the kitchen, which still smelled of Mrs. Liu's cooking. A covered pot of rice sat on the counter, the clock ticking quietly on the wall.

She climbed the stairs to the hall. The strange artifacts that decorated the elegant space were familiar to her now, turned from rare treasures into old acquaintances.

The library looked different when its great windows gazed out over nothing, the light from inside trapped by the boards Cairncross and Sam were nailing up in an effort to save the glass. There were other things changed as well. Lily was conscious of gaps in the shelves, places where Cairncross had removed the most precious manuscripts for safe storage down in the vaults below the house.

Lily had never been into the cellar. She wondered what might be squirreled away in the depths of The Refuge. There was at least one cabinet of poisons and hallucinogens. Cairncross had mentioned a book that had to be kept chained up like a rabid dog. What else might she find? The journals from Ash's travels around the world? More of his wife's unsettling paintings?

Perhaps a better answer to tonight's desperate quest lay down there, or waited somewhere in the sprawling collection of the library. If that were true, it hardly mattered. Lily didn't have time to go wading through haystacks for the chance of stumbling across a needle.

She continued up the grand stairs to the first floor.

The training room was dark and silent. The weapons mounted on the wall reflected pale slivers of light from the street lamps, fragments that managed to make their way through the boards Cairncross had already fixed to the front of the house.

She followed the hall past Ash's private rooms. The doors were shut, the space beyond dark.

Her motoring outfit was hung where she had hoped it would be, inside the guest room where she had changed after returning from the Crossness Sewer Outfall. Mrs. Liu had washed and pressed it. Her boots were washed and shined as well.

Lily shrugged out of the soaked gown. She was unsure what to do with it, eventually settling on hanging it from the rail over the tub in the adjacent water closet. On the wall beside it hung an illumination ornamented with flaking gold leaf. It depicted the cosmic spheres, red and blue and black, spinning around the oblivious men who labored through the cycle of time.

A wave of longing overtook her, strong enough that she had to cling to the sink to endure it.

This place had become the heart of her world. The fabric of it was wrought through with the souls of the people she loved. The idea that tomorrow it might be swept from the earth made her hands shake.

She pushed from the sink, forcing herself to steady. Navigating the twists of the hallway, she found herself at the foot of the attic stairs.

A light burned at the top, visible through the crack under the door.

The smell drifted down, reminiscent of damp wood and snuffed candles. She thought of her childhood church again, the drone and incense of Mass. An unexpected longing to return to St. Patrick's swept through her, as though going there would bring her closer to God—as though somehow she would be told what she was supposed to do.

That wasn't how it worked.

It would be Sunday tomorrow morning. Would the churches of London still be standing?

She climbed the stairs.

As she neared the top, she realized with cold shock that the curtains were gone.

The yards of black fabric that normally hid Evangeline Ash's last work from view had been taken down. It left the mural completely revealed in the flickering light of the candle on the floor.

The entirety of the artist's creation spun around her, dizzying in its detail and its immensity. It was far too much for her brain to absorb. Some primitive thing inside of her palpitated in the presence of it, urging flight as though the vision of Evangeline Ash represented a threat.

Lily forced herself to focus on one piece of it at a time to keep from being completely overwhelmed. She kept her eyes on the panels she had seen before, but even that was not entirely safe. More details leapt out at her, resonant with significance.

A woman in peacock blue robes danced in the skeletal arms of the dead, but now Lily was confronted by the red ribbon she wore around her neck, dripping blood onto the floor.

The physician was half-buried in a mountain of used syringes and crimson bandages, a broken helmet like a cracked egg rolling at his feet.

The scholar sat in his cave of books, an army rifle leaning against his chair, holding a volume gingerly in hands well-stained with blood.

This was too much, more than she wanted to know—an intimacy she felt she had no right to. It did not help to turn away. The same raw truth assaulted her from every angle.

A young man with a familiar fall of black hair stood with rats at his feet, holding a bouquet of white crosses in his arms. He wore a pair of raven's wings on his back made up of tiny night-dark gears and cogs, and as Lily looked into his eyes they seemed to shift from threat to grief and back again.

A few silvery strands clung to his side. They were part of a grander web, enormous and complex as it spread across the next panel. At its center was not a spider but an elegant white serpent. The web was not made up of threads but of strings of words in a dozen different tongues.

The beautiful skin of the snake was crisscrossed with ancient scars.

On another wall stood a warrior with black gauntlets on his hands. A band of shadow crossed his face, obscuring his left eye, his head crowned with a golden ring of light.

The light was no halo. Lily could see now that it was the crown of an impossible sunrise rendered in otherworldly hues. Pale flowers of kaleidescope shape twined around his boots. Mosaic leaves unfurled beneath a crystalline sky splintered into its most essential geometric structures.

Secrets slipped in and out of all that beauty.

A twist of barbed wire. The pale flag of a woman's slip blowing on a clothesline. A child's misplaced shoe.

It was an arrangement of heartbreaking beauty, and the truth of it sang through Lily like a struck chord. This was Strangford, the full scope of his gift rendered into paint on plaster. It was not just the power to know with a touch, but to peel back the surface of life and see the beauty blazing underneath.

He had been distant from that wonder lately. Lily felt responsible for that.

The painting pressed itself upon her, demanding she experience everything else it was made to reveal.

The land beneath their feet torn asunder, spiked with bones and shrapnel.

Monsters lurking in the shadows, curling their gold-trimmed tentacles out into the world.

The light cracking through the darkness, whipping threads of connection through all of it.

Evangeline Ash's work was a wheel spinning around Lily until she felt like she would be sick. It was as though she could hear the dead woman's voice whispering great and terrible secrets in her ear.

She braced herself against the impact of the mural, regaining enough of her sense to recognize that she was not alone in the attic.

Ash stood beside his own portrait. Unlike the others, whose features were rendered as stylized impressions, the man on the wall was recognizably Ash. He was younger, his beard still rich and brown, the lines of his face softer.

The eyes, though—they were old. Lily recognized the grief in them, the quiet weight that her mentor always carried.

In the portrait, he sat with his legs folded in a pose of meditation, balanced atop a pedestal built of cathedral arches and temple columns, inscribed stones and tattered scrolls.

Artillery shells and a smoldering pyre. The elegant calligraphy of an Arabic phrase.

The herbs from Mr. Wu's garden grew at his feet between a few discarded mechanical raven feathers.

When the true Ash was meditating, his hands were balanced carefully on his knees. The man in the mural was not still. His hands tugged at smoky filaments which stretched back to the other portraits on the wall.

The woman in the arms of the dead. The old soldier with a book in his hand. The snake in her web of words.

In Ash's hands, those lines of connection formed a bridge. It was not a fairy-tale whimsy but had the industrial look of something real, something Lily could almost imagine she had seen before.

It was not elegant, but it was strong, a careful structure of entwined connections that Ash held in his hands.

The artist herself was beside him.

Lily knew that face—the strong brows, the regal nose. She wore a gown in a pattern that seemed to shift as Lily looked at it, refusing to be pinned down into ordinary shapes of pigment.

There was so much more, a complex arrangement of symbols and connections, but what struck Lily with the most force was that the woman was under water.

Her dark hair floated around her, suspended in the murk. A hellish light reflected down from the surface, burnishing the depths with the color of flames.

In that moment, Evangeline Ash's features seemed to shift, and Lily felt she saw her own face hovering in the water, eyes open to the disaster that surrounded her.

She rebelled against it with a sick lurch in her stomach, and the painting resolved once more into the dead woman's form.

Lily was not comforted.

She walked into her own death . . .

If there had ever been any room for doubt as to whether Ash's wife understood what she was doing when she boarded that steamer, her own artwork banished it. Evangeline had known that the water held her fate. When the moment called to her, she had answered it.

"Why?"

The question fell from Lily's lips before she could think better of it.

"Evangeline understood better than any of us the complex relationship between destiny and will," Ash replied.

"So she had a choice."

"I do not believe choice meant to her what it does to us," he said quietly.

He stared at the portrait on the wall. The painted eyes of his dead wife were calm.

"I have tried to make what good of it I can," he went on. "After seeking every source of wisdom, plunging into every tradition, that is all I can be certain of. Evangeline is the only one who might have told me more, and what she knew, she took with her."

"You never found anyone like her? Anyone else who could do what she could?"

"Hers was a khárisma of exceeding rarity," Ash replied.

Lily didn't know how to respond. She was wading in strange waters run through with dangerous currents and the wrecks of history.

"It was her idea, you know," he went on. He gestured around the attic. "This wall was the first one that came down inside The Refuge. I used to let the house next door. The buildings had been sold as a pair but what need had I for all that space? It was Evangeline who began to unite the two sides. To suggest that this place must become something more."

"You think we are why she did it," Lily said.

She was conscious of the black stains marring the intricate mural overhead, Evangeline Ash's whirlwind of stars and gods. The room still stank of burnt paint.

Ash turned to her. His eyes were clear.

"I would not put that burden on you."

Lily heard the determination in those words, and yet they left behind them a quiet doubt.

"Finding a purpose in it—or living without one—that is my own cross to bear," he finished.

"Then why did you do it?" Lily demanded.

"Because I believe that charismatics . . . Sam and Lord Strangford. Dr. Gardner, Miss Deneuve . . . you, Lily, are capable of alleviating some of the suffering of this world. That you have a vital part to play in all of this. I have made it my work to try to help you more fully realize that potential. I cannot say I will always get it right," he added.

Lily was again conscious of the scar on her forehead, of the damage to the opus that surrounded her.

"But if I succeed in guiding you a step or two farther down the path, I will consider it time very well spent," he finished.

It was an answer. She was not sure it satisfied her. She was still too angry, an anger tangled up in her own fear, her guilt at the thought that it might not be enough.

"I don't know," Lily blurted. "I don't know if I can do this."

She knew she was not speaking only of the enormous purpose Ash tried to bestow on her. It was also the cataclysm that threatened with the dawn. The looming vision of her own death, either a promise or a possibility. It was too much, all of it, a responsibility she felt entirely inadequate to.

"You are not alone, Miss Albright," Ash replied.

Lily heard the echo of those words fly across time, across space, growing only richer in their meaning.

"Mr. Ash? Miss Albright?"

Cairncross called from the bottom of the attic stairs, breaking the spell. Ash crossed the charred floorboards to look down at him, Lily following.

The librarian's thin figure was framed in the light from the hall.

"Lord Strangford is here," he said. "And a message has arrived."

TWENTY-TWO

Sunday, August 2
Nearly one o'clock in the morning

𝓛ILY TORE AROUND RUSSELL Square on the back of her Triumph, twisting her way through the elegant streets of Bloomsbury.

Madame White had agreed to a rendezvous. Lily was grateful that the address she named was only two miles away, though Sam made it clear that the location didn't make much sense.

"It's in the middle of the King's Cross rail goods yard," he had said when they saw the note.

The warm air pressed against the light wool of her jacket and her twill trousers, gliding across the fabric of her motoring gloves where they gripped the handlebars. It felt exhilarating to tear through the near-deserted streets of London in the depths of night. The motorbike moved like a cat, whipping around bends as she devoured the road.

She flew past St. Pancras, approaching King's Cross. She could hear the clock tower ring out one o'clock. The sound merged with the echoes of other distant bells calling from across the city.

She was running out of time.

Lily swung around the corner fast enough that the bike tipped her down near the ground, then shot up St. Pancras Road toward the rail yard. She was led on by the elegant spires of the gasometers rising over the rooftops ahead.

She passed between those great rings of iron girders as she turned into the rail yard. They loomed over her like the shadowy crowns of giants.

She stopped at the glittering barrier of Regent's Canal. Lights were on in a distant reach of the rail yard on the far side of the water, but here all was dark and quiet save for the odd rat scurrying out of her path.

The address in the note was on Cambridge Street, but there was nothing on that short stretch of road but the hulking, shadowy structure of one of the coal drops.

The coal drop was an enormous building running the length of the canal-facing side of the road. It stood three stories high. The ground floor was made up of dozens of arched brick bays. Fifty years ago, this would have been a hive of activity as coal from the north was dumped, sorted, and then transported across the city by cart or barge.

Now, most of the bays on this side looked abandoned. The wooden gates hung ajar or had been ripped off for salvage.

An elevated rail line still ran against the third floor, the girders casting strange shadows onto the street.

It made little sense as a spot for a rendezvous.

The road was not entirely deserted. Lily saw a few men standing by one of the great dark bays. The sound of their laughter echoed across to where she lingered in the shadows. Lily could hear that they were drunk.

A flicker of movement drew her eyes to a woman in an off-the-rack evening gown smoking a cigarette. A man in a flash waistcoat leaned against the wall beside her, clearly flirting.

Lily cut the engine of the bike. As its rattle receded, she could hear the distant thump of drums, the thin squeal of a horn.

The pieces came together and she realized where Madame White had really brought her.

It had to be one of the illegal nightclubs that peppered the city. Dodging licensing laws and opening far past legal hours, some of these establishments took the chance of maintaining a permanent address. Others—like this one, she suspected—popped up on a whim in places they thought the police unlikely to notice.

Like the King's Cross coal drops.

Though Lily saw no sign of them, she knew Sam and Strangford must be near. Madame White's note had demanded that Lily come alone, but Sam was less concerned about the mysterious woman's ability to detect a shadow than he had been with Cannon in Limehouse.

They would be close. Strangford had a particularly important role to play in what was to come.

Lily slid her bike into the narrow gap between a pair of sheds, hiding it from a casual eye, and threaded her chain through the wheels. She looked over to where the laughter rang off the stones.

A young couple were approaching the arch by the circle of drunks. This dark bay still retained its wooden gate, the aged boards stained with soot. The woman's dress glittered in the faint light spilling across the yard. She leaned against a dandy with polished shoes.

A large bear of a man stepped away from the wall as they approached. There was a brief exchange of words and cash before the gates parted and the couple disappeared inside.

Steeling herself, Lily approached the door.

The big man eyed her as she arrived, his eyes moving from her cropped hair to her driving gloves and the leather boots on her feet.

"There's a dress code," he announced.

"Are trousers and jacket a violation?" she demanded. She had little patience for this. Issues of wardrobe had already taken up far too much of her time this evening.

He frowned. "No," he admitted. "But I'm not sure about the boots."

"Would you like to take a closer look at them?" Lily snapped.

"I suppose not," he sighed. He pulled open one of the enormous wooden doors. "Four shillings."

Lily handed him the money and stepped inside.

The bay was made of vaulted bricks, the ceiling soaring over her head. Cables snaked along the floor, powering electric stage lights rigged up with colored film. They painted the sooty walls with red light.

The music was louder here, thumping down the stairs with a wild rhythm entirely unlike the lilting violins in St. John's Wood.

She climbed the rickety wooden steps, the music escalating in volume until she stepped through a black curtain onto the upper floor.

Sound roared at her.

The clatter of a hundred voices competed with the wail of the band set up on raised staging to her right. The musicians were all of African descent. What they played sounded akin to ragtime but less cheerful and more wild. A small, thin woman in a glittering dress sang with a voice three times her size, holding court over a dance floor crowded with close-pressed bodies.

The room itself was as big as a church. The ceiling soared overhead, held aloft by ornate iron columns speckled with rust. The air smelled of sweat and whiskey, thick with heat as though the storm had never broken here.

On the far side, black curtains concealed what must be the windows that faced the canal. They were either opened or long deprived of their glass based on the way the black fabric swayed in a breeze that Lily could not feel.

More stage lights provided the only illumination. These cans had been rigged behind shreds of green film that danced in the breeze from carefully placed electric fans, painting the walls in a moving field of eerie light.

That flickering tugged at the back of Lily's brain, leaving her feeling even more uneasy than she had been already.

Little work had been done to convert the space from coal sorting floor to nightclub. The big iron hoists still loomed overhead, their massive pulleys and hooks hung from big cables tied back with a bit of rope to clear the floor for the party. Tobacco smoke clouded her view. She thought she caught a whiff of the sweet stench of opium.

The rest of the setting was a superficial lacquer slapped up over the industrial space. Potted ferns and tapestries punctuated a mismatched assortment of sofas and tables. A slapdash mural with modernist ambitions covered the wall behind the worktable they had converted to a bar. Lily suspected the paint wasn't entirely dry.

She slipped into the chaos, looking for some sign of the woman from the St. John's Wood cemetery.

A girl and a man in a pinstripe suit necked obliviously in an armchair. A drunk stumbling onto the dance floor nearly knocked over a pair of handsome young men. An older crowd hovered over an assortment of craps tables.

Lily glanced back to the door just as Strangford ducked past the black curtain.

He was still in his evening dress, but he had taken the gloves from his hands. Lily knew what that must cost him, how vulnerable it made him in this close-packed crowd. He held himself carefully, moving quickly aside when a pair of dancers veered near him.

The crash of the music, the cacophony of voices, the close press of bodies—it would strike at him like an artillery barrage.

With a tension in his jaw only Lily could see, he pushed into the room.

He would not come to her. Their plan depended upon Madame White's ignorance of their connection.

Lily put more distance between herself and Strangford. She stopped at the curtains that covered the far wall. Pulling one back, she found herself looking out of a great, glassless window over the gleaming ribbon of the canal.

The narrow water was flush with the edge of the building, punctuated by little piers that would have allowed barges to pull up and load directly from the bays on the ground floor.

The breeze caressed her skin, briefly breaking the suffocating warmth of the nightclub.

Lily stepped back, letting the curtain fall into place, and realized that she was no longer alone.

A woman stood behind her. She was a bit taller than Lily, roughly her own age and elegantly built. Her thick black hair was held back by a beaded headband. She was clearly of East Asian descent, and something about her features sang of familiarity even though Lily was certain she had never met the stranger before tonight.

"Miss Albright," the woman said, and recognition flared.

Lily knew the voice. It was the same one she had heard in St. John's Wood. The purple gown had been replaced by a pair of flowing white silk trousers and a graceful tunic of the same color.

"Madame White," she stammered in reply. "Thank you for agreeing to meet with me."

"Anything for the daughter of the illustrious Lord Torrington," Madame White replied. "Shall we sit?"

She gestured to a little table.

Lily took the chair across from her. She tried to think of what it was that set the woman so distinctly apart from the chaos of the club—the wailing horns, the roar of voices, the clatter of bottles and ice.

Control—that was the aura Madame White projected. Every gesture, every fluctuation of her expression was a master class in control. It gave her the feeling of being an island in the middle of this sea of humanity, one whose secrets were well shielded.

"Drink?" Madame White asked as a waiter approached.

"No," Lily said.

Madame White waved the man off with a twist of her hand.

"Have you come to buy what your father refused?" she asked.

"Is it still for sale?" Lily returned.

"Everything is for sale. I told your father the price. Can you pay it?"

"I was hoping you might consider an alternative."

"That depends on the alternative," Madame White said.

Lily wasn't quite ready to answer that yet.

"Your name. It's an alias," she said.

"Very astute," Madame White replied dryly.

"But it must mean something to you," Lily pressed.

"Just an old Chinese ghost story about an animal that changes its shape," the stranger returned, shrugging it off with deceptive disinterest.

"Then why use it?"

"Names have power. I prefer not to give anyone power over me."

There was a weight of truth to her words that caught Lily off guard.

"Your name," Madame White went on. "It is also an alias, is it not? I wonder if you even know what your true name is."

Lily's thoughts sucked her back to the end of the Limehouse Cut, to what the Fenian stranger had told her about her mother.

Albright was the bloke she ran off with . . . She was a MacBride.

MacBride. Albright. The Torrington family name, Carne. Which of them did Lily have a rightful claim to?

"Maybe I don't need a name to have power," Lily cut back.

Madame White absorbed this, and Lily thought she saw the slightest nod of respect.

"The information your father wished to buy was very difficult to acquire. It therefore commands a high price. What are you offering?"

"Miss Albright. What an unexpected delight."

Madame White turned at the sound of this new voice. Strangford stood at their table. He hid his discomfort carefully but Lily could still hear it, a thread of tension woven through his words.

His hands were bare at his sides.

"Mr. Rivers," Lily replied, keeping her eyes on Madame White, her tone carefully neutral. Strangford's family name tripped strangely off her tongue. "Allow me to introduce you to Madame White."

Strangford turned to the woman across the table.

"Charmed, Madame," he said.

He extended a hand, pale skin catching fragments of the strange light that flickered up the walls.

Lily's heart pounded. Everything depended upon what happened next.

The spy continued to gaze at Lily. Her mouth quirked into a cold little twist of a smile, then her focus shifted, the subtle intensity of it coming to rest on Strangford.

Deliberately, she set her long, elegant fingers against his hand.

Lily watched the impact of that touch wash over him. Strangford gasped in shock and pain. He dropped to his knees, Madame White's hand still clutched convulsively in his own. He managed to release his grasp, cradling the limb against his chest like someone burned.

"Such a pleasure to finally make your acquaintance, my lord," Madame White said calmly.

My lord.

The words were a message. Lily heard it clearly. Madame White had known exactly who Strangford was.

"What did you do to him?" Lily demanded.

"She is full of pain," Strangford rasped in reply. He leaned against the table like a boxer at the losing end of a match.

"I showed him what I wanted him to see," Madame White clarified.

The very notion of it was a firework exploding across her brain, and yet Lily didn't doubt the truth of it. Somehow this stranger had been able to direct the course of Strangford's power, the same power that tossed open the most secret corners of Lily's mind like the pages of a magazine.

"How?" she demanded.

"I have a great deal of experience hiding what I really think," Madame White replied.

Strangford's hands were shaking.

"I am so sorry," he said.

The words had weight. Lily felt the significance of them but could not say whether Strangford was expressing sympathy for the suffering the woman had experienced or apologizing for trying to violate the privacy of her mind.

"That means nothing to me," Madame White retorted.

They were losing control. No—they had never had it. Madame White held all the cards, more of them than Lily had ever suspected.

Strangford had been taken off the table. Lily needed another play.

The sense of threat provoked by the room around her grew, nearly overwhelming her with the strange urge to flee. She resisted it, grasping at the only idea that came to her. It was a wild gambit. She had nothing else to try.

Lily might not have her father's access to Britain's military secrets, but she did know what waited for the city of London with the dawn.

"You asked what I was offering," she cut in, compelling Madame White's attention. "I have an answer."

"I am listening," the woman replied.

"Your life," Lily said.

Madame White looked disappointed.

"Is that a threat?"

"It isn't me that threatens it," Lily said.

The woman across the table absorbed this thoughtfully.

"What, then?" she asked.

"First you give me the names."

"But we both know what I bring to this bargain has value," Madame White replied. "I have no assurance that what you offer is worthwhile."

More was required. It would mean revealing exactly what Lily was to this stranger—a stranger who traded in secrets and information. The notion sent a bolt of fear flickering through her, and yet the woman's playing of Strangford showed that Madame White already knew far more about Lily and The Refuge than she should.

Lily was out of options and out of time. Whatever the risks, this was her only chance to get what she had come here for.

The club roared around her. Lily pushed her focus away from the riot of noise and movement to something deeper, reaching for her power.

Instinct flashed around her, lighting on seemingly meaningless things.

A man with a glass of whiskey in his hand sitting across from a woman in a lace gown.

A waiter hovering beside a potted palm.

A table near the dance floor covered in glittering bottles.

She felt the press of imminent revelation . . . and then everything shifted.

Green flames crawled up the walls. Breaking glass rang like tiny bells. Screams cut through the air around her.

Madame White's skin shimmered, rippling over with the scales of an ivory snake.

The truth crashed over her with the force of a wave.

The warehouse at St. Savior's dock was gone. Lily's vision had never been about that physical building. It had stood as a symbol for something else, as a snake might stand for a woman she had not yet met.

The warehouse was her mind's way of filling in for a space Lily could not possibly have imagined—the place she now sat in.

What she had foreseen was happening right here—right now.

TWENTY-THREE

"I THINK THIS IS A waste of my time," Madame White said.

The words rang in Lily's ears, firing urgency through her bones. Fear crippled her, twisting her into knots. The need to run pounded against her with the beat of the music.

Lily gripped the edge of the table with her gloved hands, forcing herself to stay.

"Lily . . ." Strangford started. She cut him off.

"The bomb tomorrow morning won't be what you think," Lily blurted.

"I have my information from a very reliable source," the spy replied.

"Your source doesn't know. Nobody knows this. Just me." Lily stumbled on, aware of the time—of how little of it she might have. "It's going to be bigger than anyone planned." She closed her eyes, the memory of her vision of that apocalyptic destruction churning her stomach. "Much, much bigger."

"Collecting the materials for a blast of any substance cannot be done without making waves. How do you think I learned of this bomb in the first place? Even the trains transporting government ammunition and explosives cannot be kept in perfect confidence. The logistics of procurement and transportation are dull secrets, easily dropped when men are in the company of those they under-estimate. Were tomorrow's bomb any larger, there would be more waves. I would know," Madame White said.

"I don't think it's intentional," Lily countered. "Something is going to go wrong. The result is . . . catastrophic."

The word felt too small. Lily had no better one to describe the desolation she had foreseen.

Madame White was quiet. Lily pressed on.

"You knew what Strangford was. You knew it before he touched your hand. That's how you were able to prepare yourself."

Those last words nearly choked her. A small part of her burned with jealousy that Madame White had managed to do that, though Lily was certain that the ability came at great cost.

"You must know what I am," she finished. "And I am telling you that if that bomb goes off tomorrow morning, millions of people are going to die. If you have any desire to the see the light of another sunrise you should leave this city now. And if there is any part of you that holds some shred of human decency you will give me the name of the man involved so that I stand some chance of stopping this disaster from happening."

Madame White watched her quietly from across the table, and Lily knew that her mind must be furiously calculating.

Behind her, a man spilled his glass of whiskey on the lap of a woman in a lace gown.

To her left, a waiter dodged back to avoid being knocked into by a pair of drunks on the dance floor. His boot connected with the potted palm, tipping it over.

The sense of imminent danger crawled up her spine, but Lily was frozen in her chair, waiting for Madame White's response.

"Thank you for telling me," she finally replied. "But I will not give you what you have come here for."

Something was happening over by the doorway, shouting and a general clatter. Lily was only half aware of it, reeling from the impact of knowing she had run out of options, until she caught sight of Sam's tall, lean figure skidding his way through the knots of people.

The bouncer from the gates appeared in the doorway behind him, shouting.

Sam dodged through the crowd with the speed and nimbleness of a man who spent the better part of his childhood as a pickpocket.

"It's a raid," he announced as he reached the table. "Half a division of Peelers outside. We need to go."

He was standing right beside Madame White, but didn't bother to look at her until the words were out.

Once he did, he reeled back as though from a blow.

"Jiějie," he gasped. "Zhao Min!"

Zhao Min.

The name had power.

Madame White rose from her seat, uncoiling like a viper prepared to strike. The rage that simmered under her skin was a palpable thing, sizzling at Lily from across the table.

"Wu Zhao Min is dead," she replied. "You have no sister."

Sister. The face in a sepia photograph flashed across her mind, the stern-eyed girl in the back of Sam's family portrait. It was the same child who had been snatched from the streets of Limehouse, swallowed into the cavernous underworld of that dockside borough.

Screams rose from the dance floor as a wave of blue-clad constables pressed through the door.

The table covered in bottles tipped over, crashing to the floor in an orchestra of breaking glass.

Lily stood.

"We need to go," she announced.

Her senses were alight, her instinct buzzing. She knew what was coming next the moment before it happened. She was ready for it.

Zhao Min ran.

Lily bolted after her.

She had known Sam's sister for only a short time, but she was certain Zhao Min was not the sort of woman to walk into a room with only one exit. She would know another way out. Whatever that was, Lily and the others needed to follow her through it.

The nightclub had devolved into chaos. Dancers bolted in every direction, tripping over chairs and shoving each other aside. The police had quickly resorted to swinging truncheons. Bottles shattered. Tables rolled across the floor. The stage cans continued to burn, projecting fields of green flame across the scene.

Zhao Min raced for the side of the building that faced the canal.

Lily knew Sam and Strangford would be behind her, but there was no time to look back. Zhao Min was fast. Desperation fueled Lily's steps, lending her enough speed to keep pace.

At the back corner of the room, Zhao Min ripped a small carpet out from under a table and chairs, sending them flying.

One of the great black curtains hung behind her, blocking another window opening to the canal.

Where the carpet had been lay a hatch in the floor.

Across the room, the beams holding aloft the backdrop of the stage tipped over, crashing into the rusting iron hoist that arched overhead.

The great iron hook and pulley knocked loose, swinging down toward them on a fraying cable.

Zhao Min was turned away, her hands on the ring of the hatch, hauling it open.

Lily did not need to be psychic to know what would happen next.

There was no time for a warning. There was only a choice, one made in the space of a heartbeat.

She was Sam's sister, and Sam was family.

As Zhao Min rose, Lily leapt. She shoved the taller woman in the back, pushing her out of the way of the swinging pulley. Instead of bashing into Zhao Min's head, it struck Lily in the chest.

The wind rushed out of her. Her body flew back into the black curtain—and then through it.

She plummeted through the cool night air of the rail yard.

Then she hit the water.

Agony arced through her back, her thighs, and then the canal swallowed her like a stone.

Lily knew she should fight, should swim, but her arms refused to obey. They remained limp at her sides as she sank.

She struck the bottom hard enough to send lights flickering across the back of her vision. They melded with the green flames that flickered across the surface of the water a few feet overhead.

Her lungs had been empty of air from the moment she fell. Oblivious to the desperate resistance in her mind, Lily's body drew in a breath.

Water poured into her core, burning like liquid fire.

She was drowning.

Her will fought it with wild energy even as her body gave in. The canal blazed inside of her, tearing her apart. More lights popped and burst across her vision, tributes to her dying brain.

And then she was gone.

—

The grass goes on forever.

It is like the marsh at Graveney where Joseph Hartwell's legacy made a final procession to the sea. But this is not Graveney.

Ravens pass overhead, black wings ragged against the twilit sky. Their calls are the only sound but the quiet lap of the water that laces through the ground.

Not land. Not sea. Somewhere in between.

Stars peer through the purple velvet, adhering to no order Lily has ever known. There is no moon, not even a shadow of darkness where the moon might once again be.

A narrow road unfolds before her like a pale ribbon against the whispering green.

Whatever you do, stick to the path.

Adler's words from Graveney snake through her mind. Lily feels the truth of them in the longing distance of the marsh unfurled around her, in its silence and its space.

She walks for what seems like hours. The purple sky with its distant, intermittent stars never changes. It remains trapped between evening and night, night and dawn. Lily moves through the space that lies between the hands of every clock.

Finally, there is a shore.

The sea falls softly against a thin curve of white sand. Waves rush gently back and forth from the prow of a small boat.

The vessel is built of storm-weathered wood. It has no sail, no oars. Lily is drawn to it at the same time that the sight of it fills her with fear and regret. It seems she hears an old song in her ears, a woman's familiar voice mingling with the rustle of the sea.

The wind teases her hair, sand clinging to her boots.

A woman rises from the waves.

She stands in the water a few yards from the shore, submerged to the waist. She is naked, adorned only by the luxurious thickness of her dark hair.

Lily knows her face. She knows the strong brows, the regal cut of her nose—the eyes that see into a distance few could stand to contemplate.

"Evangeline Ash," Lily speaks.

"Yes," the dead woman confirms.

The sound of her voice summons painful memory. Lily is struck by screams and breaking glass, the cold slap of water against her back.

"I've died," Lily offers.

"Yes," Evangeline Ash confirms.

The breeze ripples the grass. The sea washes against the sand, the stars glittering overhead. A raven flutters to the bleached root of a sea-tossed tree. It perches there, impassively watching.

"What about the boat?" Lily asks.

"It's how you cross to what's next."

She can imagine so vividly how it will work. She will step inside, the old wood creaking softly under her weight. The waves will rush up, lifting her out into the water. She will pass across the sea, leaving the flat trail of a wake behind her.

She aches for it with a longing, and yet she hesitates, held back by a nagging resistance.

"Is this it, then? My fate," she asks.

"This is all of our fates," the woman in the water replies. "You want to know if you came here by the right path."

"Did I?"

"Yes," Evangeline Ash says. "And yes, and yes, and yes, and yes."

The truth of it settles into her bones.

"There is more than one right path," Lily says.

The dead woman smiles.

"More than one of many things."

Lily can see it again—the portrait this woman painted of her. A figure woven through with keys, with doors—not one but hundreds, thousands of them.

She remembers when she glimpsed it for herself, felt time split into two, three, five . . . one hundred and forty-four . . .

More than one.

"You mean the future," Lily returns.

"Yes," Evangeline Ash replies.

And yes, and yes, and yes, and yes . . .

Something in Lily trembles like a drum about to be struck. She recalls other words this woman once spoke to her, impossibly, in the throes of a drug and a vision that should not have been possible.

Stop fighting. Ask for what you want.

A pivot shifts beneath her. The raven watches from the branch with an impatient shuffle of claw.

On the wall of the attic of The Refuge, with hair of flame and a yew staff in her hand, something powerful waits to be spoken into life. To be named.

Will and fate. The dance of the Parliament of Stars. Lily feels it rage inside of her.

Ask for what you want.

What you want . . .

She knows the answer. She can still feel the fear that has always crowded it out, that dark and flapping terror of the responsibility that hushed it into stillness. But in this place, on the verge of this quiet sea, at last she knows.

"I am the Prophetess," she speaks, feeling the clear call of her voice ring across the stars. "And I want to see."

And then she does.

Cracks tear across the sky, doors splitting apart the fabric of the moment. They open to the light of a thousand futures, an infinity of possibility anchored in countless tiny movements—the swing of a woman's arm, the flight of a wounded bird.

A broken mirror.

The crack of a match.

The weight of something cold in her pocket.

The power washes over her, ripping holes in the matter of who she was. Lily is shredded by it, burst asunder into something built of shards of what-might-yet-be.

It calls for her to fall, to come completely apart, giving way for something unimaginable.

"No," Lily whispers, clinging to a remaining fragment of her voice. "Not that. Not yet."

She weaves herself back together, pulling at the strands against the blast of this becoming. The Triumph rumbling under her boots. The weight of Cat on her stomach when she wakes up in the morning. The grief in her father's eyes. The sharpness of Sam's smile. Strangford's hands on her skin.

God help me, Lily, but I want you anyway . . .

The burden of blood and bones and flesh, full of pain and need. She roots herself in it, and yet she can feel how precarious it is that something so enormous should be housed in such a frail and vulnerable shell.

Another wave hushes across the shore. The water kisses Lily's fingers where they dig into the sand. She can feel the damp through the knees of her trousers.

"Very well," says the woman standing in the waves. There is a wry twist to the words, and yet they wash over Lily like a benediction. "Now comes the choice."

On the pale finger of the branch, the raven stretches its wings.

"I have a choice," Lily echoes, because now she can feel it too, a humming potential in the soft song of the wind, the rustle of the grass. "But what about fate?"

Evangeline's mouth twists, her eyes bright and deep.

"Fate takes care of itself," she replies.

Lily takes a breath. The sea calls to her, tugs with a longing of unspeakable beauty. It is everything—the deepest love, the most lasting peace, the wildest adventure.

"I'm going back," she says.

"This might hurt," Evangeline Ash warns.

~

The hurt found her on a slab of concrete. It ripped through her body, spilling acid into her lungs and lightning down her limbs.

Lily gasped. The breath was agony. Her body heaved in response, a tide of canal water flooding out of her.

She wheezed, and air came in to fill the place the water had left. It was fire inside her body, but she did it again—another ragged inhalation forced past the pain.

"Lily."

Strangford leaned over her. His jacket was gone. He was soaked through, shirt plastered to his shoulders, his hair still dripping into eyes hollow with fear and relief.

Sam stood behind him, his face drawn into an agony of worry. He breathed out something Lily knew was a prayer, every line of him sagging as the tension uncoiled.

She reached a trembling hand for Strangford. It was all the invitation he needed. He pulled her against him, holding her as though afraid she would turn to sand and slip through his grasp.

She felt the heat of him through the soaked linen of his shirt, tasted the murk of the canal water. There was blood on her hand from where her knuckles had grazed the concrete. She relished all of it.

"You got her back," Sam croaked from above.

"What do you mean?" Lily asked, pushing back to look at them.

"I asked Gardner," Strangford replied. "After I learned what you'd foreseen. Whether there was any way to recover someone who had . . ."

He couldn't manage the word. The near pain of it choked him. It was a palpable thing, that pain, the raw edge of it so close to his surface that even Lily could feel it.

"Drowned. Someone who had drowned," she filled in gently.

"He was breathing for you." Sam's voice still shook.

"Gardner didn't know whether it would work," Strangford went on. "He said it didn't, more than half the time. I couldn't tell him why I was asking. I didn't know if I would be near enough to you when it happened. But I couldn't just . . . I had to try—"

She kissed him then, holding his rough face in her hands. She could feel the tears on his cheeks mingling with the damp of the water.

Had it been Strangford's breath that brought her back? Her sense of that other place was fading, receding like the edge of a dream, but she knew there had been a choice.

Perhaps they had done it together, him on one side of the divide and her on the other, building the slender cord of a bridge.

"Thank you," she said.

He laughed, a broken sort of sound, and then he kissed her again.

Strangford climbed to his feet, helping Lily up beside him. She needed the help. She felt shockingly weak. Everything hurt.

She could see now that they were some distance away from the coal drops, standing at the edge of the wasteland that lay beside the rail bridge over the canal.

The raided nightclub was still buzzing with activity, the lights and voices distant from where they were concealed in the gloom. The rail goods yard slept across the narrow band of water.

"He wanted to jump after you but I made him go down through the hatch," Sam offered. "The water's only four feet deep. He'd have cracked his head open. It's lucky you landed like you did. Must've been flat on your back. I didn't know you were a bloody circus diver."

Lily reached out to take Sam's hand. He squeezed back, and she could feel the tremble in his grip. It said more than words.

Knowing hummed in her. Lily turned toward the shadowy brush of the wasteland.

"Someone is coming," she announced.

"We can get clear of them this way," Sam said, nodding toward the nearby rail bridge.

Lily held back, a new instinct tugging at her, pointing like a compass toward the shadows.

"Wait," she ordered quietly.

A moment later, a pale figure emerged from the darkness.

Wu Zhao Min stopped halfway across the rough ground.

"It seems you managed to fulfill your part of the deal," she said.

Lily recalled the arc of the hoist, the block of metal swinging toward Zhao Min's head. The impact of it against her own chest. She could still feel it, a sharp ache in her ribs.

Sam stepped forward. Lily could feel the tension simmering through him. His sister glared, a look with enough force to hold him in place.

"Cannon told me you were dead," he blurted.

"And you believed him?"

"He had your slipper."

The words were a plea, one that even Sam knew had little strength.

"Because he helped the men who took me," Zhao Min replied. Her words were daggers. "They found me through you. The second time that you managed to destroy my life."

It was a blow, and it found its mark. Sam was shattered by the impact of it.

"I didn't know," he pleaded.

"But you still might have found me. You could have taken me out of there if you'd had the spine to do what was required."

Lily did not miss the implication. Sam's words on a Limehouse street corner came rushing back to her.

Would've been different if I'd had the stomach to pay the ravens their price.

Zhao Min knew. How could she not? She had grown up side by side with Sam. She was fully aware of his power—and of the powers of the animals he communicated with.

Animals like the ravens.

They can find anyone.

"Sam wasn't the one who hurt you," Strangford said. The words had more weight coming from someone who had shared that pain, thrust into it by his power and Zhao Min's immense will.

"His name is Xiang. Wu Xiang," Zhao Min retorted. "And while he stewed in his cowardice I made my own escape from that hell. I tricked secrets from the men that used me and turned them to my own purpose. I sold and blackmailed and cheated my way out and then I taught other women to do the same. I built my own security and it depends on no one but myself. All of it no thanks to you, Dìdi. You are as guilty as the worst of them."

Zhao Min's pain was a force, a raw and visceral thing. It struck her brother with devastating impact, rendering him speechless.

That it whipped at him so fiercely was a testament to its strength. Zhao Min was not a woman who easily ceded control to her passions. Even now, Lily could see her reining it back in, wrapping up all that hurt and rage in a web of mastery again.

She set Sam outside the scope of her attention, focusing on Lily once more.

"You paid for a name. It's Bexley," she said. "And now we're even."

She turned and walked back into the night, disappearing into the shadows.

TWENTY-FOUR

Sunday
Two-thirty in the morning
London

$\mathcal{L}$ILY RACED THROUGH THE night-dark city to Westminster Palace. She flowed like water through the near-deserted streets, skimming over the road on her motorbike with the wind tugging at her hair.

The wind cut at the chill in her clothes, still damp from her plunge into the canal. Lily ignored it, pressing on, grateful for the speed of the Triumph through lanes normally crowded with traffic.

As she approached the Houses of Parliament, the clock in the tower showed that it was half past two.

The urgency of that pushed her to more speed.

She wove the motorbike through the stanchions and into Old Palace Yard, skidding to a stop at the Lords entrance. The uniformed doorkeepers turned to her with alarm. Lily swung the vehicle against the wall and dismounted, stalking toward the ancient gate.

The younger of the two guards stepped into her path.

"This building is closed to the public, ma'am," he pronounced.

Lily was conscious of the wildness of her appearance—a woman in wet trousers and a jacket, her hair tangled from the wind of the ride. She knew her chances of success were slim but waded in regardless.

"I need to see Lord Torrington," she demanded.

"I cannot let you pass," the doorkeeper replied staunchly.

"This is a matter of the utmost urgency. I can assure you that he will be outraged if he learns that you turned me away."

The authority in her tone made an impact. The younger doorkeeper glanced to his older colleague, the look a question.

The older man subtly shook his head.

Lily gritted her teeth.

Her father had told her to send word. He could not have imagined that Lily might turn up herself at the gates for his help. He had told the Westminster doorkeepers to pass on a message, and that was clearly all they were willing to do.

She could not waste any more time arguing. As tempted as she was to try to force her way inside, she was without her walking stick and could see another pair of uniformed men peering through from within. Even if she managed to slip past the gate, she would not get far.

Lily stalked back to the Triumph and pulled a folded paper from her saddle bag. The message was scribbled on a crumpled receipt for carriage parts from Sam's pocket, the only dry paper available to her. Lily had folded it as neatly as she could. So much was riding on what more or less amounted to a scrap of refuse.

She thrust it at the older of the two guards, whom she could see had more authority.

"You will see this delivered," she ordered.

He accepted it from her, holding the paper gingerly between his fingers as though afraid it might bite. He read the address scribbled in pencil on the folded exterior of the receipt.

If her father had done as he promised, those words should ensure that the message—however humble in appearance—found its way into his hands.

For Lord Torrington. Urgent. Miss Lilith Albright.

The doorman bowed.

"Thank you, miss. I will ensure it reaches his lordship," he replied.

He stepped through the gate into the hallowed precincts of the building. Lily could not follow, and her urge to wait outside for a response was futile. Her message would be delivered. Her father's orders were not lightly ignored or disobeyed, however unorthodox they might appear, but there was no telling what arcane system must be used to get the message from the yard to wherever Torrington was inside.

If the note reached him in time to bring aid, it would have served its purpose.

Lily could not afford to wait and see.

She picked up the Triumph and swung her leg over the seat, pedaling the motorbike to speed and sparking the engine back to life. She tore away across the yard, heading north.

Hyde Park was a sprawling patchwork of light and shadow to her left as she rode, its pathways deserted of all but a few wandering lovers and the odd drunk finding his way home.

She crossed the canal again in Lisson Grove. Her motorbike bounced over the grooves of the bridge. The water was a silver ribbon beneath her, passing in a breath—such a slender thing to have robbed her of her life until Strangford stole it back for her.

She reached her goal a few quick minutes later—the leafy shadows of St. John's Wood Church Gardens.

The Triumph bumped over the curb and Lily wove onto the tree-lined pathways.

She found them in the cemetery.

Lily's ride had mostly dried her clothes, but Strangford was still noticeably wet under his evening coat. The canal water was apparent in the transparency of his shirt and the close hang of his trousers.

"Did you get through?" Sam demanded.

Xiang, Lily thought to herself, recalling the true name his sister had revealed back at the coal drops.

Both of his names felt right to her. It was as though she saw him with doubled vision.

Xiang, the proud and curious boy in the photograph on his father's desk.

Sam, her fierce and clever friend, as much a creature of London as the rats he ordered about her streets.

"They accepted the note," Lily informed them.

"And what happens if it doesn't make it to your old man till breakfast?" Sam said.

"We can't afford to wait that long," she replied.

"No," Sam agreed. "And there's one option none of us have had the guts to speak of yet, but it's time we stopped stalling off."

"And what option is that?" Lily demanded.

"We ask the birds," he replied.

Sam's meaning was clear as ice.

Memory rushed over her, every detail fresh. The sound of Joseph Hartwell's body sliding across the icy shingles of a roof in Hampstead Heath. The soft thump of black wings as the dark bird on the chimney stack flew down to claim its prize.

"They'll want an eye. Whose would you offer them?" she demanded, feeling sick.

"Mine," Sam retorted.

She felt the pain that lay behind the word. This wasn't about the disaster that threatened with the dawn. It was about the day Zhao Min disappeared from Limehouse, about the burden of guilt she had thrown at his feet in the wasteland by Regent's Canal.

"No," Lily said.

"It ain't your choice," Sam shot back.

"Your ravens," Strangford cut in quietly. "Would they bring you word in time?"

"They're as quick as they want to be," Sam replied, glaring back at him.

"And they are carrion eaters," Strangford noted. "Perhaps they would rather feast on what's coming than help you stop it."

Sam met Strangford's quiet challenge unflinching.

"Sacrifice means more to them than carnage," he said, and the certainty in his words chilled her.

"By how much of a margin?" Strangford pushed back.

She could see Sam hesitate, but with a sinking in her heart she wondered if he was right. Perhaps the ravens were the answer.

As she thought it, the space around her seemed to shift. The trees of St. John's Wood became walls of ancient stone beside the flat and glittering road of the Thames.

Sam kneels in the dirt, hands bound behind his back. Birds perch on rock and branch, watching with fathomless eyes. The words of a bargain are spat into the night.

The beating of black wings. A scream and a spray of blood.

Lily snapped back to the cemetery, gripping the cold the steel of the Triumph, anchoring herself in the lingering damp of her coat. She was breathless, her guts churning.

"Lily?" Strangford asked, looking at her with concern.

"There has to be another way," she ground out.

The words were a plea. An answer seemed to come in a scent on the breeze, the perfume of black roses blooming in a walled garden.

The sense of rightness set her heart pounding.

"We aren't going to the ravens," Lily declared. "We will get the location of the bomb from Lord Bexley."

"He ain't going to give it up willingly," Sam retorted. He nodded insolently at Strangford. "You going to hold him down and tear it out of him?"

"If I have to," Strangford quietly replied.

"And then he'll know exactly what you are," Sam snapped back. "Imagine a bloke like Bexley could have quite a bit of fun with that if we don't come out on top of this."

"If we don't come out on top of this, we'll all be dead," Lily cut at him.

Sam muttered a ferocious curse under his breath, but Lily could see him give way and knew that they had won the argument about the ravens—for now.

"This won't be like waltzing into Harrod's," he pressed. "Lord Bexley will have a dozen servants packed into the corners of that big house and there are only three of us. I can pick the lock, but what happens after that?"

Lily took a deep breath.

"I will get us through," she vowed.

Sam wanted to protest. He knew as well as she did how thoroughly she had failed to manage something like this in the past. All those exercises Ash had set up for her, trying to teach her to call up her power at will and use it to see a few steps ahead.

She still had bruises to prove it, mingling now with the damage she had done to herself when she fell from the coal drop.

"The stakes are high," Lily added softly.

Sam's mouth twisted and Lily braced herself, waiting for him to voice the doubt that trembled under her own surface.

He turned to Strangford instead.

"What about you? Could you read a man in his bed without waking him up?"

"I suppose that will depend upon how soundly he sleeps," Strangford said.

"This is cracked," Sam concluded.

"I'm telling you it's our best chance," Lily cut back. She felt the truth in the words, even though she didn't entirely understand it.

The scent of Bexley's garden still called to her, urging her on like a beacon in the darkness.

"Then we'd best get to it," Sam concluded.

—

Bexley's garden walls were high, the gates—including the one Lily had used earlier—closed and locked for the night.

That posed little obstacle for Sam, who easily identified a place to scale the wall. He set his boots into holds formed by the clinging roots of a neglected ivy, scrambling nimbly up to the top.

It was a practiced art and reminded Lily of how Sam had made his living before Robert Ash plucked him from the streets of Limehouse.

The latch of the gate clicked softly a moment later. Sam swung it open, offering Lily and Strangford easier access to Bexley's garden.

A scattered few of the myriad lanterns still flickered, flames guttering in their wax. Half-drunk glasses of brandy and champagne were scattered about. A woman's heeled shoe lay toppled in the middle of the lawn next to the paper remnants of a party cracker.

Sam eyed the back of the house, assessing their options. A few windows on the upper floor were opened to admit the evening air, but the facade offered no clear way to climb up. The ground floor was dark. Lily felt certain it would be locked up tight.

"Wait here," he ordered and slipped across the grass.

He stopped at the dining room door, which was sheltered from the view of the other windows by a pair of bay laurels.

Strangford stood beside her in the shadow of the holly tree, the only sound the chirp of a night bird.

"I thought I lost you," he said quietly.

Lily slipped her fingers into his gloved hand. His grasp tightened and she felt the warmth of him through the black leather.

"How much did you see?" she asked, thinking of the kiss he had given her on that slab in the wasteland by the canal.

Her own recollection of what had passed in those moments between falling and returning was strange and disjointed, the details slipping away from her the more firmly she tried to catch them.

What remained was a strange and twilit place, the pale ribbon of a path, the quiet whisper of the endless sea. Ash's wife with her eyes full of knowing and the sense of some momentous happening—of being torn apart and torn through, pulled back together into something no longer the same.

"Nothing," he replied. "It's like someone cut a hole in you right around where it ought to be."

The revelation shocked her.

"You can't see it?"

"No, Lily," he confirmed, meeting her gaze.

She had found something Strangford could not reach—something utterly hers and hers alone.

It burst over her with a feeling like relief. It became easier, somehow, to soak up the comfort of standing close to him—the brush of the damp wool of his suit, the pressure of his hand.

"There was something," she admitted carefully. "Perhaps . . . sometime . . . I will tell you about it."

"When you're ready," he replied.

She leaned into him, letting her head fall against his shoulder. His arms slipped around her back.

A whiff of smoke rose from his jacket. She felt something warm and wet against her hand where it rested on his lapel.

Lily yanked it back, looking at it in alarm.

Why did she expect to see blood?

A quick fear pounded through her.

"What is it?" he demanded.

Before she could answer, the call of a swallow whistled from the bay laurels by Bexley's dining room door.

Sam was ready for them.

She pulled herself away from Strangford, her pulse still pounding, skin still crackling with the aftermath of some strange impulse of her power. It was filled with foreboding but devoid of any detail or direction.

The whistle came again.

"Let's go," Strangford said and slipped out into the garden.

Lily had no choice but to follow.

Sam waited in the darkness, fitting himself easily into the deepest wells of shadow. He nodded to the door as they arrived.

"Your turn," he announced.

She was about to lead them into the inhabited house of a leading government minister. If they were seen, it would surely mean arrest. Lily glanced at Sam for some hint of fear, of doubt that she was capable of doing this.

There was none.

She stared at that unprepossessing rectangle of wood, trying to gather her resources. What came next must be a sort of magic, one she had a shaky history of conjuring at will. There was no way the three of them could make it through the house otherwise, even with the switchblade in Sam's boot or Strangford's tàijíquán.

It would be down to Lily—or to blind bloody luck.

She took a deep breath, recalling what Ash had taught her. She conjured his voice in her mind, echoing the patient instructions he had repeated over and over again in the studio of The Refuge.

Calm your body. Calm your mind. Listen to your deeper voice. Release logic. Release judgment. Let it speak.

She had tried it so many times in The Refuge and remembered the humiliating pangs of Cairncross's darts, the sting of his paint bombs when she failed and failed and failed.

We must raise the stakes.

If they weren't high enough now, she doubted they ever would be.

She sought for Ash's calm, felt for some hint of her power and grasped a thin golden thread of it, an instinct that tugged her gently forward.

"Follow me," she said and led them inside.

The dining room table was an enormous slab of mahogany polished to a gleam that captured even the faint light of the stars. A massive vase of sickly-smelling flowers loomed at its center under the darkened web of an elaborate chandelier.

She followed the thread to the left, taking them deeper into the house.

The hallway was dark. The space around her felt still, but Lily knew in her bones that not everyone inside was asleep. Her blood raced through her veins. She was painfully conscious of Strangford at her back, Sam slipping in and out of the shadows behind him.

The thread hummed and Lily urgently gestured them to the side, putting the grand staircase between where they stood and the back of the hall. Strangford and Sam followed without hesitation.

She peered through the rail. A light glimmered at the back of the house and a moment later the butler who had greeted her earlier that evening crossed into view, clad in his dressing gown and carrying a lamp in his hand.

The light faded, the sound of his footsteps echoing down to the kitchen.

Instinct gently tugged her up. With a glance back at Strangford and Sam, Lily climbed the stairs.

The thick carpet muffled their footsteps. At the top lay another hall lined with doors. A pair of them were ajar, the others closed.

Lily waited for the thread to pull her forward but it remained still, as though waiting.

She fought the fear that threatened to rise up in its place, trying to open herself more to whatever her power would show her. The few times she had managed that in the past, she had been granted a glimpse forward to another step, the next turn she would need to make.

This time was different. Lily pushed, and a door snapped open inside her mind. Knowledge spilled through with dizzying speed.

A sharp sound. Pounding footsteps. The flash of lights, rough impact, the scrape of carpet against her chin. Ropes on her wrists, Sam shouting, his head snapping back under the blow of a police constable's baton. A woman in silk railing hysterically, a white ball of fur yelping in her arms. The gilded sky outside the window disappearing into a great white flash as the room explodes into shards of pain . . .

Lily choked on a gasp, strangling herself to silence.

The quiet of the darkened hallway throbbed. She could feel cracks in the surface of it, myriad places where different outcomes had the potential to break through.

The possibilities tugged at her, dizzying in their variety. She felt ill. She struggled for control, reaching for it in the only way she knew how.

Get me to Bexley, she thought, clinging to the thought fiercely. *Get me to Bexley.*

The cracks resolved, focusing to a pinpoint, and the golden thread tugged at her.

"In the second room on the left there is a small white dog," she breathed to Sam, the words spilling from her before she quite knew what they were. "You have to tell it not to bark."

Sam blinked at her through the darkness, absorbing this with a silent surprise. Then he slipped up the rest of the stairs.

He moved with the light feet of a former housebreaker as he approached the cracked door. He paused there and Lily watched as he closed his eyes, his breath deepening, reaching into his own well of concentration.

His eyes still closed, that focus still held, he stepped in front of the door.

The hallway remained silent.

Sam's face was softly illuminated in the light from the half-opened room. Lily saw his eyes open, every movement careful and deliberate.

Still gazing into the room, he motioned slowly for Lily and Strangford to come.

The thread of her instinct momentarily still, Lily carefully joined him in the doorway.

The Pomeranian was a pure white snowball topped with pointed pink ears. It sat upright on a gold-embroidered cushion at the end of the huge four-poster bed.

A woman slept alone under the fine brocaded coverlet. Her window was cracked to let in the cooler night air. The other side of the bed—Bexley's side, Lily deduced, since this was clearly the master bedroom—was still made.

The dog stared at them with unblinking black pebble eyes, a small pink tongue panting out of the front of its mouth. The puff of a little tail thumped against the cushion with quiet ecstasy.

Bexley was not here. Had he gone out? It was a possibility that made her stomach drop, and yet Lily knew it was not unusual for married couples of fortune to take to separate beds. He could well be behind one of the other doors lining the hallway. But which one? Would they have to open them one by one, praying they didn't wake up the wrong person as they went?

"It wants to follow us."

Sam's whisper was a breath. He said the words without breaking his eye contact with the tiny white threat on the bed.

"I can't shut it up from a distance," he finished, soft as a falling leaf.

Lily could well imagine what sort of racket a disappointed Pomeranian might make. Bringing it with them hardly seemed any better an option. And yet even as they watched, Lady Bexley stirred restlessly. It would not take much to wake her.

Her power offered no help with this decision. It simply waited, humming with readiness, for her to choose.

"Bring it along," she whispered back.

With a jerk of his head and a low whistle at a pitch Lily could barely hear, Sam called the animal over.

It leapt from the bed with clear delight and waited at Sam's feet, tail wagging frantically.

"Bloody dogs," he cursed softly.

Lily assessed the hallway. Her mind churned with possibilities. Bexley might be in his study working, or perhaps the butler they'd glimpsed in the hall downstairs had been on his way to bring his master a final nightcap of the evening. If his lordship did keep a different room from his wife, it likely lay right beside her own—and yet which of the two doors should they try? There were too many possibilities, all of them rife with threat.

Find Bexley, Lily willed, pushing the thought into her hands, her feet, her bones. *Find Bexley.*

Instinct drew her toward a thinner door at the end of the hall.

"That one," she whispered.

There was nothing about it that made it a reasonable choice. Doubt plucked at her from all sides.

She waited for Sam to object, for Strangford to point out that they had no reason to believe that door would lead them to their quarry.

They were silent.

Forcing in a breath, she led them past the closed bedrooms. As they passed, she heard the murmur of low conversation, the bright call of a snore.

They reached the narrow door. Lily set her hand to the knob and waited for some sign or signal that it was safe to move on—or that it wasn't.

She felt nothing.

Cursing Bexley, Ash, and this blasted ephemeral gift, she pulled the door open.

It revealed a narrow wooden stair.

Lily climbed it.

She slowed as they reached the top, logic urging her to caution. The stair led to a hall in the attic floor of the house. Lily could see how the roof sloped down at the sides. The doors that lined this space were closer-set and less fine than the ones below. They had clearly reached the servants' quarters.

Why had her power directed them here? There was of course one obvious possible reason why they might find the master of the house in the attic in the small hours of the night. Lily made a silent prayer that they weren't about to walk into a seduction or something worse involving Bexley and one of his staff.

Cracks of light could be seen beneath some of the doors. At least one of them was half ajar, the scuffling sounds of closing drawers audible from within. Clearly not everyone here was asleep for the night.

The Pomeranian panted beside her boot as though eager to see what would happen next. The madness of slipping about a stranger's house with a small dog in tow struck her with full force.

Sam whispered behind her with all the urgency of hard-learned experience, his voice as low as a creak in the walls.

"We need to get out of here."

He was right, and yet she hesitated. If she trusted logic, the only reasonable course of action would be to flee the house, then the city—hide out in Highgate and safely watch the whole thing burn.

This had never been about logic.

Something inside of her had changed. Lily could feel it. She had been feeling it ever since Strangford brought her back to life by the canal. Whatever had happened to her on the far side of that impenetrable barrier wasn't entirely clear now that she had returned, but she knew it was real.

Things were different in a way she didn't yet understand, but she had to trust it. She knew beyond doubt that it was their only hope.

The power tugged her forward, sparking with a quick urgency.

Somewhere nearby a chair scraped against the floor. Nightclothes rustled. A shadow passed across the light under the door.

"Do you trust me?" she asked, not daring to look back.

"Yes," Strangford replied unhesitatingly, his breath warm against her cheek.

"Then follow me," Lily whispered back and stepped into the hall.

She moved evenly, her boots falling silent across the floorboards.

One of the wooden planks glared up at her with importance. Lily stepped neatly over it, and as she did it seemed she could hear the potential creak of a loose nail in her ear.

She paused at the open door, the regular throbbing of her heart telling her *wait-wait, wait-wait . . .*

The rhythm switched and she pressed forward, passing a room where she could see a maid turned around, bending in to retrieve something from her trunk.

Once beyond that obstacle, the wall drew her in like a magnet. She pressed herself against it, waving for Sam and Strangford to do the same.

An older servant opened his bedroom door, the wood swinging out toward her face. He walked blithely across the hallway with a towel and toothbrush in his hand, pushing into the water closet.

His room beckoned.

It was senseless. Bexley could not possibly be inside. The servant who had occupied it until a moment ago would be back in the time it took him to brush his teeth.

Find Bexley, it sang to her. *Find Bexley.*

Doubt suffused her, the certainty that this was absolute madness. She was trusting their lives to a whim. It would be proved false, as it must be, and they would see the dawn from the basement of a police station until St. Amalgaid's apocalypse ripped everything apart.

The song of her power skipped, a record losing its track. It left behind only emptiness, a frantic guessing that felt infinitely weaker than that glowing call inside of her.

She rounded the open door and stepped into the room.

Bexley was not there.

The place had to belong to Bexley's valet. A few clothes were neatly spread across a small sewing table, things far too fine for a servant's wardrobe. The coverlet on the bed was worn in places but still of good quality, clearly a hand-me-down from the man's master.

On the table lay a spool of black thread, a pair of sharp steel scissors, a half-drunk cup of tea. A silver needle shone against the black fabric of an elegant waistcoat brocaded in gold.

The dog sat in the doorway, staring at the door to the water closet. A low growl crawled from its tiny throat. Sam hissed it back to silence.

Apparently the mistress's pet wasn't fond of the valet.

"Why are we here?" Sam demanded under his breath. Even Strangford looked concerned.

Lily didn't know the answer, and it threatened another panic. She pushed back from that and posed the question to her gift.

Why am I here?

The waistcoat on the sewing table bloomed with significance. With its shimmering pattern of crowns and stars, she recognized it as the one Bexley had worn that evening at the party. One of the buttons had come off, which explained why it had landed in his valet's quarters.

Impulse propelled her forward. She ran her fingers over the fine silk, felt a bump in the slender pocket of it.

She slipped her hand inside, her fingers closing around what felt like a bit of folded card paper.

The space around her shifted as though someone had snapped off the lights. The waistcoat was just a bit of cloth, the room just a room.

They had not found Bexley.

She pushed at her power, demanding it take her further—that it show her where in the house their quarry was hiding.

There was nothing, only the slender object in her hand, and the inexplicable certainty that they had found what they had come for.

"Let's go," she announced and strode back into the hall.

She headed for the doorway at the far end of the house, moving as quickly as she dared. The dog's claws skittered against the polished wood of the floor.

They dove into the gloom of the stairs.

Lily led them down, sensing Sam and Strangford close behind her. The stairs ended on a landing that branched to the kitchen on the one hand and the garage on the other.

Flipping a mental coin, she chose the garage, cutting through it into the starlit expanse of the garden.

Strangford emerged behind her but Sam hung back.

With the quickness of a snake, he flipped the Pomeranian onto its side, then gave it a push, sending the animal sliding across the glazed cement of the garage floor. As the dog regained its feet, Sam pulled shut the door, trapping the Pomeranian in the garage.

It began barking in furious protest.

"Time to run," Sam announced.

TWENTY-FIVE

$\mathcal{T}$HEY SPRINTED ACROSS THE shadows of the garden. Lily led them past the holly trees to the gate in the garden wall as lights flickered on in the house behind them, voices rising in confusion.

She threw back the bolt of the gate. They dashed into the mews.

Sam caught her arm as the alley spilled them into the street.

"Walk now," he ordered. "Like you belong here."

She forced herself to slow though her heart still pounded. They crossed the road, and Lily glanced up to see a constable making his quiet rounds, his baton swinging at his side.

Sam led them back into the shadows of the park. Safely within the embrace of the trees, he bit out a curse.

"Too bloody close and nothing to show for it," he spat.

"Not nothing," Strangford countered quietly. "What did you take from the waistcoat?"

Lily pulled the object from her pocket.

It was a matchbook, two matches down from full. The paper cover was printed in a pattern of black and white stripes. In the center stood the emblem of an open pomegranate in a rich, dark mauve, dripping with juice.

The sense of failure was overwhelming. Sam was right. What had been the point? Lily had trusted her power and this is all it brought her.

They should have gone to the ravens, whatever it cost them.

The matchbook felt electric through the cloth of her driving gloves, buzzing in her hands with a useless sense of importance.

"Matches, eh? I've a pack in my pocket. If you'd wanted a smoke, Lily, all you had to do was ask." Sam's tone was sharp.

"It's from Mrs. Needham's."

There was a strange tension in Strangford's voice. Sam perked with interest.

"What, the cat shop up Primrose Hill?"

Cat shop. Lily had heard less polite terms for such establishments.

That Strangford recognized the emblem of a brothel carried uncomfortable implications.

"Toff like Bexley might make use of Mrs. Needham's after a swarry," Sam mused. "It's right posh, not a punter's retreat."

"You know it?" Lily asked flatly.

"It was a long time ago," Strangford replied.

There was a wealth of conflict under the surface of that quiet phrase.

Lily had some knowledge of the trade of women like Mrs. Needham. Whoring was a dark business. Women like her mother were the exception. Deirdre Albright had been happy enough with her arrangement. She had gained the support of a wealthy and reasonably attractive lord who provided her with everything she wanted in life so long as she made herself available at his convenience and didn't mind sharing him with the wife and family he left behind every time he came to Oxford Street.

Most women who made their living on their backs didn't have a choice in the matter. Lily knew that held whether she worked her trade in a Covent Garden alley or a high-class establishment like Mrs. Needham's. Abuse or drugs might drive them to the work, or blackmail or simple desperation.

The idea of Strangford making use of someone in such circumstances twisted her up, and yet she knew it must be more complicated than that.

Other men of power might easily ignore the darker side of the trade or remain happily and deliberately ignorant. That wasn't possible for Strangford—not in a situation involving any sort of intimacy.

The tension in his voice made a terrible sort of sense. She could not know the true details of what had happened in Mrs. Needham's however many years ago. She was not sure she wanted to.

She could well imagine the possibilities.

"That's why we didn't find him in the house," she declared. Her own certainty surprised her, but there it was, singing inside her mind. "He's at the brothel."

"What are our chances of getting inside?" Sam asked.

"She keeps a man at the door," Strangford recalled. He had not looked at Lily.

"Like as not there will be others 'round the neighborhood watching for some wife or mistress looking to kick up a bit of dust," Sam filled in. "We won't be getting in like we did at his lordship's manse."

Sam gave the pair of them a carefully assessing look and Lily felt a quick sense of foreboding.

"You look respectable enough if one doesn't notice the damp," Sam concluded, taking in Strangford's evening dress. He shifted his look to Lily, and she was conscious that she was dressed more or less like a dockworker, her short auburn hair windblown from her ride on the Triumph.

"Where's Mrs. Needham stand on kink?" Sam demanded.

Strangford's jaw twitched. Lily felt her cheeks flush.

"I believe she caters discretely to a range of interests," he replied.

"That's your gag, then," Sam concluded. "Paying clientele. You won't be the first lord she's met with a smack for a girl in trousers. Assuming you left last time on friendly terms, that is."

"They may have been less than ideal," Strangford said thinly.

Sam sighed.

"Let's hope she cares more for the dosh than her pride," he concluded.

—

They collected the carriage from an alley in Barrow Hill, the area northeast of the park where the city slid from wealth to genteel poverty. Sam and Strangford lifted Lily's Triumph onto the luggage rack and strapped it into place.

Sam threw a coin toward the driver's box. The huddle of gray cloth perched there looked suspiciously like a sleeping driver until it shifted, a pale little hand flashing out of the folds to snatch the coin from the air.

An undernourished boy of perhaps twelve slipped out of Sam's coat and nimbly descended to the street.

"Thanks, guv'ner," he saluted before scampering away down the narrow streets.

Sam took a moment to greet Mary and Pickford, giving the chestnut mare an extra scratch on her ear. She replied with a rough nuzzle to his shoulder.

He mounted the box and took the reins. Strangford held the door, waiting for Lily to enter.

Steeling herself for what was to come at Mrs. Needham's, she climbed inside.

The carriage rolled through the empty streets.

"It was only once," Strangford said quietly, facing the window.

"We don't have to talk about this . . ." she began.

His hands were clenched on his knees inside the black leather armor of his gloves.

"I am not proud of it, Lily, but I would rather you knew the truth."

She wondered if it were selfish of her—not wanting to hear the rest. Or was it selfish of him to tell? She couldn't say, and so she waited in silence for him to speak.

"I was nineteen. I think my father was afraid I was too much alone. It was . . . after Annalise."

Annalise. The woman Lily had known as Mrs. Boyden—briefly, before the night she found her sprawled across white sheets with her throat cut.

Strangford's first love and first kiss. His first betrayal.

"He sent me off with this son of a friend of his," he continued. "The lad caught me up in a tear of boys one night. A lot of brandy was poured and we ended up on Primrose Hill. God help me, Lily, I knew it was a terrible idea. I'm not sure that I have any excuse except that I was so . . ."

"Alone," Lily filled in.

The word conjured a cascade of memories.

Moving ignored and outcast through finishing school. The gossip of chorus girls as she sat by the mirror, separate and strange.

Rolling a wooden train across the floor as her mother laughed at the deep rumble of her father's voice in a place she was forbidden to go.

The constant feeling of being isolated by knowledge she could not share, secrets no one would believe she had.

Alone. Such a small word for such an enormous burden. It had driven her to poor choices in the past. She could hardly judge him for it.

"I could feel it everywhere, Lily. The handle of the door, the bedpost, the sheets. Lust and pain and ennui. This haze of laudanum or gin. I don't know how anyone could be in that place and stand it."

"They don't know," she replied.

"I don't see how that's possible," he retorted, his voice thick. "They sent me up with a girl. She was older, perhaps twenty-five. Everything was so loud—they play music to cover up the rest of the sounds but it doesn't really work. I was still trying to go through with it. I touched her and I saw . . . I couldn't . . . "

"You don't have to tell me the rest," she said.

He looked down at his black-gloved hands.

"If our places were reversed you would already know. I have taken all your secrets from you. What right do I have to hold my own?"

"Every right," Lily quietly replied.

He laughed. It was a sound halfway to a sob and she crossed the carriage to him.

His head fell against her chest. Her fingers found the dark velvet of his hair.

"I do not deserve you," he said, his breath warm against her collarbone.

She knew the words were driven by more than his sordid night in the brothel. It was the whole mess of what lay between them—the pain his title and class inflicted upon her because of who she was born. His unavoidable invasion of her soul. His inability to be perfectly understanding of what he encountered there—to calmly navigate the complex quicksand that was the landscape of their relationship.

All of it was true, and yet as she held him Lily knew a greater truth.

It was obvious, undeniable, and it needed to be spoken.

"You are my choice," she vowed, her hand clasped to the bare skin of his neck. "You. As you are. No one else."

She knew he would sense her certainty through every nerve, every cell.

He raised his head, dark eyes meeting her own. His gloved hands tightened on her back, drawing her closer.

"Then I am yours," he replied.

The words thrummed through her with the power of a prophecy, and Lily understood that something irrevocable had just passed between them—a contract signed with an ink deeper than blood.

Nothing was certain. The world could end with the dawn. This would still be true.

The carriage stopped and Lily knew they had arrived.

Strangford straightened. She watched him steel himself for what came next, and for a moment it was as though she saw through the damp wool of his suit to something else, something more real—the robes of a dark knight on the attic wall, armor gleaming on his hands, light flickering around his unruly hair.

The image was gone in a blink, and yet Lily knew it was still there—that it had always been there.

She was left with the feeling of an electric potential beneath her own skin, one she was not quite ready to contemplate.

The carriage was parked in front of a tidy, fine-looking townhouse that faced Primrose Gardens. The street was swept clean, the neighboring houses decked out with flower boxes and brass door knockers.

The building in front of them looked identical to those beside it save that the gas lamps by the front door were still lit, spilling a soft yellow glow across the pavement. A plaque above the house number was embossed with the emblem of the split pomegranate.

Strangford stepped down.

Sam spoke lowly from the driver's box.

"I'll stay close. Round the bend on the park drive."

"Thank you, Sam," Strangford murmured in reply.

He offered her his arm.

Lily was conscious of how odd they must look. She was not a lady but a bastard, torn and stained in rough trousers. Strangford looked the perfect gentleman in his fine evening dress, except that he was soaked through and lacking a hat.

Yet he was beautiful. The fact of it struck her like a bullet as he stood there with the light of the gas lamps by the brothel door falling across his face. He was beautiful, and he was hers.

She took his arm, her back straight, suffused with a ferocious pride, and they walked to the door.

It opened immediately at his knock. An older but still lovely woman stood inside. Behind her Lily could see the shadow of someone larger, male, and far more intimidating.

"Good evening," the woman greeted them.

"I have a special request for Mrs. Needham," Strangford said evenly.

Lily was conscious of the woman's quick assessment—her measure of the quality of Strangford's suit, his accent, his bearing. Being so blatantly screened filled her with a quick burst of rage. She contained it—this was not the time.

"Certainly," the woman said. "Do come in. Mrs. Needham will be with you in a moment."

She showed them into a small sitting room. A curtain on the far side blocked Lily's view of a doorway through which she could hear the tinkling of glassware and a burst of male laughter. That would be the true parlor of the establishment, a place where Mrs. Needham's clients could enjoy a drink in pretty company, taking their time to select from her available merchandise.

The smaller room they had been shown to was tastefully and elegantly furnished, but there was irony in the details. A Bible rested on the bookshelf next to a volume of De Sade, propped up by bookends in the shape of a pair of nymphs. A painting hung on the wall in brashly modern style, depicting a stylized nude in a decidedly erotic pose. Lily quietly judged it and determined it was not up to Strangford's standards.

Strangford had not completed his story. Lily was conscious that she was ignorant of how he had left matters with Mrs. Needham, their soon-to-be hostess. However it had all fallen out, Lily hoped that history was not about to see them promptly booted back out onto the street.

The curtain fell aside and a new woman stepped into the room. She was perhaps sixty with an upright carriage and graceful movement.

"My Lord Strangford," she said in greeting.

Strangford had been barely out of grammar school when he was last inside this building. He was a grown man of thirty now. Lily knew he must have changed, but the brothel mistress was clearly a woman who made her living on remembering faces.

Mrs. Needham had not yet looked at Lily. She was waiting, Lily realized, for some sign from Strangford. The woman understood that female companions brought to her house may or may not be people her clients wanted treated as fully human.

She had not batted an eye at Strangford's dampness or Lily's unorthodox attire. It spoke to her professionalism and to a clear policy of catering to the whims of whatever wealthy or powerful patron came through her door.

An unsettling possibility occurred to her—that perhaps Mrs. Needham also knew perfectly well who Lily was. A woman in her line might make it a point to know by sight the faces of anyone of consequence in London. Lily's father would certainly qualify.

Perhaps his bastard daughter did as well.

"To what do I owe the pleasure?" Mrs. Needham asked.

The ormolu clock on the mantle ticked, the longer hand inching forward another minute. It was twenty past four in the morning.

On the far side of the curtain, a woman squealed, barking out a decidedly Cockney retort to some unexpected liberty.

"My companion and I are looking for a bit of respite," Strangford replied.

His voice was steady but Lily could hear the strain in the words. She was glad that they had not been taken directly into the more raucous parlor. The clatter and the crowd would only have made this harder for him.

"Respite," Mrs. Needham echoed. "Of course. Were you looking for a comfortable room for a few hours? Or did you hope to add to your party?"

She glanced to Lily as she said it, as though measuring her potential performance.

Strangford's arm tensed under her hand.

"I will note that the price is the same either way. Our space is at something of a premium here, as you must understand," Mrs. Needham elaborated.

"The room will be fine," Strangford said.

"How long do you require it for?"

"An hour," he replied.

It was the wrong answer. Lily could read that in the flash of Mrs. Needham's eyes. It told her all she needed to know—they were here on tolerance. A woman with clientele like Mrs. Needham's could not afford trouble. She would be alert to the possibility of it, especially in someone who had caused a problem before.

Lily raised her hand, brushing her fingers along the line of Strangford's jaw.

"Best make it three," she said.

She felt him twitch. He closed his eyes and Lily knew he was gathering strength, fighting not to explode from the tension of this.

That tension might look like something more straightforward to a woman who did not understand the rich complications that ran under Strangford's surface.

"Three, then," he managed to say.

"A judicious choice," Mrs. Needham concluded. "I have a very nice spot for you. I am sure you will find it suitable. Payment does need to be made in advance."

She named an exorbitant sum. Strangford opened his wallet and removed two damp bank notes. Lily found herself quietly relieved that he had possessed the cash. He was not a man of limitless finances.

Mrs. Needham took the money and held it out to the enormous man who still hovered by the door.

"Hang these up on the line in the kitchen, Gustav," she said.

She rose.

"Ethel will show you up. The Elizabeth Room, if you please, Ethel. Should you decide that you wish to make use of more of our resources, you need only ask."

Strangford stood.

"Thank you, madam," he said. His tone was polite but he did not bow. Knowing Strangford's strict courtesy, that spoke volumes to Lily.

"This way m'lord," Ethel announced with a curtsy.

TWENTY-SIX

$\mathcal{T}$HEY PASSED THROUGH HALLWAYS papered in crimson silk. A pair of women in lace lingered in a doorway, giggling and eyeing Strangford with calculated obviousness as they moved by. The smaller of the pair gave Lily a wink.

A man with a gray mustache and a gold waistcoat slapped the rear of a plump girl in a bright yellow gown. She yelped in a way that spoke of actual pain thinly disguised as delight.

The walls were hung with explicit photographs. Lily had a sudden horror that she would pass one with an image of her mother. She tried not to look, staring ahead as a series of panting moans emanated through one of the doors.

A pair of men in the remnants of naval dress lounged by one of the doors. One in his shirtsleeves poured amber liquor into the glass of a commodore who still wore the bars of his rank on his shoulders. The commodore's arm was draped around the waist of a girl who could not have been much older than sixteen. Her expression was one of cultivated boredom.

"When's the shipment?" the first man asked.

"Tomorrow morning," the commodore replied. His refined accent revealed signs of inebriation. "Slightly over twenty-thousand pieces altogether, shells and mortars. Takes thirty cars to hold the lot of it," he bragged, patting the girl's side like he might the flank of a horse.

"I keep forgetting the name of the originating station," the first man replied. "Something twee, wasn't it?"

"Hugglescote," the drunken commodore replied.

The word was a thunderclap in Lily's ear.

Twenty-thousand pieces, shells and mortars.

Tomorrow morning.

And Virginia Eversleigh's voice, chattering amid the quaint loveliness of Tower Gardens.

It's on a special train through Blackfriar's at quarter past six Sunday morning.

She had stopped walking. Strangford tugged gently at her arm.

"Lily," he murmured urgently.

The woman, Ethel, had paused by one of the doors. It looked identical to the others they had passed.

Her pulse pounding, Lily forced herself to put on a facade of calm, to keep moving even as her mind whirled with the implications.

"Here you are, m'lord," Ethel announced. "Will this be suitable?"

She opened the door.

Lily felt Strangford tense beside her, but there was nothing she could see in the room that might explain his reaction. It was perfectly ordinary, a small space dominated by a large bed. Though the initial impression was one of luxury, Lily could see the scratches in the veneer.

Gilt mirrors hung on the walls. Lily could well imagine the logic of their placement.

Strangford stepped inside.

"It's fine," he managed tightly.

"Just alert the attendant at the end of the hall if you desire anything more."

Ethel bobbed another curtsy and closed the door.

"Strangford—" Lily began.

"I have been here before," he cut in, the words spilling out of him.

The revelation threw her.

"It's the same room," she stammered as understanding dawned. "The same room you had the last time you were here."

There were a dozen Strangfords reflected in the mirrors over the bed, a thousand of them—his image echoed back on itself in the glass.

Fury raced through her. The brothel-keeper made her living on memory. Lily had no doubt this was deliberate.

It didn't matter.

"Strangford, the men in the hall—they were talking about a train. A train full of munitions, coming from Hugglescote."

"What?" he asked. The word was foggy, the shock of finding himself back in this space numbing his mind.

"It's Eversleigh's train," Lily pressed urgently. "The one crossing through London tomorrow morning. Eversleigh's train is full of government munitions. Explosives."

Lily knew that the government had been ramping up production of ammunition and military equipment, preparing for the possibility of a war in Ireland or in Europe. She had not heard that they had turned to private firms to augment that effort, but it should not have surprised her. Eversleigh's factory in Hugglescote was an ironworks. It was ideally suited to turn to building and filling munitions.

Strangford's look sharpened, the urgency of Lily's revelation pulling him back to himself.

"If the whole thing went up, it might cause the sort of destruction you saw," he said. "But shells don't simply explode by themselves."

"Some kind of accident, perhaps?" Lily guessed. "A derailment?"

"It is possible," he admitted. His dark eyes locked onto her. "But there is also a bomb set to go off tomorrow morning. We cannot know which one will trigger the disaster."

Lily forced herself to absorb this. She had been ready to dash from the brothel and find Eversleigh or her father, or some other authority with the power to stop that train.

It was half past four in the morning. What authority could she find at that hour? How quickly could the bureaucracy of the railroads and the military be ground into motion?

Strangford was right. They needed more information—Bexley's information. She could not stop both the bomb and the train at once. She had to know where to focus her efforts over the next hour.

A grim determination settled over her.

"Then let's do this," she ordered.

She quickly scanned the room, looking for anything they might use to their advantage.

The trunk at the foot of the bed held only bundles of extra linens. A wardrobe contained an array of costumes—evening clothes, a maid's uniform, a sarong. Lily pulled out the drawers and found a set of flexible, tough leather straps.

She glanced to the four posters of the bed. The intended use of what she held in her hand was clear even to someone with Lily's relatively limited experience.

She pushed the thought aside and tested them in her hand as the myriad Strangfords watched her in the mirror.

"What are you planning to do with those?" he asked.

"They feel right. I'm keeping them," she replied.

There was nothing else of use.

It was time to find Bexley.

The hall they had passed through to get here had been busy with guests and attendants. Lily suspected that was deliberate, a way to ensure that no one disturbed Mrs. Needham's clients at their business.

She checked the door. Though it locked from the inside, there was no bolt.

"Could you kick this down?" Lily demanded.

Strangford was taut as a bowstring. He gave the door a measuring look.

"Yes," he concluded.

This would not be like Bexley's manor. It was not a house of sleepers but a thriving place of business in the peak hour of its operation. There would be no shadows to hide in, no doors they could duck through. No matter how well tuned her senses, a warning of imminent threat would do them no good. They would have nowhere to go.

"I think . . . that I have to see where he will be," she said.

"Can you do that?" Strangford asked seriously.

"I have to try," she replied, feeling the time slip past.

She would use Ash's methods. She was painfully conscious of how thoroughly they had failed her in the past, and that had been in the quiet and stillness of the studio at The Refuge, not the racket of a brothel where she could hear the furniture pounding against the wall in the next room.

She sat down on the trunk, folding her legs and straightening her back. She rested her hands on her knees.

She could feel Strangford hovering at the edge of the room, a room suffused with the awkward aura of his history.

High stakes, she reminded herself grimly. *High stakes.*

She pulled in a breath, bringing it deep, as Ash had taught her. She imagined it filling her body from her toes to the crown of her head. She exhaled slowly.

Her mind was not calm. It whirled with furious energy, protesting this apparent inaction.

Lily breathed in again, breathed out.

She focused on the need. It was urgent, burning inside of her. She poured fuel onto that blaze, fed it with her fear and her uncertainty.

Bexley's room, she thought. *Bexley's room. Bexley's room.*

Somewhere through the wall a woman screamed with false delight. Bedsprings squealed. There was a roar of male laughter.

They washed over her, washed through her, water over the bed of a stream.

Lily felt herself tumble in that water, felt it churn around and inside of her—and then she released herself into it.

She flows forward.

It sucks her off the trunk and out through the door. She spills along the worn carpet of the hall.

The hall turns to a dance and Lily spins through it as a walrus with a monocle barks from the bed of one of the passing rooms.

She tumbles down the stairs under stars that twinkle brightly against a crimson sky. At the bottom something whispers her back, holding her in place. A star winks out and a troll lumbers past, a sack of grain slung over its enormous shoulder.

Lily shivers over the scarred floorboards to the unassuming rectangle of another door, a sliver of lamplight glowing from the crack at its base.

A shadow moves across that light.

The connection snapped. Lily was thrown back to the trunk in the mirrored bedroom.

"Downstairs," she said, breathless. "Third on the left."

"How will we get there?" Strangford asked.

"Just . . . follow my lead," she replied, praying she was right.

She put her hand to the knob. She held there, searching for some sense of the right moment to begin.

It came.

Lily twisted the knob and strode out into the hallway.

She did not look back to where the attendant stood at the top of the stairs. She pressed on toward the back of the house.

Two women spilled from the room to her right. They were tipsy with champagne, naked to the waist. They swung around in a drunken embrace.

Lily took Strangford's arm.

"Dance," she ordered, and he turned her in a waltz, stepping her around the girls, who screamed with delight.

As they spun, Lily glimpsed a fat man on the bed, naked save for the glass glittering over one of his eyes atop the long tusks of his mustache. He lifted his glass in an inebriate toast.

The girls collapsed into a giggling puddle. Lily tugged Strangford into the stairwell.

Electric candles shone from the sconces on the walls, illuminating the garnet hue of the wallpaper. They raced down, hurrying around the dark corners.

Lily nearly stumbled out into the hall at the bottom, catching herself in time and holding Strangford back. She reached up and gave the bulb of the nearest sconce a twist, burning her fingers and casting the stairwell into darkness.

Gustav crossed in front of them. He carried a whore over his shoulder, one of her feet bare.

He turned into the hall. Lily's heart pounded with the beat of his footsteps.

One, two, three, four . . .

His head disappeared down the stair at the far end of the house and Lily tugged Strangford into the hall.

She skidded to a stop at the third door on the left.

Light shone softly through the crack at the bottom of it. The sounds through the boards were quiet—the low murmur of a voice, a rustle of cloth.

"Now?" Strangford whispered against her ear, pressed close.

"Wait," Lily said, the instinct a quick flare.

They held ready for the length of one heartbeat, another, a third . . . Lily wondered if she were mad or mistaken, knowing every second they stood here was another chance they would be exposed.

Then it came to her.

"Now. Do it now," she hissed, stepping aside to clear his path.

His movements were elegant, more dance than war. He rooted himself to the floor, body slipping into a perfect state of balance. Then he twisted, his leg flying out, weight shifting powerfully into the blow.

Somewhere downstairs, a door slammed.

At the same moment, Strangford's boot connected with wood and the lock tore loose.

The door cracked into the wall.

Lord Bexley sat on the end of the bed in a room draped with silk, buttoning his shirt. A woman pulled on her dress behind him.

Lily did not hesitate. She leapt into the room, the leather strap ready in her hands.

Strangford was ahead of her. He caught Bexley's raised arm and twisted it behind his back, throwing him down onto the bed. The nobleman's shout of outrage was muffled by the plush quilts.

Lily thrust the strap around his wrists, tugging it tight through the iron buckle.

The woman gaped at them.

"Get out," Lily ordered. "Go."

She scrambled across the bed and sprinted into the hall.

They would have only moments now before the alarm was raised.

"The bomb," Lily said. "The one the Red Branch have set for this morning. Where is it?"

"Outrageous bitch," Bexley spat. "You have no notion who you're crossing. I will see you in chains for this."

"Tell me where it is," Lily returned, pulling up on the leather strap, wrenching back his arms.

"You'll rot in an asylum," Bexley shouted back.

"You aren't the first man to promise me that," she snapped.

"Lily, can you hold him?" Strangford asked her.

Bexley was not a small man, and his rage had made him stronger.

She put her knee into his spine, holding tight to the leather that bound him.

"Do it," she commanded.

Strangford released his grip.

Bexley writhed beneath her. Lily could hear voices rising from downstairs, promising that they would soon be overrun.

Lily pressed their captive down, watching as Strangford ripped off his gloves.

She met his eyes across Bexley's body, sharply aware of the risk they were about to take.

Strangford put his hands on the nobleman's arm. His eyes fell closed.

"What the bloody hell is he doing?" Bexley snarled. "Is this some sick prank?"

Strangford's eyes flickered behind his eyelids. She saw the changing emotions shimmer across his face—a curl of distaste, something else that sent a shudder down his spine.

Lily's heart pounded. She could hear a thunder of footsteps on the stairs.

"Blackfriars," he gasped, sweat beading on his brow. "The rail bridge."

He tore his hands away, stumbling back.

Bexley lurched, throwing Lily against one of the posters of the bed. The bruises on her back from the fall sang with the impact.

"How do you know that?" he demanded. "How the *bloody hell do you know?*"

Her mind spun, reeling as the pieces tumbled into place.

Blackfriars. Quarter past six.

She could see Virginia Eversleigh by the Thames, the Gothic spires of Westminster Palace rising behind her.

. . . on a special train through Blackfriars . . .

The train, the thirty cars packed with artillery shells. A hundred thousand tons of high explosives that was set to go trundling over Blackfriars rail bridge . . . at quarter past six tomorrow morning.

The vision of St. Amalgaid's cataclysm flashed across her mind—a crater where St. Paul's should be, where Ludgate Hill and St. Bridget's and Queen Victoria Street now stood. A hole in the heart of London and at the center of it . . .

Blackfriars.

"The train," she blurted. She scrambled to her feet. "Strangford, the train . . ."

His face was drained, his eyes wide with the horror of it.

"My God, Lily—"

"In there!"

The cry came from the hall and Lily knew they had run out of time. Bexley rolled over, shouting for help.

She ran to the window, snapping aside the lock and throwing open the sash.

The roof of a portico jutted out beneath her.

She swung out, dropping to the shingles. They slid under her boots. She steadied herself, then felt the impact of Strangford landing behind her.

Bexley's curses drifted down from above.

"They're outside!" he barked.

Lily scrambled to the edge. She let herself slip over it, catching her hands on the gutter and dangling. She dropped to the ground, bones jarred by the jolt of the impact.

Strangford landed beside her. He grabbed her arm and pulled her into a run.

They bolted around the side of the house.

The carriage waited at the edge of the park, half-lost in the gloom between the street lamps. They sprinted for it as doors slammed open behind them, more shouts rising into the night.

Gustav and another man just like him burst from the front door of the house, pounding down the street. Behind them, Mrs. Needham was framed in the doorway, screaming a curse out into the night.

"Go!" Strangford shouted as he and Lily neared the carriage. "Drive!"

Sam straightened, grabbing the reins. Strangford wrenched open the door and Lily dove inside. He leapt after her and the carriage jerked into motion.

It rattled away from the curb and out into the street.

"Where?" Sam shouted down from above.

"Blackfriars," Strangford called back, the name rough in his throat.

The carriage wheeled around a turn and Lily was tossed against the door. With the impact, her vision shifted.

The water of the Thames, gilded with dawn. The stench of diesel. Sam hunching over a box of wires—*I can't do it.*

The clatter and scream of an oncoming train.

Fire tearing her into shreds.

"No," she rasped, catching herself. She grabbed Strangford's arm. "We can't go to Blackfriars."

"Where, then?"

"Hold on," Sam called from above. Lily grasped the strap as they reeled around another turn, the momentum of it half throwing her into Strangford. A glimpse out the window told her that Gustav and his companion had fallen behind. They were lost around the corner as Sam drove them furiously into a warren of streets.

"Sam, find a safe place to stop," Lily called.

They rolled to a halt a few moments later. The carriage rocked as Sam climbed down from the box and wrenched open the door.

Lily stumbled out, Strangford following.

"It's at Blackfriars?" Sam demanded. Behind him, the horses panted, shaking off the strain of the sudden run.

"The rail bridge," Strangford confirmed.

"It's the train," Lily blurted, the words falling out from some deeper place inside of her. "We have to stop the train."

"What train?"

"A freight run of artillery shells from the midlands," Strangford replied.

She could see Sam make the calculation, the same geometry that had overwhelmed her in Bexley's room at the brothel.

"Where is it coming from?" he asked.

"Eversleigh's works. Hugglescote, Leicestershire," Strangford replied.

"Leicester to Blackfriars. It'll be on the Midland line."

Reaching into his boot, he flipped out his switchblade. The wicked little knife flashed in the dim light.

Sam turned to the horses. He set a reassuring hand on the neck of the bay, murmuring something into her ear. Then he slid the blade through the traces, cutting them with a neat tug.

He set to work on the harness, loosening buckles and tugging straps.

"The Camden Tunnels," he announced as the leather clattered to the ground. "You know it?"

"Northeast," Lily replied, pulling the place from her mental map of the city. "Off Camden Square."

Sam nodded confirmation.

"A freight run on the Midland won't stop anywhere between Camden and the bridge. You'll have to drop onto it as it passes through. It'll be coming down the westernmost line." He rubbed his eyes, mind working furiously. "Your best chance is to unscrew one of the couplers that hold the cars to the engine. It's that, or knock out the engineer."

"I understand," Strangford replied grimly.

The bay mare was free. Sam led her out of the tangle of rigging.

"Take Pickford. You'll be faster on horseback," he ordered. "Lord Strangford?"

"Give me a knee," Strangford said.

Sam extended a leg. Strangford pressed his boot against it, vaulting gracefully up onto the mare's bare back. He yanked loose his tie, tossing it aside and opening the top of his shirt.

It felt for a moment as though Lily could look into the past rather than the future. She saw him as he was the day she first met him, galloping bareheaded over Hampstead Heath.

The memory was vivid, brighter than life—how he had swung down from the horse, his dark eyes and windblown hair appearing in her line of vision. A black-gloved hand pressing against her chest as she tried to rise.

You really ought not do that.

How she had rebelled against it, fought to close herself off to this stranger who had burst into her life, upsetting the careful control she had painstakingly constructed over the years. Stubbornly resisting even as her blood dripped onto the road.

It's just a scratch.

Her pain, the weight of those years of grief and failure, had been so much more than that. The strides she had made since that morning on the heath she owed to Ash, to Sam—to the family that was The Refuge—but most importantly to the man reaching down to her from that horse.

"You'll need help getting up," he said, and the words echoed across time, ringing through her like a bell.

"I suppose I do," she replied and gave him her hand.

He pulled as she pressed her boot into Sam's waiting hands, levering herself up onto the enormous beast and swinging her leg over its bare back.

Pickford grunted but held steady.

Lily slid into place behind Strangford. She was pressed against him, her arms wrapped around his waist. She could feel his solid balance on the horse, how naturally he held his seat.

Sam moved to Mary, cutting the chestnut's traces.

"Don't wait too long to jump," he said as he worked the remaining buckles of the harness. "The engineer will slow as it passes through the tunnel, but once they're clear of it he'll pick up more speed."

"What about you?" Lily demanded.

"I'm going to the bridge," he replied, giving the leather a yank. The harness fell to the pavement with a clatter of brass buckles.

The chestnut tossed her head anxiously but held her place at a touch of Sam's hand.

"There are two ways we do this," he said. "We stop the train or we stop the bomb. You work one line and I'll cover the other. Unless you know a reason I shouldn't." He glared up at her, waiting.

Her heart was twisted in her chest. She couldn't see past the fear.

"It isn't clear," she admitted.

"You'll pass Bedford Square," Strangford cut in. "Collect Ash and Cairncross, if they're still there, and take the Rolls. You may need the help."

"I will," he promised. "Set Pickford loose once you're at the tunnel. She'll find her way home."

He brushed his hand over the neck of the bay. Lily felt the horse shiver, muscles quivering under her legs. She was certain he had just communicated something of the urgency of the ride to the animal.

"Sam," she called as he stepped back. He looked up at her, his dark eyes narrow.

"Take the Triumph." Her voice broke on the words. "You'll be faster."

His mouth twisted into a wicked smile.

"If you insist," he replied.

Strangford pulled the bay into a turn. The horse leapt to his command. Lily could feel the power of it beneath her.

She glanced back and saw Sam pat the chestnut on her rear. As the horse cantered off down the deserted street, Sam sliced neatly through the straps that held the motorbike onto the luggage rack.

As though inspired by her sister, the bay kicked into a gallop. Lily buried her face in the back of Strangford's jacket, praying for balance.

Behind her, she heard the familiar cough and rumble of the engine. It slipped into a triumphant roar and Lily knew that Sam was on his way.

TWENTY-SEVEN

Sunday morning
Quarter past five
Camden, London

THEY GALLOPED THROUGH THE streets of Camden.

The sky was glowing in the east, the cobalt of night shifting to the paler blue of imminent dawn.

The time felt like water in her hands, slipping between the cracks of her fingers.

She clung to Strangford as the horse raced past tidy brick row houses, the wind of their flight tugging at her hair. A light flickered on in one of the windows, a cat scrambling out of their path. A milkman turning the corner stopped to stare at them like a thing out of a dream.

Their destination was a quiet alley bounded on the north by a few carriage houses and a tumbledown shed. To the south, a low iron fence was all that lay between the road and a twenty-foot drop to the mouth of the Camden Tunnels.

Strangford pulled Pickford to a halt. The horse was breathing heavily, her sides flecked with sweat. Lily could feel the damp of it under her thighs.

He swung down off the beast with practiced ease, placing a reassuring hand on the mare's neck.

"Shall I help you down?" he asked.

"Please," Lily said.

Black-gloved hands grasped her waist. Strangford paused, looking up at her.

"It occurs to me we have done this before," he said.

The memory of it brought a flush to her cheeks.

Their first encounter had been fraught with awkwardness, Strangford's discomfort with touch colliding with Lily's distrust of anyone with a title before his name.

When he touched her now it felt right. Lily thought perhaps it had felt right then, six months before in the yard of a farm on Hampstead Heath, only they had both been too afraid to know it.

Trusting his grip, she slid down from the mare.

"At least this time I can walk," she noted, brushing a stray hair back from his forehead.

"I think you will have to do rather more than that if we're to manage this," he replied grimly.

He worked free the bridle of the horse. Lily had no notion of how to talk to animals, but she might have sworn Pickford looked happy to be relieved of it.

The mare tossed back her mane, hooves clicking restlessly against the asphalt. She wheeled about and broke into a gallop, racing off through the twilight streets—following the orders Sam had whispered in her ear a mile back.

Strangford kept the bridle and reins in his hand as he leaned over the iron rail, assessing the distance from the road to the mouth of the tunnel below.

Lily joined him there. The cut for the rail line was deep. The top of the tunnel mouth was perhaps twelve feet below the road on which they stood, and the train likely cleared it by a few feet more.

Jumping from here to the top of a moving train would be an act of lunacy. They couldn't possibly manage it without breaking a leg or worse.

"We shall have to climb," Strangford determined.

"On what?" Lily demanded, looking at the smooth face of the wall below them.

"This," Strangford replied, raising the reins in his hands.

He threaded one of the leather straps around the iron rail. He knotted it, working quickly but carefully.

A train whistle sounded, distantly, adding urgency to the task.

The bridle and second rein were tossed over the side. They unfurled against the soot-stained bricks. With the bridle linking the two reins together, the rigging reached just to the top of the tunnel mouth.

Strangford swung a leg over the side, taking hold of the make-shift rope.

"Use your feet to brace yourself against the wall. You'll have to follow after me. Can you do that?" he asked.

Swallowing the panicked fluttering in her stomach, Lily answered. "Yes."

He slipped the rest of the way over the rail and set his boots against the soot-stained bricks. His body leaned out over the sheer drop of the cut. He carefully walked himself down, threading the reins out through his gloved hands as he went.

She watched him navigate the trickier transition where the bridle attached the two leather straps, her heart pounding. Once past, he looked up at her and Lily knew she could delay no longer.

Pulse pounding, she straddled the rail.

Their rope was already taut from Strangford's weight. Lily found a chink in the mortar where she could set her boot. Holding tightly to the line, silently grateful she still wore her motoring gloves, she swung herself over into the open air.

The train whistle called again, closer now. Though she could not see it, Lily could hear the distant rumble of the engine.

Below her, Strangford was braced against the wall at the mouth of the tunnel.

Her arms ached, hands raw even through the protection of her gloves. She moved down another step, working her way past the bridle. Her legs were shaking.

As she neared him, Lily risked a glance down to where Strangford hung suspended. His gaze was directed toward the mouth of the tunnel, the lines of his expression grimly focused.

The timbre of the engine noise changed and Lily felt a vibration through the soles of her boots where they pressed against the bricks.

A moment later, the train roared out beneath them.

Sam had told her the engine would slow as it went through the tunnel. Lily believed him, but everything was still moving far too fast, the cars flying past beneath her.

Strangford let go.

He landed on the roof of a corrugated steel boxcar, rolling once with the impact before his gloved hands caught the ribs of metal, swinging him to a stop.

The wind tore at his dark hair, and already he was three cars ahead of her.

There could be no more hesitation.

Lily slipped down the last few feet of the reins, the cars whipping past beneath her.

The impulse to jump hit her like a wall, undeniable in its intensity.

Praying she wasn't about to kill herself, Lily leapt.

She slammed into weathered boards—and then, with a sharp crack, through them. She plummeted into the darkness of the freight car in a spill of splintered, rotten wood.

The impact of hitting bottom winded her. Her teeth snapped together as her head bounced against the ground. The coppery taste of blood slipped across her tongue.

Lily forced herself to roll over, pushing her way to her feet.

New scrapes and bruises promised to add to those she had already acquired, but nothing was broken.

She had fallen through the thin planks covering a hatch in the top of the car. The dark space around her was packed with wooden crates. Most were closed, a handful open at the top. As her eyes adjusted to the gloom, Lily could make out the labels stenciled on planks that still smelled of fresh pine.

QF 18 lbs HE

MK 1 Cordite

Vickers 47mm

Artillery shells, packed with explosives.

The crates were jammed into the car, packed up to the ceiling.

Lily could feel the length of the train extending before and behind her, car after endless car loaded with the weapons of war. She closed her eyes and it seemed that the vibration of wheels on track shifted into something else—into a low tremor through torn soil and a crack of sound both like and unlike thunder, a rumbling that went on and on until the earth itself groaned in agony.

The horror crawled down her back. She shook it off, forcing herself back into the present. There was no time. She had to find a way out of here.

Gripping the top of one of the crates, Lily hauled herself up. She reached for the next level and her fingers brushed against the contents of an open-topped bin.

It was packed with rows of smooth, rounded metal that glowed with a heat Lily was certain only she could feel.

Her hand closed around one of the objects. She pulled it out for a better look.

It was a solid cylinder of brass, rounded at the top—some sort of small mortar perhaps two inches in diameter and heavy for its size.

It glowed in her hand with a significance both urgent and dangerous. Lily shook off the irrational fear that it was about to burst apart under her eyes, triggering the entire car into immolation.

She was seized by an impulse she knew was madness—but madness had been her course since Ash set his wife's last work alight around her.

Giving in to it, Lily slipped the bomb into her pocket.

"Lily!"

Strangford's face appeared between the broken boards of the hatch overhead, the wind whipping at his hair. Kneeling on the roof of the car, he reached down.

Lily braced her boot against the top of a crate full of eighteen-pounder shells, thrust herself up and grasped his hand.

He hauled her back into the rushing air.

The rail yard sprawled around them, a maze of tracks, signals and switches, warehouses and cranes. Engines seeped white clouds of steam into the sky.

She glanced back. The train unfurled behind her, cars marching off into the distance.

All of them packed with death.

The enormity of it iced her veins. The image of London blasted into oblivion, a smoking wreck of mud and iron, felt closer than ever.

"Can you jump?" Strangford demanded, shouting over the roar.

Lily nodded.

Climbing to his feet, he pressed forward against the wind, marching up to the edge of the car. Pausing only a moment, he leaped over the gap, skidding to a stop and turning to look back at her.

Caution would not help her here. Taking a shaking breath, Lily charged, boots pounding against steel. She hit the end and kept going, throwing herself into the air.

She clanged down on the next car. Strangford caught her, gloved hands firm on her arms.

"Five more," he said, dark eyes searching hers for any hesitation.

"Let's go," she replied.

They pushed on as the train clattered over the silver water of Regent's Canal. The hulking black shapes of the coal drops were visible in the distance, a shadow cut out against the paling backdrop of nearing dawn.

The iron rings of the gasometers rose before them, those crowns of circular scaffolding marking the way to St. Pancras station.

The engine lay a few cars ahead. Lily could see that the last of them was an open coal hopper, and behind that, two hoppers full of what looked like bags of grain. She pressed on, following Strangford over to another car.

From behind, St. Pancras was an open void, its iconic glass ceiling visible through a grille of iron beams, glittering with the lights of the terminus. The red brick spires of the hotel that fronted the station rose up on the far side of it, piercing the lightening sky.

A signalman threw a lever as they approached, swinging their track to the right. He looked up, eyes locking onto where Lily and Strangford stood. His mouth dropped in shock. A moment later, as he quickly receded behind them, Lily heard the shrill alarm of his whistle.

Lily cleared another car, and the train veered around the unnatural glow of the station, plunging into the darkness of a tunnel.

They fell to the top of the boxcar, flattening themselves as dark objects whizzed past overhead. The world was a deafening roar and the stink of smoke, illuminated in flashes by red signal lights or the ghastly glare of a maintenance lamp.

The train leaned into a sharp turn, the momentum of the car she clung to shifting hard. Lily grasped for a hold, her gloves sliding across the metal. She skidded over the surface until her boot bumped against the ridge of the edge. She pressed back against it, clinging to the steel as unseen dangers whipped by on every side of her.

The curve reversed and the train swung back the other way. Lily slipped across the top of the boxcar.

Strangford reached out, grasping her hand and yanking her to a stop. Looking up, Lily could see that his other hand gripped the round curve of a hoist eye bolted into the top of the car.

She held on, heart pounding in the darkness.

The train burst back into the open air. They had reached the far side of King's Cross. The tracks were sunk between close-pressed buildings—brick row houses and flats with windows cracked to let in the night air. Laundry hung on lines suspended over the tracks twisted in the wind of their passing.

Lily scrambled back to her feet, following Strangford down the train. The tracks wove in and out of tunnels between here and Blackfriars. They needed to press on as fast and as far as they could in these moments outside.

A paperboy gaped down at her from one of the streets that passed overhead as she leapt onto another car.

Ahead of her, Strangford dropped deliberately off the edge of the last boxcar. Lily crawled over, looking down to see him balanced between the boxcar and the first of the hoppers full of grain.

She slipped onto the ladder bolted to the side of the car just as the train dove into another tunnel.

Noise screamed around them, seeming more intense in the narrow space between the cars. In the flash of a passing lamp she saw Strangford unhook the safety chain, then set his hands to the enormous screw that held the coupler together.

She added her strength to the task. If they could release the screw, the train would separate here. The hoppers would rattle on while the explosives gradually rolled to a halt.

The metal refused to budge. Lily released it just long enough to tear her gloves away, tossing them into the darkness, then try again with a firmer grip.

There was a screech of brakes ahead of them. The two cars

wavered, coming a hair closer together. Lily felt the screw give under her hands.

A shout burst from overhead, loud enough for her to hear over the roar of the train and the tunnel.

A dark figure crouched on top of the hopper. Lily made out the details of an army uniform and the dark shine of a sidearm pointed at her head.

The tunnel ended, the dawn sky visible once more. The soldier shouted again, his words incomprehensible against the racket of the train but his meaning perfectly clear.

Clerkenwell Road slipped by overhead. Lily knew Farringdon Station was just ahead—and beyond that, Ludgate Hill and the approach to the Blackfriars rail bridge.

She looked at the screw. They had only moved it a quarter of the way it needed to go. There was no way they could finish without being shot.

Beside her, Strangford raised his hands.

Lily's pulse pounded. She was conscious of the weight of the mortar in her pocket.

Not yet, her heart hammered back at her. *Not yet.*

The soldier backed up, waving them onto the hopper.

Lily made her careful way across the bags of grain toward the engine.

The train had slowed as it approached the tight chain of passenger stations that marked their path to the river.

Their captor walked them down the narrow scaffolding along the side of the coal car and pointed them into the engine.

It was a small space. The engineer gaped at them with shock, a shovel of coal in his hands poised before the open door to the red flames of the boiler. A second soldier, older than the first, quickly produced his own weapon.

"What the hell is this?" he demanded.

"They were sabotaging one of the couplers," his colleague replied from behind them.

Lily was conscious of how thoroughly they were pinned. There was no room to maneuver in the confines of the engine. Why hadn't her power warned her that the shipment would be guarded?

"Should we stop the train?" the younger soldier demanded.

"Yes," Lily shouted in reply.

She felt the barrel of a gun press into her back.

"Enough from you," the older one snapped from behind her.

"There's no rail police this side of the Thames," the engineer cut in nervously. "Nearest unit is at London Bridge."

London Bridge Station was on the other side of Blackfriar's Bridge.

"Then we'll put them off at London Bridge," the older soldier determined.

Time slowed.

At a distant level, Lily was conscious of Strangford shouting beside her, of the engineer's mouth forming panicked words.

What do you mean there's a bomb?

It all moved as though through water, a ballet of metal and sound.

Coal dropped from a shovel to the floor, pinging against the ground.

Farringdon Street Station slipped by outside the open doorways of the engine.

The red mouth of the boiler sang to her and the weight of the mortar swung against her thigh. The impact rang through her like a striking gong.

With horrible clarity, Lily knew what must be done.

She could not question what it would cost her, what her own role in it must be. There wasn't any time.

But she could save Strangford.

Their hands were still in the air. Lily let hers fall closer and slid her fingers into the gap between wrist and glove.

Get out, she thought furiously, the facts of what must come next ticking around like a roulette wheel in her mind. *Get out.*

The train plunged into another tunnel and Strangford turned to her.

The soldier screamed behind him, the silver gleam of his gun flashing at the corner of her eye. Lights zipped by, turning everything into a magic lantern show.

Strangford pulled her into a kiss, one that sang of hunger and determination.

She felt his hand slip into her pocket.

"Not you," he whispered against her lips.

The implication slammed into her as the train blew back into the light. She opened her mouth to protest, to scream.

His hands pressed against her chest and shoved.

Lily fell.

The open door of the engine swallowed her.

She hit the ground hard, crushed stone ripping into the canvas of her coat. She rolled, the momentum spinning her across the rail bed, thumping to a halt against the wall of an office block.

Her ears rang, muffling sound, rendering the world around her thick and strange.

Fear pulsing through her with every heartbeat, she dragged herself to her feet, staggering forward.

Ludgate Viaduct lay ahead, carrying the train over the still-quiet expanse of Fleet Street. The dome of St. Paul's cathedral rose over the rooftops, gilded by the first rays of the rising sun.

The engineer leapt across the rail bed ahead of her, tumbling to the ground.

Lily began to run.

She glimpsed the two soldiers through the gaps between the cars, spilling out on the far side of the train.

At the edge of the viaduct, a final figure, clad in black, fell out of the engine door—and then the engine blew apart.

It was a ball of light burning her eyes. A rush of wind and darts of iron. She felt them fly past her, heard metal ping off of bricks and stone, the crystalline fall of shattering glass.

The force of it tripped her sideways. She caught herself and kept going, boots pounding against the gravel.

Train cars screeched beside her, couplings protesting at the abrupt change in momentum. The two hoppers overturned, bags splitting and spilling a wave of golden wheat across the ground ahead of her.

Behind her, cars full of explosives wrenched and strained, squealing against the obstacles ahead, forcing the overturned cars further down the tracks.

The whole enormous length of the train was grinding to a slow and painful halt at the edge of the viaduct.

Strangford lay in a heap beside it.

The sight of him there was agony, a fear that threatened to tear her in two.

His shirt was red with blood. It seeped from a vicious wound that ran the length of the left side of his face.

"No," she said, skidding to a stop at his side, grain and gravel flying, her heart wrenching as though it might split apart. "No, no, no, no."

Her hands raced over his chest, searching for damage, for signs of life.

A black glove clamped onto her arm, strong enough to hurt.

He gasped, lungs hollow, the wind coming back to him.

She sobbed with the relief of it even as the blood still ran from his ravaged cheek.

"Did it work?" he demanded, his voice like sandpaper.

"Yes," she said, tears dripping down her chin onto the wreck of his shirt. "You did it."

The remains of the engine smoked ahead of them, a dark cloud rising into a sky streaked with the red and gold of the sunrise. The black silhouette of a bird wheeled across the plume of it before coming to rest on the signal post across the tracks. The train was still now save for the lingering groan of tortured metal.

He started to rise and she pressed him back.

"You really ought not do that," she said.

The words sang, bridging past and present. The heath and the train yard. A gulf of months and the breath of a moment.

Strangford choked out a laugh, reaching up to brush his gloved fingers across her cheek.

"Just a scratch, Lily," he rasped in reply as his blood dripped onto the stones. "Help me up."

He clasped her hand and she levered him to his feet. Her ribs made a sharp protest at the effort. Strangford gasped at the movement of his other arm.

"What is it?" she demanded.

"I may have broken it," he admitted.

The gravel where he had lain was flecked with scarlet. Twisted shards of metal were scattered across the ground. Lily knew one of

343

them must have been responsible for the ruin of his face—she could not yet contemplate what that would mean, what that clear damage must cost him. She could only feel gratitude that the shrapnel had not struck somewhere more dear.

Too close—it had been too desperately close.

There was a flash of black feathers as the bird across the tracks took flight, and Lily wrenched herself away from the abyss of that thought, recalled the urgency of the hour.

The Thames glimmered at the far end of the tracks, silver in the light of the rising dawn.

"I have to get Sam away from the bomb," she said, the words clamping another vise around her heart.

"Go," Strangford ordered, his blood still dripping onto the hard ground. "Don't wait for me. Run!"

TWENTY-EIGHT

Sunday morning
Ten past six

*L*ILY SPRINTED DOWN THE tracks, pain blistering across her ribs.

Shouts echoed off the buildings behind her. She thought of the soldiers who had leapt from the train before Strangford threw the mortar. He would not be able to outrun them.

She could not look back.

Ludgate Viaduct flew past and she plunged into Ludgate Hill Station. The railmen leapt down to the tracks, carrying fire extinguishers toward the derailed train. A few early passengers watched bewildered from the platform.

Lily did not stop.

Her boots pounded against the rail bed. She crossed over Great Victoria Street, the morning traffic rising now, cart wheels mingling with the rumble of a lorry engine.

She could not see a clock, but she knew the time. It could only be moments until six-fifteen, until the bomb would detonate.

St. Paul's Station appeared ahead and beyond that the flat, open expanse of the Blackfriars rail bridge.

A conductor shouted as she raced past. She heard others jump down from the platform behind her and pushed for more speed. She bolted past a red signal at the foot of the bridge.

A long, thin, familiar figure stood a quarter of the way across the bridge, looking down over the side.

"Cairncross!" Lily shouted as she approached.

He turned to look at her. His craggy face was drawn into lines of distress.

He caught her as she reached him.

"We stopped it," she gasped, breathless. "Tell them to get out of there!"

"He can't go, Lily," Cairncross replied, desperate. "He's holding the blasted thing together."

Fear shook her.

He looked past her at the approaching railmen.

"I'll try to slow them," he said. He released her and jogged down the tracks.

She swung onto the ladder Cairncross had been standing over. Metal rungs took her down into the guts of the bridge, the nest of iron girders that made up its enormous arches.

Sam was perched in the midst of it, halfway across a narrow metal catwalk. Ash stood beside him, the wind of the river tugging at the jacket of his suit.

She took in the presence of barrels, wires. Sam's hands were wrist-deep in a box at the center of it, the hub of the bomb.

She hurried toward them.

"The train isn't coming. We have to get you out of here before this thing blows," she pleaded.

"It should have blown ninety seconds ago," Ash said.

"I bypassed the trigger mechanism but the blasted battery is bad," Sam said without looking at her. His gaze was on the maze of wires in the box, on something he was holding into place with his bare hands. "When the current goes, so does the bomb."

Sam had wired an ammeter to the terminals of the battery. Lily watched as the needle flickered dangerously.

"You have extra hands now. Let's fasten it together," she demanded.

"It needs a weld," Sam snapped back, his face pale but determined.

"Whoever built it was either an idiot or a genius. I don't have the equipment."

"But . . ." Lily started uselessly, the horror of the situation rendering her numb.

Sam looked up, his dark eyes sharp as ice.

"You two need to bugger off now!" he shouted.

The urgency of that order washed over her. From every corner of the iron lace of the bridge, wings burst forth. Pigeons, sparrows, gulls—they took to flight, exploding from their nests and perches, driven out by the force of Sam's fear.

Rats scurried down the piers, swam into the Thames.

The Blackfriars rail bridge emptied of life save for the three of them.

A train whistle echoed across the water.

"Where did that come from?" Sam demanded.

"The southern bank," Ash replied. "Lily?"

She swung back to the ladder, climbing quickly. She peered over the top of the bridge.

Cairncross shouted behind her, arguing with the railmen. To the west, a motorized launch cut across the gleaming river. Lily recognized the uniforms of the Thames Division and knew it was a police cruiser speeding toward Blackfriars.

On the far side of the water, a train wound its way slowly along the elevated track to the bridge.

"There's a train," she called down, her voice dry in her throat. "I see passenger cars."

"What color is the signal at the end of the bridge?" Sam demanded from below.

"Green," she rasped. She slid back down the ladder, dashing onto the catwalk. "It's green!"

The ammeter flickered again.

If the battery died as that train passed overhead . . .

Ash knelt on the other side of the mechanism.

"Sam. Let me see that," he quietly commanded.

It was a tone Lily knew well, the one that carried a natural assumption of authority. She was not surprised to see Sam heed it, allowing Ash to slip his hands into the guts of the bomb and take the delicate wires from him.

"I dunno what you think you're going to do with that," Sam snapped. "You don't know a thing about machines."

"I'm not going to fix it, Sam. I'm going to blow it up. As soon as you and Miss Albright get out of the way."

Lily could not react. The implication was too big, the situation too impossible.

Ash's eyes were clear. Fear flickered at the edges but there was no doubt, no hesitation.

His hands did not shake.

Sam's face registered the horror she could feel wrenching through her.

"*No!*" he gasped. The word was a wound, a blow struck at his core.

Lily gripped the iron rail of the catwalk. It vibrated under her fingers, a subtle message from the oncoming train.

The ammeter dipped.

"Go now," Ash ordered.

"You can't do this!" Sam cried, grief roughening his voice.

"There are great things ahead of you, Sam Wu," Ash replied steadily, his gaze strong. "I am sorry I will not be there to see it."

Lily sensed Sam's movement before he made it. She reacted on instinct. As he lunged for Ash, she knocked him into the pier.

Seconds ticked past and she knew with a bone-deep certainty that time was running out.

She grabbed his arm, yanking him back.

"We have to go!" she called into his ear.

He held firm against her—he was stronger than she was. His face was twisted with grief.

"Lily, we can't—"

"Make it mean something," she rasped back, forcing him to look at her, putting every atom of her own authority into the words.

The rattle in the iron was palpable now, a shaking she could feel through the soles of her boots.

Ash knelt at the bomb, his gaze steady.

There was too much to say. There was no time to say it.

The pain hit her like a blow, threatening to break her—but she could not break.

She grabbed Sam's arm and pulled him into a run.

He came with her, tearing himself from the pier—from Ash. They pounded down the clanging metal grille of the catwalk, pushing for speed.

Lily hit the end of it and kept going, throwing herself from the steel out into the empty void of the air.

She braced for impact. The Thames hit her like a whip of fire, then swallowed her, drawing her into its depths.

The water was cool, blanketing her world in silence. She gave herself to it, grief wrenching at her heart.

The darkness beyond her closed eyes flashed into daylight. Flames blazed across the surface of the water as the river roared.

She opened her eyes to the murk. Debris tumbled past her, glinting in the hot light from above.

Her body ached for oxygen, the surface tugging at her like a rope. She accepted it, clawed and kicked her way up past the slow-sinking bits of metal and stone.

She burst out into the morning, gasping for air, and whirled to face the bridge.

A hole smoked in the side of it, framed by twisted and blackened steel.

It was clear to her now, the entirety of what her vision had promised. It had not been just one moment but two that it foretold.

The flames dancing across the water. The shadow in the doorway.

Lily knew now who had been leaving.

On the southern verge of the bridge, a passenger train waited, engine venting steam over the close-packed rooftops.

The river around her rippled with the drops of an impossible rain falling from a clear sky, vaporized water pinging warmly back down onto the Thames.

Sam surfaced beside her. His mouth opened in a scream she could not hear, the world around her muffled and strange.

People crowded at the edge of St. Paul's Station, gazing in shock at the destruction. Lily recognized Cairncross, his hands raised and folded behind his head as he dropped to his knees.

The dark-haired figure beside him wore a suit soaked with blood, cradling his arm. Strangford.

His gaze found her in the water, and Sam beside her.

He would not know yet who was missing.

The grief tore through her, ripping like a claw.

Behind Cairncross and Strangford, men in uniforms pointed guns and shouted. Others ran past carrying fire suppression equipment, heading toward the smoking wreck of the bridge.

The shrill call of a police whistle slipped dully through the fog in her ears. Lily's hearing cleared to the roar of an engine as the diesel police launch skimmed to a stop beside them.

"Stand down!"

Rough hands plucked her from the Thames, tossed her to the floor of the boat. Her arms were wrenched back, handcuffs snapping around her wrists.

Sam knelt on the floor of the boat beside her. He had gone quiet, a stillness that came through gritted teeth. She could not tell if the drops that slid across his face were remnants of the river or something else.

The world around her screamed accusations, demanded answers. Lily looked past it to the tortured gap in the bridge, to the absence ripped into the heart of it. To the men and women climbing from the halted passenger train to gape at the disaster.

It would be the only hole torn in London today. The mad saint's prophecy was upended. She had changed fate, redirected the course of history—she and Sam and Strangford and the others.

The cataclysm of the morning would be entirely their own.

TWENTY-NINE

Sunday morning
Nine o'clock

*T*HE ROOM WHERE LILY sat was small and freshly whitewashed. It had the feeling of a ship's cabin. It moved like a ship as well, tossing ever so slightly in the wake of a passing barge.

The headquarters of the Thames Division was a low one-story structure built onto the floating pier under Waterloo Bridge. It rose and fell with the tides beneath the great neoclassical facade of Somerset House.

Everything hurt. Each breath felt as though someone were driving needles into Lily's chest. She was covered in bruises, her muscles aching.

Her interrogators had come and gone. Lily had told them nothing about why she was on the bridge—why she jumped, what she knew about the bomb.

She overheard the voices of the Thames Division constables in the hall. Her description had been circulated in relation to the train wreck at Ludgate. There was apparently a row sparking up between the military and the police authorities at Scotland Yard over custody of both Lily and the two men the army had picked up at Blackfriars and taken to Finsbury Barracks.

That would be Cairncross . . . and Strangford.

Sam had already been moved from the Thames Division, hauled off to Scotland Yard. Special Branch, charged with investigating the bombing, had been slower to lay claim to Lily, apparently having some difficulty imagining what a woman's role in the incident at Blackfriars might have been.

This could not possibly go well for her. She could not bring herself to regret that. What she had done was necessary. Her heart ached for what it would mean for the others—for Strangford, for Sam. It ached that Ash was gone.

Ash was gone. The thought was still foreign, strangely hard to accept. Her relationship with him had never been easy, but it had made her who she was—something much more than what she had been before.

She could almost hear his voice in her head.

Not me, Miss Albright. You have done that all yourself. I have merely been privileged to witness it.

It hurt, knowing he would never say it. Imagining that knowing light in his eyes, that quiet certainty, was all she had left.

Footsteps echoed from down the hall. Lily braced herself for the arrival of those who would take her on to the next set of consequences for her actions that morning.

"Yes, Commissioner. Understood, sir."

She heard the words through the thin boards of the door and felt a moment of surprise that she was important enough to bring the head of the entire Metropolitan Police down upon her personally.

Her little white room rocked gently in the passing of another boat. The door opened as the constable on guard outside showed someone in.

The Earl of Torrington stepped inside.

He had changed his evening clothes for a sober and well-tailored suit of charcoal gray, but Lily could see in the lines around his eyes that he had not slept.

"Are you hurt?" he demanded quietly.

"No," she lied.

Then, to her shock and dismay, the tears spilled out of her.

They came with force, the pain and fear and grief of the night overflowing in a manner Lily could not control.

Her father put his arms around her.

She let herself fall into him and the sobs came bubbling up, unleashed by the simple comfort of his presence. The feeling of being held by him was surprisingly familiar, from the smell of his shaving lotion to the brushed wool of his coat. Lily was suffused by the sense that she had done this before, many times, in a remote corner of her past she could barely recall.

"I am so sorry, Lily," he said.

Lily knew that it was true. Her father was sorry for many things—for the loss she had suffered today. For his inability to protect her from it. For all the ways he had failed her in the past.

He would never be a perfect father. He was too firmly bound in a complex web of obligations. Honor pulled him in contradictory directions he could only navigate, not resolve.

But he loved her. She knew that, and just then, it was enough.

The tears washed out of her and she pulled herself back together, releasing him.

"I wanted to come sooner," he said. "But I am afraid your companions were at rather more immediate risk."

"Are they safe?"

"They have been released. Mr. Cairncross and Mr. Wu were headed home. Lord Strangford has been taken to St. Bartholomew's. I am afraid he was in need of medical attention."

Her stomach dropped.

"How bad is it?" she demanded.

"His life is not in danger," he said firmly. "He will recover from the rest of it. He is very strong."

"You have no idea how strong," she replied.

"I received your message. It took an unconscionably long time to reach me—I am afraid the staff at Westminster were under other orders from the prime minister that we not be disturbed and it tied your message up in an excess of bureaucracy. The Home Secretary was with us when it finally arrived. He immediately dispatched a troop of Special Branch officers to Bexley's home."

She did not miss the significance of that. The Home Secretary would not have sent out the police on the basis of a few scribbled words on the back of a receipt. Her father had done that, thrown the full weight of his influence on the line on the basis of Lily's hurried note.

It had not always been like that. He had let her down before and told her that he regretted it. What he had done that morning showed that those were not mere words.

Her father trusted her.

"When we arrived, we found him surrounded by half a dozen D Division officers," he continued. "It seems he was in the process of listing your crimes to them, demanding you be brought in. We were just dragging him outside when the explosion could be heard from Blackfriars. He was quick enough to change his story once we offered him leniency."

"Why would you do that?" Lily demanded, shocked.

"He is only one of them, Lily," her father replied. "There are half a dozen others in positions of authority, including the ranks of the military. We are days from a declaration of war against Germany and Austria-Hungary. An investigation into conspiracy and treachery would tear the armed forces apart, if we could even convince Parliament to sanction it. And I very much doubt that we could. Not when it is a matter of collaborating with an enemy in Ulster half the Conservative party thinks should be our allies. Enticing Bexley to cooperate was the only way we could realistically hope to identify the traitors."

"They would have killed millions."

She closed her eyes against that terrible truth, and in that darkness she could see the smoking ruin of St. Amalgaid's prophecy, the extent of the destruction that Bexley and his collaborators would thoughtlessly have caused.

This room, the Thames Division station—the ancient buildings that surrounded it, the bridges and cathedral spires and shops and tenements—it would have been gone. All because of the hubris of a few privileged men who thought their politics worth a little treason.

"When they told me about the train it did not take much for me to put the timing together," he said. "I know what we owe you—and Lord Strangford, and Mr. Wu."

"And Robert Ash," Lily added. The name hurt.

"And Robert Ash," Torrington agreed solemnly. "I was able to arrange for the charges against all of you to be dismissed. The train derailment will be written off as an accident."

"And the bomb?" she asked.

"An industrial incident," he replied. "The peace talks the Red Branch hoped to disrupt will be postponed indefinitely. The Irish problem has dropped precipitously in priority in the face of what is happening in Europe. I cannot speak for the Nationalists, but the moderate Irish parties have expressed a willingness to wait until a more opportune time to address the issue of Home Rule. On the Unionist side, even the volunteer force in Ulster is eager to support British efforts to defeat the Germans. It will not be the end of the matter, but Lord knows we have more immediate concerns to contend with."

He paused.

"There are . . . certain aspects of what passed over the last twelve hours that I do not entirely understand," he said, his tone cautious.

Lily met his gaze evenly, waiting.

"Lord Bexley was quite fixated on an incident involving Lord Strangford in an establishment run by a Mrs. Needham," he went on.

She recalled the feeling of Bexley thrashing under her grip and Strangford's distant concentration as he put his hands on the nobleman.

Blackfriars. The bridge.

Her pulse leaped, nerves lighting to careful life at that memory of Bexley's shock, of how Strangford had been exposed.

How the bloody hell did you know?

"There was also an . . . unusual incident in the House of Lords earlier in the week. Something involving a flock of pigeons," he said.

"What are you asking me?" Lily returned.

He studied her with his cool gray eyes, and she knew the mind behind them was working, always working.

"Nothing," he finally replied. "Some secrets are dangerous enough that they are best kept close."

Lily had experienced the truth of that with terrible intimacy at the hands of Dr. Joseph Hartwell, a man who would have torn the blood from her veins to get at the power she carried inside of her.

A power he believed should belong to him, to do with as he saw fit.

Her father would keep their secret, whatever part of it he understood. That he knew it at all was a sharp reminder of what exposure could mean—of what it could cost them.

"Who were they? The others?"

"Bexley was the ringleader. Planting the bomb and blaming it on the Irish Republican Brotherhood was his idea. General Taggart was part of it, along with a personal assistant to the Foreign Secretary . . . and a duty clerk in the Prime Minister's office," Torrington finished. There was a gravity to his tone that seemed out of proportion to the position he had named until the implication of it crept through into Lily's brain.

"You wrote to the Prime Minister after Prinz came to you," she noted.

She could see that she had hit the mark.

"I told you that the sort of protection he was seeking was not something I could arrange myself."

The pieces clicked into place.

Even a confidential message to the prime minister had to be opened and screened. It would be done by men with the highest security clearance, but if one of those men had divided loyalties . . .

The duty clerk would have seen the note and understood its implications for his fellows in the Red Branch. He had leaked the information and Charlie Prinz had been plucked from his evening commute and drowned in the sewer.

She did not want to ask the next question, and yet she could not hide from it.

"And Patrick Dougherty?"

He did not flinch at the sound of the name, but then he must have been expecting it.

"The clerk wasn't there fourteen years ago," he replied. "The men I spoke with about Patrick Dougherty weren't named by Bexley tonight, but after fourteen years they are all transferred or retired or dead by now. One of them may have been involved, or the leak might have originated with the Fenians. Or perhaps Dougherty's lover realized what he'd revealed and thought the better of it. I don't know, Lily." There was a ferocity in him now, emotion riding nearer to the surface. "I don't know who killed her. Whether I am somehow responsible. I am not sure that I ever will."

"Would it matter?" she asked softly. "If you did know—if you could be certain one way or another—would it change anything?"

He did not answer. She had not really expected him to. That was his own burden to wrangle with. She could not do it for him.

"There will be a series of quiet resignations," he said. "Enterprises will be defunded, loans called due, invitations withdrawn. The nature of the situation prohibits a public justice but they will not go on as they have done. There are enough of us who know the truth to see to that. Of course, the papers help."

"What papers?" Lily asked.

He looked genuinely confused.

"The ones that came with your message. The carbon-copies of documents related to the missing arms shipment Prinz was concerned about. Manifests, signatures. It amounts to a very damning case that Bexley, Taggart and the other conspirators knowingly used government funds to purchase arms they then intentionally diverted to Ulster and delivered into the hands of a guerrilla army last April."

"But I didn't send you any papers," she admitted. Even as the words left her lips a suspicion grew in her mind.

Who else knew of her father's interest in Bexley and the Red Branch? Who else might have access to sources that could acquire such evidence?

Only Wu Zhao Min.

Perhaps Sam's sister had not considered her bargain with Lily entirely fulfilled—or maybe for once she had simply chosen to act for justice without demanding a price for it.

The thought sparked a little flame of hope that perhaps that link in Sam's family was not irrevocably broken.

She could see the calculations taking place behind her father's eyes. He was capable of drawing his own conclusion about the source of the papers. She wondered where that might lead.

"What about the Red Branch?" she asked.

"Special Branch is rounding up the rank and file of the society as we speak. I cannot say that we will find all of them—such organizations are like hydras, bound to bubble up again each time you think you have finished them off. But this war will take the air out of the Unionist cause for the near future."

"Will there be no stopping it? The war."

The word carried a weight of dread with it.

"The German army marches toward Belgium as we speak. Tomorrow we will issue an ultimatum to them to withdraw."

"Will they heed it?" Lily asked.

"I think that you and I both know the answer to that," he replied.

He looked older in that moment, the lines on his face seeming to grow deeper. She could feel the weight of his worry as though it were a physical thing he had carried into the room with them.

~

He held the door for her as she walked out of the holding cell. An officer in the hall tipped his hat respectfully as Torrington passed.

Outside on the pier, pots of geraniums and climbing fuchsia stood out brightly against the white walls of the police station, giving it more the look of a floating garden cottage than a law enforcement facility.

The Thames was busy with midday traffic. Barges and steamers glided past, mingling with pleasure boats churning up the muddy water. It was one of those rare and splendid English summer days where the sun hung brightly in a robin-egg sky. Somerset House was a gleaming palace of white before her, the towers and gables of Westminster sparkling in the sunlight. Bridges arched elegantly over the river, knitting together the office blocks, flats and warehouses, churches and wharves that were her home.

It was all here, where it should no longer have been. Lily had seen to that.

Across the water, the black scar in the side of the Blackfriars rail bridge spoke of the price she had paid for it.

"I want to extend an invitation," her father said. His tone had gone a touch awkward as he ventured into uncharted territory. "If you should wish someplace out-of-the-way to recuperate, I should be glad to have you at Brede Abbey."

Brede Abbey. It was the family seat of the earls of Torrington, her father's home in the High Weald of Sussex. The sprawling Elizabethan manor of gray stone was nestled amid lime trees, gardens, and rolling hills, dark forests and sheep pasture. Lily had been inside of it only once before, and her father's words conjured it up in perfect detail— the halls paneled in ancient wood, the ticking of an old clock. The muddy boots by the entry.

Lily could almost imagine what it would feel like to retreat to that quiet and comfortable place, spending the evenings with her father in his library, surrounded by the smell of old books and the chirp of crickets.

In another world, another universe, it might have been her home—but Lily lived in this world. What her father offered her was both generous and brave. Even if his wife and sons weren't in residence, the move would entail a potentially knotty and painful conflict. Though Lily herself might not have to face them, she would still know.

"Thank you," she said and meant it. "I appreciate the offer. But I have matters to attend to here."

He looked down at her and she was conscious of how closely his face resembled her own—of how far back her memories of it went.

"May I see you home, then?" he asked.

"No," she replied. "But you may bring me to St. Bart's."

~

London's oldest hospital loomed before her, its great, soot-stained facade rising overhead against the bright blue of the sky. A few sparrows danced around the upper stories. Their quick movements avoided the trajectory of a fat black raven that swooped in as Lily watched, settling itself comfortably by a window to one of the upper wards.

The sight of the bird made her a bit cold.

Inside, St. Bart's was much as Lily remembered it. The wide hall-ways were a syncopated clockwork of moving bodies and rattling equipment, smelling brightly of carbolic.

She was directed to a ward on the topmost floor. It was a clean and brightly-lit space of tall windows and tidy rows of beds.

Pausing in the doorway, Lily looked for Strangford and could not immediately recognize where he was. She felt a quick bolt of fear at the thought of why he might no longer be there.

A nurse paused in her rounds, eyeing Lily cautiously.

"Do you need some help, miss?" she asked.

It came to her that she must still look a sight. She had not changed since her fall into the river, since she had been thrown from a moving train. Her body ached and she knew there were scrapes and bruises she had not yet cataloged. The nurse could well take her for someone just escaped from the mental ward. It would explain her careful tone.

"It's alright, Matron."

The familiar voice rumbled from behind her, rough with the music of an Ulster accent.

Dr. Gardner also wore lines of exhaustion on his face. As she turned to face him, Lily could see that he had not left the hospital since the night before. He must have stayed on even with the threat of the explosion. Somehow it did not surprise her.

The terrible news bubbled up in her, demanding to be let out before any further pretense.

"Mr. Ash . . ." she began.

"I know," he replied. He set a hand on her shoulder. She could see the quiet weight of his grief. "I believe you're here for his lordship."

"Where is he?" she demanded.

"He's inside," Gardner said, nodding to the ward, and Lily felt a sick bolt at the notion that she had not been able to recognize him.

The doctor had not let go of her shoulder. Lily sensed he had more to say before she went rushing in.

"He's just out of the operating theater."

"An operation? What for?" she said.

"To remove his left eye. I'm sorry, Lily—there was too much damage to save it."

She let herself absorb the fact of his disfigurement, this permanent damage he had won by saving her from what might have been much worse. It hurt.

"What else?" she demanded.

"Twenty-six stitches to his face. A fracture to both bones of his left forearm. There are multiple contusions, abrasions. We had to take a piece of shrapnel out of his leg but that damage was more or less superficial."

"So he'll be alright?" she asked, closing her eyes, taking all of it in.

"He'll be fine," Gardner replied firmly.

She opened her eyes, meeting his gaze meaningfully.

"You know that for certain?"

An orderly bustled past them, pushing a cart full of clean bedpans. The nurse glanced over at where they hovered in the doorway.

"I do," he replied steadily. "Might I ascertain the same for you?"

She knew what he was asking. She didn't particularly want to—it was another minute that kept her from Strangford's side—but she knew it was the prudent choice.

She gave him a nod.

His hand still on her shoulder, she saw the doctor slip into another world. She stepped closer to him, clearing the path to the door for a nurse carrying a load of linens.

To anyone passing by, it looked as though they were having an earnest and intimate conversation . . . so long as no one noticed that Gardner's mouth wasn't moving.

He surfaced a moment later.

"That pain you've been feeling in your chest?" he said. "It's a pair of broken ribs."

"What should I do?"

"Stop running about and get some rest," he replied. "Manage that and they'll heal on their own, along with the rest of it."

He took his hand from her shoulder and nodded toward one of the beds.

"He's been etherized. It's likely still wearing off and they'll have given him morphine for the pain. I don't know that he'll be able to speak with you."

"We don't have to speak," Lily replied, already looking past him.

"I don't suppose that you do," Gardner noted. "Go on with you, then."

She walked past the rows of beds. An old woman sat upright with an IV dripping into her arm. A boy dozed on his side as his mother read him a book.

For a moment the room seemed to shimmer, and Lily saw something else—the beds closer packed, full of young men. Blankets flat where legs should be, burned limbs wrapped in white bandages.

The vision broke and she found herself looking down at Strangford.

It was no wonder she had not been able to see him from the door. He was barely recognizable, his head swathed in gauze. His arm lay on top of the sheet, encased in plaster from elbow to hand. It would be hard for him to put his gloves on like that, she thought distantly, her heart pounding in her chest.

His eye was closed. His chest rose and fell evenly. She found her respite in that steady rise and fall of his breath.

She sat down in the chair beside him. Reaching out, she pushed a lock of his too-long hair from his face.

"Lily," he said, half-dreaming out the word through a haze of pain medication.

"I'm here," she replied.

She slipped her hand into his own, skin to skin, and that was where she stayed.

~

It was drifting toward evening when she finally returned to March Place.

She had been politely booted from the ward as visiting hours closed for the day, though the duty nurse had assured her that Strangford was healing well, kindly overlooking Lily's own disheveled state.

Her aches had worsened. Walking home would likely have been an ordeal, but it had not proved necessary. When she left the hospital a discreet black carriage had been waiting for her at the curb. The driver greeted her by name and said he had been instructed to take her wherever she needed to go.

It was a small gift from her father. Lily was grateful for it.

The carriage stopped in front of her building.

"Good evening, Miss Albright," the driver said with perfect courtesy as she climbed down.

March Place had not changed. A few clerks working past regular hours were making their way home along the pavement. Children played ball at the end of the road, their laughter echoing off the bricks. The distant clatter of traffic drifted in from Tottenham Court Road a few blocks away.

The light was on in Estelle's flat. A pair of shadows moved across the window and Lily knew that Estelle and Miss Bard must have already come home. It was a comforting thought even as exhaustion settled into her bones.

It was the same, and yet everything was different.

Something leaned against the railing by the front steps. Lily noticed it with a quick flare of recognition.

She climbed up and took the yew staff into her hands. She could feel by the weight, by the familiar contours of its length, that it was her own.

A thin red ribbon tied a piece of notepaper to the top.

She loosened the string and opened up the message.

With regards. Jack Cannon.

Lily was not so foolish as to believe the return of her staff a gift. It was either a taunt or a threat.

If the latter, Cannon would find she was not easily cowed.

The paper crumpled in her hand.

She gave the staff a swing, striking a quick blow against an imaginary opponent. Her ribs protested the move, but the staff felt right. There was no taint in it from its misadventures.

A bread lorry rattled past. A pair of girls spun by on their bicycles, bells ringing.

Lily paid them no mind. The world had grown bigger than it was the day before. She would not be boxed in by something so trivial as appearances. She had gone to war with fate and she had won.

There had been a cost. She suspected there would always be a cost. It would not stop her from trying.

With her staff in her hand and an ache in her chest, Lily pushed open the door and came home.

THIRTY

August 6, 1914
March Place, Bloomsbury

$\mathcal{L}$ILY STOOD IN FRONT of her mirror in a black dress.

Rain pattered against the windowpanes. The pale morning light softened the lines of her little attic room.

There was nothing to be done about her hair. Whatever magic Estelle had worked to pin up the short strands of it the night of Bexley's ball, Lily could not recreate it. She would have to wear it as it was, though it would likely be considered too modern for a funeral.

She found she didn't particularly care.

She set her black hat into place and fixed the pins, ignoring the sharp ache the movement sent jarring through her injured ribs.

Pausing at the door, she contemplated her umbrella stand. She left the yew walking stick where it was, taking up a black umbrella instead. She doubted there would be a fight today, but there would certainly be rain.

Estelle and Miss Bard waited downstairs in the hall. Lily's friend was resplendent in her ebony fringed caftan embroidered in dark velvet. Somehow Lily was not surprised to learn that Estelle could dress splendidly for a funeral.

Miss Bard was sober and trim beside her in a dark tailored suit, a black armband around her sleeve.

"Are we ready?" Estelle asked as Lily descended.

Lily wasn't. She nodded anyway.

They stepped out into the rain.

The carriage wheels swished through the puddles as their hackney pulled out into the road. Posters had sprouted up overnight on the walls of the buildings that lined the road. They depicted brave men of generic appearance in dashing uniforms marching toward a monstrous enemy.

Enlist today. Your country calls you.

Red, white and blue bunting was hung across the storefronts and strung between houses. Discarded bottles and the remnants of paper crackers cluttered the streets, the debris of last night's celebrations.

The news had broken yesterday morning. Britain was at war with Germany.

An army lorry rumbled past, the khaki-clad soldiers in the rear hunched against the rain that slipped past the thin protection of the canvas roof.

"It's so like Mr. Ash to choose St. Giles's," Estelle commented from across the carriage. "St. George's is far more elegant, but of course he must have the poets' church."

"Really, Estelle," Miss Bard chided from beside her.

A pair of boys ran by in the rain, spinning pinwheels. The war was a game to them, an unexpected holiday. Those who had celebrated in the streets last night had no notion of what it would really mean. Lily had overheard men at the news shop chortling about how "Fritz" would be "trounced by Christmas."

Lily knew it wasn't true.

A paperboy called from under the awning of a teashop as they rolled past.

"British cruiser sunk by German mine! One hundred and thirty souls lost in the North Sea!"

A group of handsome young men ambled past him, heedless of the rain dripping off the brims of their hats. The brash call of their laughter cut through the quiet rush of the traffic.

"I saw him the night before last," Estelle offered. She was reclined comfortably in her seat, the velvet of her caftan glimmering.

"Who's that?" Miss Bard asked.

"Mr. Ash, of course," Estelle replied.

Lily did not bother to protest or to suggest that perhaps Estelle had been dreaming. She knew better than that.

"Oh, Estelle," Miss Bard said quietly.

Estelle reached over to pat Miss Bard's hand as though she were the one who needed reassuring. Knowing Estelle's level of comfort with the dead, it was probably true.

"He came to say goodbye. It is something the dead often do, though of course I am honored he decided to stop for me."

"And?" Lily demanded.

She knew there was more. She could see it in the careful look in Estelle's eyes, in the way that she had waited until they were trapped together in the carriage before she brought the matter up. Lily had run into her downstairs neighbor half a dozen times the day before and she had not mentioned a word of this. There would be a reason for that and Lily had no patience for dancing around it.

"He had a message for you," Estelle said.

"I see," Lily replied thinly.

Her grief, already near to the surface, roared up. It threatened the careful control she had built around it.

She wondered if it would be the same soft platitudes Estelle passed on to many of her clients from their departed loved ones, words of comfort about how at peace they were.

Somehow she doubted it. After all, they were talking about Robert Ash.

She wasn't at all sure she wanted to hear this. In fact, her gut was shouting for her to yank open the door and jump out of the carriage, walking to the funeral in the rain rather than listening to what Estelle was going to say.

Ash was gone. He had taken all his wisdom, his infuriating challenges, his painful truth with him. He had left her without a guide only halfway along this journey to becoming something she still did not entirely understand.

"I told him you would be like this," Estelle noted cheerfully.

"Like what?" Lily retorted.

"You know," Estelle replied with an expressive wave of her hand.

Lily's anger tightened.

"I warned him he'd have to give me something that would catch your attention. He said I should tell you that he had one foot in the boat."

Her heart skipped.

She remembered that twilit stretch of shore where a quiet sea lapped at the edge of the endless expanse of the marsh. The boat that waited on that boundary offering passage to what lay on the far side. A boat without oars.

A boat that did not return.

It was Lily's secret. The truth of what she had experienced during the moments between her drowning and her return to life was an inviolate knowledge that even Strangford could not touch. She had never mentioned a word of it to anyone.

Estelle could not have known about it. No one could—not unless they had been there for themselves.

"I presume you know what that means," Estelle went on, watching Lily closely.

"I do," Lily admitted.

"Good," Estelle concluded. "He is desperately proud of you, you know. He didn't tell me that—you know how he is when he's intent upon a topic—but I could feel it in him nonetheless."

It hurt to hear it. All Lily could think of was how he should have been saying it to her here, in the flesh. There had been so little of that before he died. It had all been struggle and work and frustration. Why hadn't he said it before?

Perhaps because he had known that Lily wasn't ready to hear it. She couldn't accept his pride in her until she had found some in herself.

"What did he want to say?" she asked. They were nearing the church and she did not want to have to continue this conversation later.

"He had a message for you from Mrs. Ash."

The chill crawled over her skin. Whatever Evangeline Ash had to tell Lily, it would be a matter of fate.

Lily had never had a very comfortable relationship with fate.

"Tell me," she demanded.

"You know how this works," Estelle cautioned her.

Lily did. Evangeline Ash's message wouldn't be in words. The dead spoke to Estelle in symbols and feeling, a vast and strange language that lay below any dialect.

"There are two seeds," Estelle said, focused now, intent on communicating clearly. "The first fades into dust. The second grows strong—sprouting branches, roots set deep into the earth. A key transforms into a weapon. She showed it to me as a sword in your hand."

"What else?" Lily demanded, knowing there was more.

"Blood," Estelle replied. "Blood on your hands. But you must understand the context, Lily. This was not a crime. It felt . . . necessary."

"Creation and destruction," Miss Bard offered thoughtfully, bringing the folklorist's perspective to the discussion. "The essential and opposing forces of every mythology."

Lily rebelled against it, every fiber of her rising up in protest. How dare Ash dictate her fate, even as messenger? He was dead and still he meddled with who she was meant to be.

She didn't want blood on her hands. She didn't want to be a weapon.

"Damn him," she said quietly into the gloom of the carriage.

Estelle said nothing. She had done what her old friend had asked of her, and they had arrived at St. Giles.

The church was just south of Bedford Square. It was a simple structure of soot-stained stone, steeple pointing into the heavy gray sky. The old churchyard that surrounded it was an oasis of violent green in the heart of the close-packed streets of the city.

They stepped out of the hackney under the canopy of an ancient oak. The rain was an unrelenting drizzle. Lily stood under her umbrella facing a monumental arch of dark stone, its iron gates chained open.

Black-clad bodies streamed slowly into the church, most of them people she had never seen before. It reminded her that Ash had been a part of her life for only a few months. Before that there had been decades of his existence that she knew nothing about. There would be school friends and colleagues, a bevy of distant relations, including the cousin who had inherited his estate.

The greater portion of Ash's fortune was entailed, tied up in an inheritance that must now devolve upon a Staffordshire solicitor Lily had never heard of before this week. Cairncross described him as a "decent enough sort" whom he admitted Ash had not been particularly close to.

What remained were the buildings on Bedford Square but not the funds to maintain a household inside of them—had it made any sense to keep a household without a master. A comfortable sum had been willed to pension off Mr. Wu and Mrs. Liu. The rest went into a trust established for basic upkeep of the structures.

Their ultimate fate remained unresolved. Cairncross and Mr. Wu had been working all week to put the contents of The Refuge into storage, starting at the top of the house and working their way down. They were leaving the parlor and library intact until later.

Until after Robert Ash had been laid to rest.

The interior of the church was cool and dim. Great brass chandeliers hung overhead but the electric bulbs only pushed back the gloom from the center of the space. The grayness still lingered at the verges, awaiting its moment to spill back in.

The funeral-goers gathered in little knots or worked their way into the pews, exchanging sympathies or gossip in quiet voices. The low murmur of that conversation echoed off the high ceiling, turning to a constant river of sound.

Mr. Wu and Mrs. Liu were at the front of the aisle. As she watched, Mr. Wu stopped and bowed gracefully before the gleaming wooden coffin.

It contained no body. The box was a delicate sham. She did not know what of Ash had survived the explosion at Blackfriars, but whatever there had been would have been carried out with the tide, swept into the broad, cold waters of the North Sea.

And yet she also knew the coffin was not empty. Cairncross had filled it, placing into it the objects he deemed fitting. He had not shared with them what it contained, but Lily could imagine.

A robe of black silk. An ancient scroll. The sand of a distant desert and a portrait of the woman Ash had loved.

Sam stood behind them looking unusually sober in his plain black funeral suit. His back was stiff. Lily had barely spoken with him since Blackfriars. He was always on his way to somewhere else, escaping her attempts to pull him into conversation. She suspected his distance hid a pain and anger that outmatched even her own, but he was not yet ready to share it.

Mrs. Liu glanced back at Sam and said something that Lily could not hear. Sam's reply was short, but he followed it with a bow of his own toward the coffin.

Cairncross was already at the front pew. One of the columns of the church blocked Lily's view of whomever he was talking to. Her perspective shifted and she realized it was Strangford.

He dressed in sober black as matter of habit, so he looked much as he always did save for the angry red wound that cut across his face. Tidy rows of black stitches still marred the line of it, which was interrupted by the dark circle of a patch where his left eye had once been.

He extended a hand to Mr. Wu. His other arm, encased in plaster, hung in a sling around his neck.

The sight of his injuries still twisted her up inside, reminding her of just how close she had come to losing him as well.

She waited in the aisle as Estelle and Miss Bard slid into their places in the pew.

"I hope you're not wearing a corset."

Dr. Gardner stood beside her, solid as a mountain in his funeral clothes.

"Really, Doctor," Miss Bard chided from the pew.

"She knows why I'm asking," he replied.

"I have been following my doctor's orders," Lily told him.

"How are the ribs, then?"

"They hurt," she admitted.

"Most likely will for another month or so," he said.

His frankness made her smile. It was a dangerous impulse. Smiling made her feel uncomfortably close to crying.

"Your bedside manner delights as always," Estelle noted dryly.

"Our Miss Albright doesn't need coddling," he replied affectionately. "If you'll excuse me, ladies."

He made his way to Cairncross.

Lily glanced back at the door to see a familiar figure framed in the gray light from the churchyard. As he stepped inside, he was caught by a pair of funeral-goers, one of whom tugged his forelock in a show of respect.

It seemed Torrington had come.

Lily's attention was snagged from her father by a bright voice calling her name. She turned to see Virginia Eversleigh hurrying over. She looked elegant even in her funeral blacks. Her arms were halfway to giving Lily a hug before she caught herself.

"Dash it. I nearly forgot," she murmured prettily. She clasped Lily's hands instead, the silk of her gloves smooth against Lily's skin. "How are you holding up?"

"I'm fine," Lily assured her.

Strangford's sister had not come alone. Her husband, Mr. Eversleigh, followed behind her. He was a tall, blindingly handsome fellow with an earnest and kind expression. He offered Lily a firm handshake as well.

"My deepest sympathies on your loss, Miss Albright. I understand that Mr. Ash was a remarkable man."

"Thank you, Mr. Eversleigh," she replied, but her mind was on the third member of their party.

Lady Strangford's expression was not welcoming. Everything in the woman spoke of caution. Lily knew she was too clever to be taken in by the thin story they had concocted about the reason for Strangford's injury.

There was no way she could guess at the truth, but she clearly intuited that Lily had been somehow involved in it. It could only deepen her disapproval of Lily's relationship with her son.

It didn't matter. Lily didn't want Strangford's mother to be her enemy, but she would not apologize for herself to this woman—or to anyone. She was done with that.

"Lady Strangford," she said politely, offering her a curtsy.

"Miss Albright," Lady Strangford acknowledged coolly.

Virginia was holding her breath. Lily silently willed her not to intervene, holding herself straight in spite of the ache in her ribs.

"Good morning, Mr. Eversleigh. Mrs. Eversleigh."

Her father stood beside her. His black coat set off the silver of his hair. Another pair of funeral-goers bowed to him as they passed up the aisle, murmuring *m'lord*. Torrington acknowledged them with a nod. Lily was conscious of how closely the distinctive lines of his face mirrored her own, of the steel-hued eyes they both so obviously shared.

"A pleasure to see you again, Lord Torrington," Virginia answered graciously.

Torrington shifted the full weight of his attention to Strangford's mother.

"Lady Strangford," he said. "I see you have met my daughter."

Daughter. The word resounded through her.

There was nothing tentative in the way he said it. It came as a statement of simple fact.

Lily knew it was more than that. It was a declaration. A promise.

Virginia's eyes widened. She had not missed the significance of it spoken aloud in the public space of the church. It was clearly taking her some effort not to exclaim over it.

Nor was the implication lost on Lady Strangford.

"I have had that honor, my lord," she replied evenly.

Lily did not know Strangford's mother well, but she could see the intelligence in her dark eyes, so like those of both of her children. She was razor sharp, missing nothing.

"She is a very remarkable young woman," Torrington said.

Every word hung with added significance. There was a negotiation taking place here, happening at a level deep beneath the actual language being spoken.

Lily did not require Lady Strangford's approval. She would not let her future be shaped by one woman's opinion, but if Strangford's mother's assessment shifted towards cautious acceptance of Lily's entry into her family, it would make things a little bit easier.

Lily supposed she was due for something easy.

"So I have been given to understand," Lady Strangford returned.

Virginia let out a breath she had clearly been holding.

An acquaintance hailed from the other side of the church.

"Lady Strangford!"

"If you will excuse me, my lord."

The older woman offered Lord Torrington a curtsy that somehow had more of the feeling of a bow.

"Miss Albright," she added with a nod of respect before moving away.

"Did I miss something?" Eversleigh asked, looking a little bewildered.

"Never you mind, darling," Virginia replied, patting his arm.

Strangford slipped through the crowd in the aisle to join them.

Lily felt herself glow a bit to be near him again even though she had just seen him the day before.

He was tired. She could see the grief in him, the way it weighed on his shoulders. It was a feeling she shared, which made it easy for her to identify.

"Good morning, my lord," Strangford said.

Torrington extended a hand.

"Lord Strangford," he said. "I am informed you have been recovering very well."

"He's a hard old nut," Virginia offered proudly. Strangford shot her a look, the smallest hint of a smile pulling irresistibly at his lip.

It warmed Lily to see that sign of the resilience of Strangford's humor.

A few chords from the organ warned that the service was about to begin. The Eversleighs moved to their seats. Torrington graciously gave way to Strangford to take the open space in Lily's pew.

The priest droned into the liturgy, the words of the traditional service ringing off the walls of the church. In front of the altar, Ash's casket gleamed even in the dim light of the gray morning.

In the front row, Cairncross handed Mrs. Liu a handkerchief. She dabbed at her eyes.

Beside her, Sam sat as though carved from stone. It tied a knot of worry in Lily's stomach. This was harder, perhaps, for him than for any of them, even Cairncross who had spent decades at Ash's side.

There had been arrangements made for Sam, just as for Mr. Wu and Mrs. Liu. Lily knew that Sam's father and grandmother had plans to use the money Ash had set aside for them to lease a plot of farmland outside the city where Mr. Wu could grow his herbs. They would let a small shop in Limehouse to sell them. It would be a tidy and profitable business for them, serving a growing population of their countrymen finding their way to England.

Before he had died, Ash had been making arrangements for Sam to attend the Imperial College. He would have a full scholarship to study engineering. The deal was all but settled. Cairncross had told Lily that Ash's contact on the college council had assured him Sam would still be welcome to start the autumn semester.

It was a wonderful opportunity for Sam to rise from servant to professional, and yet trying to gauge his feelings about it had been like reading a brick wall. There was always something urgent he had to attend to in the garage, or a part he must run out to collect.

The voice of the vicar called out the ritual Psalm.

"Lord, thou hast been our refuge from one generation to another. Before the mountains were brought forth, or ever thou hadst formed the earth and the world, even from everlasting to everlasting, thou art God. Thou turnest man to destruction; and sayest, Return, ye children of men."

It was all wrong—the church, the Psalms, the bland conventionality of it. This wasn't Ash. The funeral should have been an amalgamation of a dozen faiths. The bells of a Catholic Mass ringing over the incense of a shaman, or a scattering of ashes under a clear night sky in some distant desert. It should be more than this ordinary English service in a gloomy London church.

It was over in what felt like moments. Strangford rose to join the other pallbearers in front of the altar. Gardner and Cairncross were there along with a stranger who must have been Ash's cousin.

Sam took his place at the casket. The funeral director had likely protested that assignment—pallbearers were meant to be of the same position in life as the departed—but Ash must have made his wishes patently clear.

Strangford stepped into line at the back of the coffin across from another man Lily did not know.

The other five had to lift the casket without him, but once it was aloft Strangford slipped his good arm and shoulder under the polished wood, taking his part of the burden.

They moved past up the aisle, the church organ ringing out a hymn Lily did not know the words to. She tried to catch Sam's eye and failed.

Lily rose with the rest of the funeral guests as the coffin reached the church door, heavy with the burden of her own sadness. With Estelle and Miss Bard at her side, she walked out into the rain.

THIRTY-ONE

Later that evening
The Refuge, Bedford Square

$\mathcal{I}$T WAS NEARLY EIGHT in the evening when the last of the funeral guests departed The Refuge, leaving Lily and the others alone in the quiet of the library.

They were all there—Estelle and Miss Bard, Gardner and Cairncross. Sam stood at the window gazing out at the rain-soaked square.

Mrs. Liu offered everyone more to eat. Finally convinced that they could take no more, she began clearing the table she had heaped with sweets and food.

The mirrors had all been taken down. The fierce, multi-armed goddess Kali that stood on one of the reading tables had been covered in a red cloth. This had precipitated an argument between Mrs. Liu, who had done the draping, and Cairncross, who maintained that only the Chinese gods in the house needed to be covered up.

"Those are mine," Mrs. Liu had retorted. "This one is yours."

She brought in another pot of tea. Estelle poured a cup.

"Please, Mrs. Liu, sit down with us," Miss Bard insisted, and to Lily's surprise for once the housekeeper acceded, sinking gratefully into a chair beside the other two women.

"Where is Mr. Wu?" Miss Bard asked.

"He's in the garden burning joss and paper money," Cairncross replied. "A gesture of kindness as Ash has no sons to do it for him."

Lily was conscious of Sam's silent presence by the window. Though she knew little about the tradition Cairncross was describing, somehow it seemed to her that it should be Sam burning the money.

She didn't say it. It didn't feel like her place. Instead, she leaned into Strangford on the sofa they had pulled in from the parlor, free now from eyes that would judge her for taking comfort in his presence.

The library was cozy, the electric lights lit against the coming darkness. Cairncross's efforts to close The Refuge had not yet reached here. Lily could almost pretend that it was all as it always had been, that this place would still be here in another day, another year. The truth was a painful knot at the bottom of this moment of peace, but she would not dwell on that now.

The rain was petering off. The clouds were breaking up on the horizon, promising a glorious sunset.

Past Sam's shoulder, Lily could see the black shadows of birds on the branches of the trees that lined the square. Though they were some distance away, she was certain they were ravens.

Their presence gave her a chill, as it had since that night on Hampstead Heath, but perhaps there was something appropriate about it. They felt like a sort of honor guard overseeing Ash's transition from this world to the next.

Mrs. Liu rose to check on her son in the garden.

"It was a nice service," Estelle noted after she had left. She patted Cairncross's knee. "You gave an excellent eulogy, James."

A line of automobiles drove past. They were decked out with bunting, honking their horns. The occupants, all young men, hooted triumphantly out the windows, their tires swishing across the wet asphalt.

"This blasted war," Cairncross said.

Her old friend looked tired. It was unusual for Cairncross, who had always seemed indefatigable.

"They have no notion of what's coming for them," he concluded.

Cairncross would know better than any of them, of course. Of all the men and women in the room, he was the only one who had seen what a war truly looked like.

"I signed up with the RAMC this morning," Gardner said quietly from his place by the bookcases.

Miss Bard leaned over to take his hand. She gave it a firm squeeze.

"Good for you, Doctor," she said firmly.

The RAMC was the Royal Army Medical Corps. Lily found she could not be surprised, though the idea of Gardner enlisting still frightened her a bit. How could he do anything else? His skills would be in terrible demand, and Gardner was not one to shirk from the duty of his profession.

"Where are they sending you?" Estelle asked.

"I don't quite know yet," Gardner replied with a wry smile. "They have to train me first and I'm not exactly some young pup used to following orders."

"They'll set up military hospitals all along the south coast," Cairncross predicted. "Likely London as well. Or they might ship you to Belgium."

"I'll go wherever the need is," Gardner replied simply.

He would be alright—solid, strong old Gardner. Lily suspected it would do him more harm to remain where he was, knowing all the suffering happening on the continent. Her heart still ached at the thought of it.

The whole world was tipping on its axis. Everything that had seemed certain, everything she had assumed would always be, was revealing itself to be as fragile as glass.

Sam's voice sounded from where he stood by the window, gazing out at the passing cars, the black birds in the trees.

"I've enlisted too."

It was a lightning bolt in the room, shocking all of them to silence.

"Oh, Sam," Estelle said, clearly upset.

Lily came to her feet. She felt Strangford rise behind her.

"What about the Imperial College?" she exclaimed.

"Never said I wanted to go," Sam retorted.

Cairncross slowly set down his teacup.

"You are throwing away a tremendous opportunity to establish a life for yourself," Cairncross said.

Lily could hear the low fury in his tone.

"Ain't his job to decide what my life will be," Sam snapped in reply.

It clicked then, what she had been sensing simmering under Sam's granite surface these last few days.

It was rage.

"Sam, that isn't what Mr. Ash was doing," Estelle pushed back gently.

"Don't suppose it matters. The thing's done," Sam retorted.

"But I don't understand," Miss Bard protested. "Forgive me if I'm mistaken, but you aren't a British subject, Sam. How could they take you?"

"They don't much care what you put on your papers when you show them you know how to take a carburetor apart," he replied.

"What branch did you join?" Gardner asked.

"Army," Sam said flatly.

"You'll be bloody cannon fodder," Cairncross bit back. "They'll throw you up a hill into a line of artillery and you'll be blasted into pieces."

"James!" Estelle chided.

"They'll not waste a good mechanic on the infantry," Gardner noted.

"Sam, are you certain you know what you're getting yourself into?" Miss Bard asked.

"It doesn't matter. If he's signed the papers, that's the end of it." Cairncross stood up, pointing a finger at Sam. "Robert offered you the opportunity to make something of yourself. He gave his life for you. And now you're going to throw it all away on some pointless war."

Sam turned to face them. The stone in him was broken now, cracked wide. Grief twisted his features, tangled up with anger. Lily's heart wrenched in her chest to see it.

"I never asked for it," he shot back, the words raw with pain.

This wasn't about the scholarship. It was about Blackfriars rail bridge, when Ash took the bomb out of Sam's hands. It was about how he had blown himself out of Sam's life before Sam had a chance to resolve any of it—what it meant that Ash had plucked him out of Limehouse, whether he was a foster-father to him or a teacher or a dictator.

Ash had loved him. Lily knew that to be true. He had loved all of them. He had wanted to guide Sam to realizing his full potential but that could never be a clear path. People weren't simple. There would always be complications.

Behind Sam, through the window, it seemed as though the dark birds in the trees had all turned to look at them—to gaze through the glass at where Sam stood, tangled in the aura of his rage.

The notion chilled her.

Strangford spoke from behind her.

"You will always have a place to come back to," he announced with quiet certainty.

"I already have a family," Sam snapped back. The words were meant to hurt.

"You have two," Strangford returned firmly.

Strangford's words struck him. Lily could see how it threatened to break the anger Sam had carefully wrapped around himself, tumbling him into a less comfortable emotion.

He grabbed his hat from the table.

"I'm going out," he announced and stalked from the room.

On the trees of Bedford Square, the ravens rose up into the night, black wings flapping against a sky streaked with the gold of evening.

The door to The Refuge slammed.

"It's particularly hard for him," Estelle offered. "He'll come to terms with it in time."

"Let's hope he has time," Cairncross retorted.

Lily bolted after him.

She yanked open the door and raced down the front steps. The pain in her ribs drew her up short, forcing her to an abrupt halt.

"Sam!" she called.

The rain had passed. The sun had dropped down below the layer of the clouds, painting them with wild and strange light. The road beneath her feet was washed clean, the fresh smell of the city after rain filling the air.

Swallows flitted overhead, silently chasing through the evening sky.

Sam stopped. He turned to face her.

He had aged in these last days. When Lily met him six months before, she had still seen something of the boy in him. That was gone, wrung out by all they had been through. He was a man now and it sparked an ache in her to realize it.

He waited for her.

She strode to where he stood and threw her arms around him.

She held him because she understood, because something of the same terrible mix of feeling roiled under her own skin—the gratitude and the frustration, the resentment and the love.

He was clearly surprised by it, but it took only a moment for his arms to come around her as well. He held her back, squeezing her like a lifeline. He was bigger than she was, solid and warm, and she was full of the feeling of how very much she loved him.

"Ouch," she admitted.

"Oh! Sorry," he said, easing up.

She looked up at him.

"Promise me you'll be safe," she said.

His mouth tugged into a smile. It was a shadow of the smiles she knew, weighed down as it was by all that tangle of emotion, but it sparked something like hope in her.

"What, me?" he replied. "They won't knock me down that easy. I'm a right scrapper."

Yes, he was a scrapper—tough and smart and determined. He had made it through some rough scrapes, and yet Lily knew that what lay before him was different—bigger and more dangerous than anything he had confronted before.

But he would get through it. If anyone could, it would be Sam.

His expression shifted, growing serious.

"There's something you ought to know," he said. "About Strangford."

"What is it?" she demanded, conscious of an uncomfortable sense of threat.

"It's what he did at Blackfriars. Taking that bomb from you, blowing the train. And what it cost him."

She thought of the scars that would mark his face for the rest of his life, the black patch over his eye.

"There's some consider that a sacrifice," Sam said.

Her skin felt cold.

"Some?" she asked.

"You know," he replied.

It seemed she could hear the beating of great wings, the distant croak of a black bird on the windswept edge of an endless sea.

"The ravens," she filled in.

"He has a boon," Sam finished. "When he wants it."

She nodded, not knowing what else to say. The gesture felt somehow formal, like a contract being sealed.

"Stay well, Lily," Sam ordered, stepping back.

"You too," she replied. It was both a prediction and a prayer, a force of will she sent out into the universe in that moment as she beheld her friend in the glow of evening over Bedford Square.

—

Lily climbed the stairs back to The Refuge. She stopped in front of the blue-painted door. The knob was covered in a knot of black crepe while a white banner hung over the lintel. The latter was a gesture by Mrs. Liu. Both were signs of mourning.

Ash's voice echoed through her mind.

The door of The Refuge will always be open to you.

Those words had signaled a revolution in her life, upending everything she had thought she knew about the world, about herself.

In a few months, she knew the paint would start to chip. She had already seen it. She had seen the step covered with unswept winter leaves.

Everything was mortal. Everything changed. Even the people and places who seemed like they must be there forever passed, leaving emptiness behind them.

Soon Cairncross would lock the door and Lily would move on down this path that Ash had set her on, stumbling her way forward without a guide.

She put her hand to the black fabric of the knob and pushed the door open.

"Pardon me, miss?"

A bicycle courier waited at the foot of the steps. He held a slender package in his hand.

"This your place?" he asked.

The question carried far more weight than he could possibly have realized.

"Yes," Lily replied.

The package felt dense, heavy for its size. She noted the address as she walked inside.

Attn. Dr. Harold Gardner. Return to King's College Hospital, Denmark Hill.

The others were still gathered in the library. Cairncross had taken Sam's place by the window. He looked tired. He had been closer to Ash than any of them, sharing decades of history and who-knew-what trials and adventures. Lily understood only a fraction of what that relationship had been. She could not begin to measure what he had lost.

Strangford met her eyes from across the room. She knew he would want to know how Sam was doing. There would be time to share that with him later.

"This came for you," she said, handing the package to Gardner.

"Well, that's the end of the tea," Estelle announced, setting down the pot. "We'd best be getting on anyway. You know Mrs. Liu won't rest until we're all out of her hair and she must be exhausted from preparing all that food."

"She wants us to take one of those little red envelopes full of pennies with us," Mrs. Bard noted. "And we're to eat a piece of candy."

The package was stuffed with an assortment of papers. Gardner's frown deepened as he shuffled through them.

"What is it, Doctor?" Strangford asked.

"They're a batch of Joseph Hartwell's correspondence," Gardner replied.

"But we drowned all of it," Lily blurted in reply.

"There was a note from Dr. Saunders at King's. These were apparently mixed in with Hartwell's personal letters. The widow forwarded them to the hospital once she'd gone through everything. Thought they might have medical value and should be part of his archive."

The archive that Lily and the others had scattered into the North Sea.

"What's in there?" Strangford asked.

"Nothing of consequence that I can see. Though I can't make much of this one. It's in German."

"May I?" Strangford asked.

Gardner handed him the letter.

"I suppose Mr. Wu can burn it all out in the refuse bin in the garden," Gardner said, shuffling the papers back together. "If the army catches wind of the parcel, one of them might be clever enough to question the courier. Best there's nothing here for them to find. I can concoct some other document for Dr. Saunders to have sent to me to cover it."

"Wait a moment," Strangford said quietly, setting a hand on Gardner's arm.

"What is it?" Lily demanded.

"A page from a longer letter. There's no signature but the author is most likely a physician, based on the terminology he is using. He is thanking Hartwell for sending him the results of his latest round of experiments. 'I concur that your theory bears further investigation. In my opinion there are a number of potential applications for this research, many of them of profound interest to the Rassenhygieniker.'"

"What is that?" Lily asked. The word sent a breath of foreboding over her skin.

"Race hygienists," Cairncross replied from his place by the window. He turned to face the rest of them. "Supporters of the science of eugenics."

"It's not a bloody science," Gardner countered stoutly.

Strangford lifted the letter.

"Are there any others?"

"No," Gardner returned, finishing another pass through the pile of documents. "Just the one."

"But what does it mean?" Lily demanded.

Her urgency felt all out of proportion with the situation. This was not an asylum on Hampstead Heath. They were in the quiet and comfort of the library of The Refuge. Joseph Hartwell was six months dead. He could not hurt her anymore.

"It sounds as though Hartwell may have been sharing some of his research with a colleague in Germany," Cairncross replied.

"Where?" she asked.

"There's no address," Strangford said, meeting her gaze steadily.

"It's a single page from the middle of a longer missive. There is no way to know where it came from."

"Presumably somewhere in Germany," Cairncross noted.

"What about a name?" Estelle pressed.

"No," Strangford said.

It all felt too close again—the flames of the burning warehouse in Southwark. The sight of Estelle with blood dripping down her neck.

Hartwell's calm, thoughtful voice, planning aloud how he was going to kill her.

"That doesn't give us much to go on," Gardner admitted.

"Even if it did, we couldn't pursue it," Cairncross said. "We're at war with Germany. There's a blockade moving into place as we speak. The borders will be closed, maybe worse. Even if we knew where to go, we couldn't get there. Not now."

"Could we have destroyed it in Kent? The rest of the letter," Lily demanded.

"The archivist at King's had already written up an index of the files when they were confiscated by the army," Cairncross said. "Dr. Gardner's friend, Dr. Saunders, was clever enough to forward it along to me. I reviewed it thoroughly before we intercepted the shipment. There was nothing in German, nothing to indicate that he had shared the illegitimate portions of his research with anyone else."

"You don't actually know that this letter you have here is about the mediums," Miss Bard pointed out quietly.

"She's right," Gardner agreed. "Even Hartwell's general work on blood typing could be seen as a topic of interest by the eugenicists. They were looking for anything they could find to try to justify their notions of which humans are superior to the rest of us. And all of that was public."

Lily knew what the doctor said was true. The German's letter could be about any aspect of Hartwell's work. Despite his prestige, his hordes of fans and followers, Lily knew that here in England only his assistant, Lt. Waddington, had known the full scope of what Hartwell hoped to achieve—and what he had been willing to do to get there.

He might have justified his crimes in his own mind, but he was still intelligent enough to know that they were murder.

The fear settling into her gut was immune to that logic.

She had thought they were finished with it.

"I'll have a word with Dr. Saunders," Gardner said, bundling back up the other letters. "If Hartwell's widow sent these directly to King's, she must not realize the army confiscated the rest of her husband's work. Perhaps Saunders can convince Mrs. Hartwell to let her have a look through the rest of Hartwell's personal papers. It's possible that might turn up another bit of this correspondence." He lifted the papers. "I suppose I'd best take the rest of these out back and put them out of their misery."

"I will hold on to this one," Cairncross said, extending his hand. "I can see that it is put someplace secure."

Strangford handed him the page.

Hartwell's disguised files detailing his murderous experiments on the poor prostitutes of Southwark and the mediums he had murdered were sunk at the bottom of the sea. The man who had assisted him in that research had burned up in the warehouse fire.

Hartwell himself was dead.

The letter might mean anything. It might mean nothing. Either way, the war breaking out across Europe made pursuit of the matter impossible.

The words of the Sikh doctor Lily had abandoned by a Kentish roadside came back to her.

Progress is like water. It will always find a way.

~

It was deepening into twilight when Lily stepped once more into the open air of Bedford Square.

The others had all dispersed. Estelle and Miss Bard had taken a two-seater back to March Place. Gardner was headed to St. Bart's where he had a shift as the night on-call physician.

As Lily stood with Strangford on the pavement, she saw Cairncross turn off the lights of the library, the great windows going dark.

The night was warm, the air still fresh from the rain. Other windows flickered to life around them, their sashes open to let in the evening breeze. Lily heard a burst of laughter, the sound of someone's record player.

She studied Strangford's face in the dying light, both the familiar contours of it and the unfamiliar symbol of his scar, the dark circle of fabric that hid the place where his eye had been.

"Virginia claims I look like a pirate," he said.

Lily traced a finger around the curve of the patch.

"It is very dashing," she replied.

His mouth quirked into a tired smile.

"That's for the best, then. I'm afraid Gardner thinks I am a poor candidate for a prosthetic. Apparently there was a bit too much damage from the shrapnel."

The reminder of his injury hurt, and yet she found she could not mind terribly that there would be no replacement of what he had lost. His scars were a story of what he had risked to protect her, of how completely he trusted her even when she struggled to trust herself.

They would always be beautiful to her.

She let her hand drop and gave voice to the question that had been haunting her ever since Gardner's announcement in the library.

"Are you going to war as well?"

"I'm damaged goods, Lily," he replied. He made a gesture toward his eye. "They won't want me. Not for the fighting, at any rate."

Relief washed over her, and yet the fear refused to entirely give way. It was anchored in a fragment of a vision she had months before—of Strangford in a muddy uniform falling back as the earth around him exploded into a storm of dirt and wire.

The threat of that still felt real, however impossible it must now be if he was disqualified for service.

She would not be bowed by it. She had changed fate before. She would do it again if she must.

The door of The Refuge was closed, the lights dark. The black crepe on the knob rustled in the breeze. Night was settling in around them, the stars blinking on in the purple sky overhead.

She took his hand, sliding her fingers over his glove.

"What happens now?" she asked.

It was a question with layers of meaning, but she did not have to explain them. Strangford already knew. He would have felt it inside of her before she even admitted it to herself. The way she must know the lines of his face—every shape, every scar—better than he ever would, Strangford knew her heart.

"I haven't made this easy for you," he admitted. "I don't know that I ever can."

"I never asked for easy," she replied.

His grip on her tightened. His dark gaze burned down at her as he stepped closer. "I don't know what is coming for us. What this war will bring. What waits for us on the other side of it. But I am certain beyond all shadow of doubt that I want to face it at your side. Will you have me?"

Her world felt balanced on a pin.

It was not Lily's power to see the threads of her own destiny. Fate was the thing she warred with, the antagonist in her struggle. She did not understand it as Evangeline Ash must have done, could not know what it was like to greet it as an old friend.

Yet she swore she could feel it in that moment, thick in the air around her, and for once she did not want to fight it. With Strangford's hand in her own, with the ferocity of her love for him burning inside her chest, there was only one answer she could give.

"Yes," she said, the word echoing through her being, through everything she had been or would become. "*Yes.*"

She kissed him then in the open air of the street, regardless of the passing automobiles, the boys on bicycles and the respectable ladies at the crossing. With her hands in his hair and his taste on her lips, as the stars unfolded overhead and the world around them spun into war, there was only one word that mattered.

Yes.

NOTES FROM THE AUTHOR

Lily and Strangford will return in 2021 with *Bridge of Ash*, book three of The Charismatics. Sign up for the email list at JacquelynBenson.com/Subscribe-to-the-Newsletter to be notified when the book is available for pre-order.

—

Stay informed about other new releases, including the release of more books in The Charismatics, by signing up for Jacquelyn Benson's newsletter at JacquelynBenson.com/Subscribe-to-the-Newsletter. As a bonus for subscribing, you'll also get access to *The Stolen Apocalypse*, a free, exclusive novella featuring a young Lord Strangford.

—

Please take a moment to rate or review *The Shadow of Water*. It's a simple thing that has a real and powerful impact for independent writers like myself.

The Smoke Hunter

Jacquelyn Benson's thrilling debut novel takes you on a race for the truth behind an ancient legend.

Frustrated suffragette and would-be archaeologist Ellie Mallory stumbles across a map to a city that shouldn't exist, a jungle metropolis alive and flourishing centuries after the Mayan civilization mysteriously collapsed. Discovering it would make her career, but Ellie isn't the only one after the prize. A disgraced professor and his ruthless handler are hot on her heels, willing to go any extreme to acquire the map for themselves.

To race them through the uncharted jungle, Ellie needs a guide. The only one with the expertise is maverick surveyor Adam Bates. But with his determination to nose his way into Ellie's many secrets, Bates is a dangerous partner.

As Ellie gets closer to her goal, she realizes it's not just her ambitions at stake. A powerful secret lies hidden in the heart of the city—and if it falls into the wrong hands, it could shake the very fate of the world.

Grab your copy now at Books2Read.com/TheSmokeHunter.

ACKNOWLEDGMENTS

The past year has been one for gratitude. It's amazing how adversity and change make us appreciate what we have. This book would not be in your hands without the support and help of a wonderful group of people.

I owe a great deal to my early readers Matt Dow, Kaitlyn Huwe, Chris Mornick, Anna Brown-Leone, Cathie Plante and Christine Altan. Their eagle eyes made this whole story much tighter and more thrilling.

Zhui Ning Chan was an invaluable resource on Sam and his family, and also helped catch the rogue Americanisms that found their way into the manuscript. (Darn those washclothes.)

Carol Cottrell was kind enough to share stories of her own experiences chatting with the dead.

Sara Argue's unique vision and talent created the gorgeous covers for both *The Shadow of Water* and *The Fire in the Glass*. This series owes a great deal to her artwork

I also owe much to the brilliant Kate Benson, who worked wonders with our source image and provided general moral support throughout the writing of this book.

Cathie Plante elegantly laid out both the print and eBook editions, creating a seamless reading experience.

Mike Dunbar suffered through my dislike of Oxford commas while proofing. (And is also a wonderful musician, so do give him a listen.)

I'm grateful to Diana Clifford for her ongoing work compiling the series bible for The Charismatics, and to Mary Jane Solomon (who has no idea I've included her here) for the kind loan of her notebook at the Kensington polls so I could fill in a plot hole between welcoming voters.

I am also deeply indebted to the brilliant minds of The Lamplighter's Guild—Olivia and Nicholas Atwater, Rosalie Oaks, and Susannah Rowantree. Their advice and support has been and continues to be invaluable as I undertake this journey with Lily and her friends. If you have enjoyed The Charismatics series, I highly recommend you explore their books as well. You will find them delightful.

Of course, there is Dan, who remains infinitely patient in the face of the many evenings where I ignore him to type away furiously. He has been pelted with plot tangles and interrupted with the details of pre-war international alliances, and endures it all with grace. Our tiny people were also kind enough to entertain themselves on many quarantined mornings while I worked on drafts and revisions.

I must also credit General Moltke, Chief of the Great German General Staff, for the words I stole and put in Torrington's mouth. For those interested, the original statement is thus: "Woe to him who sets Europe alight, who first puts the fuse to the powder keg." I also provided Torrington with a riff on the infamous words of British Foreign Secretary Sir Edward Grey on the outbreak of the Great War. I invite the true history nerds among you to find it.

Lastly, there are you, my readers. I deeply appreciate how you have taken Lily, Strangford, Sam, Estelle, Gardner, Cairncross and the others under your wing. I could not do this without your continued enthusiasm and support.

ABOUT THE AUTHOR

 Jacquelyn Benson writes smart historical thrillers where strong women wrangle with bold men and confront the stranger things that occupy the borders of our world. She once lived in a museum, wrote a master's thesis on the cultural anthropology of paranormal investigation, and received a gold medal for being clever. She owes a great deal to her elementary school librarian for sagely choosing to acquire the entire Time-Life *Mysteries of the Unknown* series.

Her debut novel, *The Smoke Hunter*, was nominated for Best Historical Fiction by RT Times. When not writing, she enjoys the company of a tall, dark and handsome English teacher and practices unintentional magic.

If you'd like to be friends:

- **Join the email list on her website:** JacquelynBenson.com.
  You'll also get a free download of an exclusive novella,
  The Stolen Apocalypse.

- **Follow her on Bookbub:** BookBub.com/Authors/Jacquelyn-Benson
  and stay informed about deals and discounts

- **Follow her on Goodreads:** Goodreads.com/JacquelynBenson

- **Find her on social media:**
    Instagram: @jbensonink
    Twitter: Twitter.com/JBensonInk
    Facebook: Facebook.com/JBensonInk
    Pinterest: Pinterest.com/JBensonInk